ALLEYCAT LEADER, THIS IS GREY HEAD!

ENEMY ABOUT TO EXECUTE EVASIVE MANEUVER!

Colonel Curt Carson called on neuroelectronic "thought wave" tacomm to his GUNCO commander. *Leave vehicles and bots where they are! Put them in remote voice command mode! All Sierra Charlies of GUNCO go to ground at once! Form a base of fire to the east!*

Carson grabbed his Novia assault rifle, bailed out of the turret hatch, and rolled down the side of his OCV to the ground. His second in command was right behind him as he hit dirt. Together, they dashed across the fifty meters of open grassland to a line of trees.

Their objective: lead the Washington Greys to victory by ambushing the ambushers!

I0627765

#8 FORCE OF ARMS

WARBOTS

G. HARRY STINE

Imholt Press

Originally published by Pinnacle Books

Currently Published by Imholt Press, LLC

ISBN: **978-1-951810-01-6**

For more information contact **tim@timothyimholt.com**

TO:

Richard N. "Junior" Jurmain,
former Captain, California National Guard

"It is not the critic who counts, nor the man who points out how the strong man stumbled or where the doer of deeds could have done them better. The credit belongs to the man who is actually in the arena; whose face is marred by dust and sweat and blood; who strives valiantly; who errs and comes short again and again; who knows the great enthusiasms, the great devotions, and spends himself in a worthy cause; who, at the best, knows in the end the triumph of high achievement; and who, at the worst, if he fails, at least fails while daring greatly, so that his place shall never be with those cold and timid souls who know neither victory nor defeat."

- Theodore Roosevelt, former
colonel, United States Army

Forward

In this eighth installment of Warbots, G. Harry Stine takes us further into the world of robotic warfare that G. Harry saw as the future, we see it as the present. The technology we use for this task improves every day. G. Harry reminds us that no good weapon or tactic develop program goes unnoticed.

What happens when three nations argue over some territory in the Pacific Ocean, and all three have military units ready to pounce on each other perhaps destroying the local population in the process?

What happens when one of those nations has modern technology in the form of the newly developed Russian Warbots.

The Sierra Charlies of the United States find themselves trying to play peacekeeper between military units.

This book brings in the question of what does the United States do to prevent being sucked being a police force? Should we do it, but only for our allies or, you know, people who ask us nicely? It is a strange political discussion to even consider. I think G. Harry Stine can make you think about such things.

He also makes us wonder if we can survive a conventional war with the Russians. Something we may need to consider today.

I hope you enjoy this installment into Warbots, I give you Warbots Book 8: Force of Arms.

Timothy Imholt PhD

Chapter One

"Gentlemen, if this keeps up, one of us will be killed!"

"More likely, all of us! This is a war waiting to happen. And we all lead assault forces rather than police units. My orders, like yours, are not to provoke conflict. However, I actually have limited control over the possibility of keeping it from taking place."

"If it comes to a fight, my life is dedicated to the Motherland in any event. But I do not relish the thought of writing letters to the families of my soldiers who will be killed."

The mood of the three men clustered around the table in the little restaurant matched the weather outside – gloomy, foggy, cold and hopeless.

The sun had not shown for days – weeks, actually – so the colors around everyone were shadowless shades of monochromatic greys ranging from black to dirty white.

The damp fog permeated every nook and cranny, soaked into equipment, made clothing sticky and uncomfortable to wear, and kept the less hardy souls in a constant state of chilblains and head colds, modern biotechnology notwithstanding.

No warmth was available except in the coal-heated buildings where the higher temperatures brought only a damp warmth that did little to dispel aching muscles or to dry soggy clothing.

And it was hopeless weather because no one could forecast any end to it, only that it would get worse before it might get better. With the coming of winter in a few months, it could only get colder and more miserable.

The island of Sakhalin just north of Japan and situated in a strategic spot between the Amur Peninsula and the Kurile Islands was not the vacation spot of the world. No one wanted to come to Sakhalin, much less stay there, save the hardy ancestors of the Ukrainians and

Byelorussians who'd been settled there in place of the Japanese who were repatriated after World War II.

Except the Chinese, who wanted the island because it controlled the northern part of the Sea of Japan. Its possession would isolate the Amur Peninsula – and thus the Soviet Union – from the bustling economic activity of the Pacific rim.

Except for the Soviet Union, who'd gotten Sakhalin following World War II and used it as a shield for their nuclear ballistic missile submarines until they'd been forced to give it back to Japan after the infamous Sino-Soviet Incident, sometimes known as Space War I, which no one had won.

And except the Japanese, who'd owned part of Sakhalin in the last century and called it Karafuto, and who now controlled all of it in compensation for mediating the settlement of the Sin-Soviet Incident...provided that no military forces were stationed on the big island because no one trusted anyone else.

No one trusted the Union of Soviet Socialist Republics, the modern land-bound czarist Russian Empire no less imperial than the old British Empire. And the Soviets, following czarist foreign policy, wanted access to the Pacific. The USSR desperately needed that access. With its basket-case economy and its paranoid defensive posture, it needed to control the eastern end of the Asiatic land trade route exemplified by the Trans-Siberian Railway. And the Soviet Union was constantly on guard lest the Yellow Peril break again across the steppes of Asia and send Mongolian hordes into eastern Europe; a Russian doesn't easily forget that part of history which hasn't been rewritten to match current Party doctrine.

The Chinese Empire had become the People's Republic of China, exchanging one set of rulers for another in the twentieth century while the huge mass of humanity in China threw off the old mandarin ways – they thought – and tried to adapt to the modern world of the twenty-first century. The Chinese also continued the foreign policy of imperial China. They wanted the Amur Peninsula back from the Russians who they believed had gotten in unfairly in the 1858 Treaty of Aigun and the 1860 Treaty of Peking. Thus, one land empire faced another land empire along thousands of kilometers of border – some of it poorly defined – and argued about strategic hell holes like Sakhalin.

The Japanese, on the other hand, trusted no one else because they were – well, Japanese. They dealt with both the USSR and the PRC. The Japanese would work with anyone…as long as they could cut the cards and deal first. That was just good business. While the PRC was a huge marketplace jammed with people who were Orientals and thus thought as the Japanese did, the USSR was a resources base just as the United States was a production and technology base for the Japanese ecostate.

Why, then, were three full colonels, regimental commanders all, of these three nations sitting in the damp warmth of a restaurant in the grubby "city" with the nearby unpronounceable name of Yuzhno – Sakhalinsk?

Because they were professional military men.

Because they all had similar problems with their troops in this godforsaken place.

Because all three of them waged continual battles with their supply people trying to maintain decent logistics in this place.

Because they were answerable to higher authorities sitting behind big desks in the comfortable cosmopolitan cities of Moskva, Beiching, and Tokyo with all the amenities available and their families to go home to every evening.

Because if shooting started, they were the ones who would most likely be killed first.

In the last century, the military commanders in Berlin had faced similar problems. Except Berlin was a real city where you could get a decent meal in a restaurant if the mess hall began to sicken you, go to the theater or a night club if you got bored, have a hell of a party without too much worry that you might be drinking home brew with too much fuel oil in it, and find a good piece of ass to enjoy at a reasonable price, if you were unmarried or weren't a prude. Or sometimes even if you were both if you'd spent enough time in the hellhole.

"*Ie!* Waiter! More *chai!*" the Japanese colonel called out, raising his empty ceramic mug.

"Be careful, Mishida," warned Colonel Dao Min Qian. "That is Soviet vodka in the *chai*. It is not *saki*."

"What I would give for a good cup of saki right now..." Colonel Yushiro Mishida muttered, still holding his mug loft, "At least, you still get good vodka here, Kurotkin."

"Vodka, but not good vodka," he was reminded by Colonel Viktor Pashkavitch Kurotkin, commanding officer of the 110th Special Airborne Guards Regiment of the *Sukhoputnyye Voyska*, USSR. "That is reserved for my political affairs officer, the KGB watch dog who will try to make sense out of the recording of our meeting which he is making even as we speak..." The three commanders did not speak the language of the other two, so they spoke in the one language they all understood, the universal language of science, technology, diplomacy, and military affairs: bad English.

"You seem to be worried about him just as I am worried about my political education officer," Quan remarked.

"Is your spook as demoralized as mine?" Kurotkin wondered, although he didn't use that term which has been transliterated into colloquial English here.

Qian nodded. The regimental commander of the 44th Special Regiment, People's Liberation Army, knew his political affairs officer all too well. Captain Li Wan Xiang was part Manchurian, which meant he was part Mongol and had some of the powerful Mongol sexual drives and the more liberal sexual mores of his ancestors. Xiang had no wife and therefore didn't have to worry about birth control through abstinence. Qian had information on Xiang's proclivities that would have caused his political officer not only to lose considerable face but also placed him on the list for duty in Tibet, where he would be far away from the wives of the higher officers with whom he'd served. "He does not care that the three of us meet. He knows it is better than fighting between our troops. But I have been told that I must maintain the proper enthusiasm for representing my country in this joint military occupation which seems to be against all the treaties our countries have signed..."

"Waiter! More *chai!*" Kurotkin exploded, slamming his mug down on the table. "Treaties be damned! Colonel Qian, we do not meet to discuss politics! We meet to resolve differences and to maintain peace and public order on Sakhalin! Anything other than that will most certainly be reported to the chief of Political Administration of the Far East Military District in Khabarovsk by my political affairs officer!" Kurotkin didn't want to answer charges to General Lieutenant Druzhinin in Khabarovsk. Kurotkin's wife and two daughters enjoyed the luxuries of a two-bedroom flat, a Ural automobile, and a permit to use the Officers' Store in Kubuyshev. He didn't want them to be required to move to a one-bedroom flat sharing the bathroom and kitchen with three other families, be forced to use the crowded and unreliable public transit systems, or to wait in the interminable queues that were the lot of the proletariat. If it were not for his family, he might consider...but Colonel Viktor Pashkavitch Kurotkin wouldn't even permit himself to think about it. He'd made it up through the ranks in the Soviet Army by knowing how to treat the political officers of the KGB and GRU. He wasn't about to blow it now, even though he detested the slimy Major Alksander Semenovitch Ivanovski, his present political officer, who was suffering this morning from the results of a major drinking bout last night...with Kurotkin's vodka. Otherwise, Ivanovski might have insisted on coming this morning. Kurotkin could not automatically assume, however, that he wasn't being recorded somehow just because Ivanovski wasn't with him.

"May I suggest a possible solution to our problem of keeping our soldiers apart? And thereby preventing open conflict from occurring which might certainly result in open hostilities wherein we might be unnecessarily killed?" said Colonel Yushiro Mishida of the 9th International Peacekeeping Regiment, Japanese Self Defense Forces. Mishida wasn't worried; he had no political commissar peering over his shoulder, only the ancient warrior code of *bushido* to guide his actions. He also knew that possession was powerful...and Japan presently possessed Sakhalin under treaty. The fact that Japan had had to station troops there in violation of the treaty didn't bother him; when the Chinese and Soviet regiments had landed on the island as an extension of their classical long border disagreement, Japan could do no less in order to protect and hold what was rightfully and under treaty considered to be part of the island chain that was Japan. The Soviets were operating at the end of a supply and communications line almost ten thousand kilometers long, consisting of a single railway and an expensive airlift. China was closer but had no direct access to Sakhalin except over or through international waters, which made their logistics vulnerable, too. As for himself, he knew that four more JSDF regiments were stationed in Hokkaido across fifty kilometers of La Perouse Strait to the south. Japan was ready to play the old game of military power backing up the economic power baser that had become so effective after World War II when the Japanese decided they'd better make it instead of take it. Beyond that, of course, the Americans might also step back into Sakhalin to save their investments in Japan as they had after the Sino-Soviet Incident. He felt that Japan had an excellent strategic and economic position. He doubted that open general warfare would erupt as a result of what happened on Sakhalin, but it could get rather deadly before friends, allies, customers, and suppliers stepped in to save their investments in the Pacific rim. The United States, the People's Republic of China, and the Soviet Union were good customers and suppliers. So was the rest of the Pacific rim.

"And your suggestion may be?" Qian wondered when Mishida paused.

"We will work out a schedule and will not provide passes to our soldiers except on specific days when other troops are not given recreational time," Mishida replied.

"That will help," Kurotkin agreed. "But it will be complicated to work out the schedule..."

Mishida shook his head and withdrew a pocket computer from his coat pocket. "I have prepared a suggested schedule," he told his two counterparts as he keyed the wallet-sized machine and it spat out two hard copies of a schedule.

Such a device was the envy of the Soviet and the Chinese commanders. The Chinese government maintained that no computer more complex than an abacus was required by officers and preferred to keep its computer in Beiching or to export them to computer-poor countries that weren't up to handling or paying for the latest high-tech from Japan or the USA. The Soviet government simply maintained its long-standing policy of total control of all data and therefore saw no reason whatsoever to provide general-purpose pocket computers to its military personnel; officers had specialized computers to do what was militarily necessary, but they had no official need for general-purpose computers that could go online any more than the ordinary soldier had to be able to read a map.

"This covers recreational time, Colonel," Kurotkin remarked as he looked at the printout, "but does not prevent our patrols from encountering one another."

"I suggest that we unofficially determine spheres of influence, if you will," Mishida went on, "or regions where our individual units will carry out patrols. We shall meet weekly like this to report any activities that may be unusual or that might jeopardize the peace of Sahkalin..."

Kurotkin shook his head. "*Nyet!* That is not acceptable! It would deny access to potentially important areas of Sakhalin to Soviet forces." He didn't trust these Japanese. They were far more inscrutable than the Chinese. Kurotkin could fathom the Chinese to some extent because he knew something about the Mongolian soldiers who had served from time to time in units he'd commanded. (Now, of course, the 110th Special Airborne Guards Regiment had NCOs and soldiers mostly from Georgia, Armenia, and Turkistan - when they could get them - who had no familial or racial ties with the Byelorussians and Ukrainians who'd settled on Sakhalin nearly a hundred years ago, much less the Japanese or the Chinese who'd shown up on Sakhalin in greater numbers since the Sino-Soviet Incident.)

"I do not like the idea of not being able to send my patrols to certain parts of this island," Qian added in agreement. "We are here to see that neither the Soviet Union nor Japan makes any further military moves that could affect the security of the People's Republic of China…" Basically, Qian did not want to lose face by giving up part of Sakhalin to either the Soviets or the Japanese. His orders were quite specific and required that he maintain military vigilance over the entire island…which he knew was actually impossible, since Sakhalin was larger than the Japanese island of Honshu, but which he knew he had to attempt to the best of his ability.

Several generations of careful schooling in the fine art of marketing had made Colonel Yushiro Mishida subtly different from an officer of the Imperial Japanese Army a century ago. Mishida knew his customers as well as his competitors. And he knew them very well. Thus, he'd deliberately played his proposal in such a way as to utilize his strengths and their weaknesses-suspicion on the part of the Soviet colonel, possible loss of face on the part of the Chinese officer. He wanted no compromise on Sakhalin. Mishida wanted an open conflict. But not for the obvious reasons.

The discussion went on for several hours in the cold, damp, primitive little cafe. The three regimental commanders managed to resolve the recreational schedules so that their troops wouldn't encounter one another on passes, but they could come to no agreement concerning spheres of influence. Each commander maintained that the whole island of Sakhalin was within his purview.

As a result, each of them knew that his armed patrols would encounter armed patrols of the others. Perhaps rules of engagement might prevent some conflict, but none of them really knew how to establish ROEs; they were trained to execute orders from above, not to generate orders other than the tactical commands necessary to carry out the assigned missions of their units as determined from above. Linear command structure had its good points and its bad points; among its questionable characteristics was its restriction on a field commander's initiative. But, with the possible exception of Colonel Mishida of Japan, initiative was neither required nor desired on the part of Kurotkin and Qian.

They had completely overlooked the possibility of their armed patrols encountering soldiers of other units who were on recreational passes.

Or the actual cause of the forthcoming conflict.

It began to rain outside, a cold rain that heralded the bitter damp winter that was coming. The sunlight began to fade. Darkness was coming earlier and earlier after the autumn equinox in this northern latitude.

When the trio broke up, Colonel Mishida left by the front door of the cafe. Qian and Kurotkin put on their heavy raincoats and left by the back door. This was not only to conceal the fact that the three commanders had met there; their political officers and spies undoubtedly knew it. But it would not help to maintain the morale of their troops in this miserable place if it were known in the regiments that the three colonels held frequent and semi-friendly meetings.

Qian and Kurotkin had another reason as well to leave by the back door. Many cups of hot chai required them to take a leak. The little cafe lacked indoor plumbing, as did most buildings even in the biggest "city" on Sakhalin. As they stood in the alleyway allowing the drizzling rain to flush the convenient natural urinal that was the back wall of the building, Qian remarked to Kurotkin, "Comrade Colonel, we are both high-ranking officers in great people's armies of powerful communist countries. Therefore, we are supposed to be equal in the eyes of all men. If this is so, can you tell me why it is that when you piss on the wall it is like the rushing of the waters on the Yellow River as it makes its way to the sea while it is with me like the drip, drip, drip of gentle rain from the eaves of the Great Hall of the People in Beiching?"

Kurotkin looked at Qian and with great patience replied, "Comrade Colonel, I agree that we are both high-ranking officers, and in great armies of the people and that Marxist-Leninist doctrine decrees that we are equals. You want to know why when I piss it is like the roar of the Volga River when it is for you like the dripping of melting icicles from the roof of the Kremlin? I will tell you why this is so, Comrade Colonel. I am pissing on the wall; you are pissing in your raincoat..."

Chapter Two

"Goddammit, Colonel Carson, why the hell are you sniveling to me? You're a regimental commander now!" Major General Belinda Hettrick of the 17th Iron Fist Division, Robot Infantry. (Special Combat) exploded in frustration.

Lieutenant Colonel Curt Carson knew this lady very well, and he was mildly surprised at having incurred her sudden wrath simply because he'd brought one of his problems to her for advice and guidance. He was relatively new as the regimental commander of the 3rd Robot Infantry Regiment (Special Combat), the Washington Greys, although he'd worked his way up through the ranks of the Greys since graduation from West Point.

Belinda Hettrick had been his company commander, then regimental commander, and was now his division commander. Over the years, Curt Carson had relied on her support and guidance in addition to that of another experienced old soldier, now his regimental sergeant major: Henry Kester. In the past, he'd always been able to discuss with her the problems he couldn't work out with Henry Kester's help. Which was why he was surprised at her reaction this time.

"General, there's a reason why I'm here. I'm not sniveling. It's always been my policy to discuss difficult problems and decisions with you," Curt reminded her gently but formally, although he probably could have spoken informally with her...except for the fact that they were both on duty and this was her office. "Has something changed? If so, I'd appreciate knowing what it is."

"Damned right things have changed! A lot of things!" she snapped back. She was definitely testy today in spite of the first cool day of autumn which had brought clear, dry, sunny skies to Fort Huachuca, Arizona and broken the hot, sultry, rainy summer monsoon season. In this part of the world, people felt deprived if they didn't see the sun for several days.

The build-up of frustrations suddenly caused Hettrick to make a data dump on an old and trusted subordinate and friend.

"We're being penny-pinched again by the bean counters at OMB and GAO, to say nothing of their civvy-suited counterparts in the Pentagon! We're being hassled with more directives requiring us to report each goddamned dime we spend, justify it six times, and punch up umpteen hundred new forms to document it! We're being forced to do the sort of bitchy little jobs that could be better handled by Civil Service civilian types. This sure as hell isn't the sort of work that should be done by fighting troops! It forces us to let combat training slip in order to handle dumb-ass administrative crap! It's a goddamned waste of trained people who cost the government a lot of money to train...to say nothing of saddling them with jobs they're ill-equipped to do because of their personality profiles."

"Hell, General, this is nothing new," Curt tried to mollify her. "Our civilian bosses in Washington think we're no different than the nine-to-five terminal twerps all around them back there!"

Hettrick had spent more than a year in the Pentagon on staff assignment while she was recovering from wounds. She knew what he said was true. But she growled, "Yeah, too many industrial managers in the mud wrestling ring up there. I've got a sheep screw coming up – I can already see it happening."

"Maybe our sheep screws are the same kind but different degree, General," Curt suggested. "My combat-ready personnel aren't going to be fit to shoot a prairie dog, much less put their pink bodies up against the kind of nasty bastards who keep showing up out there in the world and making trouble for other people going about their lawful business. Am I right?"

"Partly," she retorted quickly, then sighed in frustrated resignation. "My staff is quietly going ape. It's driving me in the same direction! We've got bugs and worms and slime and pests and germs all through the new software that's supposed to tie in with the new hardware up at Diamond Point. And all because some tech-weenies and staff stooges thought the Army ought to have 'better' computers with the latest state of the art! Dammit, when are these idiots going to realize that good enough is the enemy of the best?"

Curt let her explode to get it off her chest. He nodded in agreement with her tirade. He felt the same way. He didn't know whether all the administrative bullshit was just a part of being a regimental commander or whether it was really something new. He suspected the former because he'd had temporary command of the Greys before.

"Hell, I thought it was just training problems. But my staff has been getting the same crap, General. It's driving Wilkinson, Gratton, and Atkinson right up the wall, too. Happily, good old Henry Kester can figure out ways to modify the software to get things done in spite of the system. Then Edie Sampson manages to jump-connect circuit cubes and modules in the hardware, so it does what it's supposed to do. Happily, I've got good jellyware to run the hardware and software…"

"I wish to hell I could borrow them both!" Hettrick muttered.

"Ask and ye shall receive, General," Curt offered, then added, "but please don't keep them too long or the Greys will go to slime."

"I'd damned well do it if it wouldn't raise hell with my own staff," she told him. "This whole mess has made them very insecure. So, they've taken to defending turf to cover their asses. My big problem is busting the vicious circle. By that's *my* problem…Now, *your* problem, Curt, is something that *you* as regimental commander will solve."

"As I remarked, General Hettrick, I've always been able to come to you for advice and guidance…even when you were temporarily out of the direct line of command in the Pentagon," Curt reminded her again.

"And as I told you, you are the regimental commander now, and it's your job to solve these nasty little internal problems!" she countered, then spat out, "FIDO!"

"Yes, ma'am, I will! That's my job! And my responsibility," Curt admitted. "And I apologize if I gave you the impression that I was bringing my problems to you for solutions. I wasn't. I can kick ass when I have to, and I can make the crappy decisions when necessary. And I'll stand behind them after I make them. I was trained to do that by experts: you and Regimental Sergeant Major Henry Kester. *But*...you taught me the value of discussing a bothersome or questionable decision with an experienced colleague before taking action – where time was available to do so. That's why I asked to see you today. If this is a bad time to ask you for some advice, I'll be happy to postpone it. And, General, if you tell me to run my own show, I'll do that too."

Major General Belinda Hettrick sighed and got up. Curt Carson was one of the few people she could really talk to because they'd been through some pretty rough times and very deadly fights. She walked to a side bar and turned to Curt. "Sorry I dumped on you, Curt. So now that I've done some sniveling of my own, I guess I should listen to some of your sniveling. Shot of juice?"

"No, thank you, General," Curt replied, although he knew he probably should. In the arid climate of Arizona, you had to keep up your intake of liquids or run the risk of involuntary dehydration. That could be dangerous for field troops. Water was the best remedy, but fruit juices were plentiful in this part of the world and were blessed with multi-vitamins and fructose. The byword was, never pass a drinking fountain or a juice bar.

"So, you've got motivational and training problems?" Hettrick repeated his earlier problem statement as she poured herself a glass of orange juice fresh-squeezed that morning from a crop of Arizona Sweets that had been preserved over the hot summer. "So, sit down, put your feet up, and let's discuss them separately. Maybe I can give you some free advice which will cost you nothing and may be worth just that."

"I doubt your value judgement," Curt replied informally as she resumed her seat behind her terminal table. But he didn't put his feet up on her table. She'd signaled informality, but that didn't mean he should take her "feet up" suggestion literally. "And I don't think we can discuss motivation and training separately because they're related."

The general looked askance at him. "You're right. You're faced with an old problem: how to keep special combat forces from becoming bored out of their skulls when there isn't anything for them to do that has a high pucker factor."

Curt shook his head. "Whether or not you know it, you helped us solve that one."

"I did? How?"

"You approved combat maneuvers using jelly rounds."

Hettrick smiled. "I thought that would increase the pucker factor! I remember when you and Carson's Companions snuck off into the boonies to relearn basic down-and-dirty infantry tactics by potting at each other with pellet pistols."

"You raised hell with me about that," Curt reminded her.

She nodded. "Until I saw the results in Tranidad and Namibia. I learned that training has to be risky. Getting splattered with laser blood doesn't hurt and leaves no mark. But a jelly round makes a mess and can knock you on your ass..."

"We get a few people hurt with jelly rounds," Curt admitted. "The stupid ones usually get hurt the worst. But even us experienced types get bruised and splattered from time to time. Bruises our egos more than anything else. And it keeps *everyone* very respectful and sharp. But that sort of thing isn't my problem right now."

"Okay, tell me about it in a hundred words or less, Mister Dumb John," she told him, lapsing into West Point cadet slang they both understood.

"Unlike warbot brainies who seem to be constantly enamored with warbot technology..." Curt began.

"And fight by remote control from comfortable couch safely in the rear of the FEBA," Hettrick added.

"Our Sierra Charlies face a lot higher personal risk accompanied by a lot of fear and apprehension," Curt continued. "They're out there taking the incoming with their warbots. We've been through some rough missions – Namibia, Sonora, Kerguelen, Brunei, Kurdistan.

23

That's more action than most soldiers see in an entire career. General, without naming names, I've got to report to you that some of the Washington Greys feel like they've had enough fighting to last a lifetime..."

"Burnout," Hettrick remarked briefly. "We've seen it in some warbot troops...very few, but we've seen it. And I won't ask you who in the Greys is acting burned out. If it's real and irreversible, Curt, you'll have to convince them that resignation or reassignment isn't a dishonorable thing. Matter of fact, it may save their lives."

"I can't convince them," Curt admitted. "Very few Greys have close family ties. They don't like their families, or they come from loose families or their families have broken up or their folks are dead. The regiment is their family. So, no matter how badly they're burned out, they don't want to leave. And no matter how rigorously we train, we can't seem to overcome overconfidence. They've been through it before, so they believe they'll get through it again - in spite of being scared shitless they won't survive or worried they'll do something that will let down their friends and the regiment."

Hettrick thought about that for a moment before she mused, "I see what you mean. And you were right to bring this to me after all. The Washington Greys are the first real infantry regiment since the Army went to warbots a quarter-century ago. The Greys have written the Sierra Charlie book...sometimes in *real* blood. I'm going to have the same problem in the Iron Fist in a year or so when the Cottonbalers or the Wolfhounds begin to hit burnout. Got any good ideas, Curt?"

"Not a one, General. Or I would have tried them out first instead of bending your ear this afternoon," Curt admitted. "The problem is compounded by some of our new people."

"Hell, Curt, you and your company commanders personally interviewed and selected your replacements after the war with the Kurds!" Hettrick reminded him. "What's wrong? Benning turning out cannon fodder?"

"I didn't say that; you did," Curt muttered. Then he went on to explain, "All of us in the Greys were warbot brainies once. Basically, one step removed from tech-weenies. But we were tempered by some people who liked to fight. Remember a guy by the name of Kelly?"

"Now Major Marty 'Kill 'Em All' Kelly? Gee-three with the Wolfhounds? Hell, yes! He was too aggressive for the Greys, as I recall. So, he was put to work turning warbot brainy kids playing video games into Sierra Charlie adults. He's good at that."

"He deserved better," Curt admitted. "Now I know we need the killer types. Fortunately, I've still got them in the regiment thanks to Kelly. He trained up Russ Frazier. Frazier's Ferrets are my top assault company. And then there's sweet little Adonica Sweet, the princess of the regiment; she keeps Alexis Morgan's Marauders a bit more vicious than Alexis herself would. Seems I warped Morgan's mind with my philosophy of winning without killing when possible. And Lieutenant Hassan the Assassin. And Kitsy Clinton..." Curt sighed wearily. "Well, Kitsy just tackled everything with the idea that anything worth doing was worth overdoing..."

Hettrick detected a wistful note in Curt's voice. "You miss Kitsy, don't you?"

"Who wouldn't? We all do!"

"If it will make you feel better, Rumor Control at this level says she's doing fine," Hettrick reported. "After that Kurdish bitch broke her neck in Iraq, the Walter Reed biotechs are sort of baffled that she's even able to walk again...which she did two days ago and then tried to walk out of there."

Curt grinned at this news. "Orgasmic! I'll pass it on at Stand-to tonight."

"So, back to your problem," the general reminded him. She had limited time these days, and her schedule for the rest of the afternoon was full. But as far as she was concerned, the others could damned well wait their turn with their piss-ass little administrative problems. Curt Carson was onto something new. Being the first Sierra Charlie regiment where people fought in the field alongside warbots, the Washington Greys' problems were likely to become problems for the whole 17th Iron Fist Division in due course of time. "So, what's wrong with the new people?"

"They're not tech-weenies."

"Your new people have warbot training…"

"That they do," Curt agreed. "But every one of them went through Fort Benning's warbot training because they had to do it in order to achieve their ultimate goal: become a down-and-dirty Sierra Charlie."

"So?" Hettrick was playing the role of the teacher as well as the leader. She knew if she kept at it long enough, Curt would discover his own solution to his problem.

"So, they don't really like warbots. They tend to treat warbots as something to get them out of trouble when things go to slime. They don't take care of their warbots because they don't think a warbot is as important as their Novia rifles. And they don't really know how to keep a warbot working when it starts to go tits-up, much less how to really maintain a warbot," Curt complained.

"In other words, we've swung the other way. Our new people are infantry grunts," Hettrick summed it up for him.

Curt nodded. "With your help, I turned warbot brainies into Sierra Charlies. But damned if I know how to start from scratch and turn an ordinary person into a Sierra Charlie. I'm beginning to think we've got to have them go through the full drill of being a warbot brainy in an RI regiment, then transfer to the Sierra Charlie units. But I don't know. I started as a warbot brainy. What I need is the input from someone who's come down a similar road as my new people…"

Hettrick didn't say anything for a moment. Then she growled in an official-sounding voice, "Colonel Carson, I am indeed surprised at you! Why don't you ask for help?"

"Uh, General, that's why I'm here."

"I can't help you directly. But you have a person in the Greys who probably knows more than either of us about being an infantry grunt, a warbot brainy, and a Sierra Charlie. He's been all of the above! Why don't you ask him? You never had any reluctance to ask him before!"

Curt couldn't help allowing a grin to spread over his face. "I believe I'll take the matter up with my regimental sergeant major! Thank you, General."

"For what? You found the answer yourself."

"With a little help from my division commander," Curt reminded her. "I just hope I've got time to run the solution before we have to go somewhere and be nasty to someone."

"Curt, you've become a worry wart," Hettrick told him. "Many times before we've gone out and been nasty before we were ready. A combat unit is never ready for what really happens. But we've proved we can haul somebody's ass out of a sling when the world goes to slime."

"Yes, General, but Big World has all sorts of deadly little glitches, and we really can't train thoroughly because we have no control over who's going to do what to whom," Curt remarked.

"So, worry about what you can do something about. Things have sort of gone into quiet mode around the world. So, it's unlikely we're going to be sent anywhere. Which compounds your motivational and training problem."

"Please don't remind me, General," Curt muttered. "The big budget crunch has hit again. The next move from Playland on the Potomac will be raping us with a reduction in force."

"Not if I can help it! I have my ways..."

"Indeed you do, General!"

"So, don't worry about your T-O-and-E. And if something starts to brew somewhere, we can usually see the precursor. Or have you forgotten what you were taught by the War College about the principles of escalation? Keep your eyes on the spook reports I download to you, and you won't be surprised by a sudden deployment." She straightened up in her chair, turned back to her

27

terminal, looked up at Curt, and said, "And don't think you got that advice for free, Colonel. I intend to visit your Stand-to in a few hours, and this little head session is going to cost you dinner tonight."

"With pleasure, General!" Curt told her, getting to his feet. "And thanks. You've always been able to call the big picture shots right on target."

This time, General Belinda Hettrick was going to miss calling the shots by more than a klick or two...

Chapter Three

Officially and even in the history books, the Sakhalin Incident began as a result of "cultural difference between the occupying police action military contingents." That was only part of the truth. It was more basic than that.

"Dear one, let me in!" *Serzhant* Artem Butomavich Ishkov rapped heavily on the door that had suddenly been closed in his face.

There was no response. He banged again with his huge gloved fist.

Finally, the door opened a few centimeters and was brought up by a stout chain. "Nyet! Go away!" was the sharp reply from the small blond woman inside the house.

"But we have an appointment!" he reminded her. "I have brought the *blat*, a liter of the best vodka that I could steal from *Leytenant* Moiseyev..."

"We are closed for business!" she announced after a pause. Obviously, officers' vodka was well appreciated in this cold, damp climate.

"Closed? But you never close!"

"We are closed!" Olga Suvarova was adamant.

"But why? Is it a matter of more *vzyatka*? Better *blat* like more vodka? I will..." *Serzhant* Ishkov suggested. He was eager in the strange, restrained Victorian way of Russians. It had been a rough week. His patrols had been shot at twice - once by a Japanese patrol, and once by comrade socialist Chinese.

"*Nyet!*"

"Then what is the problem, dear one?" Ishkov wanted to know. "Can I make something right where it is not right?"

"You and your soldiers can keep the *vostoki* barbarians away from us! They are *nee kultumi* and they smell bad!" Olga announced and then slammed the door in *Serzhant* Ishkov's face.

Ishkov kicked at the door. It was heavy and solid. It didn't budge. In frustration, he sat down on the steps of the squalid house on Susunayskiy Ooleetsah in the equally squalid industrial district of Yuzhno-Sakhalinsk. Like all other Red Army soldiers stationed in regions where the female social battalions didn't like to serve or where, as in this case, the High Command knew that the needs of the soldiers could be well served by local establishments. *Serzhant* Artem Butomavich Ishkov of the 110th Special Airborne Guards Regiment had taken great risks and squandered lots of *blat* in order to visit Olga's house. Others in the casern were covering for him. He would have to cover for them someday soon. In spite of the prudish attitude toward sex manifested in the Red Army - and exported by the Russians, often unsuccessfully, to the rest of their empire - Ishkov was a second-generation Georgian who had been raised in a warmer and less puritanical clime. He needed Olga that night. If not Olga, then the delicious little Mariya. And he was willing to ante-up whatever additional *blat* it took in the form of more vodka or Red Army rations.

As a result, he was more than merely pissed off. He was angry. What had those slimy yellow Chinese and Japanese done to these fine Ukrainian and White Russian women? Nursing his frustration and disappointment, he pulled the cap from the liter of vodka and took a heavy pull on the bottle.

"*Bojemoi!*" he muttered to himself in disgust and frustration.

It didn't help when a Chinese three-man military police patrol wandered down Susunayskiy Ooleetsah. They saw Ishkov sitting forlornly on the steps of the house guzzling from the bottle of vodka he'd brought along as part of his *blat*.

They spoke no Russian. In Chinese, they told him to get up and get going.

In Russian, Ishkov told them to go piss up a rope and made reference to the questionable nature of their ancestors.

The three Chinese soldiers didn't understand a word of what he said, but they knew from the tone of his voice that they'd been insulted.

Even three against one, it had been a good brawl. They left Ishkov unconscious, bloody, and barely alive on the pavement. One of their number wasn't in much better shape. Since the patrol commander knew the house on Susunayskiy Ooleetsah and had, in fact, been rebuffed there only last night, he and his companion beat down the door and made forcible entry...and not just into the house.

***

Colonel Viktor Pashkavitch Kurotkin wasn't sure he should make the telephone call at all. He wasn't certain how to report his problem without putting himself in jeopardy as a commander. And he wasn't certain exactly how to phrase his statement of the problem. "Comrade General Vlasov, this is Kurotkin in Yuzhno-Sakhalinsk. I am calling to report a serious problem with the troops of my regiment here. I am also facing a military situation that threatens to become worse. And I wish to make a request."

Sitting in his palatial Khabarovsk office paneled in light, polished spruce with the stern visages of Lenin and the current chairman staring down upon him from their honored positions on the wall behind his huge desk, General Ivan Fillipovich Vlasov, the commander of the Far East Military District, couldn't understand why his staffers had bucked this telephone call to him. He initially decided to discipline whoever was responsible for handling petty personnel details, until he remembered his own service on Sakhalin as the regimental commander of a motor rifle regiment whose mission had primarily been political control. He was having trouble hearing Kurotkin. Sakhalin had once had outstanding communications in the form of undersea fiber optics cables to the mainland, but that was when the island was under Soviet control and needed the comm capabilities for its air defense installations. Now that Sakhalin was ostensibly demilitarized, those communication facilities had been allowed to deteriorate. Vlasov strained to hear, thinking to himself that fiber optics technology was a poor "gift" from AT&T because the KGB hadn't been able to steal the maintenance technicians, too. He made a mental note to ask his general major in charge of the special signals troops to do something soldiers have been proficient at since the dawn of time: scrounge what they couldn't get through regular channels.

"Comrade Colonel, please tell me first about the military situation," Vlasov ordered. "Then we might be able to discuss your regimental problem..."

"Comrade General, the two cannot be discussed separately because one is a consequence of the other," Kurotkin reported with some hesitation. "But I am not certain what started it. Like you, I am a family man as well as a military man who has devoted his life to the defense of the Motherland. Like you, I am a graduate of the Frunze Military Academy." Kurotkin felt that this reminder wouldn't hurt his image with the general. "I was educated for military command, but not to handle the sort of difficult cultural situation in which I find myself on Sakhalin."

"This telephone connection is not very good, Comrade Colonel. Did I hear you say it is a cultural situation?" Vlasov asked.

"Yes, Comrade General. May I report, please, and it will become clear to you?" Kurotkin ventured. He explained how he had worked with the other two regimental commanders to stagger the time schedules for recreational passes. "This has virtually eliminated any off-duty conflicts between our soldiers and the Chinese and Japanese. And we had surprisingly few confrontations between armed patrols and carousing soldiers," Kurotkin went on. "Until four days ago. Now we have had several confrontations between patrols and my individual soldiers on pass!"

"Comrade Colonel!" Vlasov exploded. "This is in direct violation of orders!"

"Yes, Comrade General, I know! I have taken the necessary disciplinary steps and have punished the offenders in my regiment," Kurotkin was quick to reply, knowing that he was ultimately responsible and would have to answer for his regiment disobeying orders. But he also knew if he didn't voluntarily bring this to the attention of the Far East Military District and ask for help, things could go much worse for him. "But about twenty percent of my regiment is in detention or assigned to labor details requiring yet another twenty percent of my regimental strength to serve as guards." He also knew that as a result of the deterioration of social relationships in the city, the discipline within the 110th Special Airborne Guards was deteriorating rapidly in spite of harshly increased disciplinary measures.

Then, forgetting in the heat of the pressurized discussion that he hadn't completed his justification, he blurted out, "Therefore, Comrade General, I respectfully request that a female social battalion be assigned to my command at the earliest opportunity."

General Ivan Fillipovich Vlasov said nothing for a moment, causing Kurotkin to conclude that he'd blown his career out the window.

But in a place like Yuzhno-Sakhalinsk with something less than sparkling civic and social environs, Vlasov

knew that troops on pass didn't have much to do except get laid and get drunk, although he didn't think of it in those English terms. Female "social battalions" had been a part of the TO&E of the Red Army for decades in remote regions of the USSR because the generals were realists. But no social battalion was authorized for Sakhalin because the High Command didn't think they were needed there. Many members of the Defense Ministry had served on Sakhalin when it was Soviet territory.

Although state-operated bordellos were not acceptable to the semi-Victorian Leninist morality, private brothels were allowed to operate without official approval or notice in places like Sakhalin. Thus, the amply-endowed Ukrainian and Byelorussian women along Susunayskiy Ooleetsah seemed to fulfil the requirements of the Soviet troops at no cost to the government.

Vlasov recalled his own service on Sakhalin prior to the Sino-Soviet Incident. And he hoped that General Lieutenant Yuriy Pavlovitch Druzhinin had not forgotten the agreement the two Soviet generals had with one another: Vlasov would overlook the chief political officer's bizarre proclivities if Vlasov's own youthful indiscretions along Susunayskiy Ooleetsah were not brought to the attention of others.

One always had to have something on someone else to survive in the paranoid culture of the USSR.

But Kurotkin had nothing on Vlasov. Therefore, Kurotkin would have to bear the brunt of usual Soviet military doctrine: Only the strong units deserved help when things went to slime.

Besides, Vlasov wasn't about to reassign the social battalion now in Khabarovsk. He was much too fond of a certain captain and two lieutenants who served in that unit. He didn't want to send them to Sakhalin.

"Comrade Colonel, you request the impossible," Vlasov told him with weary resignation. "Because of the recent economic difficulties in the Motherland, my available *Tyl* forces have been reduced. For all of the tank and motorized rifle divisions assigned to the Far East Military District, there exists only one social battalion. I cannot reassign it to Sakhalin. You will just have to carry out your assigned mission with what you have…"

The telephone call that went from Yuzhno-Sakhalinsk to Beiching was almost the same except that Colonel Dao Min Qian asked for another regiment of PRC troops to help him keep order. No mention was made of a social battalion; such things didn't exist in the People's Liberation Army. China had a different culture and a far more stringent version of Marxist-Leninist doctrine. The sexual life of soldiers was something that simply wasn't discussed among the officers; it was every man for himself. When on pass, it was kept very private and discreet if it was done at all. And if it was wanted badly enough or if it could be taken without accountability, it was taken forcibly from the conquered. As for paying for it even in terms of barter, that wasn't even considered. At least among the Mongolian troops of the People's Liberation Army who were stationed on Sakhalin.

As for Colonel Yushiro Mishida, he didn't make a telephone call.

Instead, he communicated by means of a full holographic teleconference connection utilizing undersea laser links between Sakhalin and Hokkaido. It was a very secure communication channel, one which, by its very nature, was almost impossible to tap. And the person whose three-dimensional image appeared across the table from Mishida wasn't his superior in the Japanese Self-Defense Force. Mishida's general officer would hear from the Colonel in due course of time; but first, he had to report to the deputy minister of state for International Materials, Office Five, a person and position that appeared on no Japanese government organizational chart. IM-5 was clandestine and had been for decades. For an island nation almost totally dependent upon imported natural resources to support its economy and industry, IM-5 was a necessity.

They spoke in Japanese using ciphered code words to refer to people, organizations, and places. When translated into English it went as follows.

"Most Honorable Minister, the campaign goes well," Mishida told the flat-faced, bespectacled little man dressed in a dark, conservative business suit who appeared to be so lifelike and realistic on the other side of the table. "I anticipate major confrontations and significant casualties on all sides within a week."

"Make certain, Colonel, that your troops do not instigate any incidents," the deputy minister replied. His organization wasn't exactly like the American NIA or the Soviet KGB. He was part of a clandestine government pro-active intelligence group that was spread throughout the government in critical offices. Its job was to take care of the necessary covert operations required to ensure continued raw materials imports to Japanese industry. "Your regiment must he perceived to be the innocent bystanders who are merely on Sakhalin to protect Japan's northern border against the ravages of the Russian and Mongol hordes. After all, Japan must maintain its image as a non-aggressive, non-militant nation..."

"My regiment is well disciplined, Honorable Minister," Mishida asserted.

"I am certain that it is," the government official responded deferentially. It wasn't easy to manage this operation intended to gain total control over the petroleum, coal, and titanium resources of Sakhalin in the face of the Soviets and Chinese, who'd learned of Japan's earlier plan and attempted to thwart it by introducing their own troops on the island.

It was contrary to Japanese policy to commit military forces to seize and protect resources. If such a thing was necessary, Japan preferred to get other national trading partners to use their military forces instead. This policy had worked very well since Japan had learned how to do it as a matter of necessity after the end of the Great Pacific War in 1945. But when the Soviets and Chinese introduced military forces into Sakhalin contrary to treaty and flaunting various UN Security Council and General Assembly resolutions, Japan had no alternative but to counter with her own Self-Defense Forces.

"And when we manage to get the Americans to return their troops to Sakhalin as a result of your actions, we can withdraw your regiment back to the home islands."

"That cannot happen too quickly for us, Honorable Minister," Colonel Mishida admitted. "We dearly miss the civilized amenities such as baths, tea houses, and geishas."

"In due course of time and because of your efforts and sacrifices, Colonel, Yuzhno-Sakhalinsk will again regain its rightful name as Toyohara, and we shall be able to bring civilization back to the island of Karafuto after nearly a century..."

Chapter Four

Magnum One, this is Magnum Leader! Show me your target data bus on visual!

"Dammit!" Colonel Curt Carson growled in irritation. "Lieutenant Milton knows better! This isn't ordinary warbot warfare! She's got to get target data from sources other than her Saucy Cans!" He was in the turret of his OCV, accompanying the 1st Platoon "Milton's Magnums" of the GUNCO "Allen's Alleycats."

"Well, Colonel, that's all Lieutenant Milton knows. At Fort Benning, all they did was pour regular warbot procedures into her," Regimental Sergeant Major Henry Kester remarked dryly from his perch in the auxiliary hatch.

"Yeah, that's true. I guess I can't expect much more from a new officer," Curt muttered in reply over his secure intercom with his chief regimental NCO. "It's up to us to teach her how the Sierra Charlies fight."

"Sir, with all due respect, it's not your sweat. It's up to Major Allen and Sergeant Barnes," Kester gently corrected his regimental commander.

"You're right...as usual," Curt remarked. When he was a fresh brown-bar, it was his company commander who set him straight. When he got his own company, he was expected to do the training and not bother the regimental commander unless he had to. Now that he was finally in command of the Washington Greys, Curt discovered he was having more than a little trouble adjusting to the required aloof attitude of the position. The regiment was far larger and more complex than a company or even a battalion. And he was expected to keep a sharp eye on everything that was going on because he was ultimately responsible. But he had to allow his subordinates to run their own operations and gently correct them only when they were doing something obviously wrong or that would screw up the particular operation they were conducting.

Although Curt had taught the personnel of his original company, Carson's Companions, and then the TACBATT, he now knew he had the awesome responsibility of the entire regiment. The history of the Washington Greys stretched back in time to 1784, and it was an illustrious history. The regiment had never had its honor sullied, and he was very well aware that all of this was now in his hands. On top of that, generations of his family had served with honor and distinction in the armed forces of the United States, and now the monkey was on his shoulders. All of this scared him a little bit, but it was a different sort of fear than he felt when going into a fracas. Although he was a natural leader of people and a good teacher, he'd always taken those attributes for granted. Now, when he thought about them, he began to understand how hard it really was to be a leader and a teacher.

Thank God for Henry Kester! he told himself. And for Belinda Hettrick whom he could talk to when he had to.

And in spite of the fact that he was carefully watching potential successors as well as a new officer, he knew it really wasn't right for him to be with GUNCO during these war games out on the pampas north of Fort Huachuca, Arizona. His command post should have been where he could move quickly to any part of the exercise. However, he wanted to get first-hand data on the new lieutenant who was in charge of one of the regiment's light artillery platoons, a position that could be a critical one in any combat situation.

He had another fresh platoon officer, Lieutenant Dale Brown, who was running Brown's Black Hawks, the BIRD birdbot reconnaissance unit. However, Major Ellie Aarts, RECONCO commander, reported that Brown was good and his platoon personnel, the only real neuro-electronic warbot operators left in the Greys, were working well with him. And Lieutenant Dyani Motega, who was running SCOUT platoon in RECONCO, privately confirmed Ellie's assessment.

So Curt was far more concerned about GUNCO-1, Milton's Magnums, because the platoon's four 75-millimeter M5OO Saucy

Cans guns amounted to half his regimental artillery capability. If the Greys were ordered to go into action anywhere in this troubled, violent world, he had to be sure that Lieutenant Martha Milton had her platoon up to the proper level of training, even though she was new to the outfit. Curt also knew he should count on Major Jerry Allen for that, hut he felt it wouldn't hurt to stick around to see for himself. His presence with Milton's Magnums during this training maneuver against the Wolfhounds, the "enemy" in this exercise, would certainly he noticed by Jerry Allen, who would reinforce his own training regimen.

Magnum Leader, this is Alleycat Leader! came the voiceless and soundless reply of Major Jerry Allen in Curt's head, fed directly from his OCV's receiver through the neurophonic skin electrodes in Curt's battle helmet. *Stick your head out of your ACV and check those targets yourself with your own sensors! You know that the sensors on the Saucy Cans don't have the discrimination you've got in your ACV!*

Sir, warbot sensors are- Lieutenant Martha Milton started to reply.

Your LAMVAs are not - repeat not - regular warbots! They've got Mod seven-eleven AI to help them out, but they are not - repeat not - extensions of yourself like the regular bots you've been working with at Benning! Jerry reminded her. *They're like dumb, stupid humans with an IQ of about eighty! They don't see as well as you can, and they'll take only that action you tell them to take unless their internal programs override! Get your head out of your armored can and look around you!*

At the Club and in the company day room, Lieutenant Martha Milton seemed on the surface like a mousy New Englander. Only her 101 personnel file, with her personality profile gave any indication that she had no aversion to committing violence when required to do so. Her ancestors had fought at Lexington and Concord. She had her violent traits well under control. Perhaps they were too well under control. However, something told Curt that she wouldn't be mousy when things went to slime. He trusted his instincts about that. Furthermore, Jerry had expressed similar opinions after he'd inter-viewed her prior to accepting her. She was certainly a smart techie with an MIT engineering degree in applied robotics. Her desire to live and work in a highly disciplined adult environment such as the twenty-first century warbot Army made itself known when she joined the ROTC in her freshman year. But her reply to her company commander was more hesitant this time.

Major, my LAMVAs have good targets, and we've got the front well defined! We're ready to commence fire over the FEBA into the Wolfhounds' rear area when you give the word!

You don't know the Wolfhounds! I know the officer who trained them in Sierra Charlie doctrine and tactics! He's aggressive! Jerry snapped back, referring to a former member of the Washington Greys, now Major Marty "Killer" Kelly, who turned out to be too bloodthirsty for the Greys. The Greys had been the ones who developed the Army's new Robot Infantry Special Combat doctrine where human soldiers went back into the battlefield alongside smart warbots instead of directing regular warbots from far behind the lines using neuroelectronics linkage technology. *Major Kelly has taught the Wolfhounds what he learned from us...and we learned it the hard way with blood: There is no such thing as a FERA! It can be all around you! Especially behind you! And especially for GUNCO which is big and obvious! Lieutenant always check minus-x! Always! Get your head out of your armored can and keep looking around! And make sure Sergeant Carrington helps you by keeping an eagle-type eyeball peeled where you aren't looking at the moment!*

Curt was listening to all of this quite carefully, but not for reasons that might be suspected by others. Although he was interested in seeing to it that Lieutenant Martha Milton was properly trained, he had another motive, one that had been pounded into him years ago by then-Captain Belinda Hettrick, his first commanding officer when he'd been assigned to Hettrick's Hellcats, her company command in the Washington Greys:

"A good officer always trains a replacement! Preferably two of them!"

Curt hadn't understood the rationale behind that. Now he did.

A quiet "chain of command" had developed within the twenty-first century Army, an Army in which one spent nearly all of one's operational career - less time spent attending staff and war colleges

- in a single regiment. It was very unusual for DCSPERS to assign a regimental commander from outside a regiment, and even divisional commanders came up from within a division. When it had been necessary to bring in an outsider - as had been the case with the former commander of the Greys, Colonel Bill Bellamack whom Curt replaced because the man had been both wounded and brain-shocked - it was done with great reluctance.

As a result, one of the first things Curt did upon becoming the commander of the Greys was to search both the TO&E and his own soul to decide who he'd select to train as the next commander of the regiment.

No one in the Washington Greys knew he was doing this, of course. General Belinda Hettrick, now CO of the 17th Iron Fist Division, knew and had prompted Curt to begin early as she had done.

But although there was no roaring rush in making his selection and ensuring that the proper interpersonal contracts were in place, Curt was having some trouble making a selection.

He knew several Washington Greys who might make good regimental commanders.

Major Jerry Allen was only one of several he was interested in, and Jerry was handling the situation very well. He and his first sergeant, Forrey Barnes, were on the ground and hidden in the long brown grass that covered the rolling hills around them. GUNCO was dispersed in arroyos and gullies, hidden from the ASSAULTCO of the Wolfhounds, who were moving up on them from the north about two klicks away. Jerry had them ranged already, using burst laser ranging from his Jeep which he'd put up on the military crest of a slight rise where the warbot's sensors could sweep a broad plain to the north.

Curt monitored the progress of the mock battle. It was "mock" only in the sense that it involved two Sierra Charlie "ghost" regiments with equal equipment and manpower pitted against one another, and "mock" because it was non-lethal and no live ammo was being used, only jelly rounds that would hit and hurt but wouldn't do damage unless the hit was somehow in an unprotected part of the human boy.

The Greys recon was good. Curt watched as the battle elements paraded across his helmet visor. Occasionally, he'd look down at the bigger tac display inside his OCV, where Master Sergeant Edie Sampson was riding herd on the technology.

It looked to Curt like the Wolfhounds were actually maneuvering into the clever little trap he'd set for them. Morgan's Marauders were serving as bait to lure the Wolfhounds ASSAULTCO into a defile where they'd be caught from behind by Jerry's Saucy Cans barrage and from the flank by Frazier's Ferrets.

In spite of the fact that Curt was a maneuvering tactician - he liked to press the offensive and depend on the surprise of movement - he and his officers and chief NCOs had elected this morning to occupy a stronger defensive position and use the principle of offensive defense. He wanted to get Colonel Frederick Salley's Wolfhounds into a position where the Greys could pin them down, maneuver around them, and go on the offensive. The Greys saw no other viable alternative when confronted by an enemy with equal strength and equipment. As usual, Curt let his people do the planning with only gentle suggestions and direction from him.

Fred Salley was a careful tiger; Curt had "fought" him before on maneuvers at West Point when Curt commanded a cadet company and Salley took him on one day with a larger cadet battalion. The only new factor that kept Curt wary today was Salley's S-3 ops officer, the notorious Major Marty "Killer" Kelly, a former Washington Grey. Marty had been too aggressive for the Greys but had been a good Sierra Charlie; he'd been transferred to the Wolfhounds to train that regiment in Sierra Charlie doctrine and tactics. Curt knew that Kelly had trained the Wolfhounds with his own version of the doctrine: "Kill 'em all; let God sort 'em out!" Kelly's approach to warfare was very French with lots of *cran* and *elan* in his style. Curt intended to use that factor against the Wolfhounds.

The Greys wanted to let Salley and his troops charge into a strong defensive position, then move rapidly to envelop them.

As a result, Curt's standing order that morning was, "Fire on my command unless you're spotted and start taking Wolfhound fire yourself. If that happens, better have a damned good excuse ready for the critique!"

But it suddenly became apparent that the Wolfhounds had their own plans.

"Colonel, somethin' doesn't square with the tac display of the Wolfhounds," Regimental Master Sergeant Henry Kester remarked, calling his commanding officer's attention to the big board in the bowels of the OCV.

Curt ducked his head out of the turret and looked. What he saw was a three-dee topo map of the area with highlighted indicators showing the positions of the Washington Greys in blue and the known position of the Wolfhounds obtained from RECONCO and from ELINT reception of Wolfhound beacons. It was a confused array of lights to anyone not accustomed to a tac display. Curt saw nothing unusual. "What doesn't square, Henry?"

"Where are all the Wolfhounds, Colonel?"

Curt looked again.

Some of the red targets were already tagged by Grady, the regimental computer, as having been identified. Some of them were not, but a "best guess" probability had been assigned to them by the computer and by Henry Kester. "Looks like all the units are accounted for, Henry."

"Maybe, sir. Maybe. But they're either short-botted or someone has hung their individual beacons on vehicles and bots," Henry pointed out. "These beacons move with the vehicles and the bots."

"Dammit, I must be getting more stupid with increasing rank!" Curt muttered. He'd pulled this trick before on the Cottonbalers and the Wolfhounds - putting a maneuverable strike force in stealth and mounting their ID beacons on existing vehicles and warbots as a deception. It had been suggested by Lieutenant Dyani Motega when she was still an NCO. It was something she said was an old Crow Indian trick that her ancestors had once taught the soldiers of

Brigadier General George Crook on the Great Plains during the Indian Wars.

Henry Kester didn't comment on Curt's personal observation. It would have been inappropriate, and it wasn't Henry Kester's way of handling a situation.

Curt knew exactly what was happening now and what he was going to do about it.

Alleycat Leader, this is Grey Head! Marty may be trying to pull a Motega on us! Curt called on neuroelectronic "thought wave" tacomm to his GUNCO commander. *Leave the vehicles and bots where they are! Put them in remote voice command mode! All Sierra Charlies of GUNCO go to ground at once! Form a base of fire in those junipers to the east of us! But keep it spread out!*

There was a brief pause that was apparently caused by Major Jerry Allen making a quick evaluation of the situation from his own smaller tac display, but it only took a few seconds for the young officer to react. He didn't waste any time or words. *Grey Head, Alleycat Leader! We are going to ground! See you, Edie, and Henry in the puckerbrush! Alleycats all! Magnums to the right! Rascals to the left! Execute!*

"Drop your plugs and grab your slugs, Edie!" Curt called down to his chief tech NCO in the OCV. "Time to go physical!"

"Loud and clear, Colonel!" came the reply. "Give me five ticks to set up some patches!"

Curt grabbed his Novia assault rifle, bailed out of the turret hatch, and rolled down the side of his OCV to the ground. Henry Kester was right behind him but had elected to clamber out one of the side hatches instead. Edie Sampson followed.

Together, they dashed across the fifty meters of open grassland to the line of juniper trees.

On both sides of them, the Sierra Charlies of GUNCO were doing the same.

The objective Curt had in mind was reasonably simple: ambush the ambushers. He knew Major Marty Kelly's way of operating; it was all-out assault. Now that he'd had his aggressive tendencies tempered somewhat by having to work as ops officer for a whole regiment, Kelly's tendencies had been modified; Curt knew he'd now use guile as well as assault. Kelly was sneaking up on the Greys' artillery company, using the same tactic that Curt had used against him years ago in the Virgin Islands during a training exercise.

Curt reached the trees. He found a place where he could hunker down and still have a clear field of fire overlooking all the LAMVAs and ACVs of GUNCO as well as his own OCV. He tried to check his helmet display to locate Henry and Edit; their beacons did not show. No real sense in using IFF beacons in this situation; when the Wolfhounds made their assault, they'd be obvious out there in the open. Then Curt remembered that maybe Marty Kelly might be able to see his own tac beacon, so he toggled it off.

But he wasn't quick enough.

"Drop the Novia, Colonel!" came the growl of a familiar voice from behind. "Or you get a jelly round! And at ten meters, that hurts like hell even through body armor!"

Curt turned slowly to see Major Marty Kelly hidden beneath a ghilly net in the shadow of a tree behind him.

"In fact, I think I'll shoot you anyway!" Kelly's face sported a sardonic grin. "Sort of delayed repayment for decking me the last time you pulled this same stunt on me!"

The man raised his Novia and aimed.

Suddenly he took a jelly round in his side. The jelled pellet was not intended to penetrate but splatter. That is did, spraying red dye all over Kelly's side.

He was immediately hit by three more.

The combined impact of the jelly rounds tossed him off his feet and into the bushes, his Novia flying wildly in the air.

Curt saw Henry Kester and Edie Sampson through the trees. Curt had no doubt who had fired what. Henry was good enough to hit with one round. Edie tended to make sure by using three-round bursts.

Colonel, the action is to the rear! We walked into the ambush party! Henry reported.

And small arms fire broke out all around them as the Greys found and opened on the Wolfhounds.

Curt heard Jerry's order, *Alleycats all! Swing your Jeeps to put fire into these woods against all targets not showing beacons or showing Wolfhound beacons!*

The IFF beacons on the Greys appeared again on Curt's helmet display.

We're outgunned here on the left! Came the call from Lieutenant Bill Ritscher.

No you're not! Magnums swung around behind the Wolfers! Let's squeeze 'em! That was Lieutenant Martha Milton.

Maybe she was going to be okay as a Sierra Charlie, Curt thought to himself.

And the Wolfhounds forgot to check minus-x, too! That was unmistakably Lieutenant Dyani Motega. *Grey Head, this is Mustang Leader! We've got them, too! Been tracking their minus-x ever since we spotted them. Figured they might be coming after you, Colonel! Doctrine says to go for the OCV, get the head man, then fight what's left of the battle!*

Again, the fight had gone beyond Curt's ability to micromanage it. He had to let his troops fight it out their way, and they'd managed to take and keep the upper hand even without his constant monitoring. This was getting to be old hat insofar as he was concerned. The Greys were trained so well and operated together so beautifully as a team that Curt sometimes felt as useful as tits on a turret...like he did right then.

Curt heard the 75-millimeter Saucy Cans guns on the LAMVAs open up and knew that Jerry had been watching the overall battle while the skirmish was going on and had passed the order to Milton and Ritscher to commence firing. That meant things were going pretty well as planned now that the abortive ambush had been thwarted. Time to let his people get on with their jobs.

He went to where Major Marty Kelly had taken it in the shorts. He found the little man lying in a pool of red dye from the four jelly rounds that had hit him. He was trying to regain the breath that had been knocked out of him by the impacts.

Curt whipped the ghilly net off him with a flick of his Novia's barrel.

Kelly had regained his breath enough to try to sit up and yell at Curt, "You motherfucking sonofabitch! One goddamned jelly round would have been enough, you bastard!"

"You made the mistake of not watching your own minus-x. You were a target for two of my best sharpshooters, Marty. Both Henry Kester and Edie Sampson splattered you because they could see you. You made your usual tiger-error mistake. So shut the hell up, or I'll put a jelly round into you right now, and you'll get powder burns as well as another welt!" Curt growled back. "You're my prisoner, so get on your feet and come on over and watch what my GUNCO's doing to Salley's main force. Do I have your word as an officer that you're an honorable prisoner of war?"

"Fuck you!" Kelly snarled, slowly and painfully getting to his feet. "Last time I surrendered to you your people pissed on my equipment!"

"Hey, be glad they didn't piss on you, Marty," Curt told him with a grin. "Might as well resign to the inevitable. The war games are all but over for today. We're just about to win."

"Bullshit! Salley's a fighter!"

"I know it; but you trained him, so I know what he'll do. He won't do anything wrong; but he won't do things right, and he'll lose this one because I read your tactics like a book! You might have pulled it off if I didn't know you so goddamned well...and if you'd trained a combat team rather than a bunch of wild-assed tigers. Tell you what...Come over to our Club tonight, and I'll buy you dinner in compensation for the overkill on the part of my NCOs."

Curt could see that Marty Kelly, like himself, was getting older. The man had indeed mellowed somewhat in the years since he'd left the Greys. And Curt himself had become less of a fighter and more of a negotiator; Kelly saw that.

"Carson, you sonofabitch, you always were a smooth one," Kelly admitted. "Okay, I'll let you buy, but not out of regimental funds! Out of your own pocket! But look out, you bastard! One of these days you won't be able to win by talking your way out of a fight!"

Chapter Five

"Those bastards are at it again!" Al Murray of the National Intelligence Agency growled.

In spite of the fact that the National Security Council's ladies were present in the capacity of Vice-President, the secretary of the Treasury, the attorney general, and the director of the Arms Control Agency, retired General Murray didn't temper his language. In the first place, these women were as tough as the men, having fought their own ways up the greasy ladder of politics.

In the second place, Murray felt he needed to emphasize the nature of the situation on Sakhalin.

"Well, Al, the Japanese have always been a militant culture," said James B. Floyd, secretary of defense.

"True, but since World War Two they've redirected their militancy into the business and industrial sectors," was the remark by Commerce Secretary Charles S. Nagel.

"If you're referring to the Russkies and the Chinese, Al," interjected National Security Advisor William J. Barnitz, who spoke with some authority as a full major general in the Aerospace Force, and who'd come to NSC from leading the USAF Far East Command, "they're both land empires. They've been at each other's throats for centuries. I can understand why both of them would like to have Sakhalin Island for strategic reasons."

"My intemperate remark on the lack of parentage wasn't in reference to the Japanese, Chinese, or Soviets," the director of the NIA corrected them all.

Following Murray's remark, it was quiet for a moment in the NSC operational center located a few blocks from the White House and the Old Executive Office Building. It was located in an innocuous Washington office complex which possessed cleverly designed suites and even full floors that couldn't be detected from the outside. These were entered only through a closely guarded underground access from elsewhere. Who would notice that an elevator skipped two or three floors randomly layered in a building? Not if the inner door was closed and the floor indicator lights didn't reveal that a floor was regularly skipped. Or who took the time to notice that some corridors didn't lead to offices that filled out all the available square meters of floorspace?

The heavily tinted and partly mirrored external windows didn't allow anyone to look in. But the occupants had a view of beautiful downtown Washington. The windows were also made of immensely strong composite plastic "glass" that would stop anything short of a 200-millimeter antitank round. Parts of the "underground" government of the twentieth century were still located in deep, bombproof subterranean bunkers, but twenty-first century politicians preferred to meet with bright scenic panoramas that weren't artificial video windows. The threat of thermonuclear war had almost vanished, and the politicians and bureaucrats liked their new above-ground places of power that reminded them of what a good job they'd done (or thought they'd done; they often forgot the military and naval forces which had been their salvation) in eliminating the thermonuclear threat.

"Certainly, you don't mean the Bruneis?" was the astonished question from Vice-President Louise Dallas, who normally didn't speak up often in these NSC meetings."

"Yes, Madam Vice-President, I do," Murray replied quickly. "The sultan of Brunei has taken full and complete advantage of our joint military and trade treaty ever since it went into effect. Now he's calling for a joint COPRE military policing contingent of three nations to be put onto Sakhalin to keep the Japs, Russkies, and Chinks from starting a general war on the Pacific rim..."

"Al, this is news to me," admitted Secretary of State Clayton. "Why, only today we received the notice of the meeting of the Congress of Pacific Rim Economies, but no agenda was announced. Apparently, this request is the agenda. If you know this to be a fact, I'd appreciate learning of it when you find out." He didn't like the idea that the NIA chief had kept the information to himself and not informed him before this NSC meeting. It was embarrassing. It implied that the secretary of state didn't know what was going on in his own shop.

"My information came from my NIA sources," Murray admitted. He didn't add that he hadn't let State in on it for a simple reason: The Department of State was as leaky as a sieve. NIA had its own, very secure spook net, and Murray wasn't about to compromise something that had taken lots of time and money to set up...much less possibly expose his sources in the process.

Since the Army had sent the Washington Greys over to Brunei where they'd gotten into deep slime because of sloppy intelligence, Murray had activated a far more vital operation on the island of Borneo. Now he knew what was going on there. It often dismayed him because he didn't really understand the nature of the highly nepotistic Brunei government. Nor could he really fathom what the twenty-five-trillion-dollar investment portfolio of the sultan of Brunei was capable of doing in the closely linked world economy. He'd been told - but didn't really believe it - that the Sultan's long-range goal was to make his wealthy little nation the leading economic power of the Pacific rim.

The people on Wall Street and in the Valley of the Sun could have confirmed his intelligence reports. New York and Phoenix financial interests and stock exchange brokers had very good intelligence networks of their own and usually believed what these told them. Trillions of dollars were at stake.

"So, what's the nature of your concern that caused you to request that I convene this NSC meeting?" the President asked directly.

"Mister President, when we participated in the establishment of COPRE during the last administration," Murray started to explain, "your predecessor used the mutual defense clauses of the COPRE agreement to implement his basic policy of withdrawing American military forces from overseas bases. He pulled several regiments of warbot troops out of Sakhalin. The Japanese were told to use their Self-Defense Force to maintain order there. But a caveat to the protocol said that the Japanese troops were to be an airborne regiment based on Hokkaido and called in only if needed. Turned out they were needed. When the Sovs were forced to pull out of Sakhalin after the Sino-Soviet Incident, they took their internal police units with them. It was only a matter of time before the Russian population on Sakhalin got rowdy with the Japanese managers and engineers who were sent in there to operate the oil fields and mines. Then when the Sovs and Chinese put their own troops into Sakhalin in response to the Japanese billeting a regiment there to keep order, the die was cast."

"Sakhalin has been a potential trouble spot since the nineteenth century," General Barnitz observed.

"Bill, I see you've read my internal memo," Murray complimented him. "It was NIA's assessment that the withdrawal of the Panthers regiment of the Fiftieth Division would be viewed as an open invitation for others to insert their own forces there. Sure as hell, that's what happened. The three national military units now on Sakhalin are at one another's throats. Patrols are firing on each other. Patrols are assaulting soldiers of the other contingents who happen to be on leave or pass. A generally bad situation..."

Admiral Warren G. Spencer, Chairman of the Joint Chiefs of Staff, leaned forward and put his golden sleeves on the table in front of him. "Al, I find that hard to believe. Discipline in the Red Army, the People's Liberation Army, and the Self-Defense Force is among the strictest in the, world. Those people are trained from birth to obey orders. They sure as hell aren't individualists like our military personnel. With their linear command structure, they obey orders. I can't imagine that my counterparts in those three countries haven't set out some damned tough rules of engagement and operational orders to prevent just such a blow-up! What do they want? A general war?"

"Yes, Spence, because the Sovs and the Chinese have been spoiling for a general war for nearly a century," Murray fired back. Then he added hastily, "Let me amend that because I could be wrong. Let me say, 'maybe,' because if we do the right thing, we may be able to stop it before it gets going. Which is why I requested this meeting so we could discuss it."

"What's to fight about?" Betty Redfield of the ACA wanted to know. "I never heard of Sakhalin Island before this all started. What's so important about Sakhalin?"

"What's important about Sakhalin? What we've learned about it since the Russkies had to give it back to Japan," the intelligence chief explained. "The Soviets kept very quiet about Sakhalin. Now that some American engineers and geologists have gotten in there to help the Japanese, a lot of things have come to light. For example, the petroleum reserves are much larger than the Soviets suspected or admitted. That means the Japanese won't have to import so much petroleum over such a long distance from the Persian Gulf and the Ganges Cone. The coal reserves are enormous. And the titanium and tungsten deposits have turned out to be fabulous. Sakhalin is also an energy-rich island because of its geothermal activity-hot springs and such. But the island was a backwater that the Sovs didn't exploit because it was out at the absolute eastern end of their trade and supply route. The best they could do was to exploit some of the Sakhalin oil and coal to satisfy the requirements of their eastern redoubt on the Pacific rim. Now, does that brief rundown of the resources of Sakhalin give you any indication of why the Soviets, the Chinese, and the Japanese all want it...and might be willing to fight a general war to get it or keep it? So, yes, Spence, they might want a general war...or the threat of one."

The Chairman of the Joint Chiefs of Staff pondered this for a moment. "Our forces are thin in that region..."

"Thin? They're practically non-existent!" Murray reminded him.

"But that's not the issue. Can we afford to become involved in any armed conflict that might start there?" was the question posed by Treasury Secretary Harriett Thomas.

"We may have no choice," came the reply from Secretary of Commerce Charles Nagel. "American commercial interests linked in tight consortia with Japanese firms are already involved on Sakhalin."

"God knows I'm no dove," said Secretary of Defense James B. Floyd, "but I'm not sure we ought to go nose to nose with the Russkies over some north Asiatic Island. We're out at the end of our logistics pipeline there."

"So are the Soviets," said Barnitz.

"Let's not jump up the ladder of escalation here right at the start," the President advised them all with deliberate caution. He was not an international wimp, but he had been a cautious man and had gotten where he was because of a careful combination of caution and measured opportunism. He wasn't afraid to act when he believed he was right or that the conditions were right for action. "Al, you mentioned that the Bruneis have something in mind, a tripartite military police force, I believe. Do you have any additional details?"

"Mister President, the sultan of Brunei wants to become the de facto power center of the Pacific rim," Murray announced. "He sure as hell has the money to do it. But he doesn't have the capability to do it by force of arms. And military force does indeed count in some of today's world situations! So, since he hasn't got the military muscle, he's using this incident to leverage his position as the upcoming leader of the Pacific rim by getting others involved under his control."

"How in the world can a little tropical nation like Brunei even think it can do that?" asked the attorney general, who wasn't exactly the most knowledgeable person in the room when it came to international affairs.

"The same way that Hong Kong and Singapore did it. It's amazing what a twenty-five-trillion-dollar investment portfolio can accomplish," the secretary of the Treasury reminded her cabinet colleague.

"Be that as it may, the sultan has taken the leadership role in the Sakhalin affair," the intelligence chief went on. "He proposes a three-nation police contingent of Pacific rim countries be put into Sakhalin to balance the three contingents already there."

"Let me guess what Brunei's plan is, Al," National Security Advisor Barnitz commented. "Brunei will volunteer to provide a regiment plus personnel to serve as an overall joint command skeleton."

"Yes, but that's not all, Bill," Murray added. "The word has it that Brunei will request regimental contingents from the United States and a South American country."

"South America?" Attorney General Joan Crittenden put in. "You were speaking of bastards, Al? The Argentina-Brazil-Chile Alliance, the ABC Allianza, is as bad as any expansionist economic cartel in the world! Why South America?"

"Because the countries on the east coast of South America are also Pacific rim nations," was the quiet remark from Vice-President Dallas.

"Very well, this is a matter of policy. And policy is what I make or change as a result of what inputs I get," the President said. He knew full well that public national policy consisted of broad generalizations about democracy, civil rights, freedom of choice, free trade-especially free trade-that were enumerated in the Declaration of Independence. But actual national policy was very much opportunistic. It had to be. It depended on the desired position of the United States in various world affairs in reaction to what someone else was doing or threatened to do. It was a plastic policy capable of being altered to conform to pressures from the financial, banking, industrial, and other business interests. It also had to be amenable to cosmetic alterations in response to the expressed desires of the news media, Congress, and the general public, usually in that order of priority.

"The matter is both complex and potentially dangerous," the Chief Executive went on. "I would like to have each of you give me your first-blush recommendation on what we should do and a brief justification..."

"Right now, Mister President?" the Honorable John M. Clayton, Secretary of State, asked incredulously.

"Right now, Clay. Then I'll decide whether or not we can move on it today or if we'll all meet tomorrow morning. Tonight, I want you to rethink your snap decision and ask three critical questions. One: Can we win? Two: What will it cost us? Three: Is it worth it? After you've each had some time to think through the matter, you might care to revise or amend your first cut at a decision."

The three critical questions came directly from the President's experience in the business and financial world. He was markedly different from his academic predecessor. He'd come up through the ranks of corporate America to the point where, at the age of thirty-six, he'd been CEO of one of the most successful of the medium-sized multi-nationals. He was a "worlds to conquer" type, always looking for new challenges. The biggest challenge he'd faced was to win the presidency...which he'd successfully done. He tended to run his administration with a far better understanding of management than most of his predecessors but yet with the corridor-savvy and telecon-persuasion of politics that he'd quickly learned as a city mayor, a state governor, and a one-term senator.

He went on, "I think I have three options. Maybe more. Maybe you know of more. So, I want your assessments. What should I do? Number One: Send in a regiment as part of this police force? Number Two: Decline to send in a regiment and beg off, and why? Or, Number Three, something else, and, if so, what and why?" The President then pointed to his Vice-President. "Louise?"

She had solid convictions and a strong personal philosophy that came from the business of running a major high-tech catalyst think tank. "I'd buy off on Number One, Mister President. We're pitted against the Soviets and the Chinese in the eyes of the Pacific rim nations. We can't be perceived as being militarily indecisive. Not until the rest of the world renounces military force. And I don't see that out there in the foreseeable future."

"Clay?"

The secretary of state fidgeted. "I'd like to withhold comment until tomorrow, Mister President."

"You can't. I want it now. What're your first thoughts on this?"

After a moment, the Secretary of State replied, "Send troops. They don't have to fight. They can be recalled if necessary. But we should also send a diplomatic contingent and intensify our diplomatic efforts to resolve this through normal channels."

"Harriett?"

"We send a regiment. We don't have a choice," the Secretary of the Treasury replied. "Guess who owns a lot of Treasury bills as part of their twenty-five-trillion-dollar portfolio? Brunei's investment in the United States government is Number One followed by Japanese interests. We don't want a run on the dollar right now. Not with another bill auction coming up next month."

"Floyd?"

"If Harriett and OMB will cooperate with me to find the funding, I'd say we must send troops," the secretary of defense decided.

"Charlie?"

"The Secretary of Commerce shrugged. "Send in the Marines. We've done it before to protect our commercial interests."

"It'll have to be the Army, not the Marines," Admiral Spencer reminded him. "In spite of the strong objection of the Navy Department and the Marine Corps, the Marines are restricted to the roles of embassy, naval base, and shipboard security. Our naval infantry was taken away from us a quarter of a century ago, Mister Secretary. We need 'em now!"

The President ignored the complaint of his Chairman of the Joint Chiefs, an old Navy man who remembered the pre-warbot days when the Marines consisted of a few good men. Now they were even fewer. But they were just as proud. He continued to poll around the table, asking his attorney general, "Joan?"

"Mister President, Number Two is my option. We shouldn't send military forces. This isn't our fight. If it looks like it's really escalating into a general war that would affect us, then we should make a move." As a lawyer, an expert in the resolution of human conflicts, Joan Crittenden tended to take the conservative route of "wait and see" before committing.

"Al, I think we already have your recommendation," the President observed of his Intelligence Chief.

"Sir, I'd opt for Number Three right now," the intelligence director advised. "We need to see what's going to develop here. Another week or two might prove interesting and give us more intelligence data on which to base a rational decision."

"Hmmm. You surprise me, Al. But you often do that. Betty? I probably don't need to ask you."

The director of the Arms Control Agency nodded. "How can we get the rest of the world to disarm if our first reaction to every international crisis is a military knee-jerk requiring force of arms or a show of strength? I vote for Number Two; we shouldn't send military forces to exacerbate this situation."

"The loyal opposition has been heard from again. Admiral?"

The response of the Chairman of the Joint Chiefs of Staff surprised all the civilians at the table. "I would recommend that we not send military forces at this time, Mister President. In the first place, we don't have units that could be spared from other duties. All our policing-type units are deployed, and the only available regiments are either warbot assault units or the new Special Combat forces, neither of which are suitable for this sort of mission - as we learned in Iraq recently."

"Really, Admiral? It was my impression that it was the job of the Department of Defense and our military forces to be ready at any and all times to do what's required for the security of American interests," the President observed.

"Mister President, the current state of our armed forces isn't your fault, sir. We're still living for the most part with the consequences of the military policies of the previous administration."

"Are you telling me that our armed forces aren't prepared to do their job of the defense of this nation and its interests?"

"No, sir. We're prepared to do the job as detailed for us in the previous administration's white papers and policy statements. But I'm not so sure we're configured to step in between three aggressive nations squabbling over a piece of real estate, strategic or not."

"Admiral, I want you to get together with Secretary Floyd and General Barnitz immediately," the President ordered. "I want an up-to-date review of our current military policies and strengths. And I want your recommendations on how to correct any deficiencies you may find. I want you to present this to this group thirty days from now."

"Yes, sir!"

"General Barnitz?" What say you?"

"Mister President, I don't have a vote in this council," the national security advisor remarked.

"This isn't a vote. I called for first-shot opinions. You're my security advisor. I want your advice...*now!*"

"I don't see that our national security is threatened, sir. At least not to the extent of sending American men and women into a dangerous situation where they could be killed. My opinion is that Number Three option should be considered; we should wait and see."

The President had been making notes on his little pocket keypad. "Interesting! Very interesting! An even split! All my cabinet officers – with the exception of the attorney general, who's a lawyer – are unquestionably in the favor of troops. I suspected that my Arms Control Agency director would be opposed to a show of force. What I did not expect is that my top military people would come out against a military action!"

"Sir, military people are the first ones to get killed in these situations," Admiral Spencer explained. "I think I can explain the reaction of my colleagues on that basis, plus the fact that none of us likes the idea of giving orders that might send people to their deaths."

"But you and your people are being paid to face the ultimate liability option of your commissions. And giving orders that send people to do deadly things are part of your job, too. Would you give those orders, Admiral?" the President suddenly wanted to know. If the wrong answer came back, he would have a new CJCS tomorrow morning.

"Yes, sir! If I was told to do so, and if I was in the line of command, I would. I wouldn't like it. Fortunately, I don't give the orders. I am not in the line of command."

It wasn't quite the answer the President wanted. But he wouldn't rock the boat by causing an uproar in the JCS with the possibility of a general war staring him in the face. So, he looked at his terminal display and said, "Tie vote, opinion-wise. Floyd, how much time will it take to get a regiment to Sakhalin?"

"Several days, Mister President."

"Very well. My immediate decision is to get started. Floyd, initiate an order for a regiment to deploy to Sakhalin as part of the multi-national police force headed by Brunei. Clay, tell the Brunei ambassador that we'll give him a decision in a day or so." The President checked again on his portable terminal on the table before him. "I'm postponing a luncheon tomorrow with the Interior Affairs Council. We'll meet here at noon instead. At that time, I want each of you to be prepared to give me a five-minute briefing on your recommendation with verbal back-up...and a white paper if you have time to prepare one. Remember my three questions: Can we win? What will it cost? Is it worth it? And if any of this leaks before we're ready to announce officially, I'll explain that we're merely putting a regiment back on Sakhalin where they've been for years anyway as part of our worldwide peacekeeping policy. In the meantime, it's my sense that the United States must use force of arms when necessary to maintain the economic viability of the world. Provide me with back-up support if that's your position. Otherwise, convince me that I'm wrong! Meeting recessed until tomorrow noon!"

Chapter Six

Just being with Lieutenant Dyani Motega was comfortable and pleasant, Colonel Curt Carson decided.

More than pleasant, he amended his thought; delightful in a way he couldn't define.

He couldn't keep his mind on his assignment from the Command and Staff College. He found himself trying to fathom this unusual young woman and his strange feelings for her.

Although she was extremely intense and earnestly sincere almost to the point of obsession, she was slowly developing a sense of humor. Part of this was due to the Washington Greys themselves; they were a group of highly competent and dedicated people, and they used humor to maintain a sense of perspective which kept them from becoming zealots. And, although she had always had a strong internal sense of self-confidence, it was now becoming more resolute and audacious because she'd come up through the ranks on her own merits and because she'd proved her own valor under fire. Her field commission had been made permanent by DCSPERS, and her Distinguished Service Cross had been confirmed. She'd become as much a part of the Third Robot Infantry (Special Combat) Regiment, the Washington Greys, as Curt himself.

Their relationship seemed to be automatic. It happened, period. In the months since her commissioning, Curt learned that Dyani accepted him as he was: a virile man who'd known, loved, and still loved many women. Curt knew that women had their little jealousies, and long ago he'd decided he'd never really understand women, much less one whose ancestry was Crow Indian. Dyani seemed utterly happy just to be with him, even for a weekend afternoon.

As a partner, she was as tender as Alexis Morgan, as vibrant as Lieutenant Kitsy Clinton had been, and as exotic as Sultana Alzena of Brunei, but different from any of them. Even though she wasn't a publicly demonstrative person, it was quite a different matter when she was in private with Curt.

Furthermore, Dyani didn't seem to have a trace of envy or mistrust in her personality. She seemed to simply look the other way when Curt discreetly was with other women. It was as though she was unafraid of them, totally confident about who she was, and aware that a special bond had been forged with Curt. Jealousy and vindictiveness were not part of her.

She was right. He always came back; he was always there. "You're a man" was all she said privately to him, and always added, "thank heaven!"

But she was something else as well. Curt couldn't put his finger on it. In time, he hoped he'd discover what that was. She wasn't a superwoman, just the product of two cultures, one living within the other. Maybe that had a lot to do with it, but he wasn't sure yet.

But in the meantime, she was, he finally decided, just nice to be with. She made him feel ultimately happy in an indescribable and extraordinary way.

Besides, she was very pretty to look at. No, she was extremely beautiful, Curt amended his thought again. And looking at her was what he was doing at that moment on a Sunday afternoon in his quarters. He gave up on his latest Command and Staff College reading assignment; it was nicer to look at Dyani as she sat quietly on the carpet, her bright yellow and red squaw dress arrayed around her in a colorful circle as she was reading Clancy's classic, *The Cardinal in the Kremlin*.

She finally sensed he was looking at her and looked back at him, tossing her long, dark hair out of her face. "Wasting your time again?" she asked.

"I don't count as wasted those moments I spend watching Deer Arrow," he told her quietly, using the English translation of her Indian name.

"You usually like to do more than just look," she remarked, but there was no hostility or even reprimand in her tone. She was simply being factual in her own way.

"Sometimes looking is enough," he admitted.

"Then I'm not doing something right. Or doing it incompletely," she stated with a smile on her face.

"Do you know that you glow?"

"I do?"

"How do you do it?"

"I've told you many times. It's because of you." She hadn't moved from where she was sitting on the floor, but Curt had the impression she was suddenly very much closer to him. That was one thing he liked about Dyani. She was basically a non-verbal person. When she wanted to, she could convey her deepest, innermost feelings to him without a word in a way that of ten caught him off guard and overwhelmed him.

"Deer Arrow, I'll never understand you," Curt admitted, shaking his head in frustration.

"Good!" She put down her book. The next thing he knew, she'd arisen from the floor with a smooth, liquid movement in a swirl of bright skirt and was intimately almost one with him on the couch. "I like it when you use my Anglicized name as a nickname. But you don't have a nickname."

"I'm the regimental commander. It wouldn't be proper," he told her softly because she was so close he didn't have to speak in more than a whisper.

"When you and I are together, you're more than my regimental commander. So my nickname for you is Kida."

Why was it on a warm fall afternoon that her warmth was not only very comfortable but sybaritic? That her caresses gave him as much pleasure as he got from caressing her? "Deer Arrow, you can call me anything that pleases you when we're together. You're the most bewitching woman I've ever known. By the way, is Kida an Indian name?"

"Yes. It was given to both my father and my grandfather by my mother and grandmother."

"What does it mean?"

"Does a name have to have meaning?"

"Sometimes. Especially when you give it to me." Although he wasn't one to hide emotions from women he loved, Curt found himself awash in the emotion of this moment with Dyani; no woman had ever given him an affectionate nickname before.

Dyani cocked her head to one side, causing her heavy, dark tresses to cascade over him. She looked thoughtful for a moment before explaining, "An exact translation isn't possible. It includes the concepts of manly, protective strength."

"I like it. But I probably don't have any choice in the matter," Curt realized.

"You don't. But I wouldn't call you Kida unless you liked it." Dyani wasn't loquacious. She got a lot of mileage out of each word.

Curt knew that Dyani got a lot of mileage out of *everything* she did.

She almost made up for the fact that Major Alexis Morgan had changed so drastically over the years. And that Lieutenant Kitsy Clinton was still recovering at Walter Reed from a broken neck suffered in Iraq. Dyani Motega had forged a place in Curt's life just as she'd created her own place in the Washington Greys: by being honest, forthright, and very certain of what she wanted.

Besides, she was an extremely attractive woman. Although duty, honor, and country came first in Curt's book, he'd never been one to fail to notice and pursue beautiful women. However, he often found himself wondering whether he was pursuing Dyani or she was being aggressive in her own, unique way. Right then, he didn't care. As an officer, a military man who might pay the ultimate price even in a training maneuver, he tended to take life as it came. He didn't believe he should even consider marriage while he served in a combat outfit. Maybe someday he might settle down. Maybe Dyani was the sort of woman to raise a family with him. Dyani never mentioned it. Curt believed she also took things as they were.

The Sultana Alzena of Brunei had said she accepted him as a professional soldier; Curt wasn't sure she really understood what that entailed. Colonel Willa Lovell didn't care; she looked to Curt for a special sort of caring love. Kitsy had just enjoyed everything. Alexis had…well, Alexis seemed to be pursuing her own career and possibly other plans now.

The possibility of being killed, actually killed, had lurked in the back of his mind ever since the regiment had gone Sierra Charlie and soldiers had had to relearn the awful fact that they could be killed in combat again. Curt knew he'd had his share of combat, which was why the immutable laws of the Army would see to it that he got more than his share. Seasoned soldiers and units were always called upon when things went to slime for the simple reason that the high brass could count on them to do the job because they'd done it before. They could be counted on. They were dependable. That was a must when it came to military action.

He only hoped that some of his Washington Greys weren't getting burned out by too frequent combat. Some of them had expressed quiet, private opinions that they'd seen enough death and destruction to last a lifetime already. This was different than Henry Kester's repeated assertions that he was "getting too old for this sort of crap," or Sergeant Harlan Saunders' constant bitching about wanting to "get out of this chicken outfit." Curt really didn't know how to handle the burnout problem. And his call for help to Belinda Hettrick hadn't evoked a satisfactory answer or solution from her.

Dyani moved smoothly so she faced him squarely. With an expression of concern on her lovely face, she observed without rancor, "Kida, what's wrong? When I can't dominate your attention, something is troubling you deeply. What is it, Kida?"

She'd jerked his attention back to her. So, he told her, "All right, if you want to share a commander's problems, I'll bounce one off you."

"What makes you think I don't want to share your life?"

"Okay, but I warned you. You've been in the Greys for three years now..."

"Three years and four months, Kida," she replied with a proud and radiant smile.

"That covers a lot of deadly action - Kerguelen, Brunei, Kurdistan..."

"I've been shot at, yes. And more times than that when we were on maneuvers with jelly ammo."

"Have you had enough?"

A look of surprise came over her lovely face. "What ever do you mean, Kida?"

"Have you ever thought that you'd seen enough combat to last for a lifetime and wanted to get out?"

She didn't even pause before answering simply, "No."

"Why?"

"Are you growing tired of fighting?"

"Sometimes I get tired of it. But it's my career. It's been the career of my forefathers for generations."

Dyani looked pensive, then broke into a knowing smile. "You've answered the question. We both come from military backgrounds and warrior cultures." Dyani's ancestor, White Man Runs Him, had been a Crow Indian scout during the Great Plains Wars for what was then this regiment under different designation. She paused for a moment, then looked surprisingly coy. "Do you want us to renounce our careers and have a family?"

"Uh, no." He was continually surprised by Dyani's forthright approach to personal affairs. She said little but meant much.

"Good! Because we both have family honor and tradition to maintain. I never wanted to do anything but be the first woman Army officer in my family. An appointment to West Point wasn't available, so I enlisted, planning to get one by competitive examination."

"You planned on being an officer?"

"Of course! But not the way it happened. Field promotion was unexpected, but certainly not unappreciated. It made my life a lot easier, Kida."

"Yes, it did, for both of us," Curt admitted. Dyani had been strictly and properly all protocol when she was an NCO. Her field-awarded brown bar had lowered one of her personal moral barriers on the very day she'd first worn it. Those barriers had been down ever since, and more were falling constantly. Curt had been pleased; from the moment he'd first met her, she'd grown on him as a strange, admirable, lovely, and very lovable young woman. "You've always been full of plans, haven't you?"

"Yes. And I have some for this afternoon now that you've-"

The comm terminal sounded off with an insistent bleeping, the signal that the regimental commander was wanted on the net immediately.

"Damn! Why does this always happen at the wrong time? One of these days, I'm going to arrange my private life so I'm not jerked around for being a savior of the free world!" he exploded. He really wanted to share tender, languid love with her right then on that warm fall afternoon because one did not make love to Dyani Motega; one shared love with her.

"We will have other times," Dyani reminded him, seeming to sense his thoughts again. "Find out who wants us to do what and when. Then we can make plans for the rest of today because we want each other."

Can she really read my mind? Curt asked himself as he walked to the terminal.

The screen was flashing instructions for him to enter the proper crypto data. He'd guessed right. This was an incoming eyes-only, and it probably meant going somewhere and doing something nasty to some bad guys.

His fingers flew over the keypad, entering his name, code name, and password.

It wasn't a voice message, but a grey message on a black screen, one that couldn't be seen from the side but only by someone looking directly at it and accustomed to reading the low-contrast alpha-numerics of an eyes-only command instruction:

SORRY ABOUT THAT.
GREY HEAD:
EXECUTE RECALL AND GO ALERT.
SEE BATTLEAXE ASAP
RE DOD EXECUTE ORDER 34-8-1.
SS CO IRON FIST.
FAREWELL MY LOVELY.

Curt knew that the first and last lines had been added by the 17th Iron Fist Division's megacomputer, Georgie, in order to confuse any cryptoanalysis attempt by unauthorized tappers and hackers. But they made perfect sense that afternoon.

He keyed in the macro signaling receipt and compliance, saying to Dyani as he did so, "Back to cammies, Lieutenant! And back to your SCOUT platoon! Something's hit the impeller! Don't know what or why yet, but I'll pass the word in an Oscar brief as quickly as I know myself. Mount 'em up and move 'em out!"

Lieutenant Dyani Motega's aura and demeanor changed abruptly. She was suddenly a military officer as she quickly rose to her feet and seemed to shed her graceful, sensuous, catlike movements for the quick precision of a disciplined drill master. "Yes, sir! On my way, sir!" And she was. Stepping quickly to the nearby closet, she stripped out of the dress and into cammies almost in one movement. By the time Curt powered-down the terminal and gave it call-forwarding instructions, she was out the door.

The only aspect of her that remained was a vanishing fragrance.

And in his own mind, Curt knew it might be many long months before they would be able to enjoy a relaxing Sunday afternoon together in quarters at Fort Huachuca.

Somewhere in a world of danger and death, someone was about to raise sixteen different kinds of hell. Or was someone already doing it.

He knew it was going to be the job of the Washington Greys to go out there and stop it.

Hopefully, without anyone being killed or hurt.

Somehow, this time he sensed that the Washington Greys would have to keep someone from tripping the thermonuclear triggers that could send the human race back in the New Dark Ages.

Now that he was the regimental commander of the Washington Greys, he knew the responsibility might fall on his shoulders.

Like every other time, he knew it wouldn't be easy or predictable. In fact, it seemed to get worse every time.

Slipping his yellow-pommed, blue Sierra Charlie tam on his head, he went out the door and took off double-time for Division Headquarters across the quad.

Chapter Seven

It happened in a typical Soviet fashion.

Apparently out of nowhere, four Antonov An-404 Dynamo transports hearing Aeroflot colors and numbers suddenly appeared in the grey, overcast skies and landed at the Yuzhno-South aerodrome. Their massive belly doors opened, disgorging a battalion of *ahvtomahteek pehkhotah* troops and several airborne armored vehicles.

The only warning given to Colonel Viktor Pashkavitch Kurotkin had been in the form of a telephone call two hours beforehand from none other than General Ivan Fillipovitch Vlasov, commander of the Far East Military District.

The call had been terse and cryptic. Vlasov knew that the American ELINT satellites could pick up the telephone call, even though it was transmitted via hard wire and undersea cable. But he didn't know how long it would take the Americans to decipher the scramble code. It was given that the Americans with their high technology and megacomputers could perform miracles with information transfer, which included decrypting Soviet messages. Therefore, Vlasov had kept his verbal message short and used code words, a technique which is usually immune to decryption unless the other side has the code book.

But General Vlasov didn't arrive aboard the spartan Dynamo transports nominally and openly used for lifting heavy loads of industrial and mining equipment into the Siberian wilderness. He came in style aboard a Yakovlev Yak-140, again bearing Aeroflot colors and registration, although the aircraft was permanently fitted-out and used for VIP transportation in the Soviet Far East Military District. In spite of decades of reform and "demilitarization," the line between the military and civilian sectors in the USSR was extremely broad and very hazy. Especially in the Far East Military District where the Soviet Union faced its centuries-old enemy, China.

So Kurotkin was standing on the cold, damp, windy ramp at Yuzhno-South aerodrome beside General Vlasov when the Dynamo transports began to unload.

Rolling out of their huge bellies came small tank-like vehicles, each with a huge, out-sized gun installed not in a turret but in the chassis itself. For every three of these strange machines, there was a vehicle Kurotkin recognized as a highly modified BTR-218 Armored Personnel Carrier.

"Comrade General, I am confused," Kurotkin admitted to his chief. "You have told me that a new unit is to be added to the One-hundred-tenth Special Airborne Guards Regiment, but I did not suspect that it would be an armored battalion. I don't see how I can effectively deploy an armored battalion alongside my airborne infantry troops in what is essentially a patrol and military power projection mission."

"Viktor Pashkavitch, your assignment is not power projection. That is an American doctrinal concept. Soviet troops are here to ensure that this eastern bastion of the Motherland does not become the launching base for a military threat to our military and industrial facilities. And that sort of mission is precisely what this new battalion can help you carry out. I could not tell you on the telephone," Vlasov admitted, "but this battalion is the first Soviet warbot unit."

"Sir? Warbots? They don't look anything like the American warbots," Kurotkin remarked with surprise in his voice.

"Of course, they do not!" Vlasov explained with a smile. "Our scientists and engineers do not need to copy capitalist equipment. We are perfectly capable of producing our own warbots suited to our production methods, military procedures, and defense requirements."

What General Vlasov didn't say, of course, was that the USSR hadn't equipped their armed forces with warbots because they couldn't buy or steal the advanced technology of robotic linkage used by the American Robot Infantry. Nor could they duplicate the advanced artificial intelligence computers of the newer self-deploying voice-commanded Sierra Charlie warbots. The standard party line concerning warbots maintained that the Soviet Union didn't need warbots, that all Soviet citizens were good soldiers dedicated to the defense of the Motherland, and that the strength and heroic bravery of Soviet motorized infantry and armored troops was considered to be more than adequate to defend Mother Russia's empire. Furthermore, if the Soviet Union were to be provoked by the capitalistic imperialists, the soldiers, sailors, airmen, and cosmonauts of the Soviet Union could win any war and bring peace to the world at last.

"Peace," of course, was still defined by doctrine, the Politburo, and the Soviet armed services in Marxist-Leninist terms. "Peace" was that condition where the evil forces of capitalism were finally defeated everywhere, thus making the world safe for the on-going development of socialism. Even the symbolism of the USSR's flag flaunted that because its single five-pointed star officially signified the five continents that would eventually be brought under that banner.

"They look like my airborne assault guns," Kurotkin remarked carefully. Actually, they were dead-ringers for the ASU-88's in his artillery company. At least from the outside. And except for the smaller but longer gun.

"That, Comrade Colonel, is deliberate. It will serve to confuse and bewilder our capitalist foes who will believe these warbots are nothing more than regular airborne assault guns," Vlasov explained. "But they have no human crews in them. Do you see the armored personnel carriers? The warbot operators are inside these, properly protected by armor and capable of directing by radio technical means these new AASU-ninety-nine *Sye,yebro Palomneek* warbots of ours."

The name "Silver Pilgrim" didn't seem patriotic or even military to Kurotkin. With some trepidation, he commented, "Apparently we are saddled with that name because it was decided by a committee?"

"No, it was chosen by a computer. It is an excellent security measure. We do learn a few valuable things from our American adversaries. Computer-chosen names have shown themselves to be excellent for hiding the true purpose of military programs and corporations. I will show you what our outstanding scientists and engineers have managed to accomplish." Vlasov turned to his aide de camp and snapped, "Have the commanding officer bring a warbot and one of the directing vehicles over here!"

Kurotkin was no dummy. He was getting the only briefing he would probably get. It did not pay a Soviet military man to know too much about things over which he had no direct concern, such as the workings and principles behind a weapon. It was only necessary that he knew how it was to be used.

Thus, as the AASU-99 and its directing BTR-218 drove up and stopped in front of them on the airport tarmac, he immediately recognized the Soviet warbot as a cut-down, lightened modification of the ASU-88. And he listened carefully to the briefing conducted in rote memory fashion by the pink-cheeked Captain Vladimir Nikolayevich Yurasov, obviously a Byelorussian by his appearance and name, who seemed too young to be commanding a warbot battalion. But Kurotkin knew the Soviet military technical elite seemed to be getting younger every day.

Five-year plans and the glacial pace of Soviet industrial innovation might eventually catch up to the Americans and even the British, French, and Brazilians when it came to warbots. But since the Soviet military doctrine didn't call for warbots and took even longer to change than five-year plans, the USSR might never catch up as it had in fighter and transport aircraft as well as assault weapons. But, for some reason he didn't yet know or understand, the Politburo had decided to design, build, and field warbots.

To Colonel Kurotkin's eyes, the AASU-99 was a typical Soviet quick response to a western military advance, achieved only after suitable samples had been somehow obtained through outright purchase or clan-destine methods. These Soviet warbots could be nothing else. Their chassis and running gear were those of standard ASU-88 airborne assault guns. But, instead of mounting 73-millimeter cannons in topside turrets, they each carried a smaller, faster-firing, automatic-loading S-168 53-millimeter cannon mounted down on the chassis itself. The guts of the machine were stuffed with electronic equipment, fuel, and ammo, leaving no room for even a single human.

What he did not know because it was classified as a high state secret was the fact that this was the closest that Soviet technology and industry could get to a direct copy of the American M60 Hairy Fox warbots that had been recovered from the Cook Glacier on Kerguelen Island in the South Indian Ocean after the American Washington Greys regiment had been forced to abandon them there several years before.

Nor did he know that the Soviet team hadn't gotten all the abandoned warbots, only the bigger ones that were left after someone else had beaten the special Soviet "salvage" unit to the scene.

Captain Yurasov carefully explained to him that the Silver Pilgrims were directed by radio and lasercom beams transmitted from the BTR-218 armored personnel carrier. The Silver Pilgrim would then report back on the same channels. Two-way simultaneous duplex communications with the Silver Pilgrim wasn't used; the same channels had to time-share uplink and downlink data. Therefore, a command was given, and the warbot replied with compliance data and sensor information. The system was multiplexed with several tens of milliseconds available for each function. It wasn't duplex real-time data transmission like American warbot brainies were accustomed to using. But it was the best that Soviet technology could accomplish, given that the Silver Pilgrim program was a top priority crash project which had been pushed through in spite of five-year plans and the normal protocols and channels of Soviet research, development, production, and test.

The AASU-99 Silver Pilgrim was a lash-up make-do that was the best that the Soviet Union could achieve in about three years' time.

"Well, Comrade Colonel, what do you think of your new artillery battalion?" General Vlasov wanted to know when the briefing was finished and Kurotkin had dutifully clambered over and around the Soviet warbot.

"Comrade General, there is no warbot doctrine to guide me. How do I use these new warbots within existing doctrine? Or will you present me with a new doctrine? What sort of tactical plan must I follow to use them for the best military results in order to be consistent with the requirements of the Motherland? How do I integrate them into my present regimental command and control structure?" These were all legitimate questions of a Soviet regimental commander. Kurotkin had learned his lessons well at the Frunze Military Academy. "And how do I keep the People's Liberation Army and the Japanese Self-Defense Force from reacting to the fact that we have introduced warbots on Sakhalin?"

General Vlasov looked up at the dismal grey clouds that hugged the mountaintops on both sides of the valley. He beat his warmly clad arms and gloved hands against one another. "Let us retire to your quarters where we can speak in private and in comfort, Comrade Colonel. My bones ache from the miserable damp cold of this island. Fortunately, I remember my tour of duty here many years ago. Therefore, I brought with me a suitable supply of excellent vodka which I would share with you while we discuss the questions you have quite properly asked." He turned and put his arm around Kurotkin's shoulder as the two of them began to walk across the windswept tarmac to where Kurotkin's ZIL waited for them. "First of all, Viktor Pashkavitch, your ASU-eighty-eight airborne assault guns and the personnel of your artillery company will be loaded aboard the Dynamo transports for the return trip to Khabarovsk. We must not give the impression that we have escalated the military situation here by introducing our new warbots."

He paused, and just before entering the ZIL, he added, "Comrade Colonel, you and the One-hundred-tenth Special Airborne Guards Regiment have the honor of being the first war bot regiment in the Red Army. The Ministry of Defense decided to send the new warbots here in order to test them in the field. Since your regiment has such an outstanding and successful history, it was chosen to remain and have the warbots integrated into the regimental structure. Besides, Sakhalin is the best possible testing ground for such a highly secret new program. Here our warbots will be pitted against two non-warbot potential adversaries. We shall find out how to write the new doctrine for these machines."

"Comrade General," Kurotkin put in quickly, "if we test our warbots and doctrine against non-warbot forces, how will we develop doctrine that will tell us what to do when we must face the American and European warbot forces and defend the Motherland against them?"

General Vlasov motioned impatiently for Kurotkin to get into the ZIL and out of the wind. He snarled, "Come now! You don't think the Politburo intends our Red Army to fight other warbots, do you? We can always talk the Americans and Europeans out of fighting. We simply do what we have done for more than a hundred years: We promise them everything they want, giving them nothing that would hurt us. And they always buy it! They believe they can bluff us as they do when they play poker or bridge with one another; they have never realized that we are chess players..."

General Ivan Fillipovich Vlasov might have honestly believed that no one would recognize the AASU-99s as anything more than replacement ASU-88s brought in to rotate part of the 110th Special Airborne Guards Regiment back to Khabarovsk for R&R.

He had not carefully read the security assessment documents prepared by the Far East Military District's detachment of GRU intelligence troops.

A patrol of the Chinese People's Liberation Army operating on the fenced perimeter of the Yuzhno-South aerodrome watched all of this with very powerful optical instruments and cameras obtained from Japanese firms who were always interested in penetrating the huge Chinese market.

But Colonel Yushiro Mishida of the 9th Internal Peacekeeping Regiment, Japan Self-Defense Forces, was comfortably ensconced on a nearby hilltop where his intelligence company's troops were using much better Japanese optical and photo equipment - as well as highly sensitive electronic gear - to monitor the Soviet activity on the aerodrome.

But these remote intelligence-gathering activities were almost amateurish in comparison to others under way at the same time on the aerodrome itself.

These other activities were not only monitoring the Soviets close-up but were also watching both the Chinese and Japanese military intelligence activities.

The people involved were both Oriental and Western in appearance, and they blended in with the local populace. In some cases, they were members of the local populace. And they were using very, very high-tech equipment to view, listen, and record what was going on.

Later, that information would find its way quickly back to Langley, Virginia and Bandar Seri Begawan on Borneo.

In some cases, it wouldn't be analyzed and distributed quickly enough.

But it would be done much more quickly than the information being obtained on all of these spies, data that would end up at 2 Dzerzhinsky Square in Moscow where it would be backed up in the processing procedures and protocols behind mountains of other information pouring into the KGB First Chief Directorate. Even though the most powerful computers in the Soviet Union were used by the KGB, they were engaged in a failing attempt to keep track of millions of Soviet subjects as well as millions of people abroad.

But, in due course of time, as Soviet spokesmen are fond of saying, the information would get into the hands of those who would use it to do something brutal.

Chapter Eight

"Colonel Carson reporting as requested, ma'am!" He tossed a quick salute. He didn't need to, but Curt saluted as an expression of respect for the commanding general of the 17th Iron Fist Division who'd officially adopted the nickname given to her by Rumor Control: "Battle-axe."

Major General Belinda Hettrick' s office was busy. Aides and division staff stooges were at work on this Sunday afternoon as if it were an ordinary weekday. Terminals were up and working. Comm units were chirping and bleeping and chattering. And in a world where powerful computers and data processing equipment were supposed to cut down paperwork, printers were spewing forth reams of hard copy printouts.

Hettrick looked up, returned his salute, and remarked formally, "Thank you for coming so quickly, Colonel. Please close the door and sit down."

Curt did so, observing, "I don't know what DOD Execute Order Thirty-four-dash-eight-dash-one is all about, but an Execute Order always means trouble. And it always seems to happen on a Sunday."

"So did Pearl Harbor," Hettrick reminded him. "We serve the public by defending them against the bad guys. And anyone who believes that any public service job means working a mere forty-hour week should find another job! We signed on without the benefit of worker protection laws. Obviously from your tone of voice, you were enjoying the afternoon before my message reached your quarters. Who were you enjoying it with?"

"Uh, General, my off-duty activities are private affairs," Curt reminded her.

"Affairs, yes. With privates, no." She sighed. "Never mind; I know. Lieutenant Motega is a fine officer and a lovely young woman. And

I'm pleased to see you rebounding from both Major Morgan and Captain Kitsy Clinton."

"I think I had no choice in the matter once Motega was commissioned," Curt told her frankly. "As for Alexis Morgan, I've stopped believing that she really won't become the sultana of Brunei some day."

"I got that gee-two, also."

"And what's this about Captain Clinton?"

"Just because Kitsy's on the sick list doesn't mean she isn't also on the make sheet," General Belinda Hettrick explained easily, then her manner changed, and she got serious. "Okay, social small talk aside! You're going to take a little trip."

Curt breathed out heavily; it wasn't a sigh, but beyond a sigh. "Where to this time? And who's being bastardly this week?"

"Sakhalin. And three big and powerful countries."

"Jesus H. P. Christ on a crutch, Belinda!" Curt exploded. "Weren't the Panthers pulled out of there a couple of years ago by the previous administration?"

"Yup! You didn't believe our foreign policy would really change, did you?" Hettrick asked him rhetorically. "What goes around comes around. We've got to go back."

"Great! Another garden spot of the world!" Curt growled. "I talked with Colonel Mike Corcoran of the Panthers a few months ago. Even though his regiment is regular Robot Infantry, they damned-near froze their butts off there! And the Panthers were bored out of their skulls. Worse than Mid-East pipeline patrol, he told me. And why us? The Washington Greys aren't organized to hack a Foreign Internal Guardian mission," the commander of the 3rd Robot Infantry (Special Combat) Regiment pointed out. "FIG operations are a natural for regular warbot brainies."

"As to why the Greys, it's simple: You're available." Hettrick ticked off the regiments of her division on her fingers. "The Can-Do are working up to Sierra Charlie status, and they're only at Readiness

Level Three down in the Vee-Eye. The Cottonbalers just came off the line in Chad, and you know the conditions in that place! The Wolfhounds will fill in a gap in General Pickens' Persian Gulf Command. As for the other RI, RC, and RA divisions, they're already deployed and can't be moved right now...or at least, they can't do it fast enough to make a difference. Besides, I recall you were sniveling something about highly trained troops going sour because they weren't being used."

"Yes, General, but I also expressed a concern about some of the Greys bitching about having seen too much action."

"Tango Sierra and FIDO! Sorry about that, Colonel, but we go where we're told and do what we're told...or we resign or take retirement," Hettrick told him frankly. "Besides, you may not find it so cold or boring on Sakhalin. The Greys will be only one of three regiments that are part of the Sakhalin Police Detachment. The other members of the SPD are the Third Airborne Regiment of the Army of Chile and the Sixth Sultan's Own Gurkha Rifles of the Royal Brunei Legion...all under the command of General Sultan Ahmad Mahathis bin Muhamid and his staff with his deputy for Civil Affairs being his twin sister, the Sultana Alzena..."

"Well...uh...yeah...that does alter the situation," Curt stuttered, taken completely aback by this news. Many ladies were very close to him outside the Washington Greys. The Sultana Alzena had courted *him* very aggressively when the regiment had deployed to Brunei on a military exchange visit. "But I doubt that it will complicate matters..."

"I'm certain you'll perform as expected, Colonel" was Hettrick's only comment.

Hettrick picked up a memory cube from her terminal desk and handed it to Curt. "Here's the brief from JCS based on sit-reps from State, NIA, and NSC. Classified MAGIC. Don't swallow it after you read it because this, too, won't pass; it has a lot of sharp corners. Give it back to me and I'll have my Gee-two people store it."

Curt looked at the memory cube. It could contain an entire encyclopedia. If necessary, he could go into NE linkage with

Georgie, the division's megacomputer, and have it downloaded into his brain in a matter of seconds. But it would take about an hour to get safely into linkage and about two hours to get safely out after such an intense high bit-rate session. Sometimes, high-tech wasn't worth either the time or the risks. But Curt asked anyway just to make sure, "How much time do I have to read it?"

"Not much. You may be on Sakhalin tomorrow this time."

"*What?* Transpacific MAC flights take twelve hours or more! Since when can the Aerospace Farce trash haulers respond to a request to move a regiment in less than a week?" Curt wanted to know, basing his assessment on recent past experience deploying the Washington Greys to and from the Persian Gulf. "Or do we rate a MAC hypersonic contract flight?"

"None of the above. Three MD-two-thousand-one hypersonics from Royal Brunei Airlines will be on the ramp ready to load your TACBATT and SERVBATT at fifteen-hundred hours tomorrow."

"Since when is DOD permitting a foreign flag airline to haul MAC contracts?"

"When you read the sit-rep, Colonel, you'll discover that Brunei is playing head honcho for the Sakhalm Police Detachment," Hettrick explained briefly. "Sakhalin is a powder keg at the moment because of the Soviet, Chinese, and Japanese regiments there...and they're shooting real bullets at each other. The sultan of Brunei obviously sees this as a golden opportunity to enhance his position as the upcoming leader of the Pacific rim nations. So, he dipped into petty cash to ensure that the three regiments will be on the island the instant that COPRE approves the police action tomorrow afternoon in Honolulu."

Curt began to see that this operation was going to be the usual sheep screw of military activities impacting, being impacted by, interfering with, and being interfered with by diplomatic and political factors. He was wary of it all, so he asked, "What happens if we're on Sakhalin with the Bruneis and Chileans...and COPRE doesn't approve of the police action?"

"They will."

"Suppose they don't?"

"It could get messy."

"How far do we have to swim to get to Japan?"

"Not that kind of messy. We can get you off Sakhalin in a day or so if you can take and hold Yuzhno-South airport. Matter of fact, your own AIRLIFTCO can get you out."

"Uh, yeah, Belinda, that brings up something you quickly sprinted past," Curt recalled. "Am I going to get to take my AIRBATT along? Or will I be forced to operate without air support? And how is my AIRBATT going to get to Sakhalin?"

"You saw my staff's frantic activity when you came in?"

"Yes."

"They're doing what your regimental staff can't do...but your staff people are going to be goddamned busy themselves. Your AIRBATT Chippewas and Harpies are going to make the Sakhalin flight on their own, tanked to the slots several times en route by airborne refueling."

"Cal Worsham isn't equipped for air-to-air top-off," Curt reminded her.

"He will be. The fueling probe add-on kits are on their way from Dyess at the moment. They'll be installed tonight," Hettrick explained. "Ten man-hours per aerodyne, I'm told-"

"I don't have enough personnel to do that and get the 'dynes out of here tomorrow!" Curt objected.

"Dyess is sending help," Hettrick explained. "Your 'dynes will refuel once between Travis and Wheeler, RON at Wheeler, top-off in flight north of Wake, then RON aboard the Navy's SSCV-twenty, the U.S.S. *Cromwell*. They'll make the final leg Wednesday. They'll be able to airlift you out to the *Cromwell* or the *Kincaid* if the COPRE vote goes negative. You got any idea what it's taken to get the Navy and the Aerospace Force to support this?"

"An act of Congress?"

"Nearly. A DOD Execute Order backed up by an NSC order signed by the President."

Curt swallowed. This was indeed a high-power, low-drag, high-velocity mission! That in itself told him something about the importance of the memory cube data. It meant he'd have to get his staff busy right away, then take the necessary time to download the cube so he could give a proper Oscar brief. "Serious stuff," he remarked.

"Plenty. It wasn't just a matter of taking whatever regiment happened to be available. Curt, the NSC and the Bruneis specifically asked for you and the Greys on this one.

"I suspect you might have had something to do with that, General."

Hettrick shook her head. "Not me. General Carlisle."

General Jacob O. Carlisle, the Army COS, was the former commander of the 17th Iron Fist Division and, before that, the Washington Greys.

"Sometimes it doesn't help to have friends in high places, especially when it comes to going out and getting shot at," Curt said.

General Belinda Hettrick looked disapprovingly at him. "If I didn't know you had a sense of humor and perspective, Colonel, I would reprimand you for that statement which, under other circumstances and with other people present, might be considered highly insubordinate!"

She was lecturing him sternly and privately because she understood him very well and because, in her capacity as his commanding officer, she felt she had a responsibility to see to it that he didn't screw up his already illustrious career with an indiscreet remark. She had been taught by General Carlisle that a good commander always trains a replacement; two if possible so they can compete. But insofar as she was concerned, Colonel Curt Carson had no competition in sight. He'd taken her advice and guidance in the past. She felt he'd continue to do so - provided he survived all the nasty little fracases she had to send him into.

Hettrick went on in a less stern tone, "I don't want to give you a big head because your ego doesn't need inflation, but the Washington Greys weren't chosen for this operation just because they happen to have an orgasmic record of success, but also because their current commanding officer happens to have a long track record of successful operations in the international arena, especially in Kurdistan where you made your name shine. Curt, when I said that this operation could get messy, I meant just exactly that. Even if everything works out to begin with, it's likely to take every bit of expertise and tact you've got available. It's an international zoo full of snarling tigers, and it isn't going to get any better. The Soviets are already there and being their usual paranoid selves. The People's Liberation Army of the PRC is also on hand, and we haven't tangled with them officially since the Korean War - except on Kerguelen which doesn't count, of course. And the Japanese Self-Defense Force is messing around with their usual scrutible but oh-so-polite militancy. As for the Chileans, I've never been up against them or worked with them, but they could become very Hispanic and mercurial. I don't know how the Bruneis are going to behave, but the Gurkhas are legendary fighters you've worked with before. You're acquainted with the people involved except for Colonel Julio Castillo Pinedo, the Chilean commander. I don't know this General Mahathis who'll be CINC of the operation. You do. What's your opinion of him and how he'll lead this police detachment? How well did you work with General Mahathis during Operation Happy Abode in Brunei?"

"Pretty well...except he ended up working for me," Curt recalled. Mahathis, in spite of his background as a graduate of the U.S Aerospace Force Academy, was somewhat of a General Ducrot. He had mixed feelings about General - formerly Colonel - Ahmad Mahathis, the son of the sultan of Brunei and the heir apparent to the throne and the largest private fortune in the world. Mahathis was imperial in many ways. He could demand and get anything in the world he wanted...except, as he'd learned, the respect of other officers such as Curt and Major Alexis Morgan. Mahathis had found this out the hard way and discovered he'd had to earn respect.

Curt had seen Mahathis many times since they'd fought together on Borneo. Mahathis took every opportunity to pilot his personal TC-39 hypersonic Sabredancer VIP transport, visit the Washington Greys, and "get up to date on the latest Sierra Charlie warbot doctrine and techniques," according to his rationale. He also spent his off-duty time during those visits wooing Major Alexis Morgan, who didn't seem to object.

As a result of his leadership during the Operation Happy Abode on Borneo, Curt had been awarded Brunei's highest military decoration, the Sultan's Star of Brunei, which also meant that Curt was officially part of the sultan's family.

As a result, Mahathis was a friend, comrade in arms, and de facto brother. Curt could live with the man's shortcomings because he respected his strengths and accomplishments. The feeling was mutual on Mahathis' part. Curt knew it had to be because Mahathis sought out Curt for leadership advice and had raised no objections over Curt's relationship with his twin sister, the Sultana Alzena. Thus, it was a complex relationship that cut across cultures, religions, and emotions. He really wasn't too sure about Mahathis when the man was in total command. Like many powerful people, Mahathis could fall under the spell of having absolute power without accepting absolute responsibility.

"General Mahathis will do all right," Curt advised her. "He doesn't know from squat about running an international military operation. But neither do I! General, why don't you come along and teach us how to do it?" Curt was only half serious about that suggestion.

General Belinda Hettrick cocked her head to one side and looked at Curt. "Let me put it this way, Colonel. I'm the mama bird, see? And you're the baby bird, see? Well, the time has come to find out whether or not you can fly. Maybe as a result, you'll get some silver birds on your collar to help you fly thereafter. So the push you feel behind you will be the cleats of my hob-nailed boot making contact with your ass as you go sailing out of the nest. Flap your wings real hard, and you won't splatter too badly when you hit the ground. You may even get the hang of it on the way down if you happen to remember all I've tried to teach you...and you may soar to new heights. I'm betting on the latter."

Curt couldn't help but grin. His halfhearted suggestion had brought forth the sort of earthy mother-henning that Hettrick was known for when she hassled the Washington Greys through that very difficult transition from warbot brainies to Sierra Charlies, while at the same time training her own replacement in the person of Curt Carson. "Jeez, General, you really are an old battleaxe, aren't you?"

She raised her head and looked down her nose at him with a smile playing around the corners of her mouth. "Damned right! And damned proud of it! Or would you rather I used the code call, 'Iron Fister'?"

"With all due respect, it doesn't fit you as well."

"Thank you!" She leaned back in her chair, and her attitude suddenly changed to one of concern. "Curt, I know you had something going once with Alexis Morgan. Now I understand she's got it going with the man who's going to be your CINC on Sakhalin. That's the real reason why I asked you about General Mahathis. I want to get it square with you right now before the fur starts to fly. Is your brass green because of that? Did he take Alexis away from you?"

"Answer to first question: Not very green. A little liquid Brasso takes care of it. As for the second, no one owns Alexis Morgan, No one!" Curt said adamantly. "She's her own woman. You trained me to be myself. And I trained her the same way. If I'm not man enough to hold her on my own, that's my fault and my problem, if any. At any rate, if she's got her rich general to have fun with, she's been downright charitable of the fact that his twin sister boils my water."

Hettrick's expression of concern didn't change. "I just needed to clear the air. I know a lot about that. I have ways, you know."

"I'm sure you do, General. You always have had inscrutable means of G-2-ing your troops." He paused for a moment, then reassured her, "Don't worry. I haven't yet allowed my gonads to run my cerebrum when on duty or in official matters. Or in the field, for that matter."

"I'm only concerned that someday it's going to happen, whether you like it or not. It's one of the hazards of a mixed gender military establishment. I'm not at all sure we've figured out all the angles on that yet. I just hope to God you aren't the experimental hamster who has to discover it the hard way for everyone else."

"I think I've already been over the course," Curt admitted. "Had a woman officer die in my arms, remember? Almost had you check out from a poisoned Namibian Bushman's arrow, remember? Or when Alexis got her butt creased in Borneo and then got taken hostage by those Shiite Dayaks there? You weren't there when Kitsy Clinton damned near got it in Mexico or when she had her neck busted in Iraq. I think I've proved I can handle that sort of thing emotionally. At least I've proved it to myself, anyway."

"I don't know whether you have or not," Hettrick told him frankly. "We're all pretty damned unpredictable."

"And we're all former warbot brainies, General. We wouldn't have cut it if we hadn't had all our neurons straight and aligned to begin with. You can't mess around with mental hang-ups or problems if you're working with NE. Colonel Wild Bill Bellamack learned that the hard way when he linked with that Soviet Spetsnaz sergeant."

"Yes, and he made it back to the real world only because he was tougher than hell down inside," Hettrick reminded him. "Okay, Curt, I just wanted to touch gently here and there to see if I encountered any raw nerve endings. I didn't. At least, not the ones I anticipated." With that cryptic remark, she straightened up in her chair and told him in official tones, "Colonel, TACAMO! Take charge and move out! You've got a shit pot full of work to do before the sun sets tomorrow...and you'll be halfway around the world when that happens! Don't be a stranger..."

Chapter Nine

"Ready for the Oscar brief, Joanne?" Curt asked Major Joanne Wilkinson, his regimental chief of staff.

"No, sir!" she fired back as her blunt fingers continued to play over her keypad.

"Why?"

"Georgie is out of ports," she explained. "I dropped off-line for a moment to scratch, and some staff stooge at Division accessed and filled the incoming channels while I was off."

"Georgie is full up?" Curt had trouble believing this. Georgie was named after General George S. Patton of the legendary Third Army of the last century. It was one of the biggest megacomputers in the Army. It had once run almost everything when the Washington Greys and the other three Iron Fist regiments were full Robot Infantry outfits. Georgie had been only partly accessible for the past two years while the tech-weenies played around with him, supposedly updating and expanding him.

They hadn't totally succeeded. They'd run into trouble. Georgie was far faster than the human mind, and it now had about fourteen times the number of gates that the human mind had in the way of neural connections. Curt suspected the damned thing was becoming self-aware. If Georgie wasn't, it had certainly gotten nearly as temperamental as an overworked human being.

Curt would have preferred decentralizing Georgie by adding peripherals instead of expanding the main frame. This might have allowed incremental upgrading and testing as Georgie's expansion progressed. But Curt was a voice crying in the wilderness; he wasn't a computer engineer, just a field commander. His silver oak leaves cut no ice with the tech-weenies.

But he knew that's the way it had always been in the Army. The techies would always try to foist the latest high-tech on the troops, and the troops would then take it into the field and mod the hell out of it to get it to work in a useful way. From his own knowledge of military history, he felt that the squires of the Egyptian war chariots had probably spent many nights revising the "improvements" the techies of the Nile Valley had incorporated into the ancient counterpart of the light tank. In his own experience, he recalled with distaste the M-101 Hellcat assault rifle, the "one-oh-wonder," whose faulty design had nearly cost him his life and had, at a later time, saved his life in Borneo.

Curt turned to his regimental technical sergeant, Edie Sampson, and asked her, "Sergeant, any way you can kludge a patch into Old Hickory or Tiffany or whatever pile of slightly impure semiconducting crystals is available on-line to give Georgie more access capability?"

"Negatory, sir!" Edie fired back, intent on her terminal. "They took that capability away from us in the upgrade. Something to do with security..."

"Can you hack into anything out there to provide some more capability?" Curt wanted to know. It was 0200 by the clock; in less than twelve hours, he had to have plans together to load the regiment aboard the Royal Brunei Airlines hypersonics that would be arriving at Libby Army Airfield. In fact, he knew that the hypersonics were probably getting ready to take off from Bandar Seri Begawan even as he fought to get his staff enough data management power.

"Colonel, do you care where I get the extra power?" Edie suddenly asked.

"No, as long as it's legal," he told her, harried. "What do you have in mind?"

"I'll try getting into some Pentagon main frame through DODON," she told him, referring to the Department of Defense Open Network on-line system which DOD maintained in order to test its links and channels by allowing a limited number of private citizens to use it.

"Do you have a DODON access code?"

"No, but Colonel Bellamack did, and I think it's still active," she guessed. "I doubt he'll have a shit fit if we use it. I understand he's still on extended recoup leave somewhere in Missouri with his brother."

"Edie, how the hell did you learn his access code and password?" Curt wanted to know.

"Colonel Bellamack asked me to pass some electronic mail along for him before we took our little trip to Iraq. And, Colonel, I never forget a number," she admitted to him with a grin. "Better not talk in your sleep, sir!"

"Tell that to Henry," Curt fired back.

Regimental Master Sergeant Henry Kester looked up from where he was working on another terminal. "Tell what to me, Colonel?"

"As Edie just remarked, Sergeant Major, better not talk in your sleep," Curt said. The brief banter break was just what he needed at the moment.

"Since when has she let me sleep?" he muttered and went back to his terminal keypad.

"Since you locked your door," Curt replied.

"Since I locked my chastity belt, you mean," Edie retorted.

"As I recall, Master Sergeant Sampson, you couldn't; the lock was too rusty from disuse," the regimental sergeant major responded.

"My, isn't it getting juicy in here?" chirped Major Hensley Atkinson.

"Too much like the Club, so let's get back to official business," Curt advised them. "You've given Rumor Control enough data for a while. If any of this leaks to the news media, we'll be back in the old licentious Army pit, appearing before review boards and Congressional committees while being accused of frittering away taxpayer's money in orgasmic orgies."

"Sometime I'd like to find the part of the Army that's supposed to be engaged in that sort of activity - Aha! Got into Ulysses!" Edie cheered. "Okay, stand by for a non-reg hack. I've got three hundred gigabytes available to me!"

"Go for it!" Curt advised her. He was doing his best to try to hold together this staff planning all-nighter. He had good people, and he knew better than to joggle their elbows. They were used to working fast. But the task of deploying the whole regiment overnight was a bit taxing even for them. He knew they could pull it off. He kept telling himself that he was now in the position where his primary job was to untangle screw-ups, break bottlenecks, and unscrew the unscrutible. Top management in the Army wasn't much different from top management anywhere...except instead of committing corporate funds and effort, he was committing people's lives.

Major Pappy Gratton stepped up to Curt and announced, "Major Worsham's just reported back on post."

"Good! Where the hell was he?" Curt wanted to know.

"You gave him a weekend pass, remember? We finally tracked him down at the Reno Air Races," the regimental adjutant reminded his commanding officer.

"He's got a whole squadron of 'dynes to worry about," Curt said with irritation. "Tell him to report to the line over at Libby."

"He's here. He wants to talk to you," Gratton explained. The older man looked hassled. He'd been busy tracking Greys all over the Western Hemisphere. Curt wasn't one to withhold passes and leaves, especially when things were quiet, and no action was expected. The Execute Order had caught him short, but it was his G-1 adjutant who got it in the chops as a result.

"So? Why is he cooling his heels waiting for an invitation?"

"I asked him to wait for a break in the sheep screw here," Gratton advised.

"Shit, Pappy, you know I'm always available to my batt commanders!"

"Yes, sir, that's true. But that wasn't my real reason for asking

Worsham to wait. He's pissed about something. I felt a cooling-off period might calm him down a tad."

Curt sighed. "Get him in here, Pappy. Making Cal Worsham wait won't help him calm down..."

Curt was right about that. Major Cal Worsham came storming into regimental HQ and made straight for Curt's office. The commander of the Washington Greys was ready and waiting for him.

"Goddammit, Carson!" Worsham exploded as he thundered in, slammed the door behind him, and tore off his blue tam to reveal his shaved head. Worsham still sported the shaved head of the true war bot brainy, even though the new Mod 7/11 AI in his aerodynes didn't require the sort of hard linkage that the old warbots did. "What the *hell* are those Aerospace Farce tech-weenies doing to *my* aerodynes? I go off for a *quiet* weekend at the air races and not only get called *back* for this sheep screw but find *everyone* in the squadron tearing up the 'dynes to install *lash-up* refueling probes! Who the *hell* authorized that, and *where* the fuck are we going to *go* that requires mid-air top-off? And did *anyone* think to consider what it's *like* to fly a 'dyne for ten to twelve hours at a stretch? *Someone's* tit is going into the wringer for *this* one, and I want to find out *whose!*"

Curt just looked at him and said nothing for a moment. He knew how to handle. Worsham, who was the best tacair Harpy driver in the Army and one hell of a tough squadron leader - Cal preferred to call his AIRBATT a "squadron" rather than a "battalion" because he didn't consider his people to be gravel crunchers. But Cal Worsham was also one undisciplined sonofabitch in the old tradition of Air Force types dating from the origin of the service before World War II.

"*Well?*" Worsham finally asked.

Curt continued to look at him, then said quietly, "Major Worsham, I believe. Right? I'm Lieutenant Colonel Carson, your regimental commander. Remember me?"

"*What?*" was Worsham's explosive question.

"Major Worsham, in case you didn't realize it, the regiment has received a DOD Execute Order" Curt told him. "We are on duty at the moment and possibly headed into combat. This is *not* the Club, and it is *not* a Stand-to! *Or* an exercise! You are an excellent squadron leader, and I'm delighted to have you in my command. But I do insist that a minimum level of discipline be observed in a situation like this because combat may be a consequence. Therefore, I suggest you begin to observe that request from your regimental commander at once and then get your squadron shaped up as well. I will be counting on you for a lot of things starting now..."

Worsham swallowed, straightened up, and saluted. "Major Calvin Worsham reporting, Colonel! And I have a bitch, sir!"

Curt returned his salute. "Yes, I know. I heard some of it. The Greys have been ordered to carry out a minimum time deployment to Sakhalin in the Far East. TACBATT and SERVBATT will be departing Libby this afternoon at approximately seventeen hundred. AIRBATT will be ferrying the Harpies and Chippies transpacific behind us. Since you don't have the range for a transpacific flight, the Aerospace Force flew crews in from Dyess to help your squadron install refuel probes tonight. I approved it since you were unavailable. So now that you're here, I request you get the hell down there, make sure your squadron will be able to join us as planned on Sakhalin, and assist your people with the planning and implementation they're engaged in. Some of us, including your squadron people, have been working steadily for nearly nine hours already. I will conduct an Oscar briefing at oh-nine-thirty during which all details will be revealed. In the meantime, the base is closed, and maximum security is in effect. Any questions, Major?"

Worsham's black handlebar mustache quivered at its tips. He was suddenly all business. "My apologies, Colonel. I didn't realize you were under the gun and had been working all night..."

"Apologies accepted, Cal. Now get humping!"

"Roger! The Warhawks will be ready!" He shook his head. "Transpacific deployment ferry! Jesus! I've never done *that* before!"

"Consider it a learning experience," Curt told him. "Dismissed, Major! See you at oh-nine-thirty!"

Worsham saluted and turned to leave, but Curt interrupted his departure. "Sorry to break up your weekend, Cal. It caught mine, too. And I hope it didn't get Nancy pissed off too much." He knew that Worsham had gone up to the Reno Air Races with Lieutenant Nancy Roberts, one of the Warhawk aerodyne pilots. Curt had long ago recommended her for flight training. She was not only an outstanding pilot but was one of the few who didn't stand in complete and total awe of Major Cal Worsham, who was impressive in both size and bluster.

A quick grin touched one corner of Cal Worsham's mouth. "Colonel, she wasn't half as pissed off as I was...and I'll let you figure that one out!"

Curt suddenly felt tired. Weary. Fatigued. It was late at night or early in the morning, depending on how he looked at the situation. And it was going to be a long day ahead as the Greys finalized their departure from Fort Huachuca. Curt always worried about Regimental Sergeant Major Henry Kester's standing advice, "Don't forget nothin'!" Curt himself was hoping he wouldn't forget nothing, too. Or that his staff wouldn't. He knew he'd get his second wind in about an hour and be able to carry on for another twenty-four hours without rest. But getting over the hump was always tough.

So, he tried to keep himself busy to make it easier. Although he'd served as temporary regimental commander several years ago, this was really his first operation as the for-real regimental commander. He had discovered that his predecessors had trained the staff very well. Curt didn't have very much to do except worry that everyone was doing everything right. This came as a surprise to him. He'd always thought of the regimental commander as one who was constantly busy with a million details on his mind. It wasn't that way at all. It was worse. He was only *responsible* that everything was right, thar everything had been done, and that his people had done it for him. He really had very little control over the details. And he knew from his own experience as a batt commander and a company commander that this was the way it should be, was, and could be no other way. He had delegated the authority, but he could never delegate the responsibility.

No wonder it was lonely at the top, he told himself.

He was interrupted by a rap on his door and looked up to see Major Joan Ward. "Come in, Joan!" he called out to her.

She entered and saluted.

He returned the salute and told her, "You look beat to the socks. Sit down."

"Yes, sir," she said quietly in her small voice. This was always an unusual trait insofar as Curt was concerned. Joan was a classmate whom he'd known from Beast Barracks at West Point. She was a large, ample, and very plain-looking woman who wasn't without many definite female charms, but her small voice always seemed incongruous coming from such a large woman. "TACBATT is tactical in all respects and good to go, sir. So, I've told everyone to hit the snore shelf so they'll be sharp when we get to Sakhalin."

"Glad to hear that. I can always count on you, Joan," Curt told her. He had had some heartburn over who he should promote to the commander of the tactical battalion - Major Joan Ward or Major Alexis Morgan. He knew them both very well.

He'd trained Alexis from the time she'd joined the regiment as a brown bar out of West Point and had had a very close and often torrid relationship going there. But Alexis had somehow strangely changed since she'd gotten her own company. She was still a good leader, and the Marauders were one of the best assault companies in the whole Iron Fist Division. But she'd changed subtly since she'd met General Ahmad Mahathis when the Greys had trekked to Brunei for Operation Happy Abode.

On the other hand, he knew Joan almost as a sister. She wasn't a meteoric hall of military fire like Alexis, whose career progress had been accelerated at first. Joan was a solid, conventional, dependable, no-nonsense, and often quite ordinary leader. In that respect, she matched her appearance.

So, it had been a tough call to appoint Joan as TACBATT

commander. It had come as a surprise to most of the Greys who'd expected that Alexis would get it as a result of her relationship with Curt. In that regard, the new regimental commander had posted the message that he intended to rely on expertise, achievement, and military abilities. He'd let everyone know that he intended to run the Greys without favoritism.

Thus, although it had been a difficult decision for Curt, he'd gained even more respect from his regiment in the process.

A commander, he'd learned, shouldn't always do the popular or expected thing.

"And if you don't need me for anything, I'm going to trot for the cot once I leave here," Joan went on.

"Good! Go!" he told her.

She looked at him, knowing him very well. "Sure you really don't need me for anything?"

He shook his head. "My staff has everything under control."

"How about you?"

"Sorry. Late at night. Signals not getting through, Joan. Rule Ten is in effect anyway, you know."

"I didn't mean that. Yeah, signals not getting through. Obviously," she told him. "This is your first Big One as head of the Washington Greys. As I recall, we once talked a lot about that. You used to worry a lot about it. I think you still do. Want to dump anything on me?"

He thought about that for a minute, realizing that she was slowly taking the place of Alexis Morgan as a confidante because Alexis's interests had gradually shifted elsewhere. "Maybe."

"Dump!" she told him.

"I'm not so sure I like the idea of getting between the Russkies, the Chinks, and the Japs," he admitted, "especially with Mahathis as the CIC. I can count on the Gurkhas, even under the command of Colonel Payne-Ashwell; those bastards are fighters! I don't think I can count on the Chileans at all; at best, they're an unknown variable in the equation..."

"You talk as if you're going to have to run the show on Sakhalin," Joan observed.

"I just damned well may have to do that, Joan!" he reflected. "I can't count on Mahathis. I've never seen him operate in an international arena. In Brunei, he had things pretty much his own way, and that worries me. If he tries to behave in Sakhalin as he does in Brunei where he's the sultan's son and the heir to the throne, he could trigger a whole shit pot full of trouble for us. And if it gets out of hand, it could lead to escalation to general war somehow...And *that*, my dear, is something we've *got* to prevent!"

"Got news for you," Joan told him. "Your Papa brief late last night has the Greys thinking the same thing. This could be a real bucket of slime."

"Well, I'm glad to know I'm not alone."

"Hell, Curt, you never have been," she reminded him. Then, cautiously, she added, "I...uh...think you *might* just have more than a little heartburn, too, about the fact that the sultana decided she's going to accompany her brother as the deputy for civil affairs."

Curt looked her straight in the eye and asked, "Why? Didn't cause me any heartburn when the regiment was in Brunei. Or are some of our ladies letting their brass get green for some reason?"

"Some may not appreciate the competition," Joan said slowly, "which is ridiculous, as you and I know. There ain't no competition for us ladies in the Greys! But in Brunei there were few situations after we got through being nasty at Longliku. There might be on Sakhalin. And the sultana isn't affected by Rule Ten, is she?"

"Thanks for the heads-up, Joan," Curt told her. "Believe me, I'll definitely keep that in mind. I sort of have to behave a lot differently since General Hettrick gave me command."

Joan grinned. "She didn't give you command of the Washington Greys, Curt! We did! She just formalized it! And don't you ever forget it...sir!"

"I won't! But, as you put it, Joan, this is my first Big One as regimental commander. I hope to God we can pull this sucker off without anyone getting hurt or killed."

"Curt, it wasn't your fault, and we all miss Kitsy Clinton."

"Yeah, Joan, but I was there, and I should have shot that bitch before she busted Kitsy's neck!"

Major Joan Ward shrugged. "That can't be changed, so don't fret. Let's just go out there and save the free world from the scourge of war again!" A smile played over her plain face as she said this. It was an inside joke in the Greys.

"Thanks. And thanks also for allowing me to dump on you," Curt told her gently. "I didn't realize I needed to do it."

"You never did, even back at West Point," she reminded him. "But what are friends and classmates for?"

Chapter Ten

The AASU-99 Robotic Airborne Assault Gun, sometimes known by its Soviet code name Silver Pilgrim, rumbled slowly along the road between Novoaleksandrovsk and Sokol, heading north out of Yuzhno-Sakhalinsk.

If these names were difficult for Americans to pronounce, they were a nightmare for the Chinese troops on Sakhalin and an insult to the members of the Japanese Self-Defense Force stationed there. A century ago, these places had long-forgotten Japanese names, when Sakhalin was known as Karafuto. Centuries before that, the island had belonged to imperial China. But the empire of the Mongols hadn't seen any real purpose in exercising suzerainty over such a forsaken place with practically no people and no easily exploitable resources such as grazing or agricultural land. The only thing that had changed on Sakhalin was the discovery of abundant natural resources - coal, petroleum, iron, titanium - that now made the place an attractive target for exploitation. It also served as a strategic bastion because it virtually controlled the eastern marches of the Soviet empire and Soviet access to the Pacific. The Soviets had lost this in the aftermath of Space War I, otherwise called the Sino-Soviet Incident, which the Soviets had won but yet had lost in the negotiations to bring it to a close.

Junior Lieutenant Pavel Fedorovich Koslov was riding in the BTR-218 directing vehicle five hundred meters behind the Soviet warbot. He was watching *Starshii Serzant* Sergey Petrovich Zaytsev operating *Ohtryahd Seeneey Dvah*, the warbot's operational call.

"Sergeant, you idiot! You almost ran it off the road again!" Lieutenant Koslov snarled at his NCO. He was worried. This was his first patrol with a Silver Pilgrim. He didn't know how many million rubles the warbot had cost, but he knew that his meager lieutenant's pay would never be able to recoup the cost if he screwed up and allowed his NCO to wreck the machine. Worse than that, there were only twelve of them in the special battalion that had jointed the 110th Special Airborne Guards Regiment.

And Koslov had learned through the underground vodka channels that the battalion would get no more warbots if one was wrecked. The Soviet Union had only twenty-five of them, but Koslov didn't know that exact number. He only knew that the warbot was a rare, expensive, and highly experimental machine. It was his job to participate in the field tests and to bring the warbot safely home each day so that it could be properly evaluated and maintained. Like most Soviet military equipment, it was designed to be rugged and require very low-quality maintenance - just kick the tires every day and make sure the fuel tank was full. After a couple of hundred hours of operation, it would be sent back to the *Tyl* where it would be disassembled and rebuilt.

Sergeant Zaytsev didn't worry about losing the warbot. The Motherland could only take away his rank. At the worst, he'd be assigned to a labor battalion for a year or so, but even that was unlikely because he was now privy to state secrets in addition to being a top technical school graduate; they'd put him to work somewhere in a maximum security technical camp in Siberia. He knew the lieutenant was the responsible individual who would be in deep borscht if someone in the company screwed up.

But in spite of his training, Zaytsev was having trouble controlling Detachment Blue Two, as the code call translated into English. "Comrade Lieutenant, although I can see by the television camera in the warbot's sensor dome, the system is very slow to respond to my steering commands! It needs to be made faster if we are to properly command these warbots in combat."

"Nonsense! The warbot represents the work of the best academic and technical minds of the Motherland! And you have had months of training at *Dohleenah Styekloh!* You were certified by Academician Blyukher and Engineer Kolchak as a competent warbot operator! Did you cheat on your training and testing?" Koslov suggested.

"*Nyet,* Comrade Lieutenant! But directing a warbot along this primitive road is much different than handling a warbot simulator...or even driving a Silver Pilgrim along the test tracks at *Dohleenah Styekloh!*"

Koslov could bitch and snivel about it all he wanted to, and Zaytsev could sweat out last night's vodka binge until he was dehydrated, but both knew deep down inside that the Silver Pilgrim was a marginal machine. It was like all early Soviet attempts to equal western technology. It was a kludge. It was a poor copy. (Later versions might equal western warbots as KGB and GRU agents were able to obtain American components in enough quantity to permit a higher level of serial production.) In its present form, the warbot's circuitry simply wasn't fast enough. By the time it processed its video signal, sent it back to the command vehicle, allowed the computer there to reprocess and reconstitute the signal, gave Zaytsev time to respond and send back a correction signal, and then reprocessed the signal into steering commands, nearly a second of time elapsed. That was hardly real time in terms of operating a warbot.

Sometimes by the time Zaytsev saw things going to slime and gave the necessary correcting command, the warbot was either in deep goulash or conditions had changed. It was the classic time delay problem encountered by all who operated slow-response equipment.

The Silver Pilgrim contained no neural networks that would process its own steering commands based on analysis of the edge and center of the roadway from viewing of contrast-enhanced edge effects in the video-camera signal. Its circuitry was all analog, and it couldn't conduct digital processing that would have made the job easier. And it had no decision circuits that would permit it to shorten the time response by generating its own internal steering commands; the decision circuitry was so expensive and so touchy that it had, by necessity, been retained in the BTR-218 directing vehicle where it was safer.

And Silver Pilgrim not only had no computers that would allow it to make its own decisions, but no circuitry that would allow Zaytsev to override a bad internal command of Silver Pilgrim.

It was about as primitive as a robot could be.

Which was surprising to those who didn't understand Soviet practices. Soviet factories had far better industrial robots that were on par with those in America and Japan. But the Ministry of Electronics Manufacturing which was primarily responsible for the design and production of military equipment such as warbots simply could not get the Ministry of General Machine Building and the Ministry of Radio Technical Construction to provide information on industrial robotics because these were considered officially to be high state secrets. Unofficially, the information was part of the sacred turf of these ministries, and they weren't exactly willing to share it because they weren't building the warbots and wouldn't get additional resource allocations if another ministry used the information.

In short, it was a bureaucratic turf battle that had resulted in the primitive performance of the Silver Pilgrim.

Another factor entered in. Warbots were new to the Soviet military structure. Warbots had previously been officially considered unnecessary; internally, everyone knew that the Red Army had no warbots because Soviet industry couldn't make something that would equal western warbots in combat, and the Soviet military had always been very hesitant to field a weapon that wasn't perceived to be at least as good as existing western weapons systems. Warbots weren't part of the current five-year plan, much less the longer-range ten-year and fifteen-year plans for development and long-range planning.

However, the golden opportunity occurred to acquire American Hairy Foxes out of the glacier ice of Kerguelen Island because the Americans had been ordered by their president to abandon them there. That changed everything overnight.

But the monolithic nature of the Soviet industrial base hadn't changed in spite of several attempts to streamline it in the last fifty years. It had been monolithic under the czars, and it remained monolithic under the Politburo. It was Russian, and that's the only explanation that need be given to both the Soviets and the western world.

But the Soviet warbot was strong as an ox. It was an iron man. It probably wouldn't have been damaged or disabled even if Zaytsev had run it off the road. It might have become hogged down in the swampy tundralike terrain and thus become vulnerable to enemy fire if someone else decided to shoot at it, but it probably wouldn't have been put out of action. It could still shoot, even if bogged down. But it wouldn't have been able to train its 53-millimeter gun in azimuth. So, the 110th Special Airborne Guards Regiment might have had to come out and use one of its trucks to pull it back onto the road.

The Soviet high command believed that these primitive warbots probably couldn't be integrated into their highly mobile offensive doctrine that depended upon shock, mobility, and speed. But they thought they perhaps might have some utility in patrol and guard duties. It was their chance to get one-up on the KGB who controlled the Border Guards. If the Silver Pilgrim could do the job, it was a trading chip between the Army and the KGB. But the Silver Pilgrim had to prove itself. Thus, the Ministry of Defense had sent the Silver Pilgrims to Sakhalin.

They also believed that the Chinese and Japanese forces on Sakhalin would consider the Silver Pilgrims to be only a minor modification of the standard Soviet light airborne assault gun, the ASU-88. Thus, they could get some field experience with the Silver Pilgrim while maintaining security by misdirection.

It might have worked with the People's Liberation Army of the PRC except for the fact that engineers in Beiching knew that the Soviets had gotten some Hairy Foxes on Kerguelen. The Chinese recovery mission had pulled out prematurely when they'd detected the Soviet mission coming. As a result, the PRC had gotten only a few Hairy Foxes but a lot of Mary Anns. However, the PRC was a lot slower at analyzing the American warbots and hadn't attempted yet to introduce them into their military structure. Furthermore, with their billions of people and lots of young men available as both cannon fodder and guards, they really needed warbots much less than the Soviets. The only reason they were interested at all was that they would have to show warbots at some point soon to maintain the charade that the People's Liberation Army was indeed a modern military force.

The Soviet attempt at deception didn't work at all with the Japanese Self-Defense Forces. Within hours of the report that the Soviets had introduced the Silver Pilgrims into Sakhalin, the Japanese had reacted by triggering their warbot intelligence data unit. This had been standing by on Hokkaido waiting for just such an opportunity.

Thus, that very morning a Japanese oil field instrumentation unit had landed at Sokol and ostensibly began to move northward only to suddenly disappear into the hills between Dounsk and Ostromysovka, where they quickly set up ELINT equipment.

Doctor Osami Sakamoto and his graduate student assistant, Gunji Hirata, were bundled into their instrumentation truck bearing the sign, "University of Ashikawa Petroleum Logging Laboratory." The sign was legitimate; said university did indeed exist, and it had a small petroleum instrumentation laboratory because of its proximity to the newly acquired petroleum reserves of Sakhalin.

What was not advertised was the fact that Dr. Sakamoto was also a colonel in the Japanese Self-Defense Forces and his student assistant held the rank of sergeant. But they behaved as if they were civilian academicians.

"Doctor-san, I have determined and recorded the frequencies and modulation characteristics of the up links and down links," Hirata reported.

"Very good, Hirata!"

"It seems to be very familiar."

"Yes, it appears to be rather straightforward Soviet standard television transmission for the down link," the professor-soldier observed. "I suspect that the up-link can he deciphered."

"The up-link appears to be digitally coded."

"Ah, so! Yes, you are right, Hirata. It appears to resemble their spacecraft radio guidance command protocol!"

"It would seem that the Soviets continue to apply their existing technology in a universal way wherever they can..."

"Ah, yes! They waste nothing. But they have little to waste in the first place," Sakamoto remarked as he studied the characteristics of the Soviet warbot command signals. "Of course! They are using the Hotel Romeo coding! That is the same coding command structure that they have used for the Kosmos laser battle stations!"

"Then we can certainly inject a countermeasures signal that would interfere with their Silver Pilgrim warbots!"

"Let us not do so at this time, Hirata," Sakamoto advised. "It is our assignment to remain passive and to collect the information we have just discovered. ECM is not our assigned mission...although I realize that you would delight in confusing the Soviets!"

"True, Doctor-san. ECM would only reveal to them at this time that we have their warbot command codes..."

"And those for their space defense system as well! But I often wonder if they might suspect this in any event. In Japan, we have certainly been well known for our abilities to utilize electronics technology. I wonder if they might suspect what we are doing?"

The Soviets might not have suspected that the Japanese were conducting an ELINT operation this quickly, but the Chinese had reacted rapidly to the introduction of the Soviet warbots. Sentinels in the hills to the west were following the Silver Pilgrim, and a Chinese AT-106 light armored vehicle was quietly waiting at the ready near Firsovo several kilometers up the coast road. Colonel Dao Min Qian had already determined that he would act to test the Silver Pilgrim's capability to absorb the energy of the warhead of a Chinese S-100 rocket if the Soviets decided to open fire with the Silver Pilgrim on his troops. However, his orders to his troops were to watch only. They were to load and fire on the Silver Pilgrim only upon his direct orders.

What none of the military units and their commanders on Sakhalin suspected, however, was the fact that not all of the seagulls wheeling over the cold marshlands on either side of the road were real.

They were American birdbots, undistinguishable from the other real gulls in the air around them. If one were to carefully observe the birdbots and knew what he was looking for, he might have detected slight differences in the way the birdbot gulls flew, beating their wings far more often than real gulls because they weighed much more.

And the birdbot gulls had a tendency to remain flying on a steady bearing for a lot longer as they trained their sensors on the Silver Pilgrim...and the Japanese oil logging truck. They'd already spotted the Chinese T-106 armored vehicle and several others, mostly Soviet, that were deployed here and there.

A Sakhalin fishing trawler manned by nisei busies itself off the east coast of Sakhalin not more than ten kilometers away. It might have been unusual for a trawler to be fishing the water off Sakhalin this late in the season - pack ice was already becoming a nuisance – but everyone on Sakhalin knew hat the catch this year had been sparse, and many fishing boats were out there in an attempt to build up their catches by staying out longer in the season. No one realized that this trawler was manned by Americans because they looked Japanese (and several generations before, they were).

Some of the gulls were being operated by neuro-electronic linkage from this trawler.

The American skipper enjoyed this sort of thing. Insofar as he was concerned, this was tit for tat. Soviet trawlers still frequented the American coastline near military and heavy-lift space facilities. It was suitable turnabout that an American fishing trawler was snooping off the coast of Sakhalin.

But it wasn't an American military operation.

The data was being transmitted back to Langely, Virginia by sophisticated lasercom links through satellites.

General Albert Murray, USAF (Retired), sat in his office at the National Intelligence Agency watching the birdbot's direct view of the Soviet Silver Pilgrim as the warbot blundered its way up the road.

He'd been waiting for this for several years now.

It was a good thing, he thought, that the Washington Greys were on their way to Sakhalin. Insofar as he was concerned, they were the best outfit to put on the island at the moment.

He knew things were going to get interesting.

Chapter Eleven

The Washington Greys were gathered in the air-conditioned comfort of their regimental briefing room at Fort Huachuca. This was not the snake pit used by Robot Infantry regiments where briefings were carried out with a great deal of computer graphics support and neuroelectronic linkage. The Bravo Pit was a theater-like assembly room with a prominent briefing stage. It had a high level of computer graphic support available, but no part of the briefing was carried out neuroelectronically. The Greys had pioneered a return to the personal briefing techniques of pre-warbot days.

Actually, regimental commanders of the past such as Belinda Hettrick and Bill Bellamack found that they preferred personal briefings. Although NE techniques allowed people to link minds in a sort of computer-assisted telepathy, there seemed to be something lacking. Whatever it was, personal face-to-face briefings brought it back.

No one had yet determined exactly what it was. Even Colonel Willa Lovell and Captain Owen Pendelton, two of the Army's top NE researchers from McCarthy Proving Ground, had been unable to pin it down scientifically.

But any live-theater actor would have known what it was immediately.

It was some sort of empathetic feedback that came from the audience en masse. Actors recognized it when they felt they had the audience in their hands and fully involved in believing that the make-believe on stage was real. Television personalities and actors could only get a bit of it, but they played to the much smaller audience of the sound stage crew. Some very popular TV personalities were able to overcome the shortcomings of the electronic link.

Curt had experienced it in lesser form when he'd briefed a company or a battalion. He dimly recalled how powerful it was when he'd been temporary regimental commander and had to conduct the briefings under the pressures of combat.

Now he got it full blast when he stood up before the Greys. He was tired. Fatigued is a better term. He wasn't yet exhausted; that took a lot longer. But he'd been up all night with the regimental staff, working on the details of the deployment to Sakhalin. Yet the empathy of 136 people was there and washed over him.

"Good morning!" he told his troops as he took center stage. Like Bellamack before him, Curt used a two-meter pointer and held it horizontally with both hands in front of him. He recalled that Colonel Landers Duncan Abercromby Payne-Ashwell, the British-trained commander of the 6th Sultan's Own Gurkha Rifles of Brunei, had used a riding crop in the British tradition for the same reason. The pointer was, of course, a surrogate commander's sword, a symbol of authority. And he deliberately used it as such.

Without waiting for a reply because none was required, Curt went on, "Thank you for your fine work last night. The three batts were ready in all respects for a deployment by oh three hundred this morning. But the staff had to work all night alongside that of the Iron Fist Division. I appreciate the fact that you humped your butts on the basis of only an abbreviated Papa briefing last evening. I told you what I knew at that time: that I had received DOD Execute Order Thirty-four-dash-eight-dash-one with supporting orders from the National Security Council over the signature of the Commander in Chief. The regiment will execute a rapid overseas deployment to Sakhalin Island. The main non-air portion of the regiment will deploy today by hypersonic airlift which will be provided by the lead nation of the Sakhalin Police Detachment, Negara Darussalam Brunei. The flying portion of AIRBATT will deploy by transpacific ferry flight using refueling and RONs."

He looked around at the silent assemblage. Then he held up a memory cube. It wasn't the same one that Hettrick had given him; it was a stage prop which he used as such because the contents of the real one were far too sensitive to permit it to be outside a highly secured area. "Since the Papa briefing, I've had the opportunity to review the background information contained in this. So has my S-2 intelligence staffer, Major Aarts." He looked down at her. Her face showed the fatigue and strain of an all-nighter. "Major Aarts, if you please."

Curt stepped down and let Ellie Aarts take the stage. She. was a good Sierra Charlie platoon commander, and she'd seen her share of action from Namibia onward. But after receiving the Purple Heart as a result of being a member of the lost battalion on Brunei, she'd expressed a desire to get out of personal combat and back to being a warbot brainy. Curt had seen to it that she'd been promoted and assigned to run the birdbot platoon under Major John Gibbon. After Iraq, Gibbon decided he didn't want to take the chance of being KIA again – he'd been through it three times - but Curt had no slot into which he could slip Gibbon and had reluctantly let him transfer to a staff position with the reforming Gimlet regiment. One of Curt's first acts as regimental commander was to kick Ellie Aarts upstairs to command RECONCO.

Some people, he'd learned, weren't cut out to be Sierra Charlies. Some were warbot brainies to the toes of their boots. In spite of NE analysis and selection techniques, the only way to find out was to let an eager Sierra Charlie to go into the field and be shot at.

He also knew that some people got tired of being shot at and simply didn't want to push the odds any longer.

"Good morning! Georgie, please display a three-dee chart of Sakhalin Island," Major Aarts began. A holographic image of Sakhalin and its surroundings built up in the projection tank behind her as the Iron Fist Division's megacomputer responded to her order. "I need not present a briefing on Sakhalin. American units were stationed there as FIG forces at the end of the Sino-Soviet Incident when the island was demilitarized and put under Japanese civil and economic administration. The Panthers were withdrawn two years ago as a result of a change in FIG policy. I suggest that you spend your travel time reviewing the Sakhalin geophysical and demographic data that is readily available.

"The situation on Sakhalin has grown worse since the Panthers withdrew. The Soviets put a regiment on the island in response to complaints from former Soviet citizens that they were being harassed and discriminated against by the Japanese business and technical people. The PRC followed suit. So did the Japanese Self-Defense Force. Therefore, three foreign regiments are on Sakhalin today.

"It was only a matter of time before a military crisis occurred. But when it did, it came about as a result of some very strange and unusual circumstances." She grinned because she knew something that only Curt and the staff knew. She'd put a little spin of her own on it. She continued, "It seems the Soviet Far East Military District high command wouldn't put a Soviet social battalion on Sakhalin to minister to the needs of the Red Army Special Airborne Guards Regiment stationed there. The Soviet government has allowed the world's oldest profession to continue as a free enterprise operation on Sakhalin. Apparently the shackers of Sakhalin were doing quite well fulfilling the wants of the marketplace, and the Red Army was happy to have a cooperative red-light district. That is, until the Chinese and Japanese troops attempted to patronize it, too. The girls objected to the behavior of the Chinese and Japanese. The hookers didn't like their smell because they ate different foods, and it gets sort of noticeable if troops don't bathe often, which is not a usual practice in a cold climate even when there's plenty of hot water from hot springs. Therefore, the hookers temporarily went on strike as a lever to get the Soviet troops to do something about the Chinese and Japanese. The Soviet soldiers are really pushed out of shape about that. So, they've taken it out on the Chinese and Japanese troops. In spite of the harsh discipline in all three military units there, overt fighting has broken out over the past few days. And it's growing. Yesterday, the Soviets air-lifted additional airborne assault guns into Sakhalin. We don't know at this time what the next escalating step on the part of the Chinese and Japanese will be, but the conflict threatens to escalate and could lead to additional confrontations in places other than Sakhalin. The Sovs and the Chinese really don't like one another very well.

"This could impact business around the Pacific rim. So, Brunei has volunteered to lead a police detachment of infantry regiments from three non-involved Pacific rim nations: Brunei, Chile, and the United States. The mission of the Sakhalin Police Detachment, SPD, will be to stabilize the conflict and bring order again to the island. The Washington Greys Regiment has been selected by the National Security Council and the Joint Chiefs of Staff to fulfil the American commitment of a regiment that will join the Sakhalin Police Detachment.

"Why us? Answer: We're available."

"So we've been ordered to deploy immediately to Sakhalin and, without breaking Rule Ten, becoming involved ourselves, or killing anyone, bring a halt to the Whore War."

With a straight face, she turned to Curt and saluted. "Colonel."

It was something like gallows humor, Curt knew. It might not be funny if someone got killed. But Major Ellie Aarts was very perceptive in using a touch of humor right at that moment to relieve enormous tension created by both the anxiety of the pending mission and the fatigue of the all-nighter.

"Major," he replied with an equally straight face as he stood up to be seen. "The next question: How do we get there and what do we do when we arrive? Major Hensley Atkinson of Ops."

If anyone could be considered the de facto "house-mother" of the Washington Greys, it was Hensley Atkinson who'd taken over as S-3 in the reorg after Trinidad and had staunchly carried out the duties of that staff position through the hell of five very rough subsequent missions during which she'd been shot at. In spite of hours of time that Curt had spent with her on the rifle range, Hensley couldn't shoot worth a damn. However, she could point a Novia in the right direction and pull the trigger, so she'd scared the shit out of Bastaards in Namibia, Dayaks on Borneo, and Turks in Kurdistan. A large English-type blonde, she looked something like a young British nanny and sometimes behaved that way. After all, the Greys were her charges, although Pappy Gratton would dispute some of her claim.

"Colonel," she acknowledged and stepped to center stage. Looking around at the assembled Greys, she said, "All of you did an orgasmic job of preparation last night and this morning. Minimum Required Equipment lists have been posted on your company and platoon terminals. Double-check what you did last night and reconcile it with those new MRE lists. We are deploying into a climate that can best be described as wretched and dismal. It will be cold. If we have to stay there very long, S-4 will have to think about cold-weather gear because arctic pack ice will start coming down the eastern side of Sakhalin within a few weeks. However, don't worry too much about that now, but make sure you are equipped for weather that's cold and damp in comparison to Fort Huachuca.

"Three Royal Brunei Airlines hypersonic transports will be at Libby Army Airfield and ready to load at fifteen hundred hours this afternoon with wheels-up scheduled at sixteen hundred local. Yes, the sultan of Brunei can be thanked again for eliminating a fourteen-hour trans-pacific flight! But speed of deployment is necessary. The Congress of Pacific Rim Economies will meet in Hawaii today to discuss and approve a Brunei resolution to establish the SPD. Best data indicates the resolution will be adopted. We therefore want to be landing at Yuzhno-South aerodrome on Sakhalin as quickly as possible after the resolution is adopted. As a result of a lot of work last night, we're going to prevent the old Army screw-up of having bits and pieces of equipment and weapons systems arriving in such a sequence that nothing can be put together and used until everything has arrived. The regiment will be split into three deployment units with the first two hypersonics loaded with the TACBATT and its warbots. SERVBATT will follow in the third hypersonic.

"We should be landing at Yuzhno-South ten minutes behind the Sixth Sultan's Own Gurkha Rifles from Brunei who will be securing the airfield. Upon debarkation, we will form a column of ducks and proceed up the main highway - I use that term loosely; it's more like a local county road here - to Sokol, where we will occupy an apartment complex that has been empty since the Panthers mothballed it." She indicated the huge chart on the wall behind her. "It should be in reasonable shape according to the latest G-2. The

Gurkhas will not leave the airport until the Ninth Airborne Regiment of the Army of Chile lands thirty minutes behind us.

"AIRBATT will deploy by means of a transpacific ferry flight. The Harpies and the Chippies have been configured for air-to-air refueling. They will proceed ASAP from Libby to Travis. They will rendezvous with tankers between Travis and Hickam, then RON on Oahu. Tomorrow, they will air-refuel in mid-Pacific and rendezvous with the U.S.S. Cromwell, SSCV-20, south-east of Sakhalin. The final flight to Sokol airfield will be made day after tomorrow, and we will be on hand to secure the aerodrome for their arrival.

"Once we are on Sakhalin, we will be under the general command of the CIC of SPD, General Ahmad Mahathis of Brunei, code call Sink-Spud. We will provide a further operational briefing once we have arrived and gotten the word from Sink-Spud.

"Basically, this mission is to get the Sovs, Chinese, and Japanese away from each other and keep them apart while the civil side of Sink-Spud builds a series of agreements and protocols to keep the peace on the island. We don't know-how long we'll be there. Could be a few weeks. But we could winter over there. Maybe if the operation drags out, we'll be relieved by a warbot brainy regiment that can handle this sort of a mission much better than we can. We'll have to modify our standard ops procedures to convert from a special combat group to a FIG outfit like a non-warbot infantry regiment, but we did okay in Mosul last year. Sorry I can't be more sanguine about that, troops.

"The ROEs are simple and about the same as they were in Iraq: We don't shoot unless shot at, and we don't destroy non-military facilities. I'll have more and better orders and operational procedures for you as soon as we can dream them up. And I'd be lying through my teeth if 1 tried to tell you that we knew how the hell we're going to pull this one off. It's happened so fast that we really haven't gotten our teeth into it. But...well, we've got three hours over the Pacific when we won't be doing anything else, so...

"Any questions? Let me amend that: Any questions that I might have answers for right now?"

Lieutenant Hassan Ben Mahmud raised his hand and asked in a clear voice, "Yes, Major! What about the hookers? Seems to me that their strike caused this whole sheep screw. So, if we're going to restore order, how do we go about breaking that kind of a strike?"

Laughter rippled around the Bravo Pit. Everyone knew it wasn't an innocent question, not when it came from Hassan, who was perhaps the most notorious ladies man in the regiment. Hassan knew a great deal about that sort of thing. When he was growing up in eastern Iran before he was befriended by the Greys at Zahedan, he boasted that his foster-parent had essentially arranged for an open credit account at the local whorehouses so that Hassan could be properly trained.

Major Ruth Gydesen, the chief medical officer for the regiment, stood up and remarked, "Anyone entertaining thoughts of that sort of recreation should see me first. It will go rough on any Grey who shows up for sick call with a social disease! AIDS is still prevalent elsewhere in the world. Don't get it. If the Army wants you to get it, it will be issued to you!" And she sat down. Ruth was never one to mince words whether engaged in official business or not.

Captain Nelson Crile, the regimental chaplain, spoke up, "Colonel Carson, this is official business, and I think we should have a little decorum here..."

"Nellie, we've got just about as little as I'll tolerate at the moment," Curt replied. Nellie Crile was a very broadminded clergyman; he had to be in order to serve with the Washington Greys. Occasionally, like right then, his sense of propriety came to the surface. When it did, Curt knew things had gone far enough and the moment of comic relief was over. So, he told his operations officer, "Thank you, Major Atkinson. Since we've already slipped into the areas of morale, discipline, and administration, this is a good point to bring in our adjutant. Major Gratton, if you please?"

Pappy Gratton took the stage in painful and fatigued slow motion. He was tired, and he looked it. "We're deploying with the idea that this might not be temporary. We could be on Sakhalin for some time. So, I've arranged for real-time comm for official business. We'll be able to remain tied to Georgie and the Diamond Point complex for heavy computer support to handle our administrative needs. I've also arranged for twelve on-line links that will be reserved for personal communication by the Greys with anyone in the Z-I. In addition to this duplex satellite link, we'll have full television reception capability from the Armed Forces Network. Otherwise, we'll do what we can for off-duty recreational activities once we get there and see what the weather is like. Of course, recreational activities between POSSOHs will be strictly an unofficial matter. Suspension of Rule Ten will be announced when we get there. But until we're bunked in Sokol, Rule Ten is in effect.

"Next, I'll need a lot of help from our two new officers. Lieutenant Brown will be on-call as Japanese translator. Lieutenant Milton speaks Russian, and I'll be calling upon her for special duties. Colonel, you speak Chinese, so I'll be relying upon you for that. I believe that covers it for now, Colonel.'

"Thank you, Major. Finally, logistics. Captain Dearborn?" Curt recognized his supply chief.

The diminutive captain rose to her feet, took the stage; and announced, "We're deploying with full supplies which means a hundred hours of operation in the field with no external logistical support. Which means you'd all better take real good care of the food and water you've got because we won't be getting any more for at least three days. And maybe not then because the Aerospace Force has to set up an airlift to supply us. The Navy will eventually supplement that with sealift from Japan because sealift is cheaper. But it takes longer for the Navy to do things because they've got to move a lot of ships around, and those ships don't go as fast as aircraft. We'll be all right for a couple of days if no one wastes anything. Except don't worry about ammo; use it if you've got to shoot because that's what it's for. And remember: Holler at me for resupply *before* you run out of something! Sometimes I can't arrange immediate door-to-door delivery like a pizza parlor. And, no, I couldn't arrange for one of those. Sorry! Colonel?"

Curt stood up and took the stage again. "Any questions? No?

Obviously, we've caught you by surprise. I expect you'll have a lot of questions later. In the meantime, you all know what you have to do and when it has to be done. Do it! Sergeant Kester, do you have any observations you'd like to make before we shag out of here?"

Regimental Master Sergeant Henry Kester got to his feet and looked around. "Yes, sir. According to the briefing, we're going up against professional soldiers. At least I hope they are. Just keep in mind that professional soldiers are predictable, but the world is full of amateurs."

"Okay, then everyone stand for inspection at Libby at fourteen-thirty before we load the hypersonics," Curt said, thinking that was the end of the Oscar brief.

"Colonel, with all due respects, sir, we ain't got time for an inspection," Kester advised him; then he added, "Besides, it won't tell us nothin' we don't already know about the Washington Greys. This is a combat-ready outfit, sir, and no combat-ready outfit has ever passed inspection. Inspections are to readiness as field rations are to food…"

Curt grinned as laughter echoed throughout the Bravo Pit. "Okay, Greys, Libby airfield at fifteen hundred hours! TACAMO!"

Chapter Twelve

"Mister President, it just squeaked through! The proposal got twenty votes, the minimum two-thirds' majority!" Secretary of State John M. Clayton was on the secure cellular phone from the floor of the special convention of the Congress of Pacific Rim Economies in Oahu. His call came within seconds after the vote tally flashed on the board. The communication was, of course, highly scrambled as it went from the hand-held unit to the local Department of State cell and then by satellite to Washington and the White House where it was unscrambled before it reached the President's ear. "But Brunei owes us a lot of favors! A lot!"

"Give me a quick breakdown, Clay," the President requested. "Who went nay?"

"The ones we anticipated: the Soviets, China, Japan. They managed to hang on to their swing votes: Taiwan, Vietnam, Nicaragua, and Guatemala," the secretary of state reported, checking the tally board as well as his note pad. "Surprised me that the Soviets grabbed Peru. Korea was under the greatest pressure because she's surrounded by the three principle troublemakers. I don't know what the Sovs, Chinese, and Japanese had to give away to clinch their swingers, but I hope it was more than I had to do to keep Mexico and New Zealand on our side! Brunei apparently had trouble with Malaysia, and I think the price of southern Kalimantan suddenly went up for the sultan."

"Okay, so we'll have to be nice to Mexico for a while. What's the apparent attitude of the losers?" the President wanted to know. He was worried about what the Soviets and Chinese would do. The Japanese were too closely tied financially to the United States through the Tri-Partite Steering Council, the successor to the powerful Congress of Foreign Relations that had dominated most of the world's economy in the twentieth century. A former businessman, the President knew all too well the enormous clout of the quiet international power groups such as Tri-Partite that ruled the world by financial means as the kinds and emperors of old had ruled by force of arms.

"The Soviets are visibly angry. That's commonplace for them when they lose in an international forum. They're grumbling about taking necessary action to protect their interests 'in due course of time.'"

"That's a classical Russian response," the President noted. It didn't worry him. Except for the continuing massive Soviet Military threat which hadn't declined in the twenty-first century in spite of *glastnost* and *perestroika* - repeats under new names of similar softenings of the Soviet Union when they'd needed breathing space or time to consolidate or additional aid from the capitalist countries - the Soviet Union was considered by the President and the NSC as a strong but poverty-stricken bully in the international arena; the only thing that held the bully at bay was the potential of military action because the Russians who ruled the Soviet Union had always respected strength and willingness to use it.

"The Japanese were inscrutable and polite as usual," Clayton went on.

"Well, they don't have much to lose. They've got civil control of the resources of Sakhalin, which is important to them. This military action doesn't threaten the flow of oil and coal to them. In fact, this protects it," the Chief Executive reminded his foreign minister. "How about the Chinese?"

"I don't know, Mister President."

"What do you mean, Clay?"

"I have never been able to figure out the Chinese," the secretary of state admitted. "Right now, their delegation is just sitting across the aisle from us. They seem to be impassive and totally unemotional. I'm sure this resolution caught them by surprise in spite of the fact that they had the agenda in advance. But they *must* know what's going on. Frankly, the lack of response or emotion on their part scares the hell out of me, Mister President."

"The enigmatic Yellow Peril," the President remarked offhandedly.

"Good, they won't do anything quickly. They're very patient, Clay. They've got five thousand years of history behind them, and they're in no hurry."

"Their attitude worries me, Mister President. And the Soviets could indeed do something."

"Clay, we could speculate for days on this. Our military contingent is on its way. We'll just have to stay cool and wait to see what happens...and be ready to move decisively when something does," the President advised him. "If it does, we can let the Bruneis take the initial heat. It's their resolution, and they're in charge of SPD."

***

Among the high-tech western nations and especially in the United States, communications were fast. Colonel Curt Carson knew that, but he was still surprised when the petite Royal Brunei Airlines cabin attendant sought him out and told him, "Colonel, you have a telephone call," and handed him a remote telephone.

The huge MD-2001 hypersonic transport was seventy-two minutes out of Libby Army Airfield, slightly less than halfway along its flight to Sakhalin. At that point, it was at an altitude of seventy-four thousand meters moving along at nearly six times the speed of sound and covering almost three kilometers per second. The huge airframe was surrounded by the glow of a shock wave. The aircraft's skin was at a temperature of several thousands of degrees. Between the shock wave and the glowing skin was a plasma sheath layer that disrupted electromagnetic radiation from the Very Low Frequencies up through the Super High Frequencies. Thus, Curt knew the air-to-ground telephone link was on a frequency carrier using an X-ray laser at both ends. The ground stations capable of pinning such a laser on the MD-2001 certainly had no trouble finding it as it cut its ionized pathway through the near-space of the upper atmosphere. Once ground-to-air laser link had been established, the uplink could send suitable commands to the aircraft's downlink laser to aim it at the ground or satellite station. Such technology had been impossible, of course, before space-based strategic defense system research had developed the procedures and equipment.

"Colonel Carson speaking," he said into the mouthpiece as he motioned his chief of staff, Major Joanne Wilkinson, to plug her earpiece into the monitor jack on the phone brick so she could listen as well.

"Carson, this is Battle-axe" came the reply as clear as if General Belinda Hettrick had been calling from the next cabin. "Be advised that your activity has been authorized by the powers that be. But also he aware of the fact that it was barely a majority. Ivan, Chang, and Nip did not like it and are unhappy. But I don't believe they'll have time to object before you arrive. Contact me as planned arrival. Do you copy?"

Hettrick was speaking in broad generalities using code words because the HST-to-ground comm link couldn't he considered as secure in spite of the fact that most of it was riding on the very thin beam of an X-ray laser.

"Battle-axe, Carson copies and will make contact upon arrival," Curt told her.

"Have a nice trip!"

"Thank you. Having a wonderful time, wish you were here," Curt replied and signed off.

Major Joanne Wilkinson unplugged her earpiece as Curt handed the brick back to the cabin attendant. "So we're legal" was her comment.

"Just barely."

"Isn't that like being just a little pregnant?" was her question.

"Maybe. It can still be aborted," he told her and settled back in the comfortable seat, happy to relax for even a moment. He could feel the fatigue soaking his bones. He knew that this would compound the massive dislocation of his circadian rhythm caused by jetting nearly halfway around the world in three hours. There wasn't a whole hell of a lot he could do about it at this point. The time zone shift was only seven hours, about the same as for a subsonic flight to Europe. If the Greys had had time for it, Doctor Ruth Gydesen and her BIOTECO could have commenced circadian re-synchronization techniques. But it took several days of light-dark treatment and food alteration to do the job completely. The jet lag problem could he handled, but it took time to do it. The Washington Greys didn't have time.

"Who would want to abort this?" Joanne wondered. True, this was a quickly laid-on charter flight where the service wasn't as complete as it had been when the Greys had deployed to and from Brunei a couple of years ago to engage in maneuvers with what was now the Royal Brunei Legion - the Royal Malay Regiment, the 6th Sultan's Own Gurkha Rifles, and the Grey Lotus Battalion. But a three-hour hypersonic flight across the Pacific was a hell of a lot easier than a fourteen-hour subsonic flight in an Aerospace Force MAC cargo aerodyne. In the first place, a long flight of more than eight hours beats the hell out of people, and the Greys knew they had to be sharp and on the bounce when they got off that hypersonic because maybe people would be shooting at them and maybe not. They preferred to consider the former in order to CYA.

So although they were enjoying the luxury of hypersonic air travel, some of them were a bit uptight about what might happen after their arrival.

Curt tried not to worry about it. He knew the Gurkhas would be landing first. Those were tough little sonsofbitches who weren't afraid to fight when they had to. And when they fought, God help the adversary. To have the Gurkhas going into Sakhalin first was a real boon, Curt decided. It took a lot of the load off him. He'd know in advance if the Greys would be shot at when they arrived.

So he relaxed.

In his condition, he fell into a doze. Joanne Wilkinson on one side of him and Pappy Gratton on the other noticed it but did nothing about it. They were beat, too. And they dozed off because they'd been up and working at high intensity for more than twenty-four hours.

Then the little Brunei cabin attendant was insistently calling to him. "Colonel Carson? Colonel Carson? Excuse me for awakening you!"

Curt suddenly came fully conscious and alert with a start. "I'm awake," he insisted.

"Would you please follow me to the flight deck?" she asked.

Something's hit the impeller, and it doesn't smell good even from here! Curt decided as he got to his feet and followed the petite stewardess to the flight deck.

The flight deck was a windowless compartment amidships that seemed to be a sophisticated video game arcade. The two pilots - one obviously an American and the other a Brunei judging from their facial features and sizes - were monitoring systems whose performance and conditions were exhibited on display screens. During takeoff, departure, approach, and landing, some of the screens could display high definition video display of the scene in front of the hypersonic transport, but there was no need for this while travelling in the outer reaches of the atmosphere under positive air traffic control from the ground. It was also unnecessary for the pilots to actually have windows. They had much better views through the aircraft's sensor systems, and the ship's computers could enhance or concentrate on any part the outside view the pilots happened to select.

The Brunei pilot was wearing an NE harness and was in soft linkage with the aircraft. The American aircraft commander had apparently unplugged from the aircraft so he could interface with Curt.

"Colonel, we've got trouble on the ground at Yuzhno-South," the aircraft commander told him.

"What kind of trouble?" Curt asked.

"We just got a transmission from the company aircraft carrying the Brunei contingent that landed at Yuzhno a few minutes ago," the pilot explained, referring to the Royal Brunei Airlines hypersonic carrying the Gurkhas that was scheduled to land fifteen minutes ahead of the first hypersonic inbound from America. "Apparently, Yuzhno-South is under military control. We were requested to stand by to divert to Chitose. But, since this is a military airlift mission, I wanted to get your concurrence first."

"Any shooting at Yuzhno-South?" Curt asked anxiously.

"I don't know. The transmission merely said that the first aircraft was met by a military contingent and suggested that we divert."

That was hardly the sort of message that would he sent from one military commander to another. It didn't contain enough information, and it wasn't a direct order. So Curt figured he'd have to make a decision. He asked the pilot, "How far out are we?"

The pilot checked the ground track display showing the navigational situation out to a thousand klicks around the aircraft. It showed that Sakhalin was coming up fast. Very fast. More than two kilometers per second. The map on the display was changing even as Curt looked at it. "Nine minutes. We're in the profile descent and approach phase now."

"Can you divert?"

The pilot nodded. "Chitose is no problem. It's our filed alternate anyway. Required by ICAO. We've got more than five-hundred nautical miles reserve range even after two missed approaches,' the pilot reminded Curt. In spite of a nearly universal conversion to the metric system, international aerospace navigation still used nautical miles instead of kilometers. "I'm an old Aerospace Force trash hauler, Colonel. Even though I'm officially pilot-in-command, I consider this a military mission, and you're the mission commander. We can divert even after a missed approach. So what do you want me to do, Colonel?"

The system mechanics of the whole operation raced through Curt's mind.

This was a quick response deployment to be carried out before the Soviets, Chinese, or Japanese could react to it and offer trouble when they arrived on Sakhalin.

Apparently, something had screwed up. Curt didn't know what.

The report was too soft. It sounded like something that might come from General Ahmad bin Muhamid, who certainly knew how to give an order since he was a graduate of the United Aerospace Force Academy. But Mahathis tended to overlook or forget the military procedures when it came to reporting and/or giving orders to subordinates. The man was an imperious commanding officer and always had been. He was answerable only to his father, the sultan of Brunei. In the few years since the Washington Greys had taught Mahathis something about unit command and leadership, a great deal had obviously been forgotten by the Brunei military chief because he didn't need to use it every day.

Curt knew that behind them in trail of fifteen minutes' separation were four hypersonic transports cooking along at Mach six for Sakhalin. A very complex logistical operation has also been set up. His own AIRBATT could hold on the U.S.S. *Cromwell* SSCV-20 about two thousand klicks off Sakhalin, but no contingency plan had been put together for temporary positioning of the Grey and the Chileans in Japan.

Considering that the Japanese had voted against the SPD resolution at the COPRE meeting on Oahu a few hours ago, Curt felt that the Greys and the Chileans probably wouldn't even be allowed to leave the hypersonics if they landed at Chitose. So where would they go? Back to Hawaii? Or down to Brunei?

Such a major change in the plan at this point would also royally fuck up the complex logistical plan that was being set up to provide supplies to the SPD on Sakhalin. Curt didn't know what the details of his logistical plan were because he had enough to worry about with the tactical plan. But he knew if had to involve thousands of people, tons of supplies, and a lot of ships and aircraft. And because of its complexity, it was already in motion. People were doing things and vehicles were moving even as he stood there on the flight deck of the RBA hypersonic, trying to make a decision.

Actually, insofar as he was concerned, it was no decision at all.

The response to dump the plan was a typical reaction of a raw leader, which was what Mahathis really was. The Brunei general had never commanded any unit larger than a regiment in combat, and his attempts to command a multi-regimental operation in Borneo had nearly met with disaster several years ago. Only the professionalism of the Greys and the Gurkhas had saved Mahathis' ass there.

The sort of decisions that were made by a regimental commander couldn't be made at all by the commander in chief of a division-sized international military operation carried out at the end of a long logistical rope.

He recalled one of the principles Henry Kester had taught him:

"No tactical plan survives the first contact."

This didn't mean that the plan had to be abandoned, only that a commander had to be flexible enough to go with the flow and salvage as much of the tactical plan as possible once it started to go to slime.

This one was far too complex to dump because of an unanticipated initial contact.

Four more hypersonics pouring troops and equipment into Yuzhno-South might drastically change the picture, whatever it happened to be at that moment. And any of the three military commanders on Sakhalin might certainly think more than twice about damaging or destroying an 800-million-dollar hypersonic transport aircraft, much less six of them. The Japanese would hesitate because of the liability issues. The Sovs and the Chinese would hesitate because of the potential hassles in the World Court about damaging or destroying a hypersonic aircraft on the ground, there being no announced state of armed conflict existing at the time. Therefore, the hypersonics would probably be able to land without trouble.

What happened when the Greys and the Chileans debarked was another matter.

Would the Soviets, Chinese or Japanese be willing to risk even a limited war as a result of trying to stop the landings of the SPD?

Curt decided they probably wouldn't.

But if the Greys were on Sakhalin alongside the Gurkhas, he might be able to head off any general war that might result. Even if the Chileans might help once he got to know their regimental commander and could assess the Chilean potential.

It was a great risk, and it fell totally on Curt's shoulders to make the decision at this point, Sahkalin was coming up at two klicks per second. He didn't have time to ponder things. Thus far, his analysis of the situation had taken only a few seconds and was based on what he knew and upon his own experience.

"Captain," he told the pilot, addressing him by the proper honorific title for an aircraft commander, "continue the approach and landing. We will proceed as planned. Please pass the word to the aircraft following us. We're going into Sakhalin, shooting if we have to. We'll try to keep your aircraft from being damaged in the process."

He left the flight deck in a hurry. He had seven minutes to bring the Greys into combat status for debarking.

Again, they were probably going into a situation shooting.

Chapter Thirteen

"Where's the cabin announcement mike?" Curt said as he reentered the main cabin of the hypersonic transport.

"Sir, you must return to your seat!" the petite cabin attendant insisted. "We have started our approach into Yuzhno-South!"

"Young lady," Curt told her in a harried but polite way, "in about five minutes, we will indeed be on the ground at Yuzhno-South. Someone may also be shooting at us…"

"Shooting? This isn't a military aircraft!"

"Maybe not to you, but it's carrying military personnel," Curt reminded her. "The microphone, please! I've got to give some orders that may save our necks!"

With a combination of reluctance because she was uncomfortable that Curt wasn't in his seat during the approach according to the rules but also with some frightened hesitation because being shot at wasn't in her plans, the cabin attendant handed the microphone to Curt.

"Attention all Greys! This is Colonel Carson!" his voice crackled out of the multiple loudspeakers in the broad cabin. "I've just been informed that a military situation of unknown intensity exists at the Yuzhno-South airport. We were given the option of diverting to Japan, but since we don't know what the situation is and since it would disrupt the very thing we were called to Sakhalin to do, we're continuing our approach. On landing, be prepared to debark under emergency conditions! Be damned careful because you're not wearing body armor! We don't expect to have to go in fighting! So load and lock! Power-up any warbots you can get to. On my command, we'll go out the escape chutes, down the escape routes through the main wheel wells, and lower the bots on the cargo lifts. I have no idea of the situation on the ground. We'll have to play it by ear when we get there. I've passed the word through the pilot to notify the two following hypersonics, so we'll have help in fifteen and thirty minutes respectively. The Gurkhas are already on the ground at Yuzhno, but I don't know the situation there. We're going to find out! So stand by to land and to get the hell out of here fast, shooting if you're shot at!"

The descent was getting steep, and it was a little bouncy. Curt managed to return to his seat and to get his combat gear together as they were jolted around going through the jet stream. As he donned his battle helmet, he growled to Joanne Wilkinson, "Dammit! Now I wish I'd insisted on everyone wearing body armor, even for the trip!"

"Yeah," Joanne replied, "I could suffer with it for three hours or so if we'd known we were getting into this sort of a sheep screw!"

"Best thing to do is to play it cool," Pappy Gratton added. "I sure as hell wouldn't provoke any incoming if I were you, Colonel."

"We're not, but we're going out of this beast under the assumption that we're going to get shot at!" Curt said, checking his Novia.

"Well, if we can hold on for fifteen minutes, we've got more help on the way," Hensley Atkinson reminded him. "Ship Number Two will be on the ground with the rest of TACBATT then, followed fifteen minutes after that by the ship carrying SERVBATT."

"Well, we've got some help on the ground there already. The Gurkhas have landed," Curt reminded her. "You remember the Gurkhas, don't you, Hensley? Bunch of wiry little bastards who fought like demons in the jungle and looked sharp as hell on the parade ground, too."

"Yes, and I wouldn't want us to fight them at any time, Colonel."

"Colonel, when you passed the word back to the other aircraft, did you order body armor?" Henry Kester wanted to know.

"No," Curt admitted, realizing he probably should have done so. But he added, "There wasn't a whole hell of a lot of time. I've just got to assume that Frazier and Hampton know enough to do it themselves. They should. They've been in enough fights so that I shouldn't have to tell them the obvious. And they've got enough time to do it..."

He toggled the tacomm in his helmet. "Warrior Leader, this is Grey Head. Comm check."

"Loud and clear, Grey Head!"

"Joan, I want you to coordinate getting the warbots out of the belly of this beast with Kester and Sampson! We can't count on ground cargo handling equipment, so you'll have to use the on-board cargo lifts. Personnel from staff, BIRD, and GUNCO will assist you. I'll go down the chutes with the rest of TACBATT and cover you while you're getting the bots out."

Although Joan Ward was in command of TACBATT, she stood aside at this time and allowed Curt to assume command of the truncated unit made up of his staff, TACBATT staff, RECONCO, and Morgan's Marauders. There were also some GUNCO vehicles aboard along with a couple of ACVs. But the majority of their vehicular equipment was riding in the third hypersonic transport. Joan did what was necessary to meet an unexpected situation because she knew the TO&E had just gone out the window. "Roger from Warrior Leader, Grey Head!" was her quiet reply. Joan was a pro. She knew what Curt was doing, and she knew what she had to do.

He switched channels. "Greys all, this is Grey Head! Toggle to NE mode. It's faster, and we may not have a lot of time for chatter!" Then he switched. NE communication was faster because he only had to think his message and his helmet's contact electrodes resting against his scalp and neck picked up the neural signals from his brain and transmitted them so they'd be picked up by other NE tacomm receivers and presented to the Greys as words in their heads. It took a lot of computer power to do this, but the picocomputer in Curt's battle helmet had enormous capabilities and processing speed.

Avenger Leader, Mustang Leader, Marauder Leader, Curt addressed the three unit commanders who'd be working with him when they hit dirt, then realized that he'd be leading three women commanders and their outfits into an unknown fight, *organize your units so that when this plane stops they're ready to move at once to the nearest cabin exit! Deploy the emergency exit chutes and go down them! I don't know what the situation is on the ground, and I don't even know too much about how the airport is laid out or even where we'll stop. This is strictly a come-as-you-are operation. I can't do any planning. So keep this channel open, and we'll play it as we see it. Objective is to protect the aircraft and the unloading of the warbots! Don't shoot unless shot at! That's the best I can do right now! Got it?*

Roger from Avenger Leader! said Ellie Aarts, who Curt knew really didn't want to get into a shooting situation again.

Roger from Mustang Leader! was the quiet, calm reply from Dyani Motega.

Roger from Marauder Leader! Alexis's voice was excited. She was always that way going into a fracas.

The pilot was an old military type, Curt knew, because he switched the air-ground communications to the cabin speakers. Curt silently thanked him for this. It gave Curt and the Greys some idea of what was going on out there.

"Yuzhno Tower, this is Royal Brunei Charter Two over the outer marker inbound on the localizer and glide slope for ILS Runway Zero One."

"Brunei Charter Two, Yuzhno Tower. Cleared for ILS Runway Zero One approach. Ceiling three hundred overcast. Visibility one-five. Wind three-six-zero at two. Altimeter one-zero-zero-five. Report field in sight."

Curt looked up and saw that the aircraft commander had also switched the cabin video screens to show the final approach into Yuzhno-South. They were apparently descending through the overcast because the screens showed only white. Then the aircraft broke through the bottom as ragged clumps of scud dashed past. The long runway, a black strip against the dark green of the surrounding lowland area, appeared ahead, set in a long north-south valley between two mountain chains.

"Yuzhno Tower, Brunei Charter Two. Runway in sight."

"Brunei Charter Two, Yuzhno Tower. Cleared to land Runway Zero One."

Curt tried to get a picture of the aerodrome as they approached, and more details became apparent. It was merely a single long north-south runway paralleled on the east side by a taxi strip. A parking ramp and some buildings - maybe hangars, maybe a terminal - were located on the northeast side of the strip alongside a broad parking apron. A road and a railway ran along the east side of the field. Beyond, Curt could see the city of Yuzhno-Sakhalinsk, a collection of low buildings that were the homes of about eighty-five thousand people. Tall stacks were belching dense black smoke into the foggy air, and Curt knew from his briefing memory cube that these had to be the coal-burning power plants that supplied electricity to this end of the island. The Soviets apparently hadn't bothered themselves with environmental impact studies when they'd built these plants, and the Japanese hadn't bothered, either, to clean them up when they took over. Other stacks poured whitish-grey smoke into the air, and Curt knew these had to be the fish canneries, paper mills, meat packing plants, and smelters that provided the industrial base for the southern end of Sakhalin.

But he could see no evidence of military activity on the airfield. And the control tower had said nothing that would lead him to expect it.

As the hypersonic transport drew closer on its straight-in approach to the north, Curt saw the black shape of the first MD-2001 aircraft that had landed from Brunei with the Gurkhas, General Mahathis, and the Sultana Alzena aboard.

Dammit, why did Ahmad have to drag his sister into such a dangerous situation? Curt asked himself without allowing his thoughts to get into the tacomm NE channel. He was angry at his "step-brother" for endangering someone Curt was extremely fond of.

Then he saw that there were two hypersonic transports on the apron before the terminal building.

Curt wondered who else was there. Who belonged to that other hypersonic?

There wasn't much time to think about it. The hypersonic came over the fence nose-high at about 180 knots, and its massive landing gear touched the rough pavement. By the video monitor, Curt could see that the Yuzhno-South runway was built in the typical fashion of Soviet airfields - massive interlocking slabs of thick concrete separated by fat gaps filled with asphalt for hot-cold expansion and to prevent frost heave.

"Brunei Charter Two, Yuzhno Tower. Turn right when able. Taxi to the ramp. Monitor this frequency."

The pilot knew what he was doing. He turned off the runway onto the taxiway, thus clearing the runway for the approach of the hypersonic following him. If he'd stopped on the runway to discharge the Greys, the runway would have been blocked and the other hypersonics would have been unable to land.

And he left the nose camera on, added to the two side-looking cameras used by the flight crew to check the airframe integrity at low- and sub-mach speeds. Thus, Curt had a good view of the surrounding airfield.

"Tower, Charter Two. Place looks busy. Where do you want me to berth this beast?"

"Brunei Charter Two, Yuzhno Tower. Uh...say again?" It was obvious that English wasn't the tower operator's native language.

"Where do you want me to park, Tower?"

"Uh...follow commands of ramp crew, Brunei Charter Two."

God, I hope he's savvy enough about military ops to park this thing where we have some chance of defending it! Curt allowed his thought to get into the tacomm channel.

A Toyota truck with a big "Follow Me" sign roared out of the ramp area toward the taxiway.

Looks like he'll park it where he's told was the comment from Henry Kester.

As the MD-2001 swung its nose in toward the ramp off the taxiway, Curt got his first glimpse of military activities.

He could see Gurkhas on the tarmac. Their distinctive green hats marked them. They were deployed behind vehicles and the massive landing gear of their hypersonic.

Around the parking ramp, Curt could see a wall of soldiers, all armed. Several vehicles appearing to be Soviet ASU-88 Airborne Assault Guns backed them up.

On another side of the ramp were more soldiers, but they were dressed differently.

But no one seemed to be shooting at anyone else.

A lot of other people were also on the ramp, apparently oblivious to any danger.

Some of them had videocams on their shoulders.

Avenger Leader here, Soviet Guards unit in the center with the assault guns on either side of the terminal and some sharpshooters on the terminal roof lined up along the south end of the ramp was the comment from Major Ellie Aarts, the regiment's intelligence officer. *Japanese Self-Defense Forces on the left. I think the ones on the right are Chinese, but I can't see their uniforms that well yet.*

Reception committee? was Alexis Morgan's question.

If so, why the original report from Mahathis? Jerry Allen wanted to know.

I didn't talk to General Mahathis. The report I got was second hand through our pilot, Curt admitted. *But I'm taking no chances! If they're shooting or have been shooting, I want us to be ready and not caught with our bots down! And let's adhere to tacomm protocol here! Greys all, prepare to debark! Stand up and file to the doors! Stand by to dump out of here as quickly as this plane is parked!*

Curt took a chance and stood up. If the pilot had had to make a quick turn, Curt might have been thrown off his feet. But he hung on and worked his way quickly to the forward port-side passenger door where the little Brunei cabin attendant was standing by. She looked scared.

"When the pilot stops, ma'am," he told her with as much confidence as he could muster in his voice, "we'll open the door and deploy the slide. I don't want you to be exposed to any possible danger, so tell me how to open the hatch and deploy the slide."

She was made of sterner stuff than Curt had thought because she told him with shaky confidence, "Sir, it is my job to open the door and deploy the slide in an emergency. And I will do it, sir." Then she warned him, "Please be careful going out. The airframe is still hot enough to burn you."

"Thank you. I'll remember that."

"We're parked!" came the voice of the pilot over the comm system. He was also somewhat of a joker because, safe deep in the bowels of the hypersonic where he was unlikely to be hit by anything lethal, he added, "I won't give you the canned lecture about flying Royal Brunei Airlines on your next flight, but please try to have a nice stay in Yuzhno-Sakhalinsk! And I hope you try to keep the plane from being shot up; the sultan may have a lot of them at eight-hundred mill each, but this is the only one I've got to get home in…"

The thick door swung inward to disengage its seals, rotated vertically, then swung outward. A blast of hot air touched Curt, followed by cold dampness.

Whumpf! The cabin floor along the doorsill exploded at his feet. In a matter of seconds, a bright orange inflatable tube extended from the fuselage and door edges, thrust outward, then flopped downward to the ground many meters below. It created a softly inflated slide to the ground where it deployed a huge catch mattress for people to slide into.

It was a matter of jump onto it and slide.

It looked steep as hell.

Curt had jumped with a parachute before; Colonels Hettrick and Bellamack had insisted that the Greys know how to jump out of perfectly good airplanes if they had to make a tactical jump or get out of damaged airplanes that had gotten holes put in them by the bad guys. But here Curt had to leap into a steep slide with full combat gear and no parachute. It had a high pucker factor. But he knew the rest of the Greys were right behind him and waiting for him.

So, he cradled his Novia in his arms in front of him and jumped into the slide.

Then he was on the ground in the catch mattress.

He moved fast to get the hell out of there so he didn't get run over by the next jumper. Henry Kester was right behind him, followed by Sergeant-Edie Sampson. And then Joan Ward and Morgan's Marauders.

The Toyota "Follow Me" pickup truck was parked a few meters away, its driver out of the cab now and engrossed in the task of completing the final parking of the huge black craft. Other ramp personnel were tossing wheel chocks in front and behind the nose gear and main gear.

Curt headed for the truck. The engine was still running. But he didn't climb into the cab. That would have made him a prime Number One target. He reached through the open window, grabbed the keys, turned it off, then ducked quickly behind it, putting it between him and the terminal building. Both his flanks were still unprotected because he could see the Japs to the right and the Chinese to the left.

And television cameras all around him.

What the hell is going on here? he wanted to know.

No one was shooting. But he got a glimpse of some Gurkhas taking cover behind the landing gear of their hypersonic transport and behind whatever ramp vehicles they could find.

The whole operation had been set up on such a fast and slap-dash basis that he didn't even have a prearranged tacomm frequency to contact Mahathis. With the frequency-hopping tacomm equipment the U.S. had supplied to Brunei under the terms of the mutual aid treaty, Curt should have been able to contact Mahathis right away. But it was impossible for him to attempt switching through the channels because no freak-hop sequence had been prearranged. Although Curt hadn't thought about that, Mahathis should have done that bit of staff work since the Bruneis were CINCSPD. But they'd operated so long in their jungles without modern communications that Curt knew it had just been overlooked because it wasn't really necessary to them.

Curt hated to work with those he considered to be rank amateurs.

But he saw General Mahathis by the landing gear doors of the other Royal Brunei Airlines hypersonic. No, he didn't see him first. His attention was drawn to him because he was with his twin sister, and the Sultana Alzena had an aura about her that made her stand out in a crowd. He saw her first, then noticed she was with her brother. White was Alzena's color; she wore it in many forms, but today she was attired in bright white fur against the incredible damp cold wind that blew out of the north across the tarmac. And she was arguing with her brother.

Suddenly, as if she knew exactly what she was doing, she broke away from General Mahathis, left the protection of the massive main landing gear of the hypersonic transport, and boldly walked across the open ramp to where Curt crouched behind the truck.

Curt looked quickly around and swung his Novia up in an attempt to cover her because she was a perfect and unmistakable target if anyone wanted to shoot her at that moment.

Chapter Fourteen

When he saw the unarmed Sultana Alzena in her shining white fur parka separate herself from her twin brother, General Ahmad Mahathis, and leave the protective cover of the main landing gear of the MD-2001 hypersonic transport, Curt stood up behind the Toyota pickup truck that was providing him with some protection and yelled across the fifty meters, "Sultana! Go back! You'll be-"

He felt a hand on his shoulder and heard Sergeant Major Edwina Sampson's cool voice in his ear. "Cool it, Colonel! She's got plenty of protection!"

He suddenly saw that she indeed did. "Damned if she doesn't...and it's probably the world's best!"

Four members of the 6th Sultan's Own Gurkha Rifles, identifiable because of their distinctive green cylindrical caps, suddenly formed around the small woman in white fur who was walking unafraid across the open tarmac toward where Curt stood. They not only held their Novia rifles at the ready in one hand, but in the other hand each of them carried the legendary short Gurkha knife, the razor-sharp kukri. They weren't wearing cammy grease or even combat cammies. Even at a distance of many meters, no one could mistake the fearsome looks on their faces. Nor their intent, because they swept their steely eyes around, ever watchful and looking outward from the sultana, whom they were accompanying and protecting as their duty.

"Now that takes guts!" was the respectful comment from Major Alexis Morgan, who was a bit jealous of Alzena. But Alexis couldn't really bitch too much about Curt's relationship with the Muslim princess. After all, Alexis had an equally close relationship with Alzena's twin brother, who, at the moment, was behaving like General Ducrot in Curt's book. "She sure doesn't need to put herself in danger! She could be sitting at home in comfort in Brunei!"

"Well, none of us was forced to be here, either," Joan Ward remarked. "But I have to hand it to the Gurkhas. They're either nuts or stupid to put themselves in the open that way!"

"No, Major, they're doing what they're paid to do: Protect their boss," Edie Sampson reminded her.

"Well, if they're going to behave like crazies, let's join them," Curt muttered. "Nothing else around here makes much sense, either!" He stood up, stepped away from the pickup truck, and moved out across the open tarmac to meet them.

The four Gurkhas around Alzena were suddenly joined by General Mahathis and a very British officer with a gingery moustache, who Curt knew was Colonel Landers Duncan Abercromby Payne Ashwell, a graduate of Sandhurst who was following the old tradition that a Gurkha regiment was always commanded by a British-trained officer. Mahathis packed a 9-millimeter Steyer-Sauer P2000 pistol, one of the most expensive handcrafted hand guns in the world whose appearance was impressive but whose performance, as Curt knew, left a lot to be desired when it came to man-stopping; it was obviously for show, not for blow. Payne-Ashwell, on the other hand, carried no weapon but had his usual combat piece with him: a silver tipped and headed cane; a Gurkha regimental commander didn't have to carry an obvious weapon because his Gurkhas were his personal weapons.

Curt found at his side not only Edie Sampson and Henry Kester, but also Joan Ward and Alexis Morgan…plus several Greys who also had their loaded and locked Novia assault rifles carried easily in their arms.

"What the hell are you doing here?" he asked his Greys verbally. "Who the hell is covering us?"

"The rest of the Greys who are getting the bots off the ship, Colonel" was the comment from Henry Kester.

"You don't think I'm going to let those Gurkhas show up on worldwide video coverage as having more guts than the Greys, do you?" was the quick comment from Alexis.

"I respect those little guys after what we went through together in Brunei," Sampson added. "If the shooting starts. I'm damned well prepared to let the world know the Washington Greys can dish it out, too!"

In spite of the quiet bravado of their statements, Curt knew they were just as scared as he was.

"Yeah, and they're not wearing body armor, either." He discovered that Joanne Wilkinson was right behind him. As a matter of principle or honor - Curt didn't know which - the Gurkhas never wore body armor even when the U.S. Army had made it available to them; they disdained that piece of American military technology.

So it wasn't just sense of duty that made all of them, American and Brunei alike, be where they were, out on a windswept tarmac of an airport on cold, clammy Sakhalin Island surrounded by Japanese, Soviet, and Chinese troops. It was the Gurkhas' sense of pride in themselves and who they were, a statement that quietly said, *This is our job, our duty, our profession as the Sixth Sultan's Own Gurkha Rifles.* To which the Greys silently replied, *Dammit, if you Gurkhas can, we can, too, because we're the Washington Greys!*

"Where the hell did all the newshawks and news-harpies come from?" Curt wondered, suddenly aware of the multitude of video-cameras pointing at them.

"Who cares, Colonel?" Kester asked rhetorically. "Don't make any difference whether they're American or Japanese. They give us an open window. The rest of the friggin' world is lookin' through it right now. Best thing that could happen..."

Kester's observation was right, and it suddenly made Curt feel a little easier about this situation. He knew the awesome power of the world news media. In the last several operations, the Greys had fought without a videocam peering over their shoulders. Not since Sonora and Namibia had they operated with on-going, real-time media coverage. It was something in their favor.

"Yeah, the media is on our side for a change," Sampson added. "The Sovs and the Chinks probably knew better than to pop off at us here on the ramp in full view of the video screens of the world."

"Especially right on the heels of the COPRE resolution adopted about an hour ago which authorized Brunei, the U.S. and Chile to introduce troops into Sakhalin to maintain law and order," Alexis put in.

Curt knew that the quiet chatter during the short walk in the open was merely a tension relief for those who had their pink bods bared to incoming. But in spite of the video coverage, Curt didn't let down his guard. "Don't get cocky, troops," he warned them. "Soviet and Chinese commanders and troops can be very brutal on camera. Don't forget Praha, Beiching, Kaunas, Guangzhou, and Berlin."

"But the stakes aren't the same here as they were in those infamous places," Joan Ward said.

"How the hell did the news types get here before the military forces? This was supposed to be a fast, surgical force insertion!" Joanne Wilkinson wondered.

"Dunno, Joanne. Something to worry about when this is over," Curt told her. The Greys had moved fast, but these news types had moved faster. What did they have and how did they use it, and could he learn anything from them that might make the next panic deployment go faster?

When he came face to face with the Brunei contingent, Curt respectfully snapped a salute to the Sultana Alzena. It was polite to recognize the woman first, and it was protocol, but it wasn't necessary. The two knew each other very well in private; but this was in public.

The Sultana Alzena Mahathis bin Muhamid, daughter of Sultan Ahmad Iskander bin Muhamid Shah Rajang Brunei, the richest man in the world, removed the glove on her right hand and extended it to him. Curt was not a continental hand kisser, but he'd learned to from Alzena. When a man kissed a woman's hand, and when both of them knew and cared for one another, it was the polite and formal equivalent of a bear hug and a warm kiss. It excited Curt. And he could sense Alzena's reaction.

"Good afternoon, Sultana. So nice to see you again," Curt told her levelly.

She smiled at him. To Curt, that smile made the terror of the walk across the windswept tarmac worthwhile. But Alzena, too, was deliberately formal and restrained. "We're glad you're here, Colonel Carson. It will make our job much easier."

Curt then saluted General Ahmad Mahathis. Again, it was between friends and family, but military protocol before the news media demanded it. "General!"

"Colonel! I'm also glad you're here." Mahathis said with genuine friendship in his voice. The man could be imperious, a shortcoming that often alienated him to others and made relationships difficult. But with Curt and the Washington Greys, Mahathis was working with people who not only knew him well but were people he could trust. Furthermore, he knew from previous military operations as well as social visits to Fort Huachuca that neither Curt nor any of the Greys, even the NCOs, would tolerate any demand for respect from him. With the Greys, he'd had to earn respect. And he was proud that he had. But this didn't keep Curt from considering him as a boorish prince when Mahathis forgot and became the son of an absolute monarch again.

Besides, Curt and Major Alexis Morgan, who stood beside him, were officially part of the sultan's family; both had been awarded the prestigious and priceless Sultan's Star of Brunei for their bravery, valor, and contributions to the welfare of the small but wealthy and growing Abode of Peace. They were the only foreigners to have been so honored during the current sultan's reign.

Other greetings were quickly exchanged. These people knew one another from previous operations and activities. The greeting between Mahathis and Alexis Morgan was as formal and disciplined as that between Curt and Alzena. This wasn't the time or the place for a PDA - a public display of affection.

"General, what the hell is going on here?" Curt said bluntly, getting directly to the point. "We received a message nine minutes out that said you were in military difficulty here."

Mahathis swept his hand around the airfield, indicating the military forces of three nations who stood impassively, waiting. "We are," he replied. "We're totally surrounded and outnumbered."

"Well, that hasn't stopped us before, General," Curt replied.

"I wanted to make sure you knew about it before you landed. I know you don't like surprises," Mahathis went on. "And I wanted you to have the option of diverting to Chitose if you believed you needed to marshal a concentrated landing assault..."

"Hell, General, I wasn't about to turn tail and leave you here all by yourself," Curt told him. "As I said, what the hell is going on? Who are these troops, and how have they threatened you? Has there been any shooting?"

"Not yet, but I sure as hell don't like to be surprised and outnumbered at the same time!" Mahathis asserted. "I was hoping you wouldn't divert to Chitose. My Gurkhas are good fighters, but I wasn't sure we could get out of this without additional help."

Curt looked around. Although the troops surrounding the tarmac were all armed, no one seemed to have a weapon trained on them. "Have you tried talking with them? Have you contacted their commanding officer? Or officers, since it seems there's more than one nationality confronting us here?"

"No, he hasn't!" Alzena broke in. She was angry. Unlike her brother, when the sultana got angry, she wasn't just petulant. She meant it and she nearly always did something about it. "He's assumed that we've been greeted by a hostile force! I've been trying to convince him to allow me to go forward and open diplomatic contact, since that's my job in the SPD!"

"Not when we're greeted by overwhelming armed force!" Mahathis objected.

"So we've got a stalemate here," Curt pointed out, "and four more aircraft due in momentarily with more troops and warbots aboard! General, what are your intentions, sir? Do you plan to allow all the aircraft to land and then confront these people with overwhelming force?" Curt knew that the combined numbers of Greys, Gurkhas, and Chileans might perhaps equal those of the troops deployed around the airport, but Curt wasn't counting on the Chileans since they were an unknown factor.

He was a bit disgusted by Mahathis. Delaying any attempt to come forward and greet the military welcoming committee - and it was becoming apparent to Curt that the three arrayed forces might be just that – would merely serve to escalate the situation.

"Roger! I intend to wait! I prefer to deal from strength!"

That, Curt knew, was a combination of his education at Blue U, plus the parochial military attitude of one who has only fought on his own home grounds against guerrilla and insurgent forces.

"Ahmad, you can't! It will look like we're indeed trying to invade this island!" Alzena tried to warn him. "And that's just what the news media all around us here will report!"

"I wasn't expecting the news media," Mahathis admitted. "I don't know how they got here!"

"Well, General, neither do I," Curt admitted, "but I'd like to suggest that we've got to make the best of the situation as it stands. If we aren't dealing from strength, I suggest we act like we are because we will be within an hour! Opening communications now will confuse the living hell out of them! Especially the Soviets, who expect us to deal from strength! And they may already know of the other planes coming in!"

Mahathis had one saving grace at the moment. He knew very well that Colonel Curt Carson was a far better leader and tactician than he was. Military activities in Borneo several years ago had proved that. He struggled for a way to concede that to Curt while at the same time saving face as CINCSPD.

It was Colonel Payne-Ashwell who broke the impasse. "I say, General, it would seem to me that we should at least make an attempt to resolve this without fighting because we are at a disadvantage, don't you know?" he pointed out, swinging his silver-tipped cane around. "Even when the Americans get all their warbots unloaded - and that seems to be progressing extremely well behind us at the moment – we're still highly vulnerable to automatic weapon fire here on this ramp. We really don't have any place to hide, you know, and I am rather out of practice in digging foxholes in solid concrete..."

"Yes, Colonel, but I'm counting on the Gurkhas to put up a fine fight. It seems to me that they're itching to do so as we speak," Mahathis replied quickly. "An initial assault by the Gurkhas followed up by the Washington Greys and their warbots would certainly have a chance of succeeding!"

"Against deployed infantry battalions with automatic weaponry well within range?" Payne-Ashwell asked rhetorically. He knew what the chances were, and he was trying diplomatically to convince his own commanding general of this fact. It was plain to Curt that Mahathis wasn't used to the command of a large international division-sized force just as Curt wasn't yet used to commanding a regiment. The CO of the Gurkhas went on, "And we'll be the first to be targeted and cut down...General, it seems rather a shame to waste the Gurkhas under these conditions. They'll be extremely useful in the Police Detachment because of their international reputation. Which the Chinese know all too well from the confrontations in Hong Kong several years ago. When all is said and done, if we can win by reputation, who wants to kill people?"

The Sultana Alzena confronted her twin brother, looking up at him because she was much smaller than he. "General," she told him formally, "you can punish me later...if you can figure out a way to do it! Colonel Carson, will you and your Greys accompany me and my Gurkhas over to the terminal building? Perhaps we can find who's in charge here!"

"Yes, ma'am!" Curt told her. He hadn't yet been given a direct order by Mahathis not to do so. And time was passing quickly. He didn't know how itchy the trigger fingers were becoming, but he knew something had to be done fast before someone on either side panicked.

So he didn't wait for an order from Mahathis. The man was stuck on the horns of a dilemma, and they might be standing on the tarmac arguing about it when the next hypersonic landed in a few minutes...and that event might push someone over the edge and open fire. Especially when the Soviets or Chinese or Japanese saw that even more troops were coming in. Maybe they already knew, but maybe they didn't. Curt was willing to chance the latter. Otherwise, the military welcoming units could have cut down the Gurkhas nearly a half-hour ago when they'd landed; then they could have opened fire on the Greys with relative impunity when they'd come down the escape chute.

Curt guessed that something had happened that caused the Soviets, Chinese, and Japanese to rush to the airport for their arrival. But otherwise, the occupying unit commanders didn't have the slightest idea what was going on. They were probably waiting and trying to keep trigger fingers from itching, too.

In this sort of a taut situation, someone had to keep his head and do something positive. Curt knew from experience that Mahathis probably couldn't. His sister was trying to but needed backup. So, Curt did what had to be done.

Toggling his tacomm he called both verbally and by NE so that his troops as well as Mahathis would hear him, "Greys all, this is Grey Head! Continue debarkation! Get the Jeeps and Mary Anns out and covering for us. The present personnel around me will accompany us. We're heading for the terminal building to find the big man around here. Cover us! And the first Grey who shoots without taking incoming will catch holy hell from me...if we survive the consequences! Move it!"

He slung his Novia and turned to his Greys and the Gurkhas. "Let's cut the Gordian knot by making the first move here! Greys, I want you to come along, but sling your weapons; we're being covered already. Colonel Payne-Ashwell, will you and your Gurkhas here please join us? Sergeant Major Tuanku, your job is to do what you're already doing: Guard the diplomatic side of this committee. Let's go, Sultana!" He knew she didn't like to be addressed, even formally, as royalty other than with the title he'd just used.

The contingent started off across the ramp, leaving Mahathis momentarily behind.

As Major Alexis Morgan passed him, she muttered quickly under her breath to him, "Well, General, how are you going to punish Alzena? Send her home? What are you going to tell the sultan? Better yet, what's Alzena's report going to say? Remember: She can back it up with the videotape news coverage!"

Realizing that his stubborn twin sister was going to do as she pleased anyway with the help of these Americans, and since he really didn't have enough clout at that moment to stop her, he quickly joined the group, walking alongside the sultana.

They were almost immediately surrounded by video-camera operators and shotgun microphone bearers.

"Bravo Sultana!" Curt said aside. "If anyone shoots at us now, the press is in the line of fire, too. And the news media will immediately go into a violent, irrational feeding frenzy over the fact that their supposedly immune news people were mowed down by brutal, ruthless occupiers of the demilitarized island of Sakhalin in their ill-advised attempt to prevent additional military contingents from coming in to stabilize the situation."

Alzena smiled knowingly. "Yes, there is that isn't there? Strange that a military man would think of it."

"I've had a few confrontations with the news media," Curt admitted.

He sensed a little shudder go through her. "This is exciting!"

"God damned deadly, too, if you don't mind my saying so!"

As the contingent got about ten meters from the low, rusting chain-link fence that separated the tarmac from the two-story terminal building, the terminal building doors opened.

Out stepped Colonel Viktor Pashkavitch Kurotkin, Colonel Dao Min Qian, and Colonel Yushiro Mishida.

They were accompanied by their aides.

Behind the aides came three soldiers, each bearing the national colors of the USSR, the PRC, and Japan.

The three colonels remained at the top of the low flight of six steps leading into the terminal, thus deliberately placing themselves, their aides, and their national colors at a higher level than the Americans and Bruneis. An aide opened the rusting gate in the security fence on squeaking, rusty hinges, allowing the Americans and Bruneis to pass through to the bottom of the steps where they could look up at the three leaders of the national military forces that had been on Sakhalin to that time.

As the three colonels saluted, Colonel Mishida spoke up in English. "Welcome to Sakhalin! We assume that you have come in peace and friendship to assist our peacekeeping forces here. The news media told us only a very short time ago that you were coming. Otherwise, we would have prepared a different welcome!"

Chapter Fifteen

Much to Curt's surprise, Alzena took over at once, upstaging her brother and himself by advancing up the steps of the terminal building until she stood on the top step in front of Colonel Mishida. She was only a little bit shorter than the Japanese commander, but she acted as though she were looking down on him. At least, that's the impression she gave when she bowed respectfully in Japanese fashion from the waist and said to him, "*Konnichi wa! Watakushi was Sultana Alzena to moshimasu. Gokigen ikaga desu ka, Colonel Mishida?*" Then, having gotten him completely off guard by greeting him in his own language, she straightened up, extended her hand, and went on in English, "I have been appointed the deputy for Civil Affairs of the Sakhalin Police Detachment of the, Commission of Pacific Rim Economies with the equivalent rank of ambassador from COPRE."

Mishida was so stricken by Alzena's approach, so unlike that of a Japanese woman, and so dazzled by her universal beauty that he fumbled in English and said, "I know nothing of this Sakhalin Police Detachment, Madam Ambassador! Or of any action by COPRE. Perhaps we can retire to my offices in Yuzhno-Sakhalinsk so that you may present your bona fides..."

"All in due course, Colonel," Alzena replied with just the right amount of warmth and yet cool coyness. Curt noticed a subtle change in her. It was an incredible metamorphosis. It was as if she had thrown a switch and had quickly become not only extremely beautiful with the sort of allure that would completely disarm any man of any culture, but was projecting an aura of personal desire which led men to believe that she could be theirs if they did the right thing according to her lights. She had behaved this way with Curt, but in a far more personal vein, and he knew that she could quickly go from being no-nonsense and pragmatic to being soft, extremely exotic, and highly desirable. Curt didn't understand how she did it, but he was damned glad she could do it here and under these circumstances. It might be keeping all of them from getting killed.

She turned to Colonel Kurotkin and subjected him to her diplomatic warmth, again by addressing him in Russian, *"Dobree deyhn, Polkovnik Viktor Pashkavitch! Kahk pohjeevahyehtyeh?"*

Curt was astonished. He never knew that Alzena could speak several languages. But then, speaking different languages hadn't been among the subjects they'd discussed when they were together. They spoke one language when they needed to speak at all.

Curt noticed that Kurotkin was amazed as most Russians were when they heard someone who wasn't a Russian speaking their language. *"Dobree deyhn, Sultana Alzena! Ohchehn khohrohshow blahgohdahryou' vahs! Gohvohreetyeh lee Vee poh-rooskee?"*

"Ohchehn nyeh mnohgoh," she told him. Kurotkin didn't shake her hand as the befuddled Mishida had; he kissed it continental style because he wanted her to know that *he* was a civilized Byelorussian and *not* a Cossack or Mongol.

Colonel Qian was therefore expecting Alzena's ploy when she greeted him, *"Wu an, Qian tongzhi! Ni show ying-wen ma?"*

Curt, who spoke Mandarin, understood her very well and knew that she had used the proper formal and polite inflections.

Qian replied quite coolly and guardedly with a forced smile as he shook her hand. "Yes, I speak English but not very much." He wasn't going to be taken in by this lovely creature; he was a military man, a servant of the people of China, a person who had been assigned the important job of leading the first regiment of the People's Liberation Army back into Sakhalin, an island that had once belonged to China and would again become part of China once these barbaric Westerners and fanatical Japanese could be cleared from the island.

Alzena had not only done her diplomatic homework by learning how to greet each of the commanders in his own language, but she had somehow discovered their names and used them. It mattered not the culture a person lived in; a beautiful stranger greeting them cordially by using their own names was always an ice-breaker…almost as good as being able to say "please" and "thank you" in another's language. Curt didn't know how Alzena had discovered the names of the three colonels. That was information he hadn't even gotten out of the NSC/NIA memory cube briefing.

She had in the space of a minute almost completely disarmed these three powerful and dangerous military men. And she had done it in a diplomatic way using her outstanding Eurasian beauty to the best advantage.

She was, Curt decided, a far more complex young woman than she had ever let on to him.

In a short period of time, everyone had been introduced, whereupon Colonel Mishida spoke to her in Japanese with a somewhat gruff, samurai manner.

Alzena quickly moved in on this by saying quite plainly, "I know each of you speaks English and that you use it as a neutral common language when you meet together. Although I speak a little of each of your native tongues, may I suggest we use English, please?"

This statement astonished all three colonels because they'd been quite covert about their irregular personal meetings in various cafes and restaurants in Yuzhno-Sakhalinsk and Korsakov. Whereas her ability to greet each of them personally in their own language had impressed Curt, her knowledge of their "staff meetings" greatly impressed the three colonels. Each of them privately decided at the moment that the Sultana Alzena was someone to be reckoned with. Furthermore, she had information that might be damaging to each of them if she passed it along to their various political officers or government contacts.

"I shall be pleased to comply with your request, Sultana," Mishida replied with a bow. "I asked if I might inquire about this Sakhalin Police Detachment you claim to represent. We have heard no news about such a thing."

"But certainly, you knew about it," Alzena insisted. "How else could you have managed to turn out a welcoming contingent of your troops at the airport here? We certainly appreciate the effort you went to in order to greet us. It shows a sincere desire on the part of each of your governments to resolve the current situation by peaceful means."

Alzena was surely an outstanding diplomat. Curt decided, and this was an aspect of her that he hadn't suspected. She was now totally in command of the situation, and she firmly retained that control. Curt noticed out of the corner of his eye that even Mahathis showed no visible signs of distress over the fact that his sister now seemed to be in command. Curt figured the man obviously knew her better than Curt did or that Alzena's performance had been planned ahead of time. Curt suspected the former. He also suspected that she had leaned hard on her brother about her responsibility as the diplomatic side of the team. Or maybe the sultan himself had ordered it, something that Curt wouldn't put past a ruler who was no dummy. One thing for certain: Curt knew that the sultan or maybe even Mahathis hadn't been totally nepotistic in assigning the diplomatic functions to her. She was good.

But then again, Curt knew, she was good at anything she decided to do.

"We were told by the lady from the Los Angeles Times Multi-Media Corporation who flew in here with her television news people about an hour before your aircraft arrived from Brunei," Mishida explained.

Aha! Curt exclaimed inwardly. Things began to make sense to him. The good old American press was at work again using their well-established network of news leaks at high government levels, the legendary "Potomac secrecy sieve" that operated on the basis of "provide me with leaked info and I'll go easy on you when I have to reveal your particular ethical soft spot…and you know what I mean!"

Curt had to admit to himself that the network was goddamned good to have gotten the word far enough ahead of time to allow a hypersonic to be chartered, a news team put together, and the whole works landed on Sakhalin an hour before the first SPD contingent arrived. It bad taken nearly twenty-four hours for the Greys to deploy, and they'd moved about as fast as they could. On the other hand, maybe the Los Angeles *Times* Multi-Media Corporation had standing orders ready for such occasions as this, requiring only a go command to set them in motion. If so, Curt was interested in finding out how they did it. That information might help the Greys move a little faster next time.

At this point, the third hypersonic transport of the SPD came over the fence to land on Runway 01, turning off the runway onto the taxiway and the tarmac with the muted rumble of the combustion of its injected scramjets. Curt felt better. The rest of TACBATT was now on the ground. SERVBATT and the rest of the warbots would be on the next ship, followed by the Chileans.

This occasion shook up the three colonels. None of them had expected what was turning out to be a major non-violent military invasion of Sakhalin. Each of them knew that none of them could take any steps to stop it now. It was too late. They knew now they should have shot all the Gurkhas and passengers aboard Royal Brunei Charter One inbound from Brunei, the first one to land. By the time the Greys arrived in Number Two, it had been too late.

They also knew they'd been snookered, although none of them used that American billiards term. They'd been caught in the middle because the video cameras were watching them and transmitting what they were doing out to the world. They didn't really know how to handle that in a way that would have met with the approval of their individual governments. There hadn't been time for them to contact Tokyo, Beiching, and Khabarovsk for instructions. The linear decision-making process of the Soviet and Chinese military establishment had failed them. As for the Japanese, Colonel Mishida really didn't care because this was exactly the sort of thing he wanted…although he couldn't reveal that.

"Since we are here on a duly authorized and approved non-violent peacekeeping mission of the Congress of Pacific Rim Economies," Alzena went on smoothly, deliberately using some of the shibboleths utilized by both the Soviets and the Chinese in the past, "may I ask why the troops of your welcoming ceremony are deployed in such a belligerent manner around the tarmac? I, for one, would certainly feel much easier if the parking ramp were not surrounded and your troops were drawn up in a ceremonial formation..."

The way she said it and the expression on her face turned a mere diplomatic question and a mild suggestion into an order. She knew that these men had been here for months, had not seen their wives and lovers for a long time, had been denied a social release, and were therefore quite vulnerable to what she was projecting. She had a very effective trump card, and she played it well. Curt noticed it, of course, but he didn't yet know the full rationale behind her use of it. It made him a bit jealous as a result.

Mishida saw that he was quietly and rapidly assuming the position as spokesman for the three colonels, not only because he understood and spoke English better than the other two, but also because, of the three military units, the Japan Self-Defense Force had the strongest justification for being on Sakhalin to preserve law and order. Furthermore, it hadn't been his regimental troops who'd started the trouble; they'd only reacted properly to maintain law and order when the Soviets and Chinese had gotten out of hand in the seamier parts of Yuzhno-Sakhalinsk. They'd been a bit rough, but one couldn't be expected to handle Cossacks and Mongols gently...

"Of course, Madam Ambassador," Mishida quickly acquiesced in the most polite manner he could muster. He also considered himself far more civilized and polite than the Soviet or Chinese commander. He turned to Kurotkin and Qian. "I shall order my regiment to stand down from its present position and fall in as an honor guard beyond the terminal. I request that the Soviet and Chinese forces do the same. Would both of you like to join me in providing transportation for these honored guests to wherever they wish to go in Yuzhno-Sakhalinsk?"

Qian was reluctant until Kurotkin spoke up. "I shall be happy to provide an honor guard of our new assault guns and whatever transportation is required..."

At that point, Qian saw an opportunity to have some of his technical NCOs get a closer look at the new Soviet warbots, something that had been denied to him thus far because of the tight security maintained over these warbots by Kurotkin's men. "We shall join the honor guard," he added quietly and dispassionately.

General Ahmad Mahathis reassumed command at this point. "Excellent! We shall form our troops and prepare to leave the aerodrome once all the incoming flights have arrived! Thank you for your offer of transportation, but we have our own." Turning to Curt and Payne-Ashwell, he ordered, "Continue to debark your troops and equipment, gentlemen! Then be prepared to move out to your objectives!"

Curt turned to Major Joanne Wilkinson, his chief of staff. "Major, please make it so...but remain on Yellow Alert, please."

She saluted quickly. "Yes, sir! Ladies and Sergeant Major Kester, let's go; we have work to do." She tossed a quick look at Alzena; it was one of envy that Curt didn't fully understand right then.

"You have...other aircraft inbound?" Kurotkin asked with hesitation, trying to cover his disbelief while at the same time extracting some more information from them. This was a much bigger operation than he'd anticipated when the news media alerted him.

"Two more hypersonics, Colonel," Mahathis told him. "The rest of the American Third Robot Infantry Regiment plus the Third Airborne Regiment from the Republic of Chile. We will not leave the aerodrome until all have arrived safely."

Kurotkin hid his amazement and dismay. Instead, he said, "Perhaps we should offer our guests some warmth and refreshment while they're waiting, Colonel Mishida."

"So! Would the ambassador, the general and the two colonels please join us inside?" Mishida replied oh-so-politely. Things were working out well. This was playing exceptionally well to the video cameras still focused on them.

As they were passing through the heavy glass doors into the rather rudimentary terminal, Curt took Alzena's arm to assist her.

And was surprised at what he felt when he did so.

Alzena was a soft, feminine person. But now there was a hard, taut, strong, and resilient layer under her fur parka that hugged tightly against the skin of her small, slender arm.

Knowing what he felt, she looked up at him, smiled, and explained in a low voice so that only he could hear her, "I'm really not very brave, Colonel. My special body armor was tailor-made for me in Singapore."

"I'm glad," he told her with some relief; then he added, "You continue to amaze me."

"I hope so."

"Where did you learn to do what you just did?" Curt asked, referring to the dazzling display of diplomacy she'd put on outside.

She didn't look at him and appeared to be devoting her attention to her surroundings as she smiled and nodded at the few non-military people who had apparently been waiting for an outbound flight that wouldn't depart today because the inbound aircraft would not arrive. As their group walked through the old, stark, sparsely furnished Soviet-built terminal toward what was apparently a private dining room once intended for receiving high Party members and general officers of the Soviet armed services - and now reserved for VIPs - she added softly, "Dear Curt, my formal education in France involved more than the lovely, enjoyable things I've taught you. Please don't forget that the French have been the masters of diplomacy for many centuries. After all, I must make my individual contributions to the family business. I have always been more than I seem to others. *Garde-toi, tant que tu vivras, de juger des gens sur la mime.*"

"Sorry, French isn't my language," Curt admitted.

"Then, I'll happily translate for you and demonstrate as well. Later, but not too much later. *Et tout que je puis...*"

Chapter Sixteen

The group was waylaid on its trek across the nearly empty terminal waiting hall.

"Ahmad!" came the piercing shout from a feminine voice.

A short, very attractive young redheaded woman was running across the large terminal waiting room toward them. She was accompanied by a video cameraman, a mike man, and an additional person - a rather unattractive, purposeful, plain-looking woman who seemed to have it all together. The redhead did not.

"Now I know where the leak is!" was the quiet remark from Alzena.

Curt immediately recognized the woman. Few people in the free world would not because she'd been a fixture on the news for nearly ten years. Margaret MacPherson – "Maggie" as she preferred to be called, although the rolling credit lines always read, "Produced and reported by Margaret MacPherson" - was the darling of America, Europe, and Japan because of her down-home, friendly, helpful, compassionate "woman next door" image that came across so well. Women looked at her and listened to her and believed she was the sort of person with whom they could gossip over the telephone with the rest of their friends. Men looked at her and privately lusted for her as they often did for the lascivious divorcee or widower next door. Her weekly program, Maggie's Hour, was seen around the world, and it was *never* subtitled in another language because she wouldn't permit it; the world would never know how many people had learned English by watching Maggie MacPherson on video. Furthermore, when she'd broadcast her award-winning coverages of the volcanic eruption of Keli Mutu, the devastation of Hurricane Virgil, or the social unrest following the Korean unification, millions hung on her every word. She didn't need a Pulitzer; she already had three of them plus every other possible journalistic award that three continents could bestow upon her.

It was said that Maggie MacPherson knew everyone worth knowing in the world and that if she knew you and mentioned you on her show, it was better than being listed in "Who's Who."

General Ahmad Mahathis and Sultana Alzena obviously were known to her. Mahathis turned when he heard his name called, broke into a huge smile, and reached to welcome her with open arms, something very uncharacteristic of him.

It was a greeting that consisted of a prolonged bear hug, again something that Curt had never seen Mahathis do in public.

Maybe, Curt decided, Mahathis knew her better than anyone expected, because he'd often seen Mahathis greet Major Alexis Morgan in that manner when they thought they were alone.

I've probably got trouble! Curt told himself.

As if he didn't have enough already with Mahathis in command of the SPD.

Alzena greeted the newsharpy cordially but without enthusiasm. So did Colonel Payne-Ashwell, but the commanding officer of the Gurkhas made it seem quite properly British to behave in a cool, aloof, and very formal manner.

Which gave Curt some clues as to how he should behave when Maggie MacPherson chided Mahathis, "Ahmad, damn you, you're forgetting your bloody manners! Are you going to introduce me to Colonel Curt Carson, or am I going to have to do it myself? I've been trying to corner this hunk ever since Trinidad!"

If Maggie MacPherson came across as the "woman next door" on the tube, Curt suddenly discovered that she was as brash and abrasive as a person could be, plus having a decidedly fast mouth. She was cock-sure and openly super-confident. Curt decided he'd give just as good as he'd just gotten, so he saluted with his fingertips touching the rim of his battle helmet which he hadn't removed because he wanted to preserve the option of instant NE communication with Major Joanne Wilkinson. "Yes, Miss MacPherson, from a hunk to a harpy, I'm Colonel Curt Carson, commanding officer of the Washington Greys!"

"You can cut out the crap. I know who the hell you are," she told him without rancor in matter-of-fact tones that were strangely provocative. She glanced at the silver oak leaf on his helmet. "I see you're a light colonel now. Does an increase in rank also mean that you can be less of a gentleman and not remove your hat?"

Curt didn't smile. "In case you don't know, Miss MacPherson," he replied, stressing the honorific because he knew from some of her on-camera interviews with others that she eschewed all three female honorifics, "a gentleperson is one who is never unintentionally rude to anyone else. And I am only following protocol established by Colonels Kurotkin, Qian, and Mishida." The three of them had removed neither their stiff-rimmed garrison caps nor their combat helmets, whichever they happened to be wearing.

She looked at him with her head cocked and her mane of strawberry-red hair falling over her forehead and around her face. "Aha! I can see we're going to have a juicy time of it when I interview you...which I may do right now!" And her appearance, mood, and attitude abruptly changed; she became the friendly, approachable, and delectable, "woman next door" again because Curt noticed two video cameras - one looking over his shoulder at her and the other peering over her shoulder at him. In her professional on-camera voice and with her on-camera persona, she suddenly asked him, "Colonel, you're commanding the first contingent of American troops to return to Sakhalin since our warbot troops were brought home by the last administration. Seems to me and many other Americans that the President has reversed the foreign policy of the Unite States. Can we look forward to more American troops being stationed on foreign soil to protect American business interests?"

Curt didn't hesitate a moment to respond to this. Hesitation would be hazardous to his media health, as he knew from past experience with newshawks and neewsharpies. Furthermore, he had to give her sharp, quick, sound-bite answers. Miss MacPherson, I was given lawful orders to deploy the Washington Greys to Sakhalin as part of the international Sakhalm Police. Detachment authorized earlier today by COPRE. We didn't ask why; we just did it."

Maggie MacPherson knew better than to ask the next question because she had covered a lot of armed conflicts around the world. But she asked it anyway because she felt her viewers would expect her to do so. "Well, I'm glad our troops can move fast when necessary. But when it comes to orders, I didn't think you'd carry them out blindly, right or wrong..."

"We soldiers don't get involved in politics, Miss MacPherson. We've got an old American tradition about that."

"A tradition? Gee, Colonel, it seems to me that the tradition may have some gaps in it. Was your regiment just 'doing its job' when all those women and children were massacred on Borneo a few years ago?"

"You know the story on that one. Our job was to rescue American hostages, not kill people. I can't remember that I was enjoying myself at the time," Curt replied easily. He decided it was time to bring this to a screeching halt. "Look, ask me some questions I'm qualified to answer, and I promise I won't ask you if you've stopped sleeping with your associate producers yet. If you want to discuss the political and diplomatic side of things, I recommend you talk to Len Spencer in the White House...and tell him I sent you. As for the mission of the SPD, General Mahathis here is the man to talk to."

She was set back a bit; but she didn't show it, and she wouldn't give up. "Colonel, do you report to General Mahathis? Or are you still responsible to Congress and the President?"

He didn't answer her because she really knew better. But part of the reason was that he really wasn't sure how Mahathis viewed it right then. Curt knew very well that his own chain of command went upward through General Hettrick. But it did raise some nagging questions in his mind. If given an order by Mahathis that would jeopardize his regiment - and Mahathis had given such orders in the past - or would result in a breach of the ROEs under which he was expected to operate, how was he diplomatically going to tell Mahathis to go piss up a rope? He hoped he wouldn't have to confront that conundrum, but he knew that the possibility was high in this operation.

"Why ask me? You know what my commission says," he told her bluntly and walked away from her, leaving her standing there open-mouthed, looking like a girl whose blind date had just walked out on her. He got one look at the expression on her face, and he knew his troubles with Maggie MacPherson had just started.

As the group was ushered into the private room on the balcony of the terminal building, Alzena remarked to Curt, "You handled her very well."

"I don't think so," Curt snapped. He was irritated. Since they were in semi-private now, he pulled Mahathis to one side with Alzena and spoke to him as privately as possible, "Dammit, Ahmad, I could have used some support from you in handling MacPherson!"

Mahathis looked at Curt with an expression that told Curt the man was in his imperial mode. "Curt, Maggie MacPherson wanted to talk with you since she hadn't met you yet."

"General," Curt fired back, lapsing into the formal mode that Mahathis signified he wished to use, "she picked one hell of a time to do it!"

"She's opportunistic, Colonel."

"Damned right she is!" Curt observed. He felt he'd better get something straightened out on this regard with Mahathis right then, so he went on, "General, I wish to inform you right now that I don't intend to give her any interviews that haven't had prior approval first from my American command and then from you. You're the CINC, General; it's up to you or one of your aides to handle the news media, not your subordinate commanders."

"Oh, I suspect I'll mend the situation just fine when I take her to dinner tonight," Mahathis remarked in an off-handed manner.

Major Alexis Morgan was certainly going to have something to say about that, even if only privately to Curt, the commander of the Washington Greys suspected.

"Ahmad," his sister said to him in gentle warning, "you're not in

Bandar Seri Begawan now. Your actions are under scrutiny and surveillance not only by potential enemies but also by your own command which will strive to behave according to your example..."

"And what is that supposed to mean?" Mahathis asked.

"Just that you are now in command of a multi-national military police detachment in a foreign country," he reminded him. "I believe the Americans have something called Rule Ten. I might suggest that you speak with Colonel Carson about it with the thought that you might wish to extend something like it to the entire detachment, keeping in mind the source of the trouble that brought us here in the first place."

Mahathis didn't reply, and they rejoined the others. They sat down around a large circular table next to large windows that looked out upon the parking tarmac where the huge black hypersonics crowded the available space. Once the Russian-like waiter brought them all refreshments, Mahathis looked around the table at the military commanders - American, Brunei, Soviet, Chinese, and Japanese. "The days are getting short at these high latitudes," he pointed out. "We need to be in garrison by dark. Therefore, I won't wait for the arrival of Colonel Pinedo of Chile before starting this informal meeting. I shall brief him separately when his aircraft lands in a few minutes."

The young heir to the throne of Brunei seemed painfully aware that this was his first major international operation. If he screwed up, he wasn't really worried about what his father, the sultan, would do; nothing could prevent Mahathis from assuming the throne after his father. He was apparently concerned, however, that whatever he did or didn't do here might at some future time come back to haunt him and his tenure as the next sultan, whose job was to continue to make Brunei the leader of the Pacific rim nations. After all, that's why the sultan had taken the lead and backed the Sakhalin Police Detachment at the cost of some millions of dollars plus - more important - the call-in of some political and diplomatic IOUs. He also knew, however, that it hadn't been done totally on his father's initiative.

Mahathis couldn't afford a screw-up.

So, he began, "The Sakhalin Police Detachment was sent here under the auspices of COPRE, who met this afternoon in Honolulu and authorized the SPD. You may wish to check with your respective governments concerning the validity of my statements, hut I am sure they will contact you within the next few hours as the diplomatic wheels begin to turn."

"You can be certain that we will indeed be in communication with our governments for instructions," Colonel Kurotkin growled. "It is fortunate for you that my government issued me no instructions covering such an invasion as you have just carried out! This is an overt offensive action by the imperialists to take over Sakhalin which has been part of the Soviet Union for centuries!"

"The Soviet Union occupied only a part of it, Colonel," Mishida reminded him, then he asked Mahathis, "General, do you intend to occupy the island and require that the Japanese Self-Defense Forces withdraw? After all, we came to Karafuto to assist civil authorities in maintaining law and order..."

"Which was in violation of treaty," Colonel Qian pointed out.

"Which is why the Sakhalin Police Detachment is here now!" Mahathis snapped bluntly. "It is my mission to restore law and order to Sakhalin and to prevent the current occupation units from engaging in further armed conflict which might escalate to more serious confrontations on this island and elsewhere. I have no orders to demand your evacuation, only to keep the three of you from arguing with bullets."

"And how do you intend to do that, General Mahathis?" was Mishida's question.

"My orders are to remain on Sakhalin with the SPD until COPRE or the UN resolves the matter of the military security of the island which is now under the civil control of Japan with free access by the Soviet Union to a fair share of the island's resources," Mahathis revealed with an air of absolute and total confidence and assurance. He thought he was in control, in command, the top dog. And that's the way he liked it.

This was the first time Curt had really been briefed on the role of the Washington Greys on Sakhalin. He was a little pissed off about it. Insofar as he was concerned, Mahathis should have gathered together with Castillo and him to bring them up to speed and hear their comments. Mahathis was assumed that the Greys and the Chileans would and could do exactly what he'd planned. Curt knew the Greys would have a full regiment on hand when AIRBATT arrived in two days. But he didn't know about the Chileans. It would have been a minor matter for Mahathis to put off this proclamation of occupation for a few hours until the Chileans had arrived and there had been time for an SPD Oscar brief.

As it was, Curt was getting his one and only briefing as part of the instruction of an invading general - still without one-third of his force - to the officers of the defending indigenous forces under what was undoubtedly the strangest non-invasion of the twenty-first century.

Curt would have war-gamed this situation with Georgie if he'd known because he'd certainly had an hour or so to run scenarios during the flight. As it was, he was caught totally unprepared, and he didn't like it.

And there wasn't very much he could do about it without being insubordinate as well as weakening the position of the SPD in the process. It didn't project the image of a solid, organized police unit if the subordinate commanders started arguing publicly with the chief at the start.

He was even more shocked and dismayed when Mahathis went on, "It will be our task to separate the Soviets, Chinese and Japanese to eliminate further troubles. Therefore, I am making the following assignments. Colonel Kurotkin, you will continue to garrison your Guards Regiment here in Yuzhno-Sakhalinsk. Colonel Mishida, you will move your regiment to Korsakov, Colonel Qian, you will garrison your regiment at Kholmsk. As long as there is no further trouble, you may continue to mount your patrols to assure that your may continue to mount your patrols to assure that your nations' fair shares of Sakalin's resources are exported according to contract and then people on Sakhalin are being protected."

Then Mahathis did something Curt would never have done: The young sultan-to-be announced, "The headquarters of the SPD will be here in Yuzhno-Sakhalinsk, guarded by my Gurkhas under Colonel Payne-Ashwell, who will also patrol to the south. Colonel Carson, you will move at once to the old United States garrison building near Sokol where your tacair squadron will be based. I will use the Washington Greys as a mobile patrol force to the north up the east coast. When the Chileans arrive, they will take up garrison at Kostromskoye on the west coast where they will patrol along that side of the island. I will expect the Soviet, Chinese, and Japanese units to have liaison officers and communications centers at my headquarters here in Yuzhno-Sakhalinsk so that I may receive regular reports and be able to resolve any difficulties that may arise during this transition phase while COPRE sorts out the diplomatic and economic matters..."

Curt tensed, because he knew the Soviets and their Russian way of thinking. He also knew from his own proficiency in Mandarin Chinese how Colonel Qian would translate these orders into his Chinese mental operating system. Curt was glad he still had his Novia assault rifle, loaded and locked, at his side.

True to Curt's estimate, Colonel Kurotkin rose to his feet, anger on his face. "General Mahathis, you do not have authority to give me orders! You have shown me some documents that you claim authorize you to be here with an invading military force of three regiments! I wish to obtain copies of these documents and send them to Khabarovsk. In the meantime, I consider you to be an aggressor leading a military invasion force!"

Qian was also on his feet, although his expression was impassive. He was having trouble putting his thoughts into English. "I do not have orders to obey you, General. My orders are to protect the legitimate interests of the People's Republic of China here on Sakhalin! I do not like this invasion of yours..."

Curt looked up at the Chinese and spoke to him in his own

language. Translated into the nearest equivalent English terms, Curt said, "Colonel Qian, even at the time the Manchu Empire reached its maximum suzerainty at the time my country was founded, China did not exercise recognized dominion over Sakhalin. We are military men and should not attempt to justify our actions on the basis of diplomacy or politics which are not our concerns. You and I know you are here to protect the People's Republic against possible Soviet advances elsewhere. I, too, have read the 'Selected Works' of Mao Zedong in your own language. I am sure that you recall what he said about rash and reckless hot-heads in the Red Army. Or what Sun Zhou said about acting in ignorance of your opponent..."

Curt was deliberately obscure. He was trying to deal Qian out of the equation of the moment by gracefully advising him that the Chinese colonel was facing greatly superior numbers. He was guessing that it had been a decade or more since Qian had read either book; only a young officer studied them diligently and committed passages to memory; field-grade officers tended to proceed on what they remembered of their earlier readings plus what they'd learned from experience in the meantime.

Qian didn't resume his seat. Nor did he reply to Curt. Instead, he said to Mishida, "I do not take orders from an invading general when he has not defeated me in battle. But I shall do nothing until I receive instructions from Beiching."

Curt expected that. Qian was saving face.

When Curt looked at Colonel Mishida, he was a passive man who was simply listening. The Japanese apparently didn't intend to reveal any of his thoughts.

But Mahathis was getting red in the face. He couldn't answer the Chinese colonel. But he'd gotten into a pissing contest with the Soviet colonel, a position that usually didn't lead to a peaceful outcome. He glared at Kurotkin and snapped, "Those instructions will come from Khabarovsk, Colonel!"

"Until they do, I intend to confine your invasion force to the aerodrome here!"

Mahathis bristled. "I have the Gurkhas whose fearsome conduct in battle is well known! I have the warbots of the Washington Greys! I will very quickly have an additional regiment of Chilean troops-"

Kurotkin snapped back, "I have warbots, too, right on the aerodrome!"

And that statement brought Curt to a state of mental red alert.

Chapter Seventeen

Without allowing anyone in the room to know, Curt toggled his helmet tacomm to neuroelectronic mode and thought his message. *Grey Chief, this is Grey Head!*

Grey Chief here. Go ahead, Grey Head! was the immediate reply from Major Joanne Wilkinson.

The Soviet commander has just revealed he has warbots! Can you see anything that looks like a warbot? If so, what do they look like? What are their anticipated capabilities? Curt knew that was a complex series of questions and that it might be days or even months before they had the answers to some of them. But he had to ask them. Someone outside might have the answers already.

Grey Head, this is Grey Tech! That was Sergeant Major Edie Sampson, who was a whiz with warbot technology. *I've been watching the Soviet assault guns. I don't think they're regular ASU-eighty-eights. If they are, their crews are buttoned up inside them because I haven't seen anyone around them or even standing up in the hatches. And that ain't like Soviet operational doctrine which says they don't button down until action is imminent!*

Grey Major here! came Henry Kester's "voice." *Colonel, Grey Tech is right! Those Soviet Eighty-eights ain't. They've got S-one-six-eight fifty-three-millimeter auto cannons on them, not the seventy-three-millimeter guns of the regular Eighty-eights. And they don't move like Eighty-eights. Too Jerky. Like remote-control tanks with damned poor feedback.*

They're the only things around that might be warbots, Edie added, *and I sort of suspect they're a Soviet rip-off of our old Hairy Foxes. The usual quick-and-dirty Soviet technical response. Convert something already in inventory to keep from setting up new production lines, which takes too long. But, Lordy, those Eighty-eights, are big and klunky things! Sort of like the old Em-tens we used to have years ago.*

They've moved off the tarmac now, Kester reported. *They're headed out the gates on both sides of the terminal.*

Curt could see that through the huge double-paned windows. He also noted that another hypersonic transport had landed and parked far down the tarmac while yet another one was just touching down. One bore the markings of Tao Cargo while the other was an Air Khmer plane, both from air freight charter outfits. Obviously, the sultan of Brunei didn't have enough aircraft of his own to pull this off, so he'd chartered additional ones. Or maybe he owned the charter companies. With his trillions of dollars, he could have owned most of the Pacific rim, Curt thought in a fleeting moment, then turned his attention back to his big problem.

Grey Chief, cover for the Chileans as they unload and send Colonel Castillo up here at once! Curt instructed. *And get ready to move ASAP off this air patch to our quarters.*

Roger, Grey Head!

The whole exchange had taken only a few seconds. NE communication was very fast because it wasn't necessary for people to actually speak. It took measurable time for the brain to command verbal speech expression. NE communications only required a conscious and deliberate direction of thoughts. Because you have to think before you speak, NE comm is fast because you only have to think and not speak.

Colonel Kurotkin went on, "Because you are an invading military force, General Mahathis, I believe it is within the scope of my orders to confine your forces to the aerodrome until they can be reloaded into the aircraft and depart. In the meantime, all of you are my prisoners…" He started to reach for his APV *Kohbrah* pistol holstered at his belt.

Curt had been expecting that. His Novia had been slung over his shoulder in the fast response scheme. In one quick movement, he had it in his right hand ready to point at Kurotkin. "Colonel, I wouldn't try that if I were you! Basically I'm a nice guy, but just don't force me to go to work! You've got the world news media looking over your shoulder here. Everything you and the One-hundred-tenth Guards Regiment does will be seen in Moskva and around the world."

Kurotkin was a cool character. With his hand still on the butt of his *Kohbrah*, he told Curt, "Colonel, you and the other forces under the command of General Mahathis are surrounded on the aerodrome. I call upon you to surrender at once to avoid a needless bloodletting."

And Curt replied to him just as cooly, "Colonel Kurotkin, we are prepared for that needless bloodletting whenever it is agreeable to you! Colonel Qian and Colonel Mishida, presume you'll want to place your men so they are not in the field of fire. Or do you intend to follow the commands of Colonel Kurotkin?"

As anticipated, that got both Qian and Mishida where it hurt. Neither was willing to abrogate the slightest vestige of command to the Soviet colonel. Doing so would have meant fighting the Soviets afterward to get their individual military authority back.

Qian didn't reply. He was staring at Curt's steady Novia assault rifle. He knew it contained a clip of fifty rounds. It wasn't as deadly at close quarters as the legendary U.S. Army Black Maria assault shotgun, but Qian suspected that Curt wouldn't miss if he had to shoot at this extremely short range of several meters. Qian was no fool. He didn't want to start anything that he didn't think he could win. There was no indication to him at this point that he could win. If fighting broke out, maybe his 44th Special Regiment might win; but it could be a Pyrrhic victory, and he probably wouldn't be around to celebrate it. Insofar as he was concerned, a posthumous decoration for valor was poor compensation for a continued, upwardly mobile career in the People's Liberation Army. This affair was rapidly getting out of hand because he knew Colonel Curt Carson was right: China really had no legitimate claim to Sakhalin Island. He realized now he'd been ordered to Sakhalin with his regiment only to keep the Soviets off guard. China's attentions and intentions with respect to the Soviets were directed elsewhere, and he also knew that his superiors in Beiching were dutifully following the military principles of both Sun Zhou and Chairman Mao.

Colonel Mishida, on the other hand, was looking at Curt's helmet. He knew that Curt had instant NE communication with his

Washington Greys and may already have "spoken" to them silently via NE tacomm to give them orders. Mishida didn't know what those orders might be, if they'd been given. It wouldn't suit the plans of Japan to have fighting break out right at the start here or to possibly have General Mahathis or the Sultana Alzena killed or wounded in the initial foray because of the stupid, paranoid, bull-headed Soviet colonel. "General Mahathis," Colonel Mishida spoke up, breaking the awkward silence that followed Curt's question, "your sudden arrival with orders and authorizations we have not seen has put us in a situation for which we, as military commanders, have no guidance, instructions, or orders. The obvious fact that you have supporting troops strength at least equal to the combination of the three nations currently garrisoning troops on Sakhalm further adds to the delicacy of the situation. May we ask you to retain your troops here at the aerodrome until we receive confirmation of the COPRE authorizations from our individual governments?" That was an amazing statement to come from a Japanese military officer. Curt suddenly wondered if Japan, as a long-time economic partner of the United States, might have had some quiet role in the authorization of the SPD, even though they had voted against it in the COPRE meeting.

Mahathis had temporarily lost control of the situation to Curt Carson, something that he didn't like in spite of his friendship and respect for the tactical brilliance of the American colonel. He immediately took control again at this opportunity. "No," he replied bluntly. "We have our orders. If we meet resistance, we shall counter it in kind and intensity. Whoever provides that resistance will be responsible for the consequences. We have had enough discussion. Colonel Payne-Ashwell, Colonel Carson, carry out your orders. Dismissed!" He arose and said to his sister, "Sultana, please accompany me for your safety."

Alzena restrained herself from telling her brother that she would rather accompany Colonel Curt Carson in order to assure her personal safety. She would see to it, she decided, that things were arranged so that Carson and his American Sierra Charlies were nearby once things got sorted out. The Gurkhas were good soldiers who would protect her, but Colonel Payne-Ashwell wouldn't accept her as an equal the way the American did; to the Gurkhas' colonel, she was always an untouchable piece of property to protect whereas Curt and his Washington Greys looked upon her as a person. She wasn't really sure of her standing with some of the ladies of the Greys, but they treated her as an equal even if they envied her. However, for the moment, she followed her brother.

As Colonel Kurotkin slowly withdrew his hand from the holstered *Kohbrah* pistol, Curt lowered the Novia and swung it back into carry position.

Curt could feel the Russian's hatred of him. Curt had met him eyeball to eyeball, and Kurotkin had blinked. Kurotkin might respect Curt for that, but that didn't mean he liked the American. Curt spoke the language of the Chinese commander and thus knew how that man thought, but he couldn't read the Japanese commander at the moment. In his mind, he decided he'd have to keep a close but different type of watch on each of them.

"I say, Carson, old chap!" Payne-Ashwell said easily, arising from his chair. "Best we find Colonel Castillo and organize our deployment to garrison, what?"

"I think, Duncan," Curt responded informally in a like vein, using the colonel's given name, "we'd better accompany the general and the sultana back downstairs until they're safely under guard by your Gurkhas."

Grey Head, Grey Chief. Wilkinson's NE voice sounded in Curt's helmet tacomm as they moved down the broad stairway to the terminal's ground floor lobby, *there's a Colonel Pinedo here looking for you and General Mahathis.*

Curt shifted mental gears. Joanne obviously didn't know the Latin American protocol wherein a man was always referred to by his middle name just as the Soviets used a person's given name and patronymic. *You mean Colonel Castillo,* he corrected her gently. *We're on our way out of the building now! Have him meet us as we come out! Mahathis and the sultana are with us. Make sure we're covered!*

It was a sullen group that moved out of the terminal building to the cold, damp, windy ramp again. They were joined almost immediately by Major Joanne Wilkinson, Major Joan Ward, Leftenant Kumar Rawat, and Regimental Master Sergeant Tengah Tuanku.

With them was a short, wiry, clean-shaven man about Curt's age. He was attired in a rather gaudy uniform - at least, to Curt's way of thinking - that was almost as bright and colorful as Colonel Kurotkin's. He wore shoulder boards with strange pips on them. He was armed with a holstered Astra Model A-80 pistol and a short dagger in a decorated leather scabbard at his waist. And atop his head was something that looked very much like a German coal scuttle helmet out of World War II.

Curt recognized the getup as the Chilean Army's standard field officer's uniform.

The man saluted. "*Buenos dias!* I am *Coronel* Julio Castillo Pinedo, commandant of the Third Airborne Regiment, Army of the Republic of Chile! *Por favor,* I seek General Ahmad Mahathis."

Mahathis returned the Chilean's salute. "I am General Mahathis!" he replied sharply. "Debark and form your regiment, Colonel! You will be garrisoned at Kostromskoye which is on the west coast. Therefore, I suggest you begin deployment immediately."

It was ever more obvious to Curt that Mahathis was still a regimental commander and didn't know squat bout how to manage or lead a brigade-strength international force. This meant Curt would have to do most of the planning, management, and leading. And the only way he was going to be able to do it without incurring the wrath of Mahathis was to work through the Sultana Alzena...which, he admitted to himself wasn't going to be such rough duty.

"Pardon me, General, but I need more instructions than that," Castillo pointed out. "And I would like to be introduced to the other military commanders with whom I will have to work. And to this lovely lady who accompanied you."

Castillo's gentle rebuke brought Mahathis down from his sultanic pedestal and reminded him that he was forgetting the sort of ordinary military protocol and manners he'd been taught at the U.S. Aerospace Force Academy.

Once the formalities were completed Castillo reported, "General, I have no maps. I have not been given your rules of engagement. I do not know what the tactical mission plan is-"

Curt interrupted him to say, "Colonel Castillo I expect we'll all find out more about that when the general conducts his planning and orders briefing at his operational headquarters this evening." Curt knew that Mahathis had planning nothing of the sort. But the general would indeed have such a briefing because Curt was going to organize it and lead it while maintaining the charade that Mahathis was still CINCSPD. He hoped he wouldn't step on Ahmad's toes too hard, but this was turning out to be a repeat of the operations in Brunei where Mahathis tended to exercise overall control like a man on horseback while keeping his subordinates ignorant of plans until the last moment. Maybe this was because Mahathis was opportunistic in accordance with his Aerospace Force education in tactical matters or because the general simply didn't have a plan.

Mahathis caught Curt's drift, however. But, instead of being a sonofabitch over the fact that he knew Curt was exercising the real leadership here, the scion of the sultan of Brunei backed off, remembering that Curt was the genius at this sort of thing. Curt was obviously going to allow him to retain the overt mantle of leadership. Mahathis recalled that Curt had done the same thing in Brunei, and it had worked extremely well. So, the general took the path of least effort. "Colonel Payne-Ashwell will serve pro tempore as my chief of staff. Have your chief of staff arrange for suitable comm protocol with him. Colonel Carson, please do the same for the Washington Greys. I will conduct a briefing in my Yuzhno-Sakhalinsk headquarters tonight for the commanders and staffs of the Sakhalin Police Detachment."

That also sent a very strong message to Kurotkin, Qian and Mishida, who had followed the others from the building; they weren't invited. Curt suspected that in any event they'd all very quickly know what went on. But on the other hand, one does not invite the antagonists to one's planning sessions and briefings. It was a touchy situation. But this whole affair was touchy and getting touchier.

That seemed to be the final straw insofar as both Kurotkin and Qian were concerned. They saluted out of courtesy and immediately left the group.

At that point, Mahathis decided to move out. He left the, group, accompanied by Alzena and Payne-Ashwell.

"Colonel Castillo, why don't you follow my regiment? We're, going north to Sokol, and the road through the mountains to Kostromskoye goes west out of Novoaleksandrovsk which is on the way. I'll have my staff run a hard copy of the charts for you unless you can upload them into your regimental data base from mine," Curt offered. This wasn't totally a friendly gesture on Curt's part. He'd fought the ABC Allianza - the Argentine-Brazilian-Chilean Alliance - on Trinidad many years ago. The Allianza was growing to be a strong military force in the western hemisphere, one that might someday cause more trouble. Curt's offer was a bid to learn a little about the level of C-cubed-I-communications, command, control, and intelligence - in the Chilean army.

"Sir, I will be most pleased to have hard copy charts. I will have Sergeant Major Escobar contact your staff person," Castillo replied, declining to accept Curt's bid to learn something about his tactical computer capability.

"Very well, Colonel. Mount up and follow the Greys," Curt told him; then told Wilkinson, "Move out Major!"

"Yes, sir!" She saluted, and Curt heard her command over the NE tacomm. *Greys all, this is Grey Chief! Mount 'em up and move 'em out! Columns on both sides of the terminal building! High mobile road mode! On to Sokol! Execute!*

Curt really didn't like having to operate with a chief of staff acting as an executive officer. He'd had long discussions about this with General Belinda Hettrick. Curt was used to direct command as a platoon leader, company commander, and battalion commander. Hettrick had simply told him that he was now a regimental commander and he could no longer look both inward and outward. He wouldn't have time. He had to depend on his staff and on his subordinate batt commanders. He could live with the latter, but he was having trouble getting used to having a staff.

He took off for his OCV which was now unloaded from the hypersonic transport and waiting on the ramp. He could see Henry Kester in the top hatch and Edie Sampson standing alongside. Just as he reached it and began to clamber up the side stirrups to drop through the top hatch, his helmet tacomm sounded.

It was Major Joan Ward. *Grey Head and Grey Chief, this is Warrior Leader! The Sovs are barricading the exits! They're blocking the airport ramp exits on both sides of the terminal! They've stationed two of their assault guns in each exit, and they don't seem anxious to move! Do we push them out of the way? Or do we just sit here and wait for them to move their asses? And do we run over or shoot the troops and armored vehicles behind their assault guns blocking the road beyond? I mean, these guys are armed and aiming at us...and they definitely don't look at all friendly!*

Chapter Eighteen

Colonel Curt Carson looked. On both sides of the long, two-story terminal building where gates broke the continuous line of high chain-link fence with razor wire along its top, Soviet ASU-88 assault guns, the new Soviet warbots, stood impassively blocking the exits from the ramp.

Behind the Soviet warbots stood several armored vehicles Curt recognized as BTR-218 Armored Personnel Carriers. Some of these were festooned with radio antennas.

And khaki-clad Soviet infantry troops stood boldly in ranks around and between the vehicles, their AK-13 assault rifles, M200 rocket launchers, and RPK-20 light machine guns at the ready. They didn't look very happy. But Curt couldn't remember seeing any Soviet troops who looked happy.

In between the larger hangars, in some of the windows of the buildings, and along the ramparts of several structures, Curt could see more Soviet soldiers.

His first thought at seeing the Soviet infantrymen silhouetted against the dull drab sky was one of utter disbelief. Those men were perfect targets for his Jeeps and Mary Anns. Why, even his Greys with their Novias couldn't miss targets that well defined at that range!

He knew that Colonel Kurotkin was trying to make good his threat of keeping the Sakhalin Police Detachment on the airport.

But Curt knew something else as a result of his experiences with Soviet Spetsnaz battalions on Kerguelen Island and in Kurdistan.

This was a typical Soviet show of force. No commander would otherwise expose his valuable men to enemy fire as Kurotkin had done by placing his men along the tops of buildings overlooking the ramp! Curt believed that Kurotkin was bluffing.

A quick look around also told Curt that the Soviets were apparently alone in trying to contain the SPD forces on the ramp. The Chinese and Japanese troops had apparently disappeared, withdrawn until their commanders could see what would happen - if Mahathis would cave in to the Soviets, if Kurotkin and his men would get their buns shellacked by the SPD in a fire fight, or if the Soviets would back down under pressure. No matter which way it went, Qian and Mishida would come out ahead.

Curt knew what to do, and he would have done it immediately except for one factor. He remembered that Mahathis wasn't used to a high level of tactical communication with forces under his command. Therefore, the general hadn't assigned tacomm channels and codes to Curt or Castillo. He couldn't talk to Mahathis to shape a plan of action here...and Mahathis didn't seem to be taking the initiative in doing such a thing. So Curt was going to have to set it up. But first, he had to hold down the possibility of tiger error among some of the more antsy Greys.

Greys all, this is Grey Head! Hold positions! And keep your weapons stowed! You can pick targets if you want, but don't aim! Curt told his regiment. Switching tacomm frequencies to his main command freak, he went on, *Grey Chief, this is Grey Head! Sit tight! If you've got any sort of communication with the Chileans, tell them to do the same! Where the hell is Sock Head? General Mahathis?* Mahathis hadn't assigned himself a code call; Curt just gave him one in the heat of the moment and didn't give a damn whether or not Mahathis would eventually approve of it or not.

Surrounded by his Gurkhas over on the right! Joanne Wilkinson snapped back.

Warrior Leader, this is Grey Head! Curt transmitted again on the common tac freak. *I want the Marauders and the Ferrets to cover my OCV! I'm going to visit Sock Head! I want Alleycat Leader to be prepared to take out those Soviet Warbots with the Saucy Cans. If the Sovs open up on us, I want Jerry to smash 'em! Crush 'em! Pulverize 'em! If Kurotkin is stupid enough to open fire, I want him to learn a lesson damned fast: No one does that sort of thing to us without expecting and getting completely clobbered in an ultra-orgasmic fashion! But anyone who opens fire without my direct order to do so or without taking Soviet incoming first is sucking for a special court martial if we survive this sheep screw! Do you read me?*

Loud and clear, Grey Head!

He turned to Henry Kester. The regimental sergeant major was where he should be: in the aux hatch with only his helmeted head revealed. He wasn't being chicken; he was in command of the OCV, and that was his post.

Edie Sampson had dropped hack inside the OCV; she had work to do in there. First of all, she was sweeping the electromagnetic spectrum looking for the command and control channels the Soviets were using for their warbots. Secondly, that was where she was supposed to be because she was in control of the Washington Greys' communications and data links.

"Did you read that, Henry?"

"Loud and clear here, Colonel!"

"Then get this heap moving over to where Mahathis is covering his ass with Gurkhas!"

Henry didn't waste time. The OCV - code-named Phillip after the ancient King of Macedon who'd been Alexander the Great's father in keeping with Curt's desire to carry the unit name Companions over to his regimental staff - wheeled about and raced across the tarmac, dodging around two hypersonic airliners to reach the APV where Mahathis, Alzena, and Payne-Ashwell were trying to sort things out.

Curt didn't duck inside Phillip; he rode the front bonnet above the glacis plate out in the open without body armor. It was deliberate on his part. If the Soviets were going to start shooting, he wanted to give them a prominent target; he doubted they could hit him on moving vehicle before he rolled from the off-side of the OCV and into its protection. But he didn't think they'd start shooting. Kurotkin certainly wouldn't give the order, not with six hypersonic transports each worth more than three-quarters of a billion dollars sitting out there on the ramp fully exposed to fire. The Soviet Union still mined a lot of gold, but they didn't like to use it to pay for expensive aircraft their field-grade officers had destroyed in a panic.

He couldn't help but notice that Maggie MacPherson's television camera crews were still on hand with their equipment running. Kurotkin hadn't even thought to shut them down or take over their satellite dish which sat on the south side of the ramp, transmitting the video signals of this confrontation up into space and back down to where they could be sent on ordinary TV channels for the whole world to see. That was one of Curt's hole cards.

He also figured he could do a better job of bluffing than Kurotkin. The Soviet colonel might be a pretty good chess player, hut Curt had from time to time proved to fellow Greys that he was a reasonably good poker player.

Kurotkin had put himself in a very untenable and indefensible position, not for fighting but from the political point of view. Curt intended to make the maximum use of that.

"General!" he called out to Mahathis as the OCV shuddered to a halt not three meters away. "For God's sake, let's set up a tacomm procedure! Or we'll get in even deeper slime here!"

"We haven't had time to iron out those details yet, Colonel!" Mahathis snapped back. The man wasn't visibly frightened, but Curt knew he was a bit over-whelmed at the Soviet attempt to blockade the SPD on the airport. He hadn't anticipated it.

"Edie, give Twonky a code!" Curt called down to Sampson, asking her to give the Gurkha Sergeant Major Tuanku a useable tacomm frequency and hop code. "Then get someone who's close to Castillo to run a tacomm brick to him! I can't orchestrate this sheep screw without communications!"

"Colonel, a tacomm brick is classified, and Colonel Castillo is an ABC commander, not one of the good guys we share those things with!" Edie pointed out to him.

"Classified, my ass! Get one to him!" Curt fired back.

"Yessir, that's what I thought you'd say, but I had to warn you about the classified material first or my tits would be nailed to the wall! Lieutenant Milton has one on its way to Colonel Castillo even as I speak! Tell Twonky to come up on Channel Thirty, Hop Code Lima Quebec Three!"

Curt repeated this information loudly to Mahathis, then turned his attention again to the situation. "What are your orders, General?"

It was obvious that Mahathis didn't know, so he shot from the hip. "Get your Mary Anns to cover my Gurkhas and their Mary Anns on the right gate! They'll rush the assault guns, behind their warbots as cover! I want your Saucy Cans to pin down the left gate!"

"General, the Soviets expect something like that!" Curt warned. "The fifty-threes on their warbots will penetrate a Mary Ann's armor like a knife cutting hot water! And what the hell do you intend to do about the Soviet snipers on the rooftops with their automatics and light machine guns?"

"Take them out with fire!"

Mahathis had had plenty of experience in jungle fighting but apparently no urban-area combat. Snipers on rooftops could take out a lot of your own men even while you're putting Saucy Cans fire into them. The only thing that could make a dent in that sort of thing was tacair used as Curt had done in the Windhoek final rescue assault in Namibia.

"I've got a better idea, General! I've dealt with Soviet commanders before. Will you let me try something first before we start shooting?"

"What do you want to do?"

"Bluff his shorts off."

"What?"

"I intend to go eyeball to eyeball with him. I guarantee he'll blink and then we'll be on our way."

"Curt! Don't you dare do something without putting on your body armor first!" That was Alzena's comment.

"Damn, I wish I had time for that without tipping my hand!" Curt admitted. He didn't wait for the okay from Mahathis; there wasn't time to debate it or to wait while Mahathis made up his mind. "General, tell me no or stand by to move out when I get the Russkies and their warbots away from the gates!"

Mahathis hesitated. By the time he'd made up his mind, Curt had clambered back up on the front of his OCV and yelled at Kester with parallel communications in NE tacomm so the Greys would hear and do what they had to do, "Henry, move Phillip to the gate on the left, the one where I've got cover from our Saucy Cans! Take me right up until we're nose to nose with the Soviet warbots! Move this heap, man!"

As Phillip began to traverse the tarmac to the left terminal gate, Curt saw out of the corner of his eye that Alexis Morgan and Joan Ward had both put their ACVs into motion with the obvious intent of joining him.

Warrior Leader, this is Grey Head! Stay where the hell you are! Same goes for Marauder Leader! he fired off a tacomm message to them.

*The hell you say, Colonel! We're right there with you, whatever happens! Strength in numbers and all that...*Joan Ward shot back.

That's a direct order, dammit! Resume your positions! Now! Do it! Don't argue with me, dammit!

It was great to know he had that sort of leadership affection and support from his Greys, but what he intended to do required that he do it alone.

As his OCV approached the left gate blocked by the two Soviet warbots with Soviet troops standing behind and other Sov soldiers on the rooftops on two sides of him, Curt unslung his Novia and cradled it across his knees as he rode unprotected out in the open on the front of his vehicle.

He felt confident that the Soviets wouldn't open fire on him.

That didn't mean that his plan didn't have a very high pucker factor.

Phillip's sensors were good. Henry and Edie had them calibrated into a hair. The OCV stopped only a few centimeters from where the two Soviet warbots were parked in the gate.

Curt simply sat there and looked at them for a long minute.

Then he said in a loud, clear voice, "Move these tin cans out of here, Kurotkin! You've got no authority to block our entry onto Sakhalin...unless your Politburo withdrew from COPRE in the last hour or so! Which I know they didn't because our computers monitor the international news nets and our surveillance satellites snoop on the Soviet Union's telephone net!"

Colonel Viktor Pashkavitch Kurotkin suddenly stood up in the hatch of a BTR-218 armored personnel carrier. Curt expected him to do that; Kurotkin couldn't remain behind armor if his adversary had the guts to ride up to him unprotected on the front of an OCV. Kurotkin was a perfect target with his bright, electric-blue collar tabs, shoulder boards, and garrison cap band. Even the medals on the left breast of his uniform jacket glistened in the waning grey daylight of the cloud-filled skies.

"I have told you that I intend to keep you on the aerodrome, Colonel Carson! I have my orders!"

"Your orders don't say anything about detaining a COPRE Sakhalin Police Detachment, Viktor Pashkavitch!" Curt told him loudly, wishing he could speak Russian at this point.

Kurotkin laughed in derision. "How could you know that? You, a mere colonel! Only a regimental commander! Hah!" In the *Sukhoputnyye Voyska*, the ground forces of the USSR, only generals had that sort of information, not regimental commanders who were expected to do what the generals told them.

"I have better communications than you do...and you know it! Would you like to talk to the commandant of the Far Eastern Military District in Khabarovsk for instructions about what you should really be doing? It will take me less than a minute to arrange a satellite connection through one of the hot lines from Washington!"

"I know what my orders are! How could you possibly know?"

Kurotkin dodged the necessity of accepting or rejecting Curt's offer.

"Because I'm in direct communication with much better computers than you have! Comrade Viktor Pashkavitch, I know you're doing this because you hope it's the right thing, not because you've received orders from Moskva or Khabarovsk to keep us on the aerodrome! You yourself told me so at our meeting in the terminal! You're making a mistake! The whole world will know who's responsible! I see a lot of television cameras here!"

"Return to the aircraft!" Kurotkin ordered.

"No," Curt replied simply; then added, "Where are the Chinese and Japanese regiments who were here with you a few minutes ago? They're gone! So I suggest you take a look at this ramp. You're trying to stop three regiments. Not a very wise thing to attempt from a tactical military standpoint, Colonel. Or is that what they taught you at Frunze?" Curt didn't know if Kurotkin had attended the top military school in the Soviet Union; he was guessing at the same time he was stroking the man's ego and poking his paranoia.

Kurotkin might have looked, but Curt couldn't tell. Suddenly, the Soviet colonel snapped, "You have one minute to back away from the gate and begin returning your troops to the aircraft! One minute until we begin shooting!" He turned and gave an order in rapid-fire Russian to his troops. Curt didn't catch it, but he did hear the word, *"streylyaht!"* Kurotkin had ordered his troops to shoot.

Curt knew that he'd probably pushed the Soviet officer too far and too hard.

But he had to carry through this bluff.

So he raised his Novia to his shoulder and aimed. The laser rangefinder took a reading on Kurotkin's head, set the electropitcal sight to compensate for the range, and projected a red circle in the gunsight. Curt peered through the sight and centered the red circle on Kurotkin's face and aligned the aiming pips. It would take only one shot because the bullet would go exactly where he'd put the red circle.

"You want a shoot-out, Victor Pashkavitch? You've got it! But you and I will be the first of many to die as a result!"

Hell of a way to get a posthumous CMH, he thought to himself.

But he was at such an emotional high that he neglected to shielf his thought from the tacomm. It was broadcast to the Greys.

Colonel, not if we can keep it from being posthumous! Was the sudden "voice" on his tacomm helmet. *This is Deer Arrow! In the last thirty minutes, my Mustangs have maneuvered around behind the Sovs! I've got two Jeeps with me, too! These peasants are wide open from the rear!*

That was the best news Curt had heard yet on Sakhalin. Officially, he'd probably have to chew - out Lieutenant Dyani Motega for again doing what she usually did - see an opportunity and move to exploit it - but this move was probably going to get her at least a Bronze Star...if it proved to be decisive in this confrontation, which it probably was. *Roger, Deer Arrow, make yourselves known to the Soviets when I tell them about you!* he flashed to her.

Curt slowly lowered his Novia and put it across his knees. This obviously confused the Soviet colonel. "Kurotkin, the Sakhalin Police Department is already on Sakhalin! One of my units has left the aerodrome and is in your rear!" Curt announced in a loud voice while transmitting at the same time on his tacomm so the SPD could hear. "While we've been talking here, some of my troops have moved to your rear and now have you and your troops targeted from behind!"

Kurotkin suddenly looked around frantically. Then he laughed. "Oh? You do? Where?"

"I'll ask a few of them to reveal themselves." Curt then tacommed to Dyani, *Deer Arrow, have the Mustangs stand up enough to reveal where you are, but don't get the Soviets out of your sights.*

Five shapes and two Jeeps revealed themselves behind the Soviet regiment. The rapid-fire M133A 7.652-millimeter heavy machine guns on the Jeeps were aimed. So were the Mustangs' Novias.

"As I requested, Colonel, please move these assault guns and clear the road," Curt went on without hesitation in a very polite manner, co-transmitting on NE tacomm so that Mahathis, the Greys, and the

Chileans could hear. "We're moving out at once! The Greys will provide cover until the main body has passed."

An order in Russian snapped forth from Kurotkin. The Soviet troops lowered their weapons and began to move into formations along both sides of the road leading eastward away from the terminal to where it joined the main highway to Yuzhno-Sakhalinsk. The warbot assault guns suddenly backed away from the gates on both sides of the terminal. The way to Yuzhno-Sakhalinsk was now open.

"Gawdamighty, Colonel!" Henry Kester growled from the top hatch behind him. "I always tried to teach you to win without fighting if you could, which is a damn tough thing to do! Especially if the bad guys don't cooperate. But I gotta admit that performance of yours just now was worth at least a cluster on your DSC!"

"Yeah, but who's going to write it up, Henry? Sure as hell General Mahathis won't."

"But I can! A regimental sergeant major does have some perks, you know!"

Damned if he didn't, Curt suddenly realized. "To hell with the medal! Let's spend our energies cleaning up this goddamned military mess here and getting our asses off Sakhalin in one piece, Henry! Afterward, let's have a good party instead! But no vodka, understand?"

"I got some twelve-year-old scotch in a place where nobody but me can find it, Colonel..."

The lead-colored skies suddenly opened, and it began to rain - gently at first, then with an increasing downpour. It was a cold rain. The mountains on both sides of the valley had disappeared in clouds. Even the smoke-belching stacks of the power plants, paper mills, smelters, canneries, and other heavy industries of Yuzhno-Sakhalinsk to the north were gone in the haze of rain. The light of day was also beginning to fade.

Curt clambered into the OCV as Phillip moved through the gate and began to lead the way out of the airport area.

A long column of vehicles followed as the Greys, Gurkhas, and Chileans started to move out.

"Button her down, Henry," Curt told him.

"Yeah, Colonel, too bad it had to rain on your parade. But under the circumstances, I'm glad, not mad…"

Chapter Nineteen

"My God, what a hell hole!" was the explosive comment from Sergeant Major Edwina Sampson as she looked around the deserted regimental headquarters area of the Sokol casern occupied until a few years ago by the 31st Robot Infantry Regiment, the Polar Bears of the 50th Big L Division.

"You seem to fergit a place called Wadi Akhdar in Muscat." Regimental Sergeant Major Henry Kester reminded her unnecessarily of an old naval base which had once been the temporary home of the Greys for a few days. "Or what Fort Huachuca was like when we first wheeled in after it had been inactive for years..."

"Yeah, Sarge, but it didn't rain like this in Wadi Akhdar," Major Jerry Allen said, shaking the water off his cammies as he removed his helmet.

"Well, this so-called building isn't going to be much protection against this rain if the roof leaks everywhere," Major Alexis Morgan muttered, running her hand through her corn-colored curls as she looked up at the water stain on the ceiling and noted the dripping leaks at various places.

"Should have stopped at Novoaleksandrovsk," Joanne Wilkinson said with distaste, noting the rotting wooden window sashes. "It was the old Panthers' casern. I understand they left it mothballed in pretty good shape. It sure as hell looked a lot better. Why the hell did we have to give it to the Chileans tonight?"

Curt stood there looking around himself and letting the Greys bitch, moan, and snivel to get it out of their systems. It had been a long, hard, gut-busting day. They were all tired. The confrontation with the Soviets at the Yuzhno-South aerodrome hadn't helped, but everyone was relieved that no fighting had taken place thanks to Curt.

No one but Henry Kester had said anything to Curt about what he'd done by facing down the Soviets. Curt didn't expect them to. In the first place, he was the regimental commander. He'd tried to be a strong leader, and the upshot was that the Greys expected him to do such a thing. They would have done it themselves if he hadn't. In fact, Joan and Alexis had tried to join him for the face-down. And only his direct order had stopped other Greys from joining Joan and Alexis. The two women had obeyed the direct order like two cats told to do something distasteful: Just barely. If he heard anything about the eyeball-to-eyeball from his subordinates, it would occur if and when they ever got this ruin of a casern into any sort of shape to hold a stand-to.

"Because, Major Wilkinson, our colonel didn't want the Chileans to try going through a mountain pass between Novoaleksandrovsk and Kholmsk at night in the rain on a road of unknown condition," Jerry Allen explained patiently, recalling all he'd tried to learn as one of Curt's platoon leaders when the Companions was just a combat company.

"There's more to it than that, Jerry, my lad," Alexis put in. "Until we know where the Sovs, Chinese, and Japs are garrisoned, General Mahathis shouldn't split up the SPD. That's not considered to be good tactical doctrine, and it sure as hell violates the principles of war...like concentration of mass."

"Uh, Alexis, I know you have special relationship with the genera, but he doesn't seem like the kind of man who would take kindly to that sort of insubordination on the colonel's part," Jerry Allen put in, in a tentative manner.

"If the colonel doesn't tell him, I will!" Alexis snorted. "Would you look at this frayed electrical wiring! It's a wonder the place hasn't gone up in flames!"

"Probably too wet and moldy from all the rain," Joanne suggested.

Sampson started for the rear door. "I'll try to find the breakers for that circuit, and we'll see if it passes the smoke test."

"Wait for daylight, Sergeant, or a short is likely to leave us in the dark...or even burn this place down and force us to sleep in our vehicles tonight," Curt advised her; then went on, "Matter of fact, troops, I do indeed intend to bring to the general's attention the matter of proper disposition of the SPD. But not in exactly that fashion. Insubordinate I'm not, but I won't sit idly by and allow this operation to degenerate into an even bigger sheep screw." He didn't need to add that he wouldn't put up with anything that was certain in his opinion to cause real heartburn for the Greys above and beyond that which the other regiments would be expected to endure.

Major Joan Ward came into the room from a quick inspection of the casern and announced, "Well, Colonel, this place will keep most of the rain off. Hasn't got any furniture. Some buildings have been pilfered down to almost nothing. But we're used to that. At least, we have some experience with this sort of thing from the early days at Fort Huachuca."

"Situation is normal," Major Joanne Wilkinson muttered. "Nothing too good for us soldiers, and that's exactly what we get."

"Major, as the Army's most experienced combat-rated plumber," Battalion Sergeant Major Nick Gerard pointed out, also referring to the days when the Greys had moved into their present permanent post, Fort Huachuca in far-off Arizona, "I can officially report that the plumbing works, something the female side of the roster always seems to have a consuming interest in. No need to dig latrines outside tonight...and it is turning a little nippy in the rain. The casern has natural gas - I guess Sakhalin has a lot of that - so I turned it on, lit the pilots, and we'll have hot water for showers and such within an hour."

"Oh, thank you, Nick! Thank you very much!" Alexis gushed in honest gratitude. "One of the few things that makes a combat soldier's life bearable is an occasional hot shower!"

"You could use a shower yourself," Edie told Nick bluntly. "And take off your clothes when you do. Wash them separate."

Tired as he was, hyped as he was, and worried as he was, Curt couldn't help smiling to himself. He knew the Washington Greys were indeed one big family because they were acting that way again, even after coming halfway around the world that day.

"Okay, let's get settled in for the night," he told them and started reeling off a series of orders, relying on his memory. "Orders for the night: Pappy, my grizzled old adjutant, you've got the unenviable job of assigning quarters as usual. Ellie, see to it that we have some warbots programmed for casern security tonight; tomorrow I want you to find out where the Sovs, Chinese, and Japanese are garrisoned. Hensley, tacomm contact with Sink-Spud in Yuzhno is good enough for right now, but get our comm links with Huachuca and Diamond Point up tomorrow. Harriett, we can stand field rations until you get the logistics pipeline flowing, but we're going to need hots and cots ASAP; so I'll assign Regimental Master Scrounge Henry Kester to find us some furniture tomorrow while you see about hot meals. Right now, most of us are so bagged we probably don't even need air mats and sleep bags, just a place to throw our body. Edie see to it that the bots are okay in spite of the rain; they haven't gotten wet since the last monsoon thunderboomer caught us out in Huachuca boonies. Doctor Ruth, have your biotechs check the water supply; hots cots, and guard bots we need, but not trots. Did I forget anything, Joanne?"

"Rule Ten," Joanne said.

"My God, if anyone thinks they're in shape for that, I'll suspend Rule Ten!" Curt said with a resigned sigh knowing full well that combat tension also bred sexual tension. As for himself, he was just plain tired out. The weight of regimental command was far greater than he'd anticipated.

Jerry Allen grinned. "Thank you, Colonel." Adonica didn't even blush.

Lieutenant Hassan Ben Mahmud added with a smile "Colonel, may your camel always eat little and carry much!"

"And shit in someone else's mess kit! Hassan, you rake," Jerry jousted with him because the lieutenant had established quite a reputation with the ladies of the Greys, "why don't you quote one from Omar Khayyam...?"

"I don't quote anything from Khayyam in English. It loses too much in translation," Hassan pointed out. "Besides, why speak of the grape before we have the Club set up? As for the erotic parts of the Rubaiyat that Fitzgerald never translated because they were too explicit for Victorian England, none of us needs that tonight-"

"I move the adjournment of the Sierra Charlie Chapter of Mensa," Alexis cut in.

"Pappy, show me to a room, sir," Curt muttered, dead on his feet.

The room was large and bare to the walls, but it was dry and had no leaks. A single bare sixty-watt light bulb hung from the ceiling. Edie brought in his sleep sack and air mat from the OCV. Curt pulled the D-ring, inflated the mat, rolled out the sack, took off his helmet, but didn't bother to remove his boots or cammies. He reached up, unscrewed the light bulb - he didn't trust the almost-broken old light switch on the wall - and stretched out in utter exhaustion.

He didn't know how long it was before he started dreaming that a 53-millimeter cannon on one of the enigmatic new Soviet warbots was firing at him as he sat on the front of his OCV. *Rap-rap-rap!* Pause. *Rap-rap-rap!* For some unknown reason, he was invincible. The shells came out of the cannon, stopped in midair about a meter in front of his face, and just hung there. He had the impression that Kurotkin was somewhere behind those warbots saying something about retreating at once or he'd let the shells come the rest of the way to smash Curt's face.

Then a voice came to him. It sounded like the voice of his father, long dead, reaching out to him over the years. "Colonel? Open up!"

The sound of the three-bursts from a 53-millimeter cannon because knocks on a door.

Curt glanced at his glowing watch face.

2330 hours local time.

Who the hell? He thought groggily. Better be good, and the reasoning had better be damned solid, or Curt was going to bust a non-com or chew-ass an officer. He clambered to his feet and found the door.

The hallway beyond was also lit by a wan sixty-watt bulb.

Curt saw General Ahmad Mahathis and the Sultana Alzena standing there.

It wasn't necessary to be formal. They were officially family. "Ahmad, whatever it is, can it wait until morning?" Curt muttered. "I haven't had any sleep in over twenty-four hours...until you woke me."

"It's only eleven-thirty local time," Mahathis pointed out.

"And oh-five-dark-thirty where I was yesterday at this time," Curt reminded him.

"Ahmad, let's let him get some rest. We forgot the time differential," Alzena reminded her twin brother.

"It can't wait," Mahathis insisted. "And you know it! You were the one who talked me into driving all the way up to Sokol in this miserable freezing rain!"

"Oh, hell, come on in!" Curt grumbled, opening the door widely so that the hall light shone through. He stepped back, reached up, and screwed in the light bulb to give his room some illumination. "I was going to come down and talk with you tomorrow morning anyway, Ahmad! So what's a night's sleep among friends? Shut the door, please, since both of you seem to want a private palaver. Sorry I haven't got any chairs. You assigned us to an unfurnished casern, Ahmad. Three hundred rooms, unfinished, hot water and utilities, no view - which doesn't matter anyway because there isn't that much to see around here. Alzena, it may be more comfortable for you to sit on my air mat, Ahmad, you and I are combat soldiers; we can damned well sit on the floor." Curt rambled a little as he tried to get his mind back in gear.

Curt sank to the floor and sat there cross-legged. Mahathis did the same. Alzena flowed gracefully down onto the air mat.

"Curt, I need to thank you-" Mahathis began.

"And apologize to him, Ahmad," Alzena reminded him.

"Yes, and apologize," Mahathis added.

"What the hell for?" Curt asked, although he knew. It would have blown away Mahathis' image to make a public apology, Curt realized.

"My behavior this afternoon." It was obvious that Mahathis wasn't used to making apologies.

"Ahmad, my brother, we forged a contract between us a couple of years ago in the jungles of Brunei," Curt reminded him. "I was just carrying out my part of that."

"And I forgot and I didn't. You and I haven't been in action together since then. Lots of things have happened. I hope you'll forgive my oversight."

"Look, everyone survived. No one got hurt. Maybe Kurotkin got his knickers ripped, but he damned well deserved it!" Curt growled. "Damned Russkies are paranoid power-lovers! They get awfully tiresome when they think they've got the upper hand! If they'd ever get over their massive inferiority complex, the world might be an easier place to live in...and I might be out of a job. So your apology is accepted, and whatever we say here is a family matter that won't go beyond the walls of this room. Anything else?"

"Yes," Mahathis insisted. "I want to make sure our agreement still holds."

"Huh? Oh, you mean that you got the glory of command and achievement while I do the planning, organizing, and leading? That what you mean?"

"Yes."

Curt shrugged, "I operated under a similar contract with Colonel Bellamack. He did the management; I did the leading. I'm used to it. You need the glory and the image and the reputation because you're going to be the sultan someday. As for me, I'm doing my job and I get paid for it. Don't get me wrong; I like it or I wouldn't do it at all. So I've got no heartburn with our old arrangement except for one thing..."

"What's that?"

"You've got to live up to your part of the contract, Ahmad."

"What do you mean?"

"You know what I mean! If you don't, let me draw you a picture," Curt told him in frank tones. He wasn't afraid of the fact that this man was now a general officer; he'd known Mahathis as a colonel. The general officer's rank was undoubtedly bestowed upon Mahathis as the scion of the sultan so that he could properly command the SPD. Curt was far more respectful of a *real* general like Belinda Gettrick. "You're the front man and I'm the willing action stooge."

"You're more than that!" Alzena insisted.

"Maybe, but that sums it up from my point of view."

"So, what should I be doing that I'm not doing?" Mahathis wanted to know. The man was obviously searching in a rather desperate fashion for a way to overcome what he personally knew to be his short-comings. In Curt, he had once found a man who accepted him as he was, not as the son of the richest man in the world, not as the next political and religious leader of his small but powerful nation, not as the spoiled brat he'd become because he'd had to answer only to his father, who apparently doted upon him.

"You've got to realize that you haven't got all the answers. Hell, you don't have most of them. Or you sure as hell didn't today!" Curt reminded him bluntly. "Which means that you've got to be able to back down and consult with your staff instead of trying to blast your way through and snatch defeat from the jaws of victory. The Aerospace Force Academy apparently tried to teach leadership principles to you. Why it didn't take, I don't know and I don't care."

"I got a good military education at Colorado Springs!"

"You got an Aerospace Force education," Curt corrected him. "An Aerospace Force officer is a systems manager because the Aerospace Force has slowly turned into a high-tech fighting force where it's machine against machine and may the best systems manager win. The Army was trending that way before we got our clock cleaned by a bunch of Islamic fanatics in Zahedan and our warbots couldn't hack it against large numbers of insurgent troops armed with assault rifles. I've had to learn basic military principles from the ground up because that's where I fight - on the ground against people, not in the air against machines."

"Okay, Curt, I'll do my best, and I'll expect you to kick my ass across the room when I get out of line again," Mahathis promised.

"No, Ahmad, I'll do that only in private because of our contract. Then I'll kick the shit out of you!" Curt corrected him. "In public, I'll give you the usual signals from a concerned subordinate. If you don't know them, here are a few of them. I'll suggest. I'll recommend. I'll draw things to your attention. When I do that, I'll expect you to remember the contract and break off for 'consultation with your staff.' Which we do in private, just between us boys. By the way, it will make you look like a much better commander if you do that."

Mahathis put out his hand. "Deal!"

Curt took the man's hand and shook it. It was firm in his grip. "Deal! Don't forget."

"Kick my minus-x if I do." Mahathis really respected Curt to say something like that to him.

"All the way across the room. Count on it." It was a friendship. It was more than a friendship. Or a contract. These men were officially brothers because they were officially brothers because Curt wore the colorful ribbon of the Sultan's Star of Brunei.

Alzena moved over and put her two small hands atop theirs. "Sealed," she asserted.

"Alzena, nobody here but just us folks," Curt said to her. "However, my dearly beloved 'sister,' I suspect you had a hand in this."

"In a sisterly fashion only."

"Yes, I'm sure. I know your sisterly ways," Curt reminded her. He knew damned good and well that she'd raised hell with Mahathis after the airport confrontation. That's why she was here with them:

to see that her brother did what was necessary.

If it was more than that, Curt knew it was beyond his physical abilities that night.

"We need to have a planning session," Mahathis went on, getting back to the business that had brought them to Sakhalin.

"Yeah! First thing in the morning. I'll come down to Yuzhno."

"What's wrong with right now?"

Curt sighed with utter weariness. "Because I was taught not to try to make plans when I'm half asleep. Because I won't make any but absolutely necessary decision in this condition, especially when the lives of my friends and colleagues could depend on being right or wrong. So why don't you scoot back to Yuzhno and I'll see you in the morning?"

"It's late, and I don't want to drive it," Mahathis explained. "Can you get us a couple of rooms plus air mats and sleep bags?"

"Sure. We've got extra," Curt told him.

Half an hour later, Curt unscrewed the light bulb, then stretched out on his air mat surrounded by the lingering haunting fragrance of Alzena. He kept drifting off, then suddenly awakening with a start.

The door opened quietly, letting in a column of light from the hall, then was closed again with equal silence.

She knelt beside him. "I can't sleep."

"Neither can I."

"I have something for tired heroes."

"I'm sure you do, my love, but-"

She quietly took off his cammy shirt. "Roll over," she told him. Then with practiced, expert hands, she did things to his shoulders and back and legs. She was good. She knew exactly what to do and how to do it.

Soon, he wasn't quite so tired any longer, and he was still wide awake. So was she. The tension of the day was still with them. Both of them knew what to do then, and they did it with tender, loving care for one another.

"I'm glad you're not my real brother," she told him affectionately in a sleepy voice.

Chapter Twenty

When Curt Carson awoke at 0630 because of the drab predawn light filtering in through the dirty glass of the room's single window, Alzena was sound asleep on the air mattress behind him. She looked so exquisitely lovely with her captivating Eurasian features in total, relaxed composure that he didn't have the heart to wake her. How could he wake the delicate, enchanting fairylike princess who shared all, relaxed him, and permitted the fear, frustration, and anxiety to evaporate, especially when she'd been brave and as frightened as he at Yuzhno-South? He looked at her sensuous from and features for a minute in the dim light, relishing her physical loveliness. If she was indeed the work of Allah, then perhaps there was a God who was good and merciful and great after all. Maybe the world was really worth saving. But why would a God capable of such sublime handiwork also create a hellhole like Sakhalin and people only a devil might be proud of? He didn't know, but he was glad the world contained Alzena. She was one of those whose happiness and safety made a warrior's work worthwhile.

Without disturbing her, he arose, pulled on his cammy coveralls, and left the room. A quick recce down the hallway revealed two latrines with washbasins, commodes, and showers - common personal hygiene rooms called "sinks" in West Point terminology. Someone had already affixed signs to the separate doors indicating the only gender differentiation remaining in the twenty-first century American Army. Out on the farms and in the factories and slums, no such discrimination had ever existed. The Army retained it in spite of its leadership in social progress. Curt had never questioned it. He'd always understood that women never ready wanted to share all their little secrets with men.

Steaming hot water seemed to be plentiful. Some of the men were already there, shaving and showering. Curt had concentrated last night on making sure the Greys had a dry, warm place to sleep, so he'd left his personal pack in his OCV. The regimental chaplain, Captain Nelson Crile, loaned Curt the towel, soap, and razor from a spare personal pack.

As he left the latrine, Dyani was leaving the other one.

"Good morning, Lieutenant!"

"Good morning, Colonel!"

"Will you join me for breakfast?"

"Only if you don't just serve it, Colonel. I have a catalytic stove-heater. It can make field rations a little more palatable. May a lieutenant invite a colonel to breakfast in quarters?"

"I'll review the regs later…in a couple of months or so. But I don't recall any that would prohibit extending such a gracious invitation," he told her with mock politeness. "Therefore, I accept with pleasure and gratitude."

"Come. I have your personal pack in my room. Henry discovered it in your OCV. I told him I'd give it to you. I tried to return it last night."

Curt wasn't exactly sure how he was going to handle this. It had almost been easier for him to face-down the Soviets yesterday.

But once in her room, she closed the door behind them and said, "Good morning, Kida!" And she greeted him with a great deal more warmth and affection than she'd exhibited in the hallway. "You look much better this morning."

"You look pretty good yourself, Deer Arrow," he told her without hesitation because she did look good to him. She was a totally different person than Alzena. "You didn't have to bring my personal pack to me. I'm perfectly capable of getting it myself."

She picked it up and handed it to him. "It's raining outside. I knew you'd want it."

"You aren't my servant. And I don't rate an aide-de-camp in a Sierra Charlie regiment," he reminded her, thankful that she'd spared him a trek through the cold rain and gooey, slushy mud outside. He rolled out a fresh set of field cammies and retrieved his blue Sierra Charlie tam from the pack.

Her simple reply was "I wanted to. I'm not the sultana. But I'm better."

He'd gotten to know her subtle, under-stated signals. "Deer Arrow, do you have a jealous bone in your body?" he asked as he pulled on fresh, dry, clean cammies. He wished he'd had a garrison uniform along in view of the fact that he wanted to meet with the Soviets, Chinese, and Japanese today while dressed in other than combat clothing.

"I don't have any spiteful ones," Dyani stated. She got out two MRE field rations breakfast packs and began to open and prepare them on the little catalytic stove-heater.

"Does that mean you're not possessive?" he didn't feel guilty; she wasn't going to let him. But she was being very talkative that morning. Curt wanted to draw her out a bit. He wanted his understanding of this unusual young woman to grow.

A brief twinkle came into her dark eyes. "All real women want real men, Kida. But I don't own you emotionally. You're not a possession. But I made a commitment to myself. If I lose too much of you to another woman. I'll ask myself why. And I'll change myself to change that, Kida.

Curt shoot his head in bewilderment. Of all the women he'd known from a wide variety of cultures around the world, Dyani Motega was totally different. She was therefore an enigma to him. "You know I enjoy the company of other women. Doesn't that bother you?"

She passed a juice pack to him. "No, Kida. That makes you what you are. If you're dear to others, you aren't a cast-off. So I don't worry about you and other women. I intend to make my company the most enjoyable of all." Dyani had him pegged pretty well. In some ways, that was a little scary to Curt. What she was telling him in her open manner amounted to pillow talk for her. Except she never engaged in pillow talk.

Then she suddenly became a little coy and told him, "I have an advantage over the sultana and Colonel Lovell. I have more opportunities."

"You're not worried about the ladies of the Greys?" Curt wondered playfully as he began to eat the hot sausage and eggs out of the dish she handed over to him.

She tossed his question right back at him. "How about me and the gentlemen of the Greys? Hassan is certainly a fine young man. Full of smooth fire with dark and flashing eyes! Or Dale Brown? Or Russ Frazier?"

He had to think about that for a moment. "All of the ladies of the Greys are so special to me that I'd gladly do anything for or with any of them for any reason they wanted and with no regrets. Kitsy Clinton played the field, yet we're very close. Alexis and I go way back together, I have a totally different relationship with Joan Ward," Curt reminded her. He suddenly understood that part of her, and it made sense to him and for him. "You're Deer Arrow to me. So, it doesn't make any difference what you do as long as I'm Kida to you. Being in a combat outfit, we may be smart to have a lot of intimate friends and one who's first among equals. That's why I worry about Jerry Allen and Adonica."

"Yes. We're all warriors. We must keep our affairs properly balanced," she replied simply, conveying the answers to many questions in one phrase that was classic Dyani. "Have some hot tea. This is a wretched climate. We'll need all the warm things we can get!"

"I suspect Payne-Ashwell will have the teapot on when we get into our planning session today," he remarked, taking the hot cup and not missing her usual multifaceted meaning. "This climate's worse than England's."

Dyani didn't question him about the planning meeting. That was a military matter. She knew Colonel Carson would inform Lieutenant Motega and the other personnel as soon as he knew. Furthermore, she also knew that Curt ran the Greys the way that Hetterick and Bellamack had: by soliciting any and all inputs from them because they harbored valuable man-years of experience and also had the ability to see potential problems and unique solutions based on those experiences. It was also an outstanding training exercise for everyone. It took a while for a newcomer to become comfortable in that sort of command environment. But, once a person began to feel warm and fuzzy about it, their personal contributions added to the wealth of military data.

Instead, she said, "Our situation doesn't make it any better. A position between three adversaries is never a comfortable one."

"Only if they can be outflanked to the rear," Curt said. "And because I haven't seen you since we got off the airport yesterday, what you did with your Mustangs was orgasmic! You need a few more ribbons on your tunic to go alongside your DSC. When we get shaken down here, I'm going to recommend you for the Silver Star. The Bronze Star at least."

Finished with her breakfast, she began to gather up the empty disposable containers. "I did what I knew would work. The Soviets are obsessed with the offensive. They never fought wars like ours on the Great Plains. They don't know Indian tactics. They don't want minus-x. What the Mustangs did at Yuzhno-South was right out of the history books."

"Well, it might have been old hat to you, but you did it without being ordered to do so," Curt reminded her. "Other commanders might chew your ass for not telling them what you were up to. But I know you didn't want to break stealth, and you've never been known to lack initiative. So, you get a hero medal, not an ass-chew."

"Just watch your minus-x," she told him.

That might have been a Dyani double entendre since they were both officially off-duty at the moment with Rule Ten in abeyance, but Curt didn't get the chance to follow up because someone knocked on the door.

It was Major Joan Ward, and she was wearing the OOD brassard. She didn't bat an eye that Curt was with Dyani. "Excuse me, Colonel, you weren't in your room, and I thought I might find you here. General Hettrick's on the screen in your OCV and wants to talk to you."

He got to his feet and put on his blue tam. "Roger, Joan! Thank you! And thanks for breakfast, Dyani. Duty calls!"

Little change had occurred in the regimental headquarters since last night, but Edie Sampson, the rest of his staff, and SERVBATT were busy moving in equipment. Henry Kester was nowhere to be seen; Curt knew he was out scrounging furniture and other fixtures.

It wasn't just raining outside this morning. The rain was mixed with sleet and freezing rain. The ragged clouds were down over the mountains to the east and west. This late in the year, Curt knew that it was only a matter of weeks before winter set in and the island became almost ice-locked. In spite of the precip, Curt could smell the air pollution from the belching stacks of the factories, mills, and smelters that crowded this narrow north-south valley in the southern portion of Sakhalin.

He slipped and slid his way to his OCV, noticing that Ahmad's command vehicle with its Brunei markings was still parked outside the headquarters building. Curt made a mental note to suggest that Ahmad remove the insignia marking the command van headquarters of the sultan of Brunei's son. Sometimes it didn't pay to advertise...

Major Hensley Atkinson, S-3 ops, came out of the OCV as Curt arrived. "Good morning, Colonel!" she said in an attempt to be bright and on the bounce. It was a valiant effort because Curt could still see the fatigue on her face and the glazed look of too little sleep in her eyes. The enfolding weariness of too much work and not enough sleep wasn't helped by the wretched, cold, damp, gloomy weather. "I've got the updates on the Warhawks. Worsham is bitching and foul-mouthed as usual, so everything's going according to plan. The Chileans have agreed to remain in Novoaleksandrovsk until the general solidifies the operational plan. And we'll be ready to secure the Sokol aerodrome for the Warhawk arrival whenever you give the word."

"Thanks, Hensley. Anything you need?"

"Yes, sir. A hot shower. Some dry clothes." She thought about that for a moment, then added, "And about two days' sleep."

"Get your personal pack, duck out of this freezing rain, have a shower and shampoo, and climb into something reg and dry. You'll feel better after you do. And the world will wait while a lady prepares for her day," Curt told her. "So, do it! That's an order."

"Thank you, Colonel!" She was having trouble maintaining formal protocol. It was difficult for many of the Greys to address Curt by rote formality as their regimental commander; he'd been one of them for a long time. So, formality was used only to denote respect.

Inside the OCV, the main ops compartment was warm and dry. The size of a small bus, the armored shell of the M660B held Grady, the regimental computer, and all the necessary C-cubed-I equipment Curt and his staff needed to fight the Washington Greys as well as stay in touch with the 17th Iron Fist Division and the Georgie megacomputer complex in Arizona...which was where Curt wished he was at the moment. The weather was sure a whole hell of a lot better there.

The comm screen was in stand-by, so Curt activated it with a pass of his hand over the switch/control panel. The red light beside the uplink video camera lens came on, indicating that he was transmitting. The video screen burst into life and color.

Major General Belinda Hettrick's image came into view. She was seated at the terminal desk in her office. Curt could see the wonderful blue sky of an Arizona afternoon through the window behind her. "Battleaxe, this is Grey Head on the line and standing by," he spoke so the mike could hear his call-up.

Hettrick finally looked up from a terminal keypad on her right and faced her own pickup. She didn't appear to be very happy. "Good morning, Colonel!" she told him, signaling that this wasn't a formal protocol teleconference. "Getting settled in?"

"Yes, ma'am. But this is a hellhole."

"We rarely get sent out to the garden spots of the world," she reminded him. "This teleconference isn't scrambled, but it doesn't need to be. The Sovs already know what I'm going to tell you. I have a gee-two heads-up to pass along. The Soviets have introduced warbots to Sakhalin, the first time we've seen them. Hell, it's typically the Soviet way of introducing new military equipment. This is the first time we've even had an inkling about what they've been doing!"

"Yes, General, I know about their assault gun warbots. They're Sov versions of the Hairy Foxes," Curt reported. "I confronted two of them yesterday afternoon at Yuzhno-South aerodrome."

"That I know, too. Colonel, it's been all over the goddamned TV here!" Hettrick complained bitterly. "I know I didn't tell you to give me real-time reports, but it's embarrassing as hell to get my reports by way of Maggie MacPherson's on-the-spot video coverage!"

No wonder Hettrick was pissed, Curt thought. That was one of the problems with modern instant worldwide communications, something the Army never really got used to because its procurement regulations kept it continually at least two technical generations behind commercial users. Furthermore, the commercial stuff always seemed to work, probably because a lot of money rode on the fact that it had to do so under widely varied industrial conditions with wide environmental factors. This meant sloppy tolerances, long life to allow it to be expensed out over a multi-year capital depreciation period that would make the banks and financiers happy, and de-rated performance. On the other hand, military equipment wasn't developed under cost restraints because it didn't have to show a profit. So, it had very tight specs and almost impossible performance requirements that pushed the state of the art…but not the state of technology.

"Well, thank God she was there with those cameras rolling, General," he told her. "She was one of my hole cards. I was counting on the fact that the Soviets and Chinese - and especially the Japanese – wouldn't start any shooting with the world looking over their shoulders and therefore knowing exactly who started what at the moment it happened."

"Frankly, Colonel, I was greatly disappointed in your performance at the Yuzhno-South aerodrome yesterday afternoon," Hettrick said suddenly, and it was apparent from her facial expression as well as her tone of voice that she wasn't joking with Curt.

That statement surprised Curt. So, he asked, "Pardon me, General?"

"You're not running a combat company any longer, Colonel," Hettrick went on in explanation.

"Yes, ma'am, I know that."

"You may think you know it, but what you did sure as hell shows that you don't understand it!" she snapped. "Do you remember the exploits of Marshal Achille Bazaine?"

Curt realized that he was getting a mild ass-chewing from Hettrick. Furthermore, she was doing it in her PMS&T - Professor of Military Science and Tactics - persona and using the ancient Socratic method of teaching: Ask leading questions. Curt remembered who Bazaine was from his studies at West Point. "Yes, ma'am."

"Tell me what he did."

"At the Battle of Vionville during the Franco-Prussian War, he left his post leading his army, rallied the troops on the line and led an infantry battalion into action."

"And what didn't he do?"

"He didn't tell his staff where he went. So, his leaderless army went down to defeat. He got twenty-three years in prison, not for lack of courage, but because he abandoned his post in the face of the enemy," Curt recalled.

"Okay, you get a four-oh on that! Now, why the hell didn't you pay attention to what you'd learned?"

"General, are you chewing me out because I put myself out in front of my troops yesterday?"

"Yes! I know you've got guts; I've seen you do similar things before! But that's when you were commanding a company! You're a regimental commander now!"

"Excuse me, General, but General Heinz Guderian had his mobile

HQ right on the front line with his Panzers. He won the Battle of France in nineteen-forty."

"And the Germans lost the war."

"Certainly not because of Guderian's leadership style. General, you've seen only news media coverage of what happened," Curt told her quietly. "I haven't given you a report yet. Hell, there hasn't been time!"

"Care to set me straight, then?"

"Yes, ma'am!" He told her what had happened from his point of view, then added, "I welcome a critique, General. As I saw the situation, Sink-Spud was surprised on the ramp by the Sovs and had no plan of action. And couldn't come up with one. I'd just met Kurotkin, and I've dealt with Soviet colonels twice before. I knew I was covered by my own people as well as by the news media. It wasn't a matter of being a hero; it was a matter of facing down a possible adversary by playing a game at which he wasn't adept. Allow me to ask a question, please. When the Soviets were confronted during the Cuban Missile Crisis, what worked for Kennedy? I took him as my guide sergeant in this maneuver. And it worked for me as it did for him. Should I have done something differently, or not done anything at all?"

"I'll buy your explanation. But your ploy might not have worked without Lieutenant Motega," Hettrick pointed out.

Curt shrugged. "That can be debated just as earnestly as whether or not McDowell would have won First Manassas if Jackson hadn't arrived in time from the Shenandoah Valley: You were quite correct in giving Motega a direct appointment, General! What she did was in the best tradition of the courage and initiative of the Washington Greys!"

"I agree! She deserves a decoration for that!"

"I'm putting her in for the Silver Star as soon as I can draft the recommendation and citation."

"You'll have better luck with the Bronze Star and a sure shot at the

Soldier's Medal," Hettrick suggested. "No actual combat was involved, and the Soviets aren't considered to be an actual enemy of the United States."

"Shit!" Curt muttered under his breath.

But Hettrick heard it nonetheless. "The rules, Colonel, the rules! We must follow the rules! Otherwise, we'll end up looking like African generals with chests full of pretty medals that don't mean diddly squat! But we'll push the rules a little bit for Motega if we have to. Other than increasing pay and promoting, the best thing we can do to recognize a soldier who's shown outstanding performance is to pin on a medal. So, you take care of Motega..."

Curt grinned. "I think it may be the other way around."

"Oh? I suspected as much! But that may be your problem, and it had better not become *mine!*" the division commander warned him unnecessarily. "In the meantime, you might want to get to know Maggie MacPherson better. It never hurts to co-opt the news media rather than confront them. Len Spencer began behaving himself in Namibia once we had a little chat, and we got excellent coverage as a result."

"I don't think I'll have any trouble doing that, General."

"I'm sure. But I'm certain you're aware that she didn't get where she is solely on the basis of her expertise in reportage. She's gotten people in trouble for revealing sensitive information as a result of her horizontal interviews."

Curt replied carefully, "I'll be sure to conduct a little recce before I commit the main body."

"A wise approach, Colonel. Now, what are your intentions, sir? I suspect you'll be meeting with Sink-Spud soon to impress them with your tactical expertise and keep this fracas from becoming deadly?"

"That General is the next order of business, but I got a leg up on it last night. General Mahathis and I will get along famously, I assure you. After all, we're officially step-brothers."

"I'd forgotten that. Very well, just don't engage in any of that sibling rivalry crap or fratricide."

"General, this operation already has a high pucker factor!" Curt told her. "The Washington Greys are caught between three dangerous outfits who don't like each other, much less us. And we've got some questionable allies...with the exception of the Gurkhas. I don't like the idea of being called in to settle someone else's argument with force of arms if necessary. It's dangerous as all hell!"

General Belinda Hettrick smiled. "Yes, Curt, but don't forget: It's all a matter of bluff. Really!"

"Unless Kurotkin or Qian calls my hand," was Curt's somber evaluation.

But he'd missed the third party who could cause him trouble.

Chapter Twenty-One

"Our mission of Sakhalin is to stop a war from starting! This doesn't mean we won't shoot or suffer casualties. Our first task is to keep the Soviets, Chinese, and Japanese regiments apart so they can't start shooting at each other or harassing each other's personnel. Our next task is to keep them from sabotaging our efforts here. Then we will provide support for the reorganization of civil authority in such a way that some measure of peace can return to Sakhalin. That is my estimate of the situation and an abstract of the orders I was given by COPRE."

If General Sultan Ahmad Mahathis sounded like a stiff and pedantic version of Colonel Curt Carson, it should have been no surprise.

Curt had spent almost two hours with the CINCSPD. He'd carefully gone over the situation with Mahathis, coaching him on what contract teamwork was all about. Only his twin sister had been present at Curt's discrete request to make sure that her brother behaved himself. Curt need not have worried because Mahathis might have been an imperious royal snob, but he wasn't stupid. The sultan's scion knew he was in over his head, and he was perfectly willing to work privately with Curt under the terms of their contract: Mahathis got the glory but Carson got to lead. It suited the temperaments of both men.

This initial conference was "commanders only," restricted to CINCSPD and its three regimental commanders plus the SPD deputy for Civil Affairs, the sultana.

"We will function as a multi-national brigade, not as a joint command," Mahathis went on. "We will not split the SPD into widely separated caserns where they might be individually assaulted or harassed. We will be garrisoned here in the Yuzhno valley astride the main north-south road and railway. The Brunei Gurkhas will be based here in Yuzhno-Sakhalinsk. The American Washington Greys will remain at Sokol. The Chilean regiment will garrison at Dachnoye. This will put all three regiments in an area about sixty kilometers long with excellent ground transportation and access to two aerodromes - Yuzhno-South and Sokol."

Curt had prevailed in contention that Mahathis should not split up the brigade but should keep it in the center of action, in "Happy Valley." He'd reminded Mahathis of the principles of war they'd both studied at their respective service academies. He stressed the importance of the principle of mass as well as that of command. Spreading out the brigade would only cause communication and coordination problems as Curt knew from his own experience, some of it in Mahathis' own backyard in Brunei.

Mahathis wasn't used to having a staff and had brought none along. So later a CINCSPD staff would have to be patched together from the individual regimental staffs to iron out the details. But Curt had worked out a lash-up procedure with him, and Mahathis tackled this chore next.

"I have no staff, so I will create one. I'm hereby appointing Colonel Carson of the American Washington Greys as my second-in-command, chief of staff, and operations officer. This is a difficult set of jobs, Colonel Carson, but I've worked with you before and have confidence that you can do it. I anticipate you'll build your operations staff as needed with personnel acquired with consent from other regimental commanders," Mahathis announced, looking around the table at the other colonels. He knew this might cause Colonel Payne-Ashwell some heartburn, but Curt had advised him of an acceptable way to massage the Gurkha commander's ego.

"I'll do my best, General," was Curt's answer, although he already knew the assignment was coming and had made some plans of his own about how to carry out the tasks he'd just been assigned.

Mahathis went on carefully, consulting the notes he'd taken during his meeting with Curt, "Colonel Payne-Ashwell, you will serve as chief of air staff in addition to commanding the Gurkhas. You may build your staff by borrowing cognizant air personnel from the three regiments on a contingency basis and with the approval of the regimental commanders. We will have air support. The Air

Battalion of the Washington Greys will arrive tomorrow and be based at Sokol to provide both tacair support and tactical airlift. The Royal Brunei Air command's Cloud Leopard tacair squadron and the Snake Eagle airlift squadron will also arrive tomorrow and be based at Yuzhno-South. We shall also have logair service into Yuzhno-South from Air Khmer and Tao Cargo, both owned by Brunei. Just make sure we have whatever air support we want when we need it. Any problems?"

"Not at all, General, as I fully expect to have the total cooperation of my colleagues. I shall be inquiring as to their recommendations concerning which of their personnel will be available for these staff duties," Payne-Ashwell came back in his clipped British accent.

Curt expected that Payne-Ashwell and Major Cal Worsham might have some initial confrontations. But, since he knew both men, he had no doubts that the couth, stuffily mannered, British-educated Payne-Ashwell was certainly more than a match for the egotistical, maniacal, and mercurial AIRBATT commander. Payne-Ashwell had his own large ego and was a master at the verbal riposte. As a former British SAS officer and member of His Majesty's Royal Welch Guards, the Gurkhas' commander was no military pansy. Curt knew that the only way Cal Worsham would learn that was the hard way.

"Very well!" Mahathis said, then turned to the third and most enigmatic regimental commander, the only one in the group that hadn't worked with the others thus far. "Colonel Castillo, I wish to place you in charge of the SPD's tactical communications and intelligence activities."

That had been a tough assignment for Curt to agree with, but someone had to be CINCSPD G-2. Curt was concerned about protecting the security of Ellie Aart's birdbots and the classified equipment used to program the frequency skip program of the tacomm units. Curt relented only when Mahathis reminded him that the Gurkhas now had tacomms and that the NE linkage technology of the birdbot platoon could be protected by keeping actual command of that unit under Majoe Ellie Aarts. Curt then realized the assignment of Castillo as G-2 might also give the

Americans a look at what the ABC Allianza had in the way of C-cubed-I equipment and procedures.

Colonel Julio Castillo Pinedo knew that, too. He wanted to get a look at American technology, but he was also bound by his own national security laws. He spoke excellent American English as a result of being a foreign honor legacy graduate of the Citadel in South Carolina where he had been cadet batt commander. "Sir, I know little about current American C-cubed-I. I don't consider myself qualified, sir."

Mahathis merely looked at him. "Colonel, you are a field-grade officer of the Chilean army, are you not?"

"I am sir!"

"I would therefore expect that you've had additional military training including education relating to the duties of a staff officer. Mahathis hadn't, of course, because the sultan of Brunei didn't require it of him. What Mahathis knew about staff work came only from his education at the Aerospace Force Academy. But this didn't exempt him from expecting it from other field-grade officers.

"Sir, my country does not have a staff school. Our company commanders who are expected to become field-grade officers now attend staff school in Belen, Brazil; but I have not had the opportunity to attend, and I have served only as a regimental staff officer."

"Then I'm certain that you know what's involved with staff work," Mahathis responded easily. "The assignment is additional duty, of course, but I do need someone I can turn to regarding communications and intelligence. This is a joint military operation, Colonel, in which we are all cooperating, and no country need reveal any classified information. But we certainly can't expect to do a first-class job on Sakhalin unless we have good C-cubed-I, and that will be your responsibility. You will be free to get assistance from the other two regimental commanders and to request the services of their cognizant personnel."

With that sort of deal, it was obvious that Castillo couldn't refuse without damaging his own *dignidad de hombre*, something far stronger than any laws or military regulations insofar as he was concerned. He'd just have to be extra careful regarding Chilean classified material, but he realized that the two other colonels would be just as concerned for their own.

"Very well, sir. I'll do what I can," Castillo replied, although he really wasn't very enthusiastic about any of it, especially about being on Sakhalin when he'd been looking forward to spending a nice, comfortable summer in Chile. His regiment was well armed and well disciplined, but the 3rd Chilean Airborne personnel were considered to be elite troops. As such, they were privileged. In Chile, they got the first new rifles and other equipment. They rated special privileges when it came to off-base housing near Santiago. Even the enlisted men had perks when it came to store discounts, the ability to go places and do things other soldiers couldn't, and the payment of greatly reduced taxes on personal autos and other goodies of civilian life. All they had to do was show up at muster daily or, at times, weekly. Every once in a while, they had to march or ride their airborne vehicles through Santiago as part of a holiday parade or festival. Occasionally, they'd have to jump out of IA-90 *Avanzar* transports in a military display to impress visiting Brazilians or Argentines. It was a good life, and the 3rd Airborne of Chile was a lazy outfit. When they'd been assigned to the SPD on Sakhalin, a mission in which they really didn't want to participate, the officers hadn't had enough time to properly pull strings with politicians who'd taken occasional bites of *mordida* from them for special privileges.

Chile was one of the most laid-back of the ABC Alhanza nations. It was also the smallest of the three and the least influential. The only thing it really had going for it was the fact that German *Bundeswehr* sent drill instructors and other military advisors annually under contract to train the Chilean Army in the latest techniques. The German military influence was apparent in the Chilean uniforms and the super-perfect, oppressive, militarily correct protocol...but little else. The greatly out-numbered Chilean Army had greased the skids of the Peruvian and Bolivian armies simultaneously, and some of the troops were hardy enough to garrison several

216

strategically important posts in Tierra del Fuego. But otherwise, Chile was the weak military link in the ABC Allianza.

"Good! Now," Mahathis went on, checking his notepad to make sure he didn't miss anything that Curt had told him would be necessary for a commander's Papa briefing, "intelligence reports indicate that the northern part of the island is reasonably quiet and stable. All the troubles have occurred here in the south where the Soviets, Chinese, and Japanese regiments are stationed. So, we will concentrate our limited resources here."

"Our first task is to find out where the three regiments are located and where they're patrolling. We can then set up the SPDs patrol and recce operations. Once that is accomplished, I'll call a conference at which I'll inform the Soviets, Chinese, and Japanese that our SPD patrols will operate between theirs so that no contact ensues that could escalate. Do any of you have any comments about this general plan?"

Curt did. There were some things about it that were the wild pipe dreams of Mahathis, who obviously didn't know squat about international affairs. But neither Curt nor Alzena could get these mistaken military notions out of his mind. Although he looked to Curt for tactical planning and leadership, Mahathis felt he knew as much about international affairs as his sister. So, Curt had to comment at this point with great subtlety. "No question that this initial plan is a compromise between our overall SPD mission and good military horse sense. Let's get it going and then be opportunistic about modifying it as necessary when the situation jells, and we get a better handle on our ability to control it."

But even Colonel Castillo spotted the obvious flaws in Mahathis' overall plan. Chilean he might be; but he'd gotten an outstanding military education at the Citadel, and it showed right then. "It will not be easy to get the Soviets, Chinese, and Japanese to do what we want them to do. They won't just sit and listen, then take orders. We must be ready to use armed force to convince them to do what we want. Unfortunately, we are nearly matched in military strength."

"My dear Julio!" Payne-Ashwell put in. "We greatly outnumber them when it comes to fighting effectiveness. My Gurkhas have an awesome reputation which they are ready and willing to test in battle at any time! The Washington Greys are certainly well known and highly respected throughout the world for their campaigns in Namibia, Sonora, and Kurdistan. Your Third Airborne enjoys a similar reputation because of Tacta and Calacto."

Castillo smiled. "I'm glad you know about those campaigns, Colonel Payne-Ashwell! I proudly took part in them! I know I am indeed in the presence of a well-read military officer. But military reputations are often something for an adversary to challenge."

Curt knew exactly what Castillo was hinting, even though the Chilean might have been a bit hesitant about arguing with a general. Generals to him were sacrosanct. Curt didn't feel that way. He'd known a lot of generals before they'd become generals, so he knew the truth of the statement of Napoleon's Marshal Saxe: *I have seen very good colonels make very bad generals.*

So, Curt drew on his knowledge of military history. "You're right, Castillo. If you remember, when Clive went into Bengal, his strategy was to break up the alliance of India's princes. They wouldn't come over to his side until he showed that he could chew up an enemy on the battlefield. Which he did at Plessy. There's no doubt in my mind that we're going to have a fight, and the winner is going to determine the future of Sakhalin. We've got to win that fight. Then we have a chance of making the rules, not before!" Curt paused for a moment. "The Soviets are spoiling for a fight with me right now after what happened yesterday at the airport. Kurotkin must want a rematch, and he's likely to provoke one the first chance he gets. Our only hope of winning is to keep the fights short and intense using the strategic plan that allowed General Stonewall Jackson to hold the Shenandoah Valley against Union forces which outnumbered him..."

"Curt, my dear boy, at Sandhurst we never paid a great deal of attention to the skirmishes of your slavery war," Payne-Ashwell remarked dryly in his prudish, superior, and usually irritating British fashion.

"Pity," Curt mocked him. "We certainly studied your civil war with Cromwell..."

"Well, then, please do refresh our recollections of Stonewall Jackson's exploits," the British commander of the Gurkhas asked, adroitly extricating himself from the trap he'd built for himself and which Curt had tripped.

"Simple," Curt said offhandedly because he had no intention of holding a class in military history here. "Jackson maneuvered to keep the Union forces from gathering enough strength to whip him. Then he took them on in small groups where he was more evenly matched in terms of manpower and firepower. And he took and kept the initiative! So that's what we've got to do! We've got to maintain the integrity of the SPD, and if any of the three Far East regiments want to take us on, they'll be up against a bigger force."

"They'll know that," Payne-Ashwell pointed out. "That strategy is obvious!"

"Not if we don't look like we're doing it that way," Curt told him. "We'll garrison separately. That will give the illusion that we're operating separately. But we'll be tied together on comm nets, which they can't snoop because we'll use tacomm and tight beam lasercom. And with our airlift capability we'll be able to join up and move quickly. That's been the secret of success for the American Sierra Charlie warbot regiments. And General George S. Patton. And the old horse cavalry. Speed! Maneuverability! Shock! Surprise! Security! Those are the elements the Sierra Charlies stress. Duncan, you learned that from us in Brunei. Julio, you're Airborne, so you're probably familiar with our tactics, even though we've never operated together before."

"Yes, I studied what you did on Trinidad," Julio Castillo said, nodding.

He would have, Curt realized. That was one of the ABC Allianza's covert attempts at imperial expansion in South America. The Washington Greys was the highly mobile cavalry-like element that did an end run around the ABC-backed Trinidad forces and caught them in a pincer attack at Sangre Grande...along with the ABC military advisors.

"This plan will work," Curt stated. "Anyone here think it won't?"

Mahathis didn't comment; he knew Curt's strong points, and he upheld his part of their contract.

Surprisingly, Alzena spoke up in objection. "We're not here to fight. We're here to prevent fighting."

Curt shook his head. "Sultana, we were sent here to do a nearly impossible job. We're standing between three very nasty outfits. They don't like us being here. That should have been obvious at the airport."

"It's my job to talk them out of fighting. You're here to back up the diplomatic effort," she reminded him.

"We'll be behind you in the classical military role of picking up if diplomacy fails," Curt told her in short, emphatic sentences to drive home his point. "I hope you're successful because I don't like to fight. I don't think anyone in this room likes to fight. We're the first ones likely to get killed. And I've got a lot of other things I like to do better. So, we'll do our best not to fight. But given the situation, we'll probably have to resort to force of arms to get peace on this island."

"You did a magnificent job of diplomacy at the airport yesterday! Why do you say that?" Alzena asked, not really understanding the situation because, although she'd been educated in foreign affairs, she really didn't understand the basic reason why people fought each other.

"Because I'm a realist, Sultana. Don't worry; we won't start it. They will. And when they do, we've got to be ready with a plan such as this, or we'll be shipped home in plastic bags...and the rest of the world can start to dig shelters and graves."

Chapter Twenty-Two

When Colonel Curt Carson got back to Washington Greys Headquarters in the late afternoon, the place was frantic with activity.

Burly Russian-looking men were moving truck loads of brand-new wooden furniture into the buildings of the casern. They were carrying desks, chairs, filing cabinets, beds, cabinets, and tables.

Regimental Master Scrounge Henry Kester had obviously come through again.

But what had it cost the Washington Greys and the Treasury of the United States of America? Curt wondered. Or would this be docked from his pay for several years?

He sought out his regimental sergeant major in the main regimental day room. Kester was looking smug and giving a cursory and random inspection to selected pieces as they were brought in.

"Okay, Henry, how'd you do it this fast?" Curt wanted to know.

The old soldier shrugged. "It was easy, Colonel. Only a three-cushion dicker."

"But this stuff looks brand-new! I expected you'd find some used stuff, but we can't afford new!" Curt started to object.

Kester held up his hand. "Colonel, when you gave me the assignment, nothing was said about that. But you didn't need to. As I say, it was an easy three-bounce swap. And new furniture is easier to come by here than used."

Curt was getting curious. "Okay, explain!"

"They grow a lot of timber on Sakhalin. Damned little else grows naturally," Kester explained. "So, in addition to paper mills, there are more than a couple of furniture factories in the neighborhood. I paid one of them a visit and asked them what they needed.

Lieutenant Milton translated for me because the plant boss spoke only Russian. He needed more glue and was having trouble getting it. On my way to the furniture factory, I passed a meat packing plant. So, I went back to the meat packer and asked him what he wanted in exchange for stuff to make animal-based glue. He needs to wrap meat cuts in moisture-barrier type paper so they can be frozen for shipment. He can't get any because the paper mills are shipping it all to Australia where the price is better. So, I went over to a paper mill and asked the super what he needed, and he's in a hard way for special high-tempera lubricants for the press roll bearings on his high-speed newsprint machines. It don't take much, and we've got a lot of Mil-LH-eighty-ninety-B which is still on our logistical sked but which we don't use anymore because the bearings on the new ACVs are sealed now."

Kester paused and looked at the furniture coming in. "So I traded three hundred-liter drums of lube for the paper the meat packer needs and took the bones and stuff from the meat packer to the furniture factory and told them how to boil them up and make the best damned glue in the world. So, we got furniture, and it never shows up on a sight inventory list..."

"Henry, you're a goddamned genius, and I knew you could do it!" Curt told him with a grin. It was the first time he'd felt good since he'd left Sokol that morning.

Kester shrugged. "As I told you, Colonel, only a three-dicker deal. Give me a tough one sometime so I don't get out of practice."

"Yeah, Henry, I don't want your level of training to slip," Curt remarked, then shook his head. "Damn, it's too bad we're going to have to pull out of here so quickly and leave all that nice stuff behind..."

Kester just smiled.

Curt caught it. "Regimental Sergeant Major, just don't tell me what sort of a deal you've cut on the furniture when we leave."

"Sir? Me? Deal?" Kester managed to look innocent.

Major Pappy Gratton came up to the two of them. "Colonel," he said with a quick salute, "Maggie MacPherson's been waiting for a couple of hours to see you."

"Send her to my office, Pappy. Then find Jerry Allen and Martha Milton and send them in on the bounce! After that, I want to talk to Ellie Aarts about locating the three regiments we're supposed to be keeping off each other's ass and our minus-x as well!" Curt rapped off a quick succession of orders to his adjutant. He started to move out, then stopped and turned to Gratton. "By the way, where the hell is my office?"

"I gave you the corner office, Colonel," Gratton told him with an impish smile on his older, round face, "with the panoramic view overlooking the paper mill, the smelter, and the fish canning factory..."

"And I trust you oriented my terminal desk so that it's all at my back!" Curt grumbled in return.

The office wasn't bad considering that the roof leaked, making an artistic stain running down one of the walls. And the floorboards creaked as Curt walked over them; no one would take him by surprise here! And the ancient cast-iron steam radiator of the sort found only in the Soviet Union these days sat under the window and went "ph'd-ph'd-ph'd" at him, causing him to remark to his adjutant, "At least you gave me an office with an educated radiator with multiple Ph.D.'s."

"Sir you're the regimental commander, and nothing's too good for you!"

"Looks like that's just what I got, too," was Curt's riposte. He settled himself into the new chair behind the new desk - the furniture sort of helped make up for the utter drabness of the room in a typical Soviet building. Edie had his terminals up and running, so he had communication with the world, with Georgie, and with his regiment when he needed it. She hadn't yet set up the comm with CINNSPD, but he knew he wouldn't get it any faster if he tried to rush her. "Send in the newsharpy," he told Gratton and steeled himself to deal with the woman.

It was going to be tough, he decided, when Maggie MacPherson walked in.

She was wearing a white furry jacket with a parka hood over an incredibly tight black leather dress that didn't come far enough down to offer her any real protection against the Sakhalin weather. Curt didn't understand why a woman would wear such a skimpy sheath in the Sakhalin climate until he saw that she was also wearing skin-tight, skin-colored tights that covered her legs and booted feet. Her dark red hair exploded around her head and face when she threw back her parka hood.

There was no question in his mind that Maggie MacPherson could easily live up to her lascivious reputation...one which Mahathis apparently already knew very well.

The evidence was overwhelming: Maggie MacPherson was a gourmet dish. Furthermore, it was apparent that she knew it, too, and was both unashamed of it and willing to use it against a man's weak points.

Curt knew he had weak points, so he anticipated he was going to have a hell of a lot of trouble with Maggie MacPherson. Under the right circumstances, he might even enjoy it. He wondered if she was as good in the sack as she looked. Or as her reputation rumored.

Right out of the box, Maggie MacPherson did something that threw Curt off guard: She apologized. No news harpy had ever done that with him before. "Colonel, I'm sorry if I came on so strong in the airport yesterday. I think you'll agree that it was a rather tense time," she said to him in a liquid voice, and she strode up to his desk with a clicking of her high heels on the wooden floor. She put out her gloved hand.

Curt took it, decided that the continental custom of hand kissing would be inappropriate at this point because it really wasn't part of military protocol, and told her levelly with what he thought should be the proper concern of a regimental commander in his voice, "Your apology is unnecessary, Miss MacPherson. But, if it will make you feel better, it's accepted. Please sit down."

She did so, crossing her extremely attractive long and slender legs. Curt had discovered years ago that female television personalities were always extremely slender because, for some unknown reason, a television camera tended to make a person look broader and heavier. Maggie looked around. "Colonel, I'm impressed," she said.

"Certainly not at the luxurious office I've got!"

"But you did indeed manage to furnish it nicely in less than twenty-four hours! I never expected to find anything but military spec desks and chairs in a regimental headquarters. These look like you got them from some Tokyo corporate office!"

"You can thank the Washington Greys, Miss MacPherson. They scrounged and bartered it from a local furniture factory. Didn't cost the United States taxpayer a cent. When we leave, we'll trade it back for something we need then."

"I know that Army NCOs have always been good at this sort of thing. Especially supply sergeants. But I'll repeat: I'm impressed. You've got some good ones in your outfit." Abruptly but easily, she changed the subject and played to his last remark. "You don't expect to stay here long, then?"

Curt shrugged. "I hope not. But we stay until we get orders to return to Fort Huachuca." Then he went all business and asked directly, "Now, Miss MacPherson, what can I do for you?"

She tossed him a look that intimated that she might be able to do a lot for him. But she said, "I want an in-depth interview with you, Colonel. Several. You're an interesting man. The American public has wanted to know more about you for years, but you're an enigma. You tend to ignore news coverage."

"I'm a professional military officer," he told her quietly. "I'm also a combat soldier. That's my career. I don't have any political ambitions. I intend to serve my country for as long as my country wants me to do so. Then I'll retire and maybe do something else. So I don't need news media attention."

"You might discover that it would help you do what you just said you wanted to do," she told him. "It's helped others."

"Didn't help Westmoreland much...or even General Wild Bill Bellamack."

"Bill Bellamack got the Greys because of it and is sitting in the Pentagon today. Be that as it may, Colonel, don't discount what I can do for your career." She was certainly up-front about it, Curt decided. "In addition, you've got one shit-hot high-and-tight outfit here. The Washington Greys are a legend in their own time..."

"And going back to seventeen-eighty-four," Curt reminded her.

"Yes, but only military historians are interested in that. The American public still wants to know how you managed to out-flank the chauvinists in the Pentagon and get women into combat. True, other regiments followed suit, but you were the first. So, you're special. So, I want to cover the Washington Greys in-depth as well. The regiment is the American contingent of Ahmad's police force. You're far more interesting than the Gurkhas or Chileans." She said it like she meant it personally to Curt.

"Miss MacPherson..."

"Maggie, please..."

"Okay, Maggie, I want you to understand something. I've not only got to look out for the Washington Greys, but I'm supposed to play a major role in the SPD as the ops staffer..."

"Ahmad told me."

"Okay. So, you know. So, until I organize what I'm responsible for doing, I haven't got much time. Hell, I don't have any time! Period!" He tried to be firm. He knew it wasn't working.

"Oh, we'll find some time, I'm sure!"

"Maybe. But right now, I'm on the run, catching meals when I can and grabbing what sleep I can get whenever I can get time. I've got an in-file full of jobs I've got to do. So, if we can make this short and sweet, I can get on with doing what I'm paid to do."

He checked the clock ticking up on his terminal screen. *Where the hell are Jerry and Martha Milton?* He wanted these two to get MacPherson off his back and keep her out of his way. Jerry wouldn't be busy with Allen's Alleycats unless real combat started; furthermore, his roaring relationship with Captain Adonica Sweet would help keep him from having a hormone attack over Maggie MacPherson. Lieutenant Martha Milton was new in the Greys, but she could cover the woman's angle for MacPherson; Milton's New England attitudes would help Jerry steer MacPherson away from any obvious attempts on the news harpy's part to set up her infamous horizontal interviews with critical male members of the Greys. Curt pushed the matter by keying his comm. "Major Gratton, send in Allen and Milton!"

As if on cue, three raps sounded on the old wooden door to his office. But it wasn't Jerry or Martha.

Major Ellie Aarts stuck her head in the door and announced in an excited voice, "Colonel! Lieutenant Dale Brown and his bird-botters found the Chinese regiment! They're garrisoned in Krasnetskoye up in the hills about twenty klicks from here! But we haven't found the Soviets or Japanese yet-" She suddenly stopped when she saw Maggie MacPherson in the office. "Oh! I'm sorry, Colonel! I didn't know you had a visitor! I'll come back!"

"No, wait! Don't go!" Maggie said quickly, holding up her hand. She turned back to Curt. "Don't you know where the three enemy regiments are?"

Curt shook his head. "They're not officially the enemy since we aren't in a state of war," he corrected her. "No, we didn't know where they are. We had no intelligence data when we got here because this deployment was done in one god-awful hurry. So, we're engaged in heavy reconnaissance at the moment. We'll find them all the way Major Aarts here just reported that our bird warbots found the Chinese."

"Why don't you ask me?" the news woman wondered.

"Pardon me?" Curt replied. "Do you know where they are?"

"I had dinner with Colonel Mishida in his casern in Yuzhno-Sakhalinsk last night," Maggie MacPherson revealed, "and had a spot of *chai* with Colonel Kurotkin at his headquarters in

Novoaleksandrovsk this morning before I came over here, By the way, they're both charming men, Colonel. Very cooperative! And Colonel Qian has invited me to visit his garrison which is located in a most beautiful canyon that's nearly invulnerable to assault - as you've discovered, Major."

Curt was initially dismayed for a moment at this statement from her but quickly recovered. Of course, Maggie MacPherson would have such information! Information was her job!

"Okay, then, I'll ask you, Maggie: Where the hell are the Sovs and the Japanese?" Curt asked her.

She smiled. "I should let you find out for yourself! Information is a valuable commodity. I make my living because of that fact."

"Goddammit, Maggie, I can't pay you a snoop fee!" Curt objected.

"I didn't say I wanted money. I'm not that sort of a woman!" MacPherson quickly put in, "Although I understand from Kurotkin that this whole thing got started because of the girls over in the Yuzhno red-light district. I've refrained from calling it the Whore Wars on *Maggie's Hour*. In any event, I don't want to be an additional burden on the taxpayer, so my price isn't in terms of money."

Curt sighed. "What do you want, Maggie?"

"Just a little more cooperation from you. Like taking you to dinner tonight. General Carrington once told me that if you want to get a soldier out of quarters, ring the dinner bell. That will be the first payment for value received." Maggie MacPherson was certainly straight-forward, Curt decided. She knew what she wanted, and she had no compunctions about asking for it.

"Okay, dinner, but we'll eat chow here with the troops."

"No, I meant at my hotel in Yuzhno."

Curt shook his head. "Sorry, but I can't accept that part of the deal. We don't eat indigenous food for the first couple of days after we deploy into a new location. And after our biotechs have checked for alien organisms, we watch it pretty closely for bio-war thereafter.

Besides, I can't let you buy a meal for me or any of the Greys."

"Damned ethics regulations, right? I forgot that you're not allowed to sell your integrity for a simple meal...Never mind! We'll hassle about that later! Chow at your mess hall tonight. I can take another MRE."

"We should have hots by that time," Curt hoped. "Okay, stand by while I get a map keyed up here!" He turned to his terminal and began to key in commands. He didn't use verbal commands, not in front of Maggie. He didn't want her to know that he could verbally access a megacomputer halfway around the world in Arizona.

"My God, you Army people really are Stone Age, aren't you?" Maggie broke in as Curt was keying. "Has Congress really cut you back that much? I thought the Sierra Charlies had more C-cubed-I than an old grunt infantry outfit! I can tap into the whole LA Times morgue and data base from my portable using verbal colloquial commands! Why, even a regular warbot unit can verbally command any of the military megacomputers back in the States!"

"Georgie, Grey Head here! Come up online, please!" Curt commanded his terminal; then said to the news woman "I underestimated you. You know a lot about the military, don't you?"

"Colonel, I've been working and playing with soldiers about as long as you've been a soldier! Get that three-dee holo up from your Diamond Point megacomputer, and I'll finger the Sovs and Japs for you! Major, stick around and take notes."

When the miniature holo came up on Curt's desk tank, Maggie stuck her finger down into it and pointed out, "Soviets are here in Novoaleksandrovsk just a block or so from where the railway and the highway fork and go through the Zapadno Sakhalinkiye to Kholmsk; they get most of their supplies either airlifted into the aerodrome at Kostromskoye or by ship at Kholmsk. You probably went right past them last night and didn't know it."

"Wasn't looking for them then, Miss MacPherson," Ellie Aarts remarked.

"Whatever. The Japanese are right here in Yuzhno-Sakhalinsk, down in the southwest side of the city in the old Soviet KGB barracks," MacPherson explained, pointing into the holo with her long finger. "Their supplies come in from Hokkaido to Yuzhno-South aerodrome and by ship through Korsakov. Everyone harasses the hell out of each other's logistics activities. And both the Soviets and the Japanese have the advantage over the Chinese because Qian is in an excellent military position at Krasnetskoye but has to sneak his supplies past the Soviets and the Japanese...and usually they don't cooperate."

"You sound like you've done a War College analysis of the situation, Maggie," Curt told her, impressed.

"As I said, Curt, I've been around the military for over fifteen years," she admitted. "I've learned a few things. And I've been able to hire some pretty sharp research staffers in the past few years. They're pretty good. They get paid to do the leg work."

Curt straightened up. "Got it, Ellie?"

"Better yet," the intelligence officer replied and spoke to the terminal. "Georgie, this is Avenger Leader! Mark the holo to indicate the following unit caserns. Soviets at Novoaleksandrovsk where Miss MacPherson put her hand. Chinese at Krasnetskoye. Japanese at Yuzhno-Sakhalinsk where MacPherson indicated. Save to memory. Execute. Report compliance. Wipe the holo and replace with what you saved to memory for cross-checking."

"Well, Colonel, I see that at least one of the Washington Greys can verbally instruct a megacomputer!" Maggie observed.

Curt said nothing while he watched the feedback check holo build up from Georgie's memory banks. Everything seemed to be in the right place.

"Look okay, Maggie?" he asked.

"Right on!"

"Good! Georgie, give me a voice circuit to Sink-Spud!"

"What's up?" Maggie asked.

"I need to notify General Mahathis," Curt explained, "and tell him where I'm going."

"Oh? Where are you going?" Maggie wanted to know.

"Over to pay a social call on Kurotkin. Alone!"

"The hell you say! I'm going with you!"

"The hell you say, Maggie! I won't risk your safety."

"Safety, my ass! Kurotkin knows me!"

"I embarrassed the hell out of him yesterday afternoon. I need to see him alone."

"Okay, I get it now! Yeah, you did shake him up, and he's pissed at you! So much that he'll probably try to put a hole in you with that pistol of his! So, I'd better go along and be a neutral intermediary," Maggie suggested.

"On second thought, Maggie," Curt replied after a pause during which he ran a few permutations and combinations through his mind, "that's not such a bad idea. But let me go pull on my body armor while you call Kurotkin and tell him we're coming. Nothing shakes up a Soviet more than a Big Surprise."

Chapter Twenty-Three

As Curt slowed the PTV "Trike" to cross the bridge over the railway at Kurskoye, Maggie MacPherson emerged from her rain poncho to yell, "I don't like your goddamned convertible! Especially on a day like this!"

It was raining cold water off and on. The Trike was a twenty-first century version of a motorcycle with a sidecar...except that the sidecar was large enough to hold an M3A2 Jeep warbot. Maggie MacPherson was almost lost in the metal tub of the sidecar. She was nowhere near as large as a Jeep. The Trike and its sidecar had no protection from the elements except windscreens. "Sorry the roof leaks!" Curt yelled back over the roar of the wet wind whipping past. They could converse a bit now that he'd had to slow down to stay on the slick, winding road with an increasing amount of truck traffic as they neared more populated areas. "You want I should go back and get an ACV...and maybe get shot at by the Sovs?"

"They won't shoot! They know we're coming, and I'm with you!"

"If you'll pardon the expression since you've been around soldiers, bullshit! If Kurotkin showed up in an armored vehicle at my casern, I'd be more than just a little antsy," Curt replied. "And the Soviets have a tendency to get real paranoid about stuff that appears to be military showing up on their doorstep." He wanted to meet with Kurotkin to see if he couldn't head off an inevitable confrontation."

Lieutenant Marth Milton had contacted Kurotkin by ordinary telephone. Parts of Sakhalin still followed old Soviet procedures, including the face that no telephone books are ever printed or circulated. The telephone number of the Soviet casern was something Maggie MacPherson had managed to get from the Soviets themselves. Milton spoke Russian because Kurotkin wouldn't speak English over the telephone, although Maggie revealed that all three commanders of the occupying regiments spoke English as a common language.

Kurotkin had been mildly annoyed at the call and Curt's request for a social call, couldn't think of an excuse to refuse, but insisted that Curt come unarmed only with Maggie and a non-armored vehicle. That was agreeable to Curt, who didn't want any of his ACVs or weapons possibly falling into Soviet hands.

But Curt was wearing basic body armor covering his torso and limbs. It helped keep him warm. It also gave him a little more of a warm, fuzzy feeling knowing he could probably survive the close-range impact of anything up to a 9-millimeter Magnum. Body armor wasn't classified; let the Soviets try to figure out how to make its KrisFlex composite linear polymer! Such engineered materials were easily identified but almost impossible to make unless the exact process was known.

He was also wearing a button beacon that Edie Sampson had snapped onto his shirt before he left. When he asked about that, Edie had replied that Major Wilkinson had told her to do it so that Curt's whereabouts could be tracked in an emergency. No one was really very happy about their regimental commander going off alone and unarmed to meet with a potential enemy. Some of the ladies of the Greys were quietly disturbed that Curt was going off with a beautiful news harpy.

"Colonel, don't force me to exhibit what I know about soldiers' profanity!" Maggie yelled back.

"Someday it might be interesting to discovery that!" Curt fired back.

"This is not the time to compare notes!"

"Agreed!"

The highway - a narrow, paved two-lane road that followed terrain contours - crossed a stream. Looking in his rearview mirror, Curt saw a Soviet warbot pull onto the road behind them after they'd crossed the bridge.

"Got company! One of them ASU-eighty-eight Soviet warbots!" Curt pointed out to Maggie.

"Kurotkin told me it's called an AASU-ninety-nine Silver Pilgrim!" Maggie corrected him. "It's a remote-controlled light tank!"

Curt wondered where the human controller was located. He kept looking in his rearview mirror with one eye while keeping the Trike on the road.

Two more klicks down the road suddenly found another AASU-99 ahead of them.

Curt saw that he was boxed.

In the narrow streets of Novoaleksandrovsk, the Soviet Silver Pilgrim warbot turned right onto another narrow street. Curt had to turn as well because all other options were blocked by AASU-99's.

Finally, the leading Silver Pilgrim stopped.

"We're here! Thank God! I'll be able to get warm and dry again!" Maggie exclaimed. "Kurotkin has some of the outstanding vodka!"

Curt didn't dismount or even stop the Trike's motor. The AASU-99 ahead had wheeled about so that its 53-millimeter cannon faced them. On his left and behind him, two more AASU-99's stood with their guns levelled at him.

In spit of the cold rain, two human sentries stood under cover on either side of the casern entrance. Their uniforms were spotless. They both carried the new Soviet APSh-25 submachine guns. At least, the intelligence snoops thought they were submachine guns because they weren't very big, looked like miniature Novias, and had been seen for the first and only time being carried by an Airborne Guards regiment in the last Soviet Army and Navy Day parade in Moskva. Both sentries immediately came to present arms with that unique Soviet style of eyes left/right with an elevated chin and looking down the bridge of the nose.

Curt dismounted, helped Maggie get out, walked up to the entrance, and saluted the sentries. Then the casern door opened.

Colonel Viktor Pashkavitch Kurotkin was standing there with members of his staff and Major Aleksander Semenovich Ivanovski, his political affairs officer.

A young officer stepped forward and saluted Curt, who returned it. "Colonel Carson, I am Captain Andrei Gulaevitch Glinka, regimental staff, One-hundred-tenth Special Airborne Guards Unit of the Ground Forces of the Union of Soviet Socialist Republics!" he announced formally using his full rank and unit designation. "I will serve as official translator today. Welcome to our casern!"

"I'm pleased to come in peace and friendship," Curt replied, then faced Kurotkin and saluted. "Thank you for receiving me, Colonel!"

The conversation between Curt and the Soviets proceeded only through Captain Glinka as translator. This bothered Curt a little. It would have been friendlier if they could have talked in one language. But, on the other hand, Curt knew that it could happen only if a neutral third language was spoken...and he didn't know if Kurotkin spoke Chinese that well. Even Curt's Chinese was rusty, but he hadn't had time for a quick cram brush-up by neuroelectronic methods.

Kurotkin introduced the officers with him - Ivanovski and Captain Vladimir Nikolayevich Yurakov.

"Captain Yurasov is the commander of their new warbot battalion," Maggie revealed to Curt. "He told me he was anxious to meet an American warbot officer."

Ivanovski, the political officer, apparently understood Maggie because he shot a sharp look at Yurasov, who had probably made that remark privately to Maggie earlier.

From that point, it was a formal social visit with typical Soviet protocol laid on. Curt and Maggie were relieved of their wet outer clothing. They were escorted through the casern to a covered courtyard where a welcoming honor guard consisting of a company of riflemen was drawn up for Curt's inspection. While Curt and his hosts stood at attention and saluted, the national anthems of the Soviet Union and the United States were played in that order. Then Curt and Maggie, accompanied by Kurotkin and the company commander, walked down the line of rifle men.

This was exactly what Curt was after. He knew the military and diplomatic symbology. He was being officially welcomed as a military officer of equal rank to the highest ran ked Soviet officer on Sakhalin. The rifle company drawn up for his inspection was a signal that the Soviets were indeed here on Sakhalin and were capable of using force of arms if necessary. In fact, Curt knew that only official protocol might be keeping him from being taken and held prisoner at this moment if Kurotkin's feelings were as strong as Curt feared. In any event, Curt had deliberately forced this social call. He did it to defuse Kurotkin by giving him the opportunity to make a verbal dump on Curt in front of the Soviet political officer who was, as Curt knew, also a KGB/GRU man who reported t o a different boss than Kurotkin. Curt was giving Kurotkin a chance to regain face which, because of the influence of Oriental invaders on Russia over the centuries, was just as important to Kurotkin as it was to Qian and Mishida.

Curt also knew that some of his own staff and subordinates didn't really approve of what he was doing. But he had diplomatically pointed out that he was the regimental commander. And the standing orders he'd left were quite specific concerning what the Greys should do if something happened to him at the Soviet casern. Curt's conversation with Mahathis hadn't gone that well because the CINCSPD objected and relented only when Alzena, who understood what Curt was up to, intervened with her brother. She also knew that Mahathis could be the boor who brought this whole thing to a shooting was if he behaved like a despotic monarch.

There was no discussion of the situation until Kurotkin and his officers had treated Curt and Maggie to a lavish (for Soviets) dinner with lots of meats and starches. Many toasts were offered and drunk with that wonderfully smooth but potent vodka the Soviets never export. Curt knew he couldn't drink very much of it, so he managed to take diplomatic sips at each toast...until Kurotkin arose, toasted peace and friendship, and insisted on linking arms Slovic-style and looking Curt directly in the eye while they both tossed down full tumblers.

The vodka was smooth going down, all right, but when it hit bottom, it spread out across his guy with a warming feeling...and suddenly he was warm all over. But, of course, that's why the Russians drank vodka in their semi-arctic climate.

As Curt finished the glass, looking Kurotkin directly in the eye, the room shook.

He didn't think the vodka would be that powerful.

The overhead lighting fixtures swayed, and the crockery and glassware on the table rattled.

"What the hell?" Curt burst forth.

"Minor earth tremor," Maggie said, steadying him with her hand as he sat back down when the room stopped moving. "I'm an Angelino. Seen thousands of them."

"Here on Sakhalin?"

"Why not?" She was enjoying the vodka. "We're on the edge of the so-called Pacific Rim of Fire - earthquakes and volcanoes and such. And this is a tectonic valley...

The dinner was over, but the vodka toasting might go on for hours. It was rapidly turning into a typical wild Slavic drinking party. Curt knew the Soviets well enough to realize that they might have had some reservations about his visit. On the other hand, he also knew that their lives were so abysmally boring that they never turned down an excuse for a dinner party or a drinking binge. Kurotkin began to mellow once he had a few vodkas in him, realized that Curt wasn't ten feet tall and covered with hair, and saw that Curt was willing and able to go drink for drink with him - or so he thought.

Kurotkin remained very careful while Ivanovski was present. But the political officer didn't eat dinner and quickly drank himself into a semi-stupor; he was gently escorted from the room by two junior officers just as he began to get the dry heaves.

The only ones left in the room were Curt, Maggie, Kurotkin, Yurasov, and Glinka.

At that point, Curt carefully directed the conversation to his main purpose for coming.

"Viktor Pashkavitch, I would be interested in knowing the orders you received from Khabarovsk," Curt said to him, speaking slowly in basic English. "I hope they do not demand that you fight me. I do not want to fight with you. Many of our soldiers in both regiments would be wounded or killed. I hope we can agree that it is best to allow the diplomats to try to do their jobs first," Curt said to Kurotkin with serious conviviality.

The Soviet colonel answered Curt in good English because his political officer was no longer present, only his subordinates. "Curt Carson, I can respect you for your bravery. You faced my new Silver Pilgrim warbots with courage. I knew then that you are a soldier like I am. And like Colonel Qian and Colonel Mishida. We are ready to fight if it is necessary. But killing and being killed is not good if it is not necessary."

Curt realized that Kurotkin was reluctant to discuss his orders, so Curt took the lead. "My orders tell me that I am not to fight you unless you attack my troops and warbots. My orders also say that I am to keep your troops from fighting with the Chinese and Japanese troops. But I am prevented from taking the offensive."

"So? Hah! Invaders without claws!" Kurotkin laughed.

"You're both invaders. By treaty, this island shouldn't have any soldiers on it at all," Maggie MacPherson pointed out.

"The Soviet Union always follows the treaties it has signed," Kurotkin insisted. "Sakhalin has been Russian for centuries! It even now has a Russian population! Maggie MacPherson, I will tell you personally that I think that is Russian soil. It is part of the Motherland! I am here because a treaty was broken by others. But that is not my problem. You are the invader, Curt Carson! I go where I am ordered, and I do what my orders tell me. If the diplomats are not successful in giving Sakhalin back to the Motherland, that is another matter. But you are right. We should not fight each other until it becomes necessary."

"And personally, I think we probably shouldn't be here, either," Curt said. "But I'm like you. I do what my government tells me. At the airport, I had to do what I did because we came to Sakhalin under orders to be a police force and stop the fighting. I had to carry out my orders. Do you understand that Viktor Pashkavitch?"

"I do not like it, but I understand it. And I understand you, Curt Carson. Let us hope we do not have to fight each other before this problem on Sakhalim is solved," Kurotkin told him earnestly.

Curt had done what he came to do. He hadn't apologized to Kurotkin, and Kurotkin hadn't given in, either. Neither man had retreated. But Kurotkin's anger at Curt had been blunted. Maggie had helped in some ways, and he couldn't have done it without her. He didn't know at the time, however, that he'd gotten himself into very deep trouble.

It was 2300 hours when Curt decided he had to break up the party. He was still sober, having surreptitiously sipped the vodka during toasts and having downed the full tumbler only once on a full stomach. These Russian drinking bouts could go on all night, and Curt wanted to bug out while he was still sober and vertical. Besides, he was beat from the day's activities and anxieties. And from the pressures of commanding a full regiment under difficult conditions with no clear military objectives.

He had to hand it to Maggie; she was holding her vodka very well. Exceptionally well. Much better than Kurotkin, who insisted on embracing her and Curt as he bid them farewell at the casern main door. Curt decided there was real basis for the story about the Russian bear hug. It was only when Kurotkin released him that the Soviet Colonel remarked, "Hah! You are a prudent man, Curt Carson! You wore body armor! You were probably right in thinking that I might shoot you when I saw you! Before our meeting tonight, I wanted to shoot you! But now I know that if we are not friends, we are professional soldiers! We can depend on each other!"

And that was exactly what Curt had been hoping to achieve that night.

It was very cold in the streets of Novoaleksandrovsk as Curt and Maggie boarded the Trike for the twenty-two-kilometer drive back to Sokol. The rain had stopped, but it was nearly zero degrees Celsius. A little ice spotted the street here and there.

Maggie was huddled in the sidecar. As they drove down the narrow street and turned left onto the highway that quickly led them out of the small town and into the surrounding farmland, she remarked thickly, "Miserable night outside! Vodka will keep me warm until we get back to Sokol. Then you can-"

"Damn!" Curt swore when he realized he'd turned the wrong way. "I was going to take you back to your hotel in Yuzhno! It's only five klicks, and you'll be home sooner."

"Who says I want to go home? On the other hand, my hotel is closer, and we can get there sooner! I need you to get me warm all over-" Maggie started to say through full lips that were turning blue with cold.

Before she could finish her sentence or Curt could reply, he was hit hard in the side.

He never heard the snap from that bullet. But he heard the shock wave of the others that went past him, followed quickly by muzzle blast sounds he knew had to be from Chinese A-99 assault rifles. He'd heard that before in many places.

He slammed on the breaks just as the Trike hit an icy spot on the road. He and Maggie were saved only by the Trike skidding out of control across the road and into the muddy ditch. As it hit the edge of the road, it flipped, sending Curt and Maggie through the air.

Curt found himself headfirst in the icy water and mud of the ditch bottom. His side hurt like hell, but his body armor had saved him from being penetrated by the Chinese A-99 5.56-millimeter round.

Maggie was in the ditch, too. He didn't know if she had been hit. She wasn't wearing body armor. But she lay there in the mud, her white parka plastered with mud and dirt.

Curt heard more A-99 rounds snapping overhead. Some of them hit the mud at the top of the ditch. He couldn't tell where they were coming from, but he knew the two of them had a little safety in the ditch.

He scrambled through the gooey, cold mud caked with a thin layer of ice and rolled Maggie over. She was still breathing through the cold mud that covered her face; she'd gone headfirst into the ditch. Curt could see no obvious bullet wounds anywhere. But to protect her, he put his armored body over hers.

The sound of the A-99's stopped for a few seconds.

Then all hell broke loose above him.

He heard the reports of Soviet APSh-25's and 53-millimeter automatic cannon.

These were quickly followed by the unmistakable blasts of Novia assault rifles and the ripping, tearing sound of 7.62-millimeter heavy machine guns from a Jeep.

Somewhere above his head, a battle now raged with Washington Greys, Soviets, and probably Chinese troops involved.

He could do nothing but lay there and wait, hurting and cold in the mud and water, trying to protect the unconscious woman he was with, and thinking that all his efforts that night had been in vain.

Chapter Twenty-Four

Curt decided that the best thing he could do right then was to lie quietly in that ditch and try to keep from being hit by a wild shot. His body armor would stop most of it, but it wouldn't do much good against the 53-millimeter stuff from the Silver Pilgrims that was going overhead at the moment. Besides, he was unarmed and unable to add to the fight. At best, he'd be a target.

Someone knew he and Maggie were in the ditch. Somehow, the Greys, the Chinese, and the Soviets knew. He had no idea what was happening, so the only thing he could do was to lie quietly and wait. It was a damned tough thing to do.

Maggie seemed to have been knocked unconscious by her arrival in the ditch after being catapulted out of the Trike. In the semi-darkness, he tried to get some of the liquid mud off her face and away from her mouth so she wouldn't breath it in and choke. She had been so beautiful just a moment before, and now she was a muddy, wet mess.

Curt was surprised that she was so much smaller than he was.

And her leanness hid the fact that she was really somewhat frail.

But being frail didn't keep her from being tough.

She apparently regained consciousness, discovered someone atop her, and brough an arm and a fist around to clobber Curt in the chops.

"Goddammit, you sonofabitch, get the hell of me unless you want to get kicked in what you think is your manhood!" she yelled.

"Shut up and lie still, Maggie!" Curt whispered in her ear, his jaw throbbing from where she connected. "You're not wearing body armor. I am. I've got you covered against wild shots and possible shrapnel from air bursts…"

"Oh, Curt, Curt, I'm sorry! What's going on!"

"Someone's fighting. Over us, I think. Maybe the Chinese took shots at us. Maybe tried to ambush us or take us prisoner. The Greys and Soviets also seem to be involved now," Curt tried to explain. "I'll tell you more when I find out myself. You okay? Anything broken?"

"I don't think so...maybe we can find out later..."

"What do you mean, 'we' news lady? I think a war just started, and I'm going to have to go fight it. You're going to be busy covering it-"

A three-round burst hit the mud less than a meter above them. Splotches of mud sprayed them.

Maggie started to tremble.

"Cold or scared?" Curt asked her.

"A little of both," Maggie admitted.

"Welcome to the club," Curt growled.

"You? Scared?"

"Damned right! Anyone who says they're not scared when someone's shooting at them is a goddamned liar!"

"But you're wearing body armor!"

"Not over my hands or head! I've got a sort of sentimental attachment to my head. It's where my brain is. It's where my brain is. It may be only enough brain to run the colonel, but it's all I've got..."

"You do have a colorful way of expressing yourself, Curt," she admitted.

The shooting was over as quickly as it had started. This didn't surprise Curt. He knew that fire fights were usually brief. The more intense they were, the briefer they were. This one was intense. But he lay still for a moment.

Maggie MacPherson heard it, too. She tried to move under Curt, "Let me up! It's over!"

"Those are the final words of the last person killed in every battle! Stay put!" he told her.

"I'm getting wetter and colder by the second!"

"Better wet and cold than catch the last bullet of the fight!"

He heard the squishy footsteps of someone on the muddy bank of the road above them.

"I hate to break up a cozy situation," came the voice of Major Alexis Morgan, "but it's safe for you and Miss MacPherson to get up now. It's stopped raining water and bullets. So, you've got no excuses, Colonel!"

Curt got to his feet, muttering, "Major, I don't need an excuse!"

"That's right! You never have! Nor have you ever offered one! But that's excusable in your case!" Only Alexis Morgan could get away with addressing Colonel Curt Carson that way. Then her tone changed from mildly sarcastic to one of serious concern. "Are you all right? Both of you? Need some help getting out of the muck?"

"We got here on our own. We'll get out okay," Curt told her, helping Maggie slip and slide up the bank.

"My God, Maggie, you're a mess!" Alexis noted. Even though the only illumination on the road was now the headlamps of a couple of Jeeps and an ACV, it was obvious that both Curt and Maggie were covered with mud and soaked to the skin. She then called out to Captain Adonica Sweet, her Alpha Platoon commander, "Princess, you and Ginny get over here! Bring some wipes! And a couple of survival blankets! Both the colonel and Maggie look okay, but I want Ginny to check them for injury!"

Maggie MacPherson wasn't going to give in just because she was wet and cold. "I'm okay, Major Morgan! I've been shot at before. I've been wet before. And I've been cold. Part of the job. I didn't get my Pulitzers and Cronkites by trying to stay comfortable. Let anchor people worry about that."

Whether she was bragging or complaining or just talking so she could be glad she was still able to talk, Maggie MacPherson obviously had guts, Curt decided. Maybe he'd discounted her too much.

He looked around. To the north stood two Jeeps and an ACV along with eight Sierra Charlies recognizable by their big combat helmets. To the south he could see two of the Soviet AASU-99 Silver Pilgrim warbots, a BTR-218, and about a dozen Soviet infantrymen with their distinctive helmets. "So what the hell's going on here, Major?" he asked Alexis. "First of all, what the hell are you doing here with your Marauders?"

"You didn't think the Greys were going to let you go into the Soviet casern at night without shadowing you at a respectful and non-threatening distance, did you?" Alexis asked unnecessarily, then added, "And you didn't think I was going to let you do it, either did you? I'm here with Sweet's Scorpions. Jerry Allen and Martha Milton came along to help out with Maggie if needed. You do remember that you assigned them that duty, don't you?"

He did, and he was happy they were all there at the moment. "So the Soviets saw you, and it drew them out of their casern, and they attacked both my Trike and your outfit!" Curt snapped. Glad though he was that the Greys had been there when he'd been ambushed, he was irritated that Alexis had done what she did, although he should have expected it. Most of all, he was upset because she'd done it without telling him. Or maybe the whole damned regiment had been in collusion on it. He'd find out.

"No, sir! If you'll let me give you a brief sit-rep, you'll understand," Alexis fired back at him without rancor.

Adonic Sweet and Sergeant Charlie Koslowski appeared with survival blankets and began wrapping them around Maggie and Curt. Biotech Sergeant Ginny Bowles rushed up, apologizing, "Sorry, but I thought I could maybe save that Chinese soldier we wounded; but I didn't get to him in time…"

"Thought I heard A-ninety-nines," Curt remarked.

"You did," Alexis reported. "We were shadowing you a couple of hundred meters ahead of you on the road. When you left the Soviet casern, you were shadowed from behind by the Soviets. Your Trike was ambushed by a Chinese patrol. I don't think they were after you specifically, just any military person who happened along while they were here..."

"Milton! Go talk to the Soviets!" Curt told his Russian-speaking new officer. "Whoever the officer is, ask him to come here so I can talk with him and compliment him, please. Put it in the kindest and friendliest terms you can!"

"Yes sir!" Lieutenant Martha Milton snapped and disappeared toward the Soviet contingent.

"So, a Chinese patrol jumped us?" Curt wanted Alexis to confirm what he'd just heard.

"Damned near got you, too, if your Trike hadn't hit that icy spot and skidded. We missed seeing them. Even the Sovs didn't spot them until they opened fire."

"This is the sort of harassment that's been going on around here, Colonel," said Master Sergeant First Class Carol Head, the first sergeant of the Marauders. The large, round-faced Bohemian-American was another one of those top NCOs who actually ran things in the Army while the officers did the management and leadership chores. "We had been talking to some of the locals about it today."

Curt was getting angry. He was dog-tired after a long day which had culminated in being ambushed. Now it seemed that what had happened to him was standard operating procedure for at least one of the illegal regiments on Sakhalin. He found himself wondering how many more ambushes would occur while they were here. Most of all, he was making up his mind he was going to do something about it, that he wasn't about to let this sort of crap continue, that if someone like Maggie MacPherson was killed in one of these ambushes, the conflict could quickly escalate and get totally out of hand. In fact, Curt would be damned upset himself if any member of the Washington Greys ended up being killed as a result of one of these covert assaults.

Lieutenant Martha Milton showed up with an equally young Soviet officer. She introduced him as Lieutenant Pavel Fedorovich Koslov. Through Milton as translator, Curt said to him, "Lieutenant, I want to thank you for helping out tonight. With your important help, Major Morgan and her company rescued Miss MacPherson and me. I am in debt to you."

Koslov was astounded. He hardly knew what to say. Here was an American field officer of the same rank as his new regimental commander complimenting him for helping. It caught him totally off guard. "Comrade Colonel, I was following orders. I was told to carefully guard you on your trip back to Sokol. I just did my job."

"You did it very well," Curt responded. "I thank you very much. I will talk to Colonel Kurotkin tomorrow and give my commendations for your outstanding behavior. Now, tell me if you can, is this sort of ambush warfare common between your regiment and the Chinese and Japanese regiments?"

Lieutenant Martha Milton was having some trouble getting exact translations of what Curt was saying to Koslov. But Koslov obviously understood the gist of Curt's conversation, even though Milton might have missed translating a few words properly. "No, Colonel, ambushes are usually carried out by the Chinese and Japanese against our patrols. Soviet forces are here only in a defensive posture."

"Colonel," Martha Milton interrupted her translation, "with all due respects, sir, I believe Lieutenant Koslov is spouting a lot of straight doctrine here. It sounds almost exactly like some of the writings in *Red Star.*"

"Maybe, Lieutenant, but he's already told me something important," Curt remarked to her. Maybe the 110th Special Guards Airborne Regiment was also engaging in ambushing the other two units. But it was Curt's guess that it was primarily being done by the Chinese and maybe the Japanese. Ambush tactics were best handled by human soldiers backed up by sophisticated voice-controlled warbots like the Jeeps. The Soviet AASU-99 warbots were too big and clumsy for ambush work; they'd obviously been brought in by the Soviets to help them defend against ambushes. "Give Lieutenant Koslov my thanks for being helpful and tell him that the Washington Greys can take over from here. He can go home and get dry and warm."

"I think you'd better get dry and warm, too, Colonel," Alexis advised him. "Your Trike is totaled. You and Maggie come and ride in my ACV."

"Good idea!" Curt decided. If it hadn't been for the little bit of vodka he'd consumed with Kurotkin, he would indeed have been very cold by now. Maybe that was why Maggie looked cold but insisted she wasn't. "You've got communications with Grey Chief and Grey Major. I need to talk to them."

Alexis's ACV was full with Curt, Maggie, Alexis, Head, Martha Milton, and Jerry Allen aboard. Normally, an M660 ACV would carry six people. It was only a twenty klick ride back to Sokol, so Adonica and her Scorpions either rode on the Trike she'd brought along or mounted the outside of the ACV like tank riders, the two Jeeps hauled up on the rear ramp.

Caballo! Lleveme al Sokol! Pronto! Alexis commanded her ACV in Spanish once they were inside and all tank riders were mounted. She maintained her military formality with her commander. "Colonel, be my guest with the tacomm! But I doubt that anyone except the OOD is awake in Sokol!"

"They'll damned well get up pretty fast!" Curt growled. "You up to paying a little visit to Krasnetskoye tonight?"

"I think all of us are bushed out, but what the hell are you thinking about, Colonel?" Alexis wanted to know.

"I want to show up on Qian's doorstep at dawn in a non-violent ambush," Curt told her. "I want to damned well let him know that I'm not going to put up with this ambush shit on his part any longer! Once is enough!"

"Curt!" Maggie broke in. "Krasnetskoye is well defended! The only access is by a single road up the canyon! And I barely got up there with a four-wheel-drive Toyota Big Horn! I don't know how you'd get warbot forces - even Sierra Charlie forces - over those mountains tonight without using the road!"

"Goddammit, Maggie, I've got to hit back fast and strong!" Curt exploded in a combination of rage, frustration, and fatigue. "Otherwise, this crap will continue, and someone's going to be killed! We were damned near greased tonight except for the fact that Alexis and Koslov happened to be shadowing us!"

Alexis knew Curt very well. She knew he was tired almost beyond reasoning at the moment. So, she looked at her first sergeant and asked, "Carol, where's Ginny?"

"Riding the glacis, Major."

"Get her in here! She needs to check the colonel!"

Even a biotech sergeant could rule the commanding officer unfit to continue commanding because of physical fatigue. It was a hold-over from the pure warbot days when the biotechs weren't as much like the old medics as they were monitors of a warbot brainy's physical well-being in combat. Ginny was a P.N. and could make a determination that would put Curt temporarily out of the game; she would have to justify it to Major Ruth Gydesen, the chief regimental medical officer, but she could do it. And Curt knew it.

"Alexis, dammit, I'm running this show!" Curt insisted.

"Not very long in your current and worsening condition, Colonel!" she fired back respectfully but honestly. "Hettrick and Bellamack taught all of us, including you, not to make hasty decisions involving the whole regiment when tired, hungry, cold, or a combination of those factors!"

"Goddammit, I was colder and more tired on Kerguelen and in Borneo and in Kurdistan!" Curt pointed out. "I ran it then! I can run the regiment now!"

"Uh, Colonel," Jerry Allen interrupted, "I understand your feeling of urgency to do something quickly. But I think we can probably come up with a better plan if we back off, look at our capabilities, and see if we can't come up with an ops plan that makes the best use of what we've got against the known weaknesses of the adversary. At least, that's what you tried to teach me as my company commander...and I think you were pretty successful at it, sir."

Curt sat back and let his shoulders slump. He had to admit to himself that he was tired. He also knew he was fighting mad. That wasn't a happy combination for a commander who wanted to be successful and not waste his people or resources. And he knew it now. "We were also taught to listen to our subordinates," he recalled. "And I always have. Okay, Major Allen, do you have something in mind?"

"Yes, sir!"

"And what is it?"

"What sort of psych warfare tactic did we use in Kurdistan?" Jerry asked rhetorically. "Answer: We let the beaten force go back and tell its story of how it was greased by vastly superior forces using weapons of amazing firepower. So let that Chinese patrol go back to Krasnetskoye with its exaggerated report! They'll be more careful next time. You probably should have a chat with the Chinese colonel. And the Japanese commander, too. And let them know that if they ambush anybody, we'll smear them hard!"

"You're not here as an offensive force, Major," Maggie reminded him.

"Yes, ma'am, I know what our ROEs say," Jerry admitted. "If the Sovs or Chinese or Japanese don't knock off their harassment, our ROEs say nothing about setting ourselves up as patsies to get them to ambush us. Remember, we've got a few things they don't. We've got very maneuverable warbots that can hose a lot of steel jackets out into the pucker brush in a big, fast hurry. Tomorrow, we'll have our tacair as well as our airlift capabilities; we'll be able to move fast and hit hard from the ground and the air. We can do a lot of things once we're all up and tactical. We can use our old tactics: Hold 'em by the nose with fire while we kick 'em in the ass with maneuver! And we'll be in a condition where we can actually appear to be an attractive target for an ambush. Let them pick about two good fights and be whupped. Things will get real quiet around here real fast when they find out we can grease their skids any time we want to with what appears to be a smaller force. Which it isn't because we'll work with the Gurkhas and Chileans as a combined ops and make it seem that way. After all, Cal Worsham's Warhawks and the Royal Brunei Air Command can control the major aerodromes to prevent them from escalating this. If we want to quiet this thing down like a police force, we've got to start acting like a police force. The bad guys will still be there, but they'll be reluctant as hell to move."

In spite of his weariness, Curt listened to this with a sense of warm inner satisfaction. He'd trained both Alexis and Jerry. They'd both been raw brown-bar second looies when they'd joined his then-new warbot company, Carson's Companions, those long years ago. Now he was listening to his own teachings being fed back to him as suggestions. He had the happy feelings of a teacher whose teachings have. taken root, of a manager who discovers he's been successful at training his own replacement.

"Major Allen, I think you and Major Morgan are probably right," Curt decided. "Let's go home for tonight, then put this thing together tomorrow. Keep those thoughts, Jerry. We'll build around them. I've done enough for one day. You've done enough for one day, all of you. There isn't a whole hell of a lot more that we can really do tonight to save the free world. And, by the way, thank you all. It was cold and dangerous in that ditch..."

"Well, Colonel, I wasn't about to let the two of you lie there together all night," Alexis remarked.

Chapter Twenty-Five

"You want me to do *what?*" Major Cal Worsham exploded.

"I need a Chippie to fly me into the Chinese casern at Krasnetskoye ASAP, Cal," Curt told his AIRBATT commander, who'd just arrived at the Sokol aerodrome with the rest of the squadron. "Any reason why it can't be done?"

"Damned right there is!" Worsham snapped back with a combination of frustration and fatigue in his raspy voice.

"You ought to have a Chippie available. After all, you just made a transpacific flight with all of them," Curt pointed out.

"Yeah, we did, and that's the reason, Carson!" Being a fly boy, Worsham paid a lot less attention to formal military protocol than the Sierra Charlies of TACBATT. He'd worked as a tacair squadron commander alongside Curt when they both wore gold oak leaves. Just because Curt was now a light colonel and regimental commander didn't mean that Cal Worsham was going to kiss ass in private. In the first place, Curt didn't demand respectful protocol (and probably wouldn't have gotten it from Cal if he had demanded it). In the second place, both men knew that formal expressions of respect really had nothing to do with the inner respect both men had for each other.

Cal slumped down into a chair and began to massage his thighs. "We've just flown twelve thousand klicks. Normally a two thousand klick flight is a long one! We've been three days in the air with our butts welded to the airframes! We've made two in-flight refuelings and one carrier landing in goddamned lousy weather! Then we hit this place. A hundred-meter ceiling! Freezing rain! An approach that doesn't match our approach plates! Air traffic controllers who don't speak good English and never handled more than two aircraft in the pattern at once! And a strange field! The Warhawks are not operational at this time, Carson!"

"Everyone in the Greys knows damned good and well they've got to hit the ground shooting at the end of any deployment, Cal," Curt reminded him.

"And you're being a shithead...sir...if you think you can push my people beyond their limits! You won't push your Sierra Charlies beyond theirs! Why do you expect me to push the Warhawks?" Worsham was just barely respectful when he said that, but he was too tired to care. Even the tips of his long, black handlebar mustache were drooping. "Besides, we've got a shit pot full of squawks for AIRMAINCO! Some of our Chippies and Harpies made it here only because my pilots and their crew chiefs elected to continue flying even with marginal aircraft and inoperative equipment that would normally signal a no-go! Once I get a chance to get a shit, shine, shower, shave, and shampoo, I'll give you a squadron status report! But my best guess right now is that we won't be able to put anything into the air except on a dire emergency basis before oh-eight-hundred tomorrow!"

"Any chance of a volunteer pilot...?"

Worsham got to his feet, and Curt could tell that the man had sat too long in a Harpie's seat. Cal could barely stand erect, and the way he moved indicated that his muscles were still stiff and cramped. "I'll ask, but the way my pilots are feeling, I'm likely to get my ass in a sling..."

"It might help your posture," Curt cracked, trying to lighten up a bit.

It didn't work. Worsham was too tired to joke. "I don't read you loud and clear, Carson. Your foot's in your mouth!" He saluted in the perfunctory flyboy manner and started to limp out of the office.

Curt realized that he was being over-zealous again. Cal Worsham was beat to the socks. Otherwise, the man would be far more foul-mouthed. He realized that his plan to pay a visit to Colonel Qian and his PRC regiment up in the canyon at Krasnetskoye wasn't going to materialize today. He should have known that the Warhawks would be out of it, even though they'd arrived at 1300 as planned. "Okay, Cal, my apologies. Stand down and take care of personal and equipment maintenance. Get a hot and a cot. I'll see you at oh-eight-hundred tomorrow."

"Your compassion is exemplary, Colonel," Worsham muttered in reply.

And Curt said nothing. He was pissed off at himself. He was behaving in a way he never expected he would and reacting in a manner he would have detested in any other regimental commander. He knew he had to get straight with himself again. The pressures of commanding the Washington Greys plus those of trying to operate in a strange, hostile, and uncomfortable land with no clear military objective and an incompetent general were all getting to him. Maybe he should go see Dr. Ruth Gydesen...or his favorite little biotech, Captain Helen Devlin, who had always provided thoughtful and pleasant therapy for him since the warbot brainy days.

What the hell, he told himself. *The Washington Greys are in position. We're ready to do our part...with the possible exception of AIRBATT which needs eighteen hours of stand-down to recuperate. I've got no orders from Mahathis. I defused the Soviet threat yesterday. Why should we bust our asses to shock the Chinese? So screw it!*

He passed his hand over his comm terminal panel and said to it, "Connect me with Major Gratton!"

"Gratton here!" came the voice of the regimental adjutant.

"Pappy, do we have anything like the Club set up yet?"

"Colonel, we've been pretty busy..."

"Damn!"

"But some of the eager youngsters who still have iron in their blood rather than lead in their asses have managed to cobble-up a reasonable substitute," Gratton went on. "Wade Hampton and Harriett Dearborn managed to scrounge up something resembling food as well as some Class Six Supplies. The AIRBATT people brought in some stuff from Oahu, including seafood. Doctor Ruth's people are checking samples now. I don't expect her to report that one of the local horses has kidney trouble. We expect a green light on everything shortly. But I'm not so sure the place is in shape yet for a real Stand-to, Colonel."

"Is it in shape at all?"

"Considering the time, place, and circumstances, Colonel, affirmative!"

"Good! Crank that sucker up for operation at eighteen hundred hours! Except for those on guard duty, notify the regiment to stand down to off-duty Green Condition at eighteen hundred. And the Club will be open by my edict!"

"Is this an official Stand-to, Colonel?"

"Negatory! Attendance optional!" Curt knew that his people needed the relaxation plus the time to let off steam and do a little unofficial bitching and sniveling. He needed it, too. He felt himself growing more distant from those he commanded but who were also his friends and comrades. He had to get down off his pedestal so they could look him in the eyes at the same level.

Command was a powerful, heady brew, but he wasn't sure he liked it as a constant diet.

Then he punched up the command net to CINCSPD. Sergeant Major Tengah Tuanku of the 6th Sultan's Own Gurkha Rifles came on the line, sharp and spiffy as usual. "Ah, good afternoon, Colonel Carson!"

"Twonky, I'd like to request that the planning and staff meeting scheduled at ten-hundred tomorrow be rescheduled until fourteen hundred," Curt told him, figuring he'd put off the Chinese visit until the morning; if it didn't look good to go then, he'd scrub it then and have time to make the Papa and Sierra briefings. "Please tell General Mahathis that we haven't completed our staff work here yet. Plus, the fact that our AIRBATT crews are suffering from fatigue and won't be able to shuttle us to the meeting by air."

"Excuse me, sah, but Colonel Payne-Ashwell just overheard your message and wishes to speak with you," Tuanku replied.

The image of the Gurkha commander appeared on the screen, "I say, Carson, but that's an unusual development! I can appreciate that the Warhawks are tired from their long journey. Please tell Major Worsham that I hope to see him here tomorrow for a coordination meeting. But I'm surprised that you efficient Americans have fallen behind the schedule this early in the game."

"Duncan, after yesterday and last night, my people are beat to the socks...and so am I," Curt admitted. "The difficult we do immediately; the impossible takes a little longer. Sorry, but that's just the way we Americans are. No staying power compared to your Gurkhas, so you don't need to remind me of that. The regiment is too strung out at the moment, and we need some breathing space. Tell the general that we've still got a cesspool full of alligators up here to deal with. We're operational if absolutely necessary, but..."

"The general won't like it," Payne-Ashwell told him unnecessarily.

"Scroom!" Curt exclaimed.

"Excuse me, but that's an American term with which I'm not familiar."

"I'll give you the translation privately tomorrow afternoon, Duncan."

"Very well, Carson! I can use a delay to good advantage myself," Payne-Ashwell admitted while not willing to admit that he, too, was both tired and under more pressure than he liked. Stout British attitude and stiff upper lip and all that. But he went on to say, "But I do have some information that might be of interest to you in the meantime. Can you scramble, please? Code Quebec Seven November."

"Roger, scrambling!" Curt replied punching in the proper program.

The image didn't even waver. Edie had done an excellent job, as usual. Payne-Ashwell continued, "It seems we have our adversaries a bit confused. The only orders we've intercepted have been for the Chinese. They have been told to stand by and wait for further orders from Beiching. I suspect that the COPRE resolution caught the Chinese government unprepared to respond to our presence here. We think the Japanese regiment may have received orders.

However, their C-cubed is as sophisticated as ours, so we may not be able to put their messages through our thresher to separate the wheat from the chaff. And we have intercepted no orders for the Soviets. By the way, you did an outstanding job of temporarily defusing any possible threat from them. Good show, old chap! Up to your usual form! Therefore, I agree that it might be an acceptable move on our part at the moment for all of us to back off and let matters develop. I'll recommend that to the general. I presume you will concur with my recommendation?"

Curt replied that he did, and he would, and he'd see Payne-Ashwell tomorrow afternoon. He punched off and got back to work taking care of a raft of administrative details. Command was still plagued with "paperwork" and "computer puke," although computers and data management systems had relieved much of the burden. Army regulations, however, required Curt's personal attention to the individual reports from his staff-S-1 Personnel, S-2 Intelligence, S-3 Operations, and S-4 Logistics as well as the regimental medical report, the maintenance report, and the morning report.

CINCSPD wasn't requiring any formal reports yet, an oversight on Mahathis' part for which Curt was profoundly grateful at this point.

The Greys had discovered a barracks basement that was amenable to being quickly cleaned up and turned into the Club. It didn't have fancy electric lights, but someone had found some kerosene lanterns in Dolinsk. The result was a cozy, warm, dimly lit, and dry place to gather and let off steam. Most of the Greys were there.

A party was needed by the Greys right then. They made the best of it because no one knew when they'd have another one.

Curt was enjoying the relaxed camaraderie when he looked up and saw Maggie MacPherson in the room. She had only a single male videocam operator with her. And she headed straight for him.

"Maggie," he said to her sternly when she got within earshot in the noisy room, "I'd appreciate it if you'd put that videocam down! This gathering is private and personal to the Washington Greys! I don't want video footage of a Stand-to squirted out all over the world making the United States Army look like a bunch of wild, unruly, drunken sots! I'll not only catch hell but maybe lose my command!"

"What the hell, Curt, it's not running! I don't want tape of a wild party. *Maggie's Hour* is a family show," she replied, sitting down at the table where Curt sat with Alexis, Jerry, Adonica, Dyani, Hassan, Henry, and Edie. "I want to talk to you on tape! If this isn't a good place to do it, let's go find a good place."

"Look, I'm relaxing with my regiment at the moment!" Curt snapped at her, irritated that she'd crashed a private party. "I don't get the chance to do this often enough! Get that camera and mike out of here, Maggie! I'll see you tomorrow sometime! Check with Major Wilkinson."

"I'll be with Colonel Castillo and the Chileans tomorrow," she told him. "I'm putting together this week's show, and I've got tape of everyone except you and Castillo. You wouldn't want to have the American forces left you, would you?"

"Quite frankly, my dear, I don't give a damn!"

"Come on! Give me thirty minutes!"

"Not only no, but hell no! This is the first time I've had the chance to relax in days!" Curt told her forcefully.

"Fifteen minutes?" she coaxed. She could coax real well, and it was obvious that she knew how to do it.

"Miss MacPherson, the freedom of the press goes only so far," Alexis broke in, her tone of voice indicating that she wasn't exactly happy that this news harpy, tough and likable as she'd been last night, had broken into a private party of the Washington Greys without an invitation and unannounced. To Alexis, that was a major breach of etiquette. And she wasn't about to let it pass without telling Maggie that. "Having known Len Spencer, the presidential press aide, I can assure you that I know what I'm talking about. This is a private party, and you wouldn't want your private. parties interrupted by an uninvited guest, I'm sure. Nor would you want them videotaped! Dyani, sit down! Anything we do, we'll do together!"

But Dyani was even more a stickler for protocol and good manners. She'd caught all the signals that Maggie MacPherson wanted to bed Curt Carson. It didn't bother Dyani that Curt might enjoy one or more nights with Maggie; she'd already told him as much without specifying the woman. But she wanted to get Maggie off Curt's back so she didn't bother him when he had serious work to do and people's lives as his responsibility. So, she didn't sit down. But she let Alexis do the talking.

"Miss MacPherson," Alexis went on, "none of the men here would lay a hand on you, but that wouldn't keep the women present from escorting you out the door. I really suggest that you leave on your own!"

"Hold it, both of you!" Jerry Allen piped up. "The colonel has already assigned me as one of his press aides. Colonel Carson, we'll still be here after fifteen minutes, so why not give Miss MacPherson her interview and get it over with? True, we'll be a drink or two ahead of you, hut I'm sure you can make it up real fast."

"Jerry..." Alexis began, resenting his intrusion.

"Hey, Alexis, one of my 'incidental duties regularly or as assigned' is to help Miss MacPherson get her news coverage while keeping everyone as happy as circumstances warrant," Jerry reminded her. "What's fifteen minutes? That will give you ladies time to hit the powder room..."

Curt realized that Jerry was indeed developing some tact in handling difficult situations.

He arose from the table and said, "I'll be right back. Don't worry, ladies; duty calls." Those last two words had become Curt's signal that Rule Ten was going to be observed, or at least a civilian version of it by him.

Curt's office was in a nearby building, so he selected that because the national and the regimental colors were properly displayed on staffs behind his desk. It looked like a regimental commander's office should look. Furthermore, it had good lighting so that Maggie's cameraman wouldn't have to blind him with brilliant lamps.

Curt was very tired, but he was suddenly jolted because when Maggie MacPherson went in front of that video camera, she literally underwent a transformation. She had something possessed by all great female television personalities, a projected aura that suddenly made her seem incredibly beautiful, desirable, attainable, friendly, and warm. It was so powerful that it could be transmitted as a dance of electrons through equipment and space, and it still came out on the receiving screen. In her actual presence, it was an order of magnitude greater, almost overwhelming. He'd never witnessed anything like it.

Maggie began by gently drawing him out about how he'd confronted the Soviets at Yuzhno-South aerodrome. She didn't attempt to get him to portray himself as a hero, and she didn't intimate it, but the inference was there. She then got him to talk a little about his background and how he was the sixth generation of his family to serve in the United States Army. Finally, she shifted back to their dinner at the Soviet casern the previous night.

"Colonel, it seemed to me that you were stepping unarmed into the very maw of destruction," she remarked. "Colonel Kurotkin had confronted you as an enemy yesterday. Can you explain to me why you went to see him?"

"Maggie, it was military courtesy and something else," Curt told her, not looking at the camera but looking at her. He couldn't take his eyes off her. "I've dealt with Soviet field officers in Kurdistan and elsewhere. They bluster and threaten when they think they're being threatened. But they respect strength, and they honor personal bravery. At the aerodrome, Colonel Kurotkin lost face because I called his bluff and he backed down. He'd threatened me, and he discovered I wouldn't cave in. I had to meet with him to let him know that I wasn't about to roll over him like a barbarian invader in spite of what he'd done. I had to show him that I wouldn't threaten him in the future if he behaved himself."

"So you really don't want to fight with his Soviet regiment?"

Curt nodded. "That's right! We're not here on Sakhalin to fight.

We're here to stop the fighting!"

"But why are the Soviets here in the first place? And the Chinese? And the Japanese?"

Curt shifted in his chair and rubbed his hand across his chin. "I really don't know. I haven't gotten a full intelligence and diplomatic briefing. But I can make a guess because I know something about Sakhalin's history. The Russians and the Japanese have contested this island for centuries. They both believe it's theirs."

"Then why are the Chinese here?"

Curt shrugged. "I don't know. The Chinese have never had any legitimate territorial claims to Sakhalin. Maybe they're just bothering the Russians. The Russians and the Chinese don't like one another. Never have. So, we're here to stop them from starting a fight that could escalate into a general war."

"Does the United States have any claims to Sakhalm or its resources?"

"No, but there may be some business deals between American and Japanese corporations covering that."

"So you're here protecting American business interests after all?"

"If so, I don't know about them."

"Should you be here?"

"Maggie, that's not my decision to make or argue about. I'm a soldier. I go where I'm ordered and do what I'm told."

"Wha''s your personal opinion, Colonel? Last night you remarked to Colonel Kurotkin that you didn't think your regiment should be here."

"It's my personal opinion that the Washington Greys shouldn't be here. Why? Because we're not matched to the mission. Our Sierra Charlie personal combat doctrine is intended for counter-insurgency and anti-terrorism operations. Peacekeeping with patrols is better suited to a regular Robot Infantry outfit. However, we may be here because we were available. So, we'll do the best job we can to keep this thing from bubbling over into a bigger war while the diplomats iron out the details of restoring equitable peace."

"Are you married, Colonel?"

Curt grinning. "Not yet."

"Got a girl?"

"Several."

"Anything serious?"

"Maybe. Time will tell. Marriage and a family don't exactly go with a combat soldier's life. It's a dangerous world. Because of warbots, people seem to forget that real soldiers can and do get killed in combat."

"I hope you don't," Maggie said earnestly.

"I hope so, too. All soldiers do. But if it happens, I hope it won't be in vain. Now I must get back-"

"Cut!" Maggie told her cameraman. "Thank you, Curt."

He got to his feet as the cameraman began to pack up. "You're welcome. You'll use it all?"

"Probably. My editors in LA usually do some editing, but I tell them to keep it at a minimum." As the cameraman left and Curt moved to escort her out of his office, she asked plaintively, "Do you really have to go back to your party?"

"Yes." At the moment, still stunned by her incredible television personality, he found himself wishing he didn't.

As they walked down the hallway, she sighed. "Dammit, Curt Carson, when can we be alone?"

"We were very alone in that ditch last night."

"You know what I mean!" Maggie said as she stopped at the building's outer door and blocked their path.

"Damned right! But I hear you get your choice of some very

interesting men. So, I want to know: Why me?"

She looked up at him. "I'm curious."

"Is that all?"

"No! I don't know why you excite me like you do! Don't you feel it?"

"Damned right I do!"

"And?"

"And I'm curious, too," Curt admitted.

"Allow me to repeat your question: Is that all?"

"No." And he fell silent.

She finally exploded, "Dammit, what the hell do I have to do to get you?"

"Are you so certain I won't get you, Maggie? Excuse me, but I promised the ladies..." He reached around her to open the door.

"You're a goddamned heart-breaker!" she told him as they stepped outside in the cold, damp air.

"Not when the time and the place are right. At the moment, I have a duty to others."

Chapter Twenty-Six

It was Major Joan Ward who awakened Colonel Curt Carson the next morning by knocking on the door of his quarters. When she was told to come in, she found him alone. With a note of concern in her voice, she remarked, "I noticed you missed breakfast call. Want me to bring you something to eat?"

"Thanks for checking on me, Joan. Yeah, I know I missed chow call. But I'll grab something on my way to Yuzhno," Curt responded listlessly. He hadn't slept well, although he'd slept alone. He didn't tell Joan that. But it was obvious that she knew.

"Some of the ladies were a bit upset last night that you were gone for thirty minutes," Joan observed.

Curt strapped his belt pouch around him and picked up his hat. "So I thought it was important to do a good job!" he snapped in irritation. "And I broke it off as quickly as I could! Damnation! I ought to reprimand Alexis and Dyani for leaving a Stand-to before their commanding officer did!"

"Oh, don't get hyper-reg on me, Curt! As I recall, it wasn't an official Stand-to anyway. Optional attendance, I was told. And you had indeed left," she reminded him, then asked solicitously. "But is there anything I can do?" Curt and Joan had been classmates. Although they'd dated while cadets, the relationship between them became more like brother-sister. Each knew the other was there at any time for any reason. It was rarely physical.

He straightened up and picked up his blue tam. "Yeah provide me with a friendly shoulder and a listening ear...maybe tonight when I get back from the rat race in Yuzhno today. Our first Papa and Sierra briefing...and a day late, at that!"

"Yes, and you'll be late for that, too, unless you shag ass. The Chippie is waiting! I told Nancy I'd come get you before Cal Worsham has another one of his shit fits over wasting aerodyne fuel sitting on the pad at idle waiting for the Big Man to haul his butt out of bed. Don't scowl at me! That's what Worsham said!"

"He would!"

"Better take your Novia," Joan reminded him. "People shoot at us around here. Or didn't you notice the other night?"

"Oh, I noticed, all right! In spite of Maggie Macpherson! And I appreciate your kind concern, especially since you're not the OOD."

"Anything to keep the Big Man out of trouble," Joan said to him privately.

A UCA-21C Chippewa airlift aerodyne was sitting in the open field behind the barracks when Curt came out. Its turbines were spooled up and running at idle. Some of his staff were already inside while others waited for him on the ground outside the gaping maw of the open cargo doors. The weather had improved somewhat, although it was still cold and damp. The clouds had lifted clear of the thousand-meter mountains on both sides of the valley. And Curt could now see they were indeed rugged mountains. Maggie had been right about trying to take ground forces into them at night to pay a surprise visit to the Chinese casern.

Curt didn't have anything to say to his staff except a morning greeting as they boarded. And he said little on the six-minute flight from Sokol to CINCSPD headquarters in Yuzhno-Sakhalin. Majors Wilkinson, Gratton, Atkmson, Aarts, Hamptom, and Dearborn said little because it was difficult to talk over the roar of the 'dyne. Major Cal Worsham sat back and seemed content just to ride along for a change. Regimental Sergeant Major Henry Kester sat there with his eyes closed, taking an old soldier's opportunity to relax because sometimes, he knew, one had to come off the wall quickly and go into full action. There was none of the chatter that sometimes accompanied the approach to combat where some people tried to talk their fears away by idle conversation or gallows humor. But no one expected combat today. This was business with all the excitement of Plans and Staff meetings. This was just part of the job of being a soldier.

Lieutenant Nancy Roberts landed alongside the CINCSPD building which was part of the city administrative complex built around a downtown park. There was plenty of room because there were still few automobiles on Sakhalin in spite of Japanese civil administration. The Soviet architecture and decades of occupation by Soviet people were still evident in the feel of the place. It would take several more decades before the Japanese again put their stamp on the island they called Karafuto…if indeed COPRE agreed to let them stay and the UN didn't change the protocols that supposedly had demilitarized the island under Japanese civil control.

Mahathis greeted them all cordially while Payne-Ashwell and Sergeant Major Tuanku renewed old acquaintances among the Washington Greys in somewhat less stressful circumstances than the Yuzhno airport. Alzena's welcome to Curt was warm but reserved because she knew Curt would behave in the quite proper manner of an American officer in public while she had to maintain her reserve as the chief civil deputy of SPD.

When they all sat down for the initial briefing, Curt had absolutely no idea how he was going to present Jerry Allen's tactical concept of drawing out the three adversary regiments to engage in individual skirmishes against the combined forces of CINCSPD. He didn't feel he had the full picture yet, and as a result, he didn't want to foul up any CINCSPD plans already in existence.

It turned out he need not have worried about that.

Mahathis apparently had no concrete plans at the moment.

But the intelligence briefing, carried out by Colonel Castillo, gave Curt a much better picture of who was doing what to whom and where they were doing it.

The three adversary regiments were garrisoned according to previous reports. Patrols from the three regiments were mainly confined to the Yuzhno valley - now becoming known at CINCSPD as Happy Valley - that ran north and south through the capital city from Staroduhskoye on the north to the Zaliv Aniva on the south. There appeared to be "control patrols" at platoon strength whose function it was to keep watch on the other two regiments and their patrols and to harass them if the opportunity arose. This information obtained by Castillo confirmed the preliminary findings of Dale Brown's birdbots as reported to Curt the previous afternoon.

Mahathis finally said, "Curt, you're my ops man with the tactical brains. Do you have any recommendations about how we can handle this situation and keep these patrols from firing on one another?"

"From an overall point of view, General, I do, and I've mentioned this earlier to Colonel Payne-Ashwell," Curt replied. "We don't want to take them on in any one-on-one, evenly matched confrontation. We'll take them on a patrol or a regiment at a time."

"We can't assault their patrols, Curt!" Alzena reminded him.

"The sultana is quite correct," was the comment from Colonel Castillo. "Our standing orders from Santiago are to participate in the Sakhalin Police Detachment but to take no offensive action here."

A rumbling sound reminiscent of a regiment of assaulting heavy RTVs grew louder. Then the room began to tremble. Two brief ground shocks like artillery shells landing nearby shook the room. Then it subsided.

"Ah, minor earth tremor!" Castillo commented. "We have them in Chile, too. I forgot that we are on the other side of the Pacific rim here."

"We won't attack their patrols," Curt promised, ignoring the tremor. It was unnatural to him, but Maggie had pointed out that such things were common in the vicinity of earthquake zones such as the Kamchatka-Kurile region. "I don't think we have to. On the other hand, we must let all three regimental commanders know very quickly that we won't stand for their patrols hassling other patrols, regardless of who's who."

He looked at Mahathis and went on, "I've told Colonel Kurotkin that. He may not believe me. But he will if he pulls an ambush like the Chinese did night before last. When ambushed, we must respond in an overwhelming manner. Fast. With crushing force. Not a lot of killing - none if we can get away with it - but with enough zip that the ambushers know damned good and well they've tickled a tiger. How do we do this? Well, we must set up a situation that invites or provokes the Chinese, Japanese, or Soviets to ambush one of our patrols. When they do that, it's got to trigger a response not just from our patrol that's attacked but from pre-positioned and trigger-ready portions of the three SPD regiments acting together to absolutely blow them away. In brief, keep your nose clean and your patrols peaceful. We're nice guys, but you don't want to meet us at work. And we go to work immediately if you force us to do it."

"I like it," was Castillo's comment. "I did the same thing in the confrontation with Peru and Bolivia. It will work. I know it."

"It's rather deceitful," Alzena observed with distaste.

"Sultana, the military forces of Brunei, America, and Chile are here to stop the fighting and to give you a chance to do your job," Curt reminded her. "Like it or not, we have a 'low intensity war' going on here. Very low intensity, to be sure. But warfare nonetheless. When someone ambushes and shoots at me with intent to inflict serious bodily harm - which happened night before last – that's war to me. The art of war must therefore be brought into action. Sun Tzu laid out the principles behind the art of war. One of these says, 'All warfare is based on deception.' If we want to get off this island alive and well in the near future, we'd better act like we mean business and treat it like a war."

"But I met with Colonel Mishida yesterday," Alzena revealed. "The Japanese casern is only a few hundred meters from here. He assured me that his regiment is not the one carrying out ambushes. He wishes to cooperate."

"My dear Sultana," Payne-Ashwell told her in a patronizing manner, "this is also what Curt was told by Colonel Kurotkin. While I should not doubt the word of another officer, I would also be somewhat remiss if I did not rely on deeds rather than words when the lives of my officers and men are involved. Therefore, I intend to recommend that all SPD patrols go out armed and ready for ambush and that our air support remains on stand-by alert to provide tacair, since it is apparent that the other side has no air support. As we gain experience here on Sakhalin, we will certainly discover who is doing the ambushing and who is being ambushed."

"Curt, that's an interesting tactical proposal. How do you propose to do what you suggest?" Mahathis wanted to know, steering the meeting back on track again.

Curt looked at him and smiled. "General, that's what we're here today to work out! We've got good military minds from three nations and military commanders and their staffs who have actually fought, been shot at, and won other engagements and campaigns. So, we'll use that expertise. After all, that's what staff meetings should be all about!"

A Gurkha lance corporal unobtrusively entered the room and spoke quietly to Payne-Ashwell, who in tum spoke to Mahathis.

"Colonel Carson, you have an urgent communication via videophone. You are excused in order to take it. If it has anything to do with the situation, please report as quickly as possible," the CINCSPD general told Curt.

Curt got up and tossed a look at Joanne Wilkinson that asked, *Who the hell could it be?* He took it in a private office nearby.

It was Major General Belinda Hettrick, and she was angry as hell from the look on her face and the fire in her eyes. As soon as Curt came on, she skipped the hellos and got right to the point.

"Colonel Carson," she began formally, at which point Curt knew he was somehow in very deep trouble, "you gave an interview to the correspondent, Maggie MacPherson, last night?"

"Yes, ma'am, I did," Curt replied in a forthright manner. It was apparent that she knew he had, and it wasn't his manner to waffle in response to a question from her anyway.

"What did you talk about?"

"Oh, she asked me a lot of things about myself, General," he told her, recalling the warmth and attraction of the woman and the ease with which she'd drawn him out. "She wanted some background about the situation on Sakhalin from my point of view."

"What did you tell her?"

"Basically, what I'd been told and what I knew. None of it is classified. If it is, I wasn't informed of the fact," Curt remarked. "General, it's obvious you've either seen the tape she made or know more about something than I do. What's the situation? Why the call?"

"I just watched that favorite prime-time television show, *Maggie's Hour*," Hettrick told him.

Curt did a quick calculation in his head; it was early evening in Arizona. Maggie's show must have been squirted via satellite to Los Angeles after his interview last night, Sakhalin time, which was morning, California time. It had probably been edited into final form there during the day and then broadcast in American prime time.

"I haven't seen it yet," Curt admitted. "I thought the interview was pretty innocuous. Should I have Edie Sampson pull it off a satellite and have a look?"

"I think you should!" Hettrick replied forcefully. "My comm hasn't started to get hot yet, but it may in the morning. I expect to hear from everybody from the White House on down."

Curt was mystified. He knew he must have screwed up somewhere during that interview, but he didn't know where or why or what was causing Belinda Hettrick to have a real case of heartburn at the moment. "General, why am I in trouble? Did I say something wrong?"

Hettrick seemed to relax a little, but Curt could see that she was still very angry. "I want the ungarbled truth from you, Curt! Did they edit you poorly in Los Angeles, or did you really tell Maggie MacPherson and the world in general that you didn't think the Washington Greys should be on Sakhalin at all?"

"Yes, ma'am, I said it," Curt admitted candidly. "But I wasn't speaking for the Department of Defense or the United States Army. I explained to Maggie in the interview that it was just my personal opinion."

Hettrick leaned forward, and her transmitter's video-camera had trouble keeping her face in focus because she came that close to the set. Her face turned red, and she said nothing for a moment. Then she exploded, letting Curt have the impact of her wrath, "Personal opinion, hell! Curt, as long as you wear that uniform, *you don't have a personal opinion!*"

Curt closed his eyes and gritted his teeth. So that was it!

Major General Belinda Hettrick glared at him for a whole minute, letting the words sink in. Curt could feel how angry she was.

"General, I will apologize to you and anyone else. But I said it, and there isn't a whole hell of a lot that I can do about it now," Curt replied slowly and carefully, aware that he must not sound either too smug or too devastated; he was still the commanding officer of the Washington Greys. But he wasn't sure now how long that would last. "Do you want me to pack my things and be ready for orders posting me to Uganda? Or should I find a good tailor to fit me out in civvies?"

"Just shut up, don't say anything about it to anyone, and keep your personal opinions to yourself and away from Maggie MacPherson," she advised him, some of her anger gone. "It probably won't blow over, but it may if we don't make a big deal about it by going around apologizing for it. If someone wants to use it to get General Carlisle, me, or you, let them come after us first. Let's not give them any more ammo to use."

"My God, I didn't realize it could get that bad!"

"It hasn't yet. But it could. We'll deal with it if and when it happens." Hettrick sat back and said in a hurt but motherly tone, "Curt, I thought you'd watched me handle Len Spencer in Namibia. But now I realize that you were far more concerned with your company and with Spencer romancing Alexis. Be that as it may, I obviously neglected part of your education. Best I can do right now is to try to remedy that and cover for you if I can."

"Can I do anything about it?"

"No. As I said, shut up and soldier! And handle Maggie MacPherson as the regimental commander of the Washington Greys of the Army of the United States, not as Curt Carson, U.S. citizen. Got it? Understood?"

"Yes, ma'am. In Maggie's case, that will be hard to do…"

"I know. I watched her perform. And I watched your reaction to her."

"Was it that obvious?"

"Curt, you're a man. All man. I'd be concerned if you hadn't reacted. I'd worry that maybe you got something shot off in the last skirmish and hadn't reported it," Hettrick admitted. "I'm glad to see that didn't happen! So, go back and do your job!"

Chapter Twenty-Seven

Curt was riding on the flight deck of the UCA-21C Chippewa with Lieutenant Nancy Roberts when he saw it. They were on a shuttle flight from Sokol to CINCSPD in Yuzhno-Sakhalinsk, and it was the usual sort of dark grey day with the clouds just topping the mountains with a ragged thousand-meter ceiling and light drizzle.

"Soviet Air Lift Six Four, this is Yuzhno Approach," the air traffic control receiver sounded off. "Turn right to heading of one-four-zero, join the localizer for Runway One-Niner, Yuzhno-South. Descend and maintain niner hundred meters until established on the localizer and glide slope. Cleared ILS Runway One-Niner Approach, Yuzhno-South. Contact the tower on Channel Four. Traffic below you at three hundred meters southbound on visual, an American Chippewa aerodyne, landing Yuzhno Centrum, should he no factor."

"Yuzhno Approach, Soviet Six Four, right turn to one-four-zero, down to niner hundred, cleared ILS Runway One-Niner," the Russian pilot's voice replied, speaking excellent aeronautical English because, almost a hundred years after World War II, the international language of air transport was still English. "We are descending through one decimal one thousand, ceiling is very ragged."

"Hauler Two, Yuzhno Approach, a Soviet Antonov four-oh-four will pass over you at niner hundred on ILS approach to Yuzhno-South. Should be no factor," the air traffic controller - obviously a Japanese from his accent - told Nancy.

Nancy Roberts looked up since she was only in partial linkage with the Chippie and using her own eyes rather than the aerodyne's sensors. Even the Mod 7/11 AI which was directing the autopilot really didn't have good enough resolution for Nancy at their low altitude, so she preferred piloting these shuttle hops with a minimum of robotic assistance. Taking her right hand off the control stack, she pointed upward and to the right for Curt's benefit and replied on the comm, "Yuzhno Approach, Hauler Two. Tally ho! Traffic in sight!"

Curt saw the huge Soviet airlifter breaking in and out of the low cloud deck above them. The Soviets had always been obsessed with very large airplanes, and the An-404 was no exception. This was an airlift logistics flight for the 110th Special Airborne Guards Regiment. With six regiments being supplied mostly by airlift, Yuzhno radar approach control was a busy operation now. The Chinese brought their supplies directly into Krasnetskoye using H-8 license-built MDH helicopters and H-13 license-built French Delauney aerodynes. Because of airport congestion, the Greys were being supplied through Sokol aerodrome. By mutual agreement, all military commanders on Sakhalin had agreed not to harass one another's logistics flights just as they'd come to a similar agreement not to ambush one another's patrols. Alzena had put that agreement together with Curt's help. Thus far, everyone had honored it for two weeks.

Out of the corner of his eye, he saw the bright flare and the dark black smoke trail coming up. It was fast. Too fast for him to spot the ground launch site. It looked like a Soviet SA-77 *Ossah* baby SAM, but he couldn't tell without countermeasures equipment to identify the i-r and radar signatures. The smoke trail converged with the An-404, and it seemed to Curt that the right inboard fanjet took the SAM. What happened afterward occurred quickly. It seemed that the explosion also severed the right wing of the huge transport. The monstrous plane began to slowly roll over and over to the right as it began to fall from the skies toward the green meadows of Sakhalin below.

"Yuzhno Approach, Soviet Six Four has an emergency! Number Three engine has exploded. Emergency! We are going down! We are going down! *Bojemoi!*" The rest of the panicky message was in rapid Russian which terminated in an obvious expletive, undoubtedly the Russian equivalent of the words usually uttered by nearly all pilots everywhere just before they crash: "*Oh, shit!*"

When an aircraft the size of an AN-404 hit the ground going nearly straight down, it made a huge fireball. Although Curt didn't know how anyone could have survived the impact, he told Nancy, "Change course! Head for the crash site! Maybe we can rescue survivors, if any!"

Nancy didn't answer him, but the Chippie suddenly heeled over and began to descend toward the fiery field. "Yuzhno Approach, this is Hauler Two! We saw what happened! It looked like Soviet Six Four was hit by a SAM fired from the ground! It has just crashed, and we're declaring an emergency and heading for the crash site to give aide to any survivors!"

"Tell him to call Sink-Spud and the Soviet casern!" Curt added.

"Hauler Two, Yuzhno approach, roger your last! We are notifying medical and fire units! We will also call the military headquarters! Please give me any reports you wish to have relayed to authorities!"

"Yuzhno, I don't think there are any survivors! It had a wing blown off, and it went straight into the ground!" Nancy replied, her voice shaky.

The Chippie was the first on the scene, and there wasn't anything left but a smoking hole in the ground. Pieces of the aircraft and its cargo were scattered by the impact and explosion. Curt saw no bodies. He cautioned members of his staff who were numbed with shock as they exited the Chippie and saw the crash site, "Don't touch anything! I don't think there're any survivors, but let's make a quick search!"

"Damned lucky it missed the railway!" Henry Kester observed. "And another couple of hundred meters to the east would have wiped out those houses! Colonel, there ain't much left, but I think this pile of stuff over here is what's left of one of their Silver Pilgrim warbots..."

"Goddammit!" Curt swore. "Kurotkin wasn't supposed to bring in any reinforcements!"

"Could be a couple of replacements," Henry surmised. "The Sovs rotate their equipment a lot, especially when it reaches its TBO limits whether it needs overhaul or not. That way, a Sov commander is always sure of having fresh equipment on hand if the balloon goes up."

They found that no living creature had survived the crash, so they stood around and waited for the fire trucks and unnecessary ambulances to show.

Colonel Kurotkin was there before the Yuzhno fire department made it to the scene. He roared up in a BTR-218 with Major Ivanovski and Captains Yurasov and Glinka. His first reaction as he debarked from the armored personnel carrier was one of stunned silence. Then he erupted in Russian.

Curt called Lieutenant Martha Milton over. "Need a translator."

"I can't translate that!" she told him.

"Why not?"

"It's very strong language! Invective, mostly. But he's pretty angry at you."

"At me?" Curt suddenly wished he hadn't left his Novia in the Chippie.

At that point, Kurotkin turned on Curt and let loose with a torrent of Russian.

"More invective," Milton reported. "He wants to know why you intercepted the aircraft on final approach and shot it down from the Chippie."

"What the hell! Can't he see? Doesn't he know a Chippie is an unarmed tactical transport aerodyne?"

"No, not in his present emotional state," Milton advised him.

"Tell him to cool it," Curt instructed her. "Nancy and I both saw the SAM come up from the ground and hit the plane."

Although Kurotkin spoke good English, he wasn't speaking it right then. Captain Andrei Glinka walked up to Curt and Milton, his eyes also angry but his demeanor a bit more under control. He spoke in English to them, "Why did you do this?"

"We didn't, Captain. But we saw it," Curt told him earnestly. "And why do you think we would shoot down one of your airlift planes?"

"You knew it had replacement Silver Pilgrims aboard!" Glinka snapped.

Curt shook his head. "Like hell! We didn't even know the cargo manifest until Sergeant Kester here spotted the remains of a Silver Pilgrim on the ground over there! Tell Colonel Kurotkin that! And tell him we're as shocked as he is about this because *we didn't do it!* Tell him that and tell him that I speak as one honorable officer to another!"

Glinka did so, whereupon Kurotkin engaged in animated conversation with his political officer, Major Ivanovski. Finally, Kurotkin whirled on Curt and snapped in English, "Full investigation is to be done! You are not trusted by me until investigation shows truth is what you say!" The man was obviously strung out because he spoke better English than that; he was now speaking Anglicized Russian, dropping articles and using almost direct translation of Russian grammar structure.

"I'll cooperate fully with your investigation," Curt told him, then said to Milton, "Tell him that in Russian, too!"

She did, where upon Kurotkin said nothing but began to move away to inspect the smoking remains.

Curt summoned up what little he knew of Russian. *"Kay sohjahlyeneeyoo.* I'm sorry," he called after the Soviet commander.

Back in the Chippie, he told Nancy, "Spool up and get back to Sokol!"

Keying his tacomm brick, he called, "Grey Chief, this is Grey Head! I'm coming back to Sokol right away! In the meantime, go to Condition Red and advice Sink-Spud to do the same! I'll explain when I get there! Do you copy!"

Edie Sampson had been monitoring the tacomm in Sokol. "Grey Head, this is Grey Techie! I copy! Will pass the word to Grey Chief and Sink-Spud immediately!" She didn't waste time asking why.

She knew how to react when Curt declared an emergency, which he'd just done.

Nancy Roberts didn't waste any time, either. She didn't go for altitude. With the possibility of SAMs in the neighborhood, she stayed right down on the deck, flying a harrying nap-of-the-Earth path back to the Greys casern in Sokol. Five minutes later, she settled the Chippie on the ground in front of the headquarters building. As quickly as Curt and his staff debarked, she was in the air again and heading for Sokol aerodrome to get refueled and configured for tactical airlift, which was her job under Condition Red.

The regimental headquarters was quietly but tensely Condition Red when Curt burst in. "Sampson, I'm going on the line to Sink-Spud to report. I want all Greys plugged in on the circuit. We may not have time for a separate briefing."

"I take it the slime hit the impeller?" Edie asked unnecessarily.

"A big Soviet log bird took a Golden BB," Henry Kester told her briefly and went to his Condition Red post.

"Oh, shit!" seemed to be the generally voiced comment that came almost simultaneously from about a dozen people in the room.

When Curt contacted CINCSPD, he insisted that Mahathis and Alzena get on the line along with anyone else who was there at the moment. He also waited until they got Colonel Julio Castillo on the net. Then he explained what had happened.

"We just heard," Mahathis told him.

"Where? From who?" Curt wanted to know.

"Yuzhno Approach Control called us," Mahathis said. Curt had forgotten he'd given that order.

"This is not good," Castillo remarked with deep concern in his voice.

"And Colonel Kurotkin informed me," Alzena added. "He's withdrawing from the non-harassment agreement. He said to tell you that he doesn't believe the Greys did it, but he's going to find out who did and take what he termed 'appropriate action.'"

"That figures! Great!" Curt growled, then quickly said, "General, as your tactical ops officer, here's what I recommend we do in order to keep this from escalating. We've got to prevent any Soviet confrontations with the Chinese or Japanese until things cool down a little bit. If you and the sultana would, please call Kurotkin, Qian, and Mishida and explain that this is a police emergency. Tell them to recall all their troops to their respective caserns and stay there until we declare the emergency over."

Colonel Castillo broke in, "My regiment should occupy Yuzhno-South aerodrome as quickly as possible to prevent anyone else from taking it. We'll make certain that the aerodrome continues to operate normally and that all scheduled flights can come in and out on flight plans."

"The Washington Greys will secure the Sokol aerodrome," Curt assured them.

"Right-o! We must hold the aerodromes," was the comment from Payne-Ashwell. "Otherwise, we'll have to be supplied by sea through Korsakov and Starodubskoye, and that would place us on short rations for several days."

"I can still act as C-cubed-I staff officer from Yuzhno-South. That is mostly communications, and we have that well established at the moment," Castillo remarked.

"How do you suggest we keep those regiments in their caserns, Curt?" was Mahathis' question.

"Roadblocks," Curt said. "Put the Gurkhas between Yuzhno-Sakhalinsk and Novoaleksandrovsk. The Greys will block the road between Novoaleksandrovsk and Krasnetskoye. The Chileans can serve as an airborne reserve to be moved somewhere quickly if they're needed."

"If the triumvirate of Soviets, Chinese, and Japanese try to break through the roadblocks by force of arms," Payne-Ashwell added, "we can call in tacair support. We have it. They do not. At least, not at the moment. That could change in a day or so."

"Well, we'll let them start it," Curt said. "But we've got to respond in strength when they do."

"Colonel Carson, may I remind you again that we're not here to fight?" Alzena put in.

"Sultana, the circumstances are now such that we've got to do our job, which is to keep the triumvirate apart...and one of them is pretty pissed off at the other two right now. And when they learn about it, one of them may decide to make a preemptive strike because they're evenly matched and they want surprise on their side," Curt explained. Then he went on more gently, "Alzena, we won't fight unless they insist. But right at the moment, I think Kurotkin would try to blast his way through anything to get at either the Chinese or the Japanese, but not both. He hasn't got that sort of superiority at the moment, and he won't move against superior forces. Soviet doctrine prevents him from doing that. Since we don't know which way he'll move - or if Qian or Mishida may move first – we've got to get this thing organized fast! And when he moves, we've got to show him that we do indeed have the superior force and thus take him off the dangerous-to-our-health list. That will leave only two regiments to worry about."

"Do you have any idea who might have fired that SAM at the Soviet aircraft?" Mahathis wanted to know.

"Yeah, I do, but I could be mistaken," Curt replied. He was. "So, I won't say who right now. He'll reveal himself in due time. We've got something else to worry about right now. When we get this situation cooled off, we can team with Kurotkin in an investigation."

"Kurotkin might have shot down his own airplane just to get something started," Mahathis suggested.

"Not a chance, General! The Soviets are indeed chess players, but I seriously doubt that Kurotkin would throw away a piece as expensive and important as an Antonov Four-oh-four," Curt insisted, then recalled what he'd read in one of the armed forces professional journals about a month before. "The Soviets have only twenty of them. And they're mostly used for air logistics to isolated

Siberian locations. And the production line has shifted to making Four-forties for foreign sales to boost hard currency reserves. Would you deliberately throw away one of your hypersonic transports?"

"I don't know. Would the United States throw away a LoadStar and its crew if the government thought it was somehow worth the price?"

"General, not a chance! Not in peacetime! Probably not in wartime, either! We've never deliberately sacrificed that sort of thing," Curt assured him. "We don't think or operate that way, even when things get really desperate."

"Under certain circumstances, it might be an acceptable move in a chess game…" Maha this pointed out.

"We're poker players," Curt said. "And we wouldn't throw away a jack of the same suit when we're working on a royal flush with a good chance of making it."

Mahathis suddenly seemed to take a different course. "Shouldn't we stay in caserns ourselves and not move out? Our roadblocks could be interpreted as a threat in the wake of the Soviet aircraft shoot down," he continued. "Shouldn't we consider putting up birdbots and recon aerodynes to spot when one of the regiments starts to move? We'd have time to intercept them instead of putting the troops out in the field in this cold and damp weather."

Curt knew what the man was doing. He was trying to investigate all the permutations and combinations, trying to find the best way to move, and perhaps yielding to what he thought his twin sister's wishes might be. Curt knew Alzena. He knew she was committed to a non-violent diplomatic solution if she could get one.

But Curt also knew that waiting might be interpreted as waffling. And waiting never made it better, only worse.

"General, it's my serious recommendation as your tactical expert and chief of staff that we start moving *now* before the triumvirate decides to do so!" Curt insisted.

"General Mahathis, I agree," Payne-Ashwell added.

"You would!" Alzena snapped, frustrated because all her attempts and overtures toward gaining a peaceful diplomatic settlement on Sakhalin seemed to be coming apart bit by bit in spite of all her efforts. "Anything to keep your Gurkhas in fighting trim and spirit! And practice, too, I imagine!"

"Your Highness," Payne-Ashwell responded formally "your grandfather wanted and needed real fighting men to keep Brunei from being swallowed in the post-colonial wars of the last century. He got them when he agreed to employ and maintain the Sixth Gurkha Rifles after the United Kingdom withdrew from the Far East. Without wanton destruction or senseless killing, the Gurkhas have helped three sultans expand Brunei and turn it into the Abode of Peace and the shining new jewel of the Pacific rim. The ancient words of Sun Tzu are as applicable today as they were twenty-five centuries ago: 'War is of vital importance to the State; the province of life or death; the road to survival or ruin.'"

"I'm interested in life, not death," Alzena remarked.

"So am I," Payne-Ashwell responded without hesitation. "Or I would not do this as a profession."

"Alzena, I think," Curt ventured to suggest, trying to blunt her assault which might strongly affect the decision he had to get from her twin brother very quickly now, "that you should talk with Major Alexis Morgan about this sort of thing. I guarantee that she's also a woman, although she's different from you. But later, please. We have work to do and little time in which to do it if we're going to keep it from becoming deadly! General Mahathis, you're the commander in chief. Colonel Payne-Ashwell, Colonel Castillo, and I need your approval. We agree on what must be done. May we have your orders, sir?"

Mahathis hesitated, then he said, "Execute your plan, gentlemen, with the following rules of engagement: You may not attempt by force of arms to halt the movement of the other three regiments."

"General Mahathis," Colonel Castillo asked, "how do we execute the plan and still obey your rule of engagement?"

"You gentlemen are the tactical experts," Mahathis said imperiously. "We are not here to fight. We are here to stop the fighting. Remember that!"

Curt knew at that moment that he was going to have to take command away from this man.

But he would have to do it in such a way that he wouldn't ruin his career if he did...because he was likely to be killed if he didn't.

Chapter Twenty-Eight

It was a rapid response maneuver. Curt's orders to the Washington Greys were quite simple to understand but extremely difficult to carry out:

3RI/SC OP ORD SPD-001. PASSWORD: star*lever/goombah. War can protect but cannot create. GREYS to deploy ASAP south to Kurskoye and Sinegorsk. Objective: prevent movement of Soviet personnel to Krasnetskoye and PRC personnel to Novoaleksandrovsk. Units deploy as follows: SCOUT move to northwest and place PRC casern under surveillance; report any PRC movement. BIRD to base at Kurskoye and engage in recon of Soviet units in base at Novoaleksandrovsk; report developments. ASSAULTCOs to bridge road/ railway at Sinegorsk and form roadblock. GUNCO to deploy on high ground to northwest of Sinegorsk where Saucy Cans can sweep road. AIRBATT: Use AIRLIFTCO to emplace TACBATT. TACAIRCO to come to pad alert for tacair support as called upon by company commanders. Companions and BIOTECO to base at Kurskoye. Remainder of SERVBATT to secure Sokol airfield. Full Oscar briefing to be made by tacomm in the field once deployment complete. CC. Carson LTCOL Commanding. Tact consists in knowing how far to go in going too far.

The nonsense phrases inserted at the beginning and end of the text had been carefully selected by Curt to convey a message as well. The Greys knew he did that sort of thing from time to time, and his company and platoon commanders were accustomed to reading double meanings into them. Since they were part of orders and often ambiguous, they could be interpreted by subordinates. It was a trick he'd learned from both Hettrick and especially Bellamack, who had not only given deliberately vague orders but often incomplete orders.

The Greys also knew the bitter truth of the old saying, *Turn the other cheek and get two Purple Hearts.*

A copy of Curt's orders to the Greys went to CINCSPD, of course.

Curt was counting on the fact that Mahathis didn't know how to write the kind of order for land forces that would given them some leeway in operations. Mahathis had been educated in a different style of fighting by the U.S. Aerospace Force Academy - system against system. Furthermore, the Brunei general was accustomed to giving a simple, direct order and then expecting others automatically to obey and carry it out; he wasn't good at follow-up because, as the sultan's son his orders were, in effect, royal edicts that one disobeyed at one's peril. At least in Brunei. But this was Sakhalin, and Colonel Curt Carson was a citizen, not a subject.

Curt's orders as land ops commander were less vague and more direct in instructing the Gurkhas and Chileans.

But difficult orders or not, the Washington Greys moved out of Sokol within an hour. Every Grey was anticipating the order, and they were eager to *do something*. Very shortly after the An-404 crash, the unofficial word had gotten around on the Rumor Control net, the only means of communication facetiously believed to be faster than the speed of light. Some of the Greys were already powering up warbots and starting vehicles when the move-out order came.

Curt established his operational headquarters on the western outskirts of the little village of Kurskoye only ten kilometers from Sinegorsk where Joan Ward had established Morgan's Marauders and Pagan's Pumas across the road and railway. Curt's direct view of Sinegorsk was blocked by both a heavy forest of Manchurian oak and some high terrain. But he had two visuals from two birdbots being operated in NE linkage by Jenny Volker of Brown's Black Hawks.

The Oscar briefing was by means of comm, sat, and NE links where everyone got the ungarbled word in their ACVs thanks to Georgie and Grady. It was almost redundant. Most of the Greys had already figured out what was going on and what would be expected of them because of the way Curt had deployed the regiment.

Then it became a matter of settling down and waiting for something to happen.

Curt tried to relax as he sat with Joanne Wilkinson, Henry Kester, and Edie Sampson in his OCV, watching the holographic display of the area projected in the tactical tank. The position of all units was marked. Curt studied the situation again, then remarked to Joanne, "See anything we missed?"

She shook her head. "It's a good tactical plan," she told him.

"Henry?" Curt asked his highest expert and most experienced critic.

"Good start, Colonel, but don't forget: No tactical plan survives the first contact" was Henry's candid comment.

"Edie?" Curt requested input from his regimental technical sergeant.

"It may work if tacomms work," Edie warned. "This whole operation depends pretty heavily on tacomms. It's been so cold and damp here on this friggin' island that I worry about whether or not we've got all the slime and rats out of them because we haven't used them in this sort of climate before..."

"Worries me, too," Henry admitted. "Comm gear always fails when you need it desperately...usually for fire support."

"Henry, you are a veritable encyclopedia of little bits of tactical know-how," Edie told him. "Did you ever think about writing them down?"

"Might. Someday," Henry told her.

"Henry, when this sheep screw is over and we're not watch-on-watch, do it. It'll be one of your 'additional duties regularly or as required,'" Curt told him.

"You and your big mouth, Sampson!" Henry muttered to Edie.

"Grey Head, Sink-Spud!" came the call from Mahathis in Yuzhno-Sakhalinsk.

"Fort Fumble calls," Joanne gave a heads-up to Curt.

"Grey Head here! H-A, Sink-Spud!" Curt snapped back as he toggled the tacomm channel.

"Be advised I've received a land-line message from Maggie

MacPherson's assistant producer at their operating base in the hotel in Yuzhno," Mahathis told him. "Maggie went up to Krasnetskoye with her team this morning to get some more tape of Qian and the Chinese troops. Her SatNet transmission from Krasnetskoye to her Yuzhno taping facility was interrupted by the Chinese. Before the signal died, it appeared that Qian's troops were taking her prisoner along with her field crew! Don't you think you should move on them with vertical envelopment and get her out?"

"Oh, shit!" was the quiet remark by Major Joanne Wilkinson.

"Told you so, sir!" was Kester's comment.

"Sink-Spud, if I try to move in there without real good recce, it could be very dangerous to our health. Let me get a handle on it first. I'll have recce reports from Krasnetskoye shortly," Curt told him. "In the meantime, Maggie will be all right. They won't harm her."

"How do you know that?" Mahathis wanted to know.

"The PRC Chinese have never harmed a Western reporter since they took over," Curt said. "They may put her away in a room for a while so she and her Bohemian Brigade can't videotape things that might be embarrassing later."

"But they might torture her! Or even shoot her!"

"Not a chance! Torture takes time and manpower, and Qian may have neither right now. And Chinese shoot other Chines, but not foreign devils!" Curt tried to put the CINC at east. Mahathis should know better because Brunei was full of Chinese merchants and traders, some of whom were from the PRC because even mainland China needed hard-currency international bankers in foreign locations.

Mahathis wasn't totally convinced but didn't have enough data to argue with Curt or to give him a direct order to get Maggie. Lieutenant Dyani Motega and her Mustangs were on the way to look things over, and there was nothing that could be done right then but wait until Dyani reported in.

Curt passed the word along to Dyani by NE tacomm, *Mustang Leader, Grey Head has received information that Maggie MacPherson and her field crew have been detained by Qian in Krasnetskoye. When you are able to do so, try to check that out.*

Grey Head, do you want the Mustangs to carry out a rescue and recovery? Dyani's thought voice came back.

Ah, negatory at this time! Report when you have some info!

Roger, Grey Head!

"The Chinks know something's happening," was Henry Kester's comment.

"Sure, especially if they were the ones who shot down the Soviet plane," Curt agreed. "They've probably prepared for this. Which is why I expect them to move out of their casern shortly and move down the canyon to take on the Soviets in Novoaleksandrovsk."

"They should have moved into position before they shot down the Soviet transport," Joanne remarked.

"I think the SAM attack was opportunistic," Curt said. "They might have planned to do it, but Qian didn't know exactly when it would take place. The Soviets have deliberately been irregular when it comes to the arrival of their log birds."

"Or maybe it ain't deliberate irregularity; maybe the Russkies do it on demand when they need supplies or when one of the big Four-oh-fours is available," Henry mused, then added sagely, "But when it happened and Qian got the word, he had to get those news media people out of his hair so he could move. I'd guess he'll get his regiment moving out within the hour. He sure as hell ain't got no maneuvering room where he is."

"But he's in an impregnable defensive position," Joanne point out.

"Major, there ain't no such thing. Any defensive position can be taken..." Kester began.

"...if the attacker is willing to pay the price," Joanne finished for him.

"So we change plans on the fly and pound the shit out of them with the Saucy Cans, then let Major Worsham expend a little ordnance on them, and then send in the warbots followed by the Sierra Charlies," Kester hypothesized.

"But since we ain't about to attack Krasnetskoye anyway, that's a moot point, Henry," Edie Sampson said. "Our assumption is that the Russkies are going to come at them first."

"We hope. We assume. It may not work that way. Assumption is the mother of all fucked-up, sheep-screwing fur balls." Kester thought a moment, then added, "Too bad we can't let the Russkies waste themselves going up against the Chinks in that strong defensive position. Then we could take the Russkies from behind and make a caviar sandwich out of that regiment!"

"Tattoo it on your brain, Henry, that we're not going to do it that way because we've been told we've got to do it Sink-Spid's way without force of arms," Curt reminded all of them, then added unnecessarily, "But, as you pointed out quite succinctly just now, our approved tactical plan will not survive first contact and is also based on an assumption. So, we'll just have to change our plans, won't we? And that is what's going to keep us from being chewed up by the Soviets."

"Just in time, too, Colonel! Here they come!" Joanne Wilkinson pointed out the targets that began to appear along the road leading out of Novoaleksandrovsk. "Looks like regimental strength, too. Silver Pilgrim warbots in the lead. Column of ducks."

"Well, at least something's working right for a change!" Henry muttered.

"Edie, I feel pretty sure those Russkie warbots are remotely controlled by some sort of radio link. See if you can't find their control frequencies with a spectrum sweep," Curt instructed his top tech sergeant.

"Looking" was the brief reply as she got busy with her equipment rack.

"He's not expecting anything," Joanne pointed out. "He hasn't got any flank guards out on either side of the road. He's wide open for a flank assault..."

Warrior Head, this is Grey Head! Our targets are coming up the road as anticipated. Activate the roadblock! Curt passed the order along through his NE tacomm to Joan Ward.

Grey Head, Warrior Head is activating roadblock! I assume the tac plan is still solid?

Roger! If they shoot at us first, take out the Silver Pilgrims! If Curt was right and the Soviet AASU-99 Silver Pilgrim warbots were unmanned and remotely commanded like the old American Hairy Foxes, destroying the warbots wouldn't mean killing Soviet soldiers. If Kurotkin didn't back off after Curt had destroyed the warbots, then Curt felt no compunctions about shooting at the Soviets themselves. He'd play CYA with Mahathis and apologize to Alzena later.

"What's them targets over there on the railway line through the pass to Kholmsk?" Henry indicated some blips that Grady had marked as "unknown."

"Railcar maybe?"

"Nope, Major, it ain't movin'. And there's more than one of them. Looks like three targets sitting on or alongside the railway line."

"Which sensors are picking them up?" Curt wanted to know, anxious to identify these potential hazards if possible. He didn't like commanding and leading in this manner, safe behind armor ten klicks from the action, making decisions that might send friends and colleagues to death or mutilation. He was no longer scared shitless for himself. He was now scared shitless for *them!* He knew now why Belinda Hettrick had never married anyone who also served in the Washington Greys; it would be impossible to send your spouse into this sort of thing!

"Active laser illumination and single pulse micro radar," Kester reported, checking Edie's equipment because she was busy with the frequency sweeps. "They're also transmitting some short bursts of some sort of coded control groups, looks like digital stuff..."

"Soviet style stuff?"" Joanne asked.

"Don't know."

Black Hawk Leader, this is Grey Head! Curt thought into the NE tacomm to his birdbot platoon leader, Lieutenant Dale Brown. *See if you can't get a visual and an i-d on three targets marked unknown by Grady over on or near the railway line south of Sinegorsk where it goes through the pass to Kholmsk. Do you see the targets or do you want me to hang a pointer on them?*

Brown's Black Hawks had six birdbots aloft at this time. They were huge warbots disguised as hawklike birds. They flew by wing beating and were controlled mostly by the Mod 7/11 AI which did most of the flight work and left Brown and his warbot brainies free concentrate on general direction and sensor evaluations. The birdbots were the only neuroelectronic warbots left in the Sierra Charlie TO&E of the Washington Greys.

Roger! Have targets! Three klicks south of Sinegorsk! I'll have a bot over them in thirty seconds! Stand by!

"Russkies are closing quickly on our roadblock!" Joanne reported as she kept watch on the tac display. "The Marauders and Pumas both have the targets. Alleycat Leader is laying Mademoiselle Saucy Cans at this time!"

Greys all, this is Avenger Leader aloft in a birdbot over the Soviet regiment! The road column is headed by twelve Alpha-Alpha-Sierra-Uniform niner-niner warbots followed by eighteen Alpha-Papa-Tango one-zero-six light tanks and twentyfour Bravo-Tango-Romeo two-one-eight armored personnel carriers. Vehicles are not buttoned down. All personnel appear to be riding in vehicles behind armor. I see no flank guards or skirmishers of any sort. That was Major Ellie Aarts helping out by being in linkage with one of the birdbots. An experienced Sierra Charlie who had expressed a desire to stay with the Greys but to go back to being a warbot brainy, Ellie knew what she was seeing, how to report it, and what it meant to the Sierra Charlies on the ground.

Warrior Head, this is Marauder Leader! Our Smart Farts can take out the warbots, but they won't touch the Alpha-Papa-Tangos! Request a couple of Saucy Cans up here loaded with IRP Heave rounds as backup! Alexis was anticipating the worst, and Curt didn't blame her. She'd been up against the Russkies twice before, and she didn't trust them, either.

Alleycat Leader, this is Warrior Head! The Magnums are farthest west and closest to the roadblock. Send them at high cross-country mode to Sinegorsk ASAP!

Damn! We just got 'em laid! But anything to protect the Free World! Magnums on the way! Expect arrival in four minutes! was the quick reply from Jerry Allen, who had apparently shunted the order directly to Martha Milton even as he received it. Communications time while in NE tacomm mode was very fast because of the elimination of the need to vocalize messages.

Thirty-six spit-shit points toward your next DCS! was Joan Ward's comment.

Two klicks! The Russkies should see us soon! Captain Russ Frazier was excited, but he was a man who liked to fight. Curt's big worry right then was how to keep Russ from triggering at the slightest provocation. He hoped to God that discipline held; he'd hate to have to ramrod Russ.

"Give me a visual from any of the Warrior forward vehicles or warbots!" Curt said to Henry.

"You got it, Colonel!"

A visual came up on a bulkhead screen showing what the visual sensor on Alexis Morgan's AVC was seeing: the road as it stretched through the little village of Sinegorsk.

Warrior Head, this is Grey Head! Did you evack the civilians from Sinegorsk?

S-O-P, Grey Head! Affirmative!

Grey Head, Black Hawk Leader here! I have a make on the unknowns! was the sudden report from Dale Brown. *Japanese sixteen-wheeler semitrailer trucks! I can read the markings on the side of one of them. Says in Japanese: University of Ashikawa, Petroleum Logging Laboratory. That's on Hokkaido! I can just discriminate something like antennas on them!*

"What the hell are the Japs doing snooping on this fracas?" Curt said to no one in particular, "Edie, do you have any make on the EM emissions from those Jap trucks?"

"All over the place! They're scanning and sweeping like they're looking for something! Probably trying to snoop on our warbot voice-command and data downlink channels! Hah! They'll never spot those! They're looking in the wrong part of the spectrum!"

"Scroom!" Curt blurted out. He was getting over-communicated now, pushed by a plethora of data was beginning to pour in...and no fighting had started yet! "Put Phillip on watch and have him report directly to Grady. I want to know if there's any change in what the Japs do. If they're just going to sit up there and snoop, and if they're not looking up our assholes at our linkage freaks, I've got other things to worry about!"

Marauder Leader reporting! Magnums are here! Martha, dammit, don't straddle the road! You make yourself and your Lambs into perfect targets for those Russkie warbots! Alexis called over the common tactical freak.

Marauder Leader, this is Magnum Leader! I'm not going to trust the sensors and computers at a range of less than three hundred meters! I'm going to boresight with calibrated eyeballs! Martha Milton fired back, indicating that she didn't think the automatic gun-laying equipment would be accurate enough at this short range, especially for anti-tank work where it was important to put a HEAV round as close to where you wanted it as possible. Milton's training had taught her where the vulnerable points of the Soviet APT-106 light airborne tanks were; put a round in the wrong place so it bounced off, and you became meat for the next round from its 76-millimeter gun. Curt could see from the visual display that Milton was already out of her ACV and mounting a LAMVA to boresight it.

Curt thought she was nuts to do what she was doing. But he didn't have time to do anything about it.

The Soviet column suddenly came within sight of the roadblock.

But it didn't stop. The two lead Silver Pilgrims running alongside one another on the road kept right on coming, but they did slow down so that Captain Andrei Gulaevitch Glinka could run forward between them.

"Americans clear this road! We are coming through!" Glinka called out.

Joan Ward stood up in her ACV hatch and called out "No. *Nyet!* We are under orders from the Sakhalin Police Detachment to prevent your unit from proceeding to the Chinese casern at Krasnetskoye!"

Martha Milton heard and looked up. She repeated Joan's announcement loudly in Russian.

Glinka looked confused. He picked his battle communicator from his belt and spoke into it. Someone – probably Kurotkin - spoke back to him. Glinka looked directly at Joan and said, "You will clear this road at once and permit us to pass, or there will be very bad problems!"

"We're ready for them when you start them, Captain!" Joan called back.

"We will not shoot, but we will run you down and push you off the road!"

"Be my guest…if you can do it! You'll have to run over some people in the process!"

The Soviet warbot on the right suddenly fired its 53-millimeter cannon point-blank into the Washington Grey roadblock of vehicles and people.

Chapter Twenty-Nine

The Soviet warbot's aim was atrocious.

The 53-millimeter shell glanced off Lieutenant Martha Milton's Jeep, knocking it over from the force of the impact, then ricocheted at an angle to slam into the LAMVA where she was bore sighting the 75-millimeter gun.

The reaction from Frazier's Ferrets was almost instantaneous. Lieutenant "Hassan the Assassin" Mahmud launched an M-100A "Smart Fart" AT/AA rocket and hit the Soviet AASU-99 Silver Pilgrim on the low right side in among its suspension gear. Since the Smart Fart's special warhead could penetrate up to 300 millimeters of armor, its tongue of fire went right through the side of the Silver Pilgrim. The concussion was sharp and brisant. That Silver Pilgrim would never shoot again.

One of the four Magnum Saucy Cans fired once, its 75-millimeter HEAV round at the short range of 200 meters not only holing the other Silver Pilgrim but picking it up and throwing it back into the Soviet column.

"Cease fire! Cease fire!" Joan Ward was both yelling at the top of her lungs and transmitting on NE tacomm as well. "Glinka, what the hell...?"

In response, the second wave of Silver Pilgrims fired dead into the Greys at about two-second intervals.

This time, they got even more violent, immediate, and overwhelming response from the Greys in the form of a barrage of Smart Farts and withering direct fire from three of the Magnum Saucy Cans.

Curt could see Soviet soldiers breaking from their vehicles and heading for the houses, huts, barns, and other cover on both sides of the road.

"Greys all, go to ground!" Curt ordered.

Greys all, this is Grey Major! Kester's quick comment almost stepped on Curt's verbal and NE transmission. *Stay out of the houses! If you make it tough for the enemy to get at you, then you can't get out of there!*

Dyani Motega's NE voice cut in. *Grey Head, Mustang Leader! We have the PRC casern under surveillance. Be advised that an armored column of approximately regimental strength minus service units is now leaving Krasnetskoye by road!*

Watch 'em, Mustang Leader! We have a fight going here! Curt told her, then said to Joanne, "Have Ellie keep track of the Chinks out of the corner of her eye. Let me know when they're close enough to increase the pucker factor!"

There was now the strong possibility that the Chinese 44th Special Regiment would catch the Greys in the rear while they were dealing with the Soviets. In between two regimental-strength forces was no place to be. Curt found himself getting into deeper and deeper trouble by the minute. He punched up the CINCSPD freak. "Sink-Spud, this is Grey Head! The Chinese are leaving Krasnetskoye in regimental strength by road! Stand by to airlift the Chileans to give us some help! Where the hell are the Japs?"

"Roger, Grey Head. Sink-Spud copies! Are you in trouble there?" Mahathis asked.

"Yeah, deep shit and getting deeper! The Soviets opened fire on us! Get me those Chileans and put 'em on the road northwest of Sinegorsk to deal with the Chinese!" Curt fired back. It was obvious that Mahathis either wasn't watching his tac display or had reduced the sensitivity so that he was watching only gross regimental movements, not individual actions as Curt was.

"Colonel, I've cracked those Japanese EM emissions!" Sergeant Edie Sampson broke in. "They've come on the air with a strong signal that matches what the Soviets were transmitting to their warbots! The Japs are transmitting a signal that swamps the real one from the Soviets and causes the Silver Pilgrim receiver AGCs to jack up to accept only the higher-power signal!"

"So, the Japs have taken control of the Russkie warbots," Kester summarized what Edie had just said from the techie viewpoint.

"You got the Soviet warbot freaks, Edie?" Curt asked, trying to juggle all fifteen battle balls in the air at once.

"Roger, but I don't know the control codes. I can't make the Japs stop making the Silver Pilgrims shoot at anything and everything!"

"So jam 'em! Jam 'em hard! Take them out of the game!" Curt told her.

Edie grinned. "Yessir! With pleasure, sir!"

Warhawk Head, this is Grey Head! Scramble two Harpy flights! Scramble! I have two targets for you! Curt relayed over another tacomm frequency to Cal Worsham whose aerodynes were idling on the ground at Sokol.

I was wondering when you'd get yourself into such deep shit that you'd have to call for us to extricate, resuscitate, or exacerbate! Cal Worsham's "voice" came back. Even in NE linkage, it seemed raspy and rough just as his real voice did when talking. Curt had long ago decided that there was no way anyone could get Worsham and his wild-assed flyboys and flygirls to adhere to tacomm protocol except when dealing with Air Traffic Control. They were wild and wooly and just wanted to get out there and do their jobs because they liked to fly. Curt had taken a fam hop with Cal over to the Barry M. Goldwater Aerospace Force Range one day and had decided that Cal and his Warhawks weren't "Kill-'em all" types like Frazier's Ferrets; the Warhawks just liked to fly and got some sort of perverse high out of wreaking havoc from on high. The Warhawks were also different from the Ferrets in that the Warhawks usually never saw the human targets they were shooting at in spite of their objectionable and tasteless beer-call song, "Strafe the Town and Kill the People!"

Okay, Warhawks are up! Guns and ordnance hot switches to hot, ready to lay heat. Feed us the hot scoop with the ground, Colonel!

It's on the data bus! Curt told him. *Take out the Jap trailers! Flat-hat the Chinese column!*

Well, at least you took only half the fun out of it! Shoot-if-shot-at still valid!

Roger! If the PRC boys try for the Golden BB, slap their wrists! But don't cream them!

Roger! Any anticipated bogeys?

Negatory! You may be joined by the Broonies, but they're flying the same stuff you are!

Colonel Pain-In-The-Ass told me! We'll mix well. I helped train the Broonie flight leaders!

Medic! Medic! We've got wounded! was the sudden cry from Sinegorsk.

Remember, ladies and gentlemen of the Greys, this is a polite war! Do not return fire unless you are fired upon! Then apologetically return the fire! And please be sure to grease the bastards when you do, so they aren't impolite and try their barbaric ways again! Joan Ward's sarcastic voice was dripping with false sweetness and light.

Warrior Head, this is Grey Head! And that's exactly and precisely what you uill - repeat, will - do! Curt told her. *We've got the ungarbled word here now! Edie Sampson discovered that the command link of the Silver Pilgrim was overridden by a Japanese contingent up on the high ground to the southwest! The Russkies didn't shoot at you! And the Warhawks will be taking care of the Japs in a minute or so!*

I don't much give a shit who shot at us, Grey Head! We've got wounded!

Who?

Don't know yet! We're all sort of scratching mud at the moment! But the shooting has died down!

Get Milton and try to talk to Glinka or Kurotkin! Give them the word about what happened!

If I can find Milton, I will! She was blown off the top of a Lamb by the first Soviet shot!

Oh, shit! Curt swore. This was Lieutenant Martha Milton's first combat engagement. The girl's ancestors had fought at Saratoga and a place called The Parrot's Beak. She was trying to follow a family tradition. It would be tragic, Curt decided…No, even more tragic than usual if she ate the big one the first time out of the box.

Phillip shook with a rumble.

"Sounds like Cal Worsham leaving his calling card by flat-hatting us again!" Joanne Wilkinson remarked.

"What the hell is he doing this far east of the action?" Curt wanted to know.

The rumbling continued and the OCV began to shake.

"Christ, Colonel, that ain't Major Worsham's people!" Henry shouted over the noise.

"Are we taking incoming?" Curt wanted to know.

"Negatory! Negatory!" Edie snapped.

Then Phillip, his OCV, began to bounce up and down.

Curt had to sit down and hang on. So did everyone else inside the ten-ton armored vehicle which was being tossed about like a Trike. For a moment, Curt thought the vehicle was going to be overturned by the violence of the shaking which now was side-to-side as well as up-and-down.

"*Earthquake!*" someone yelled.

The word came over the tacomm network from several sources almost simultaneously.

The visual from Alexis's ACV in Sinegorsk was blurred and showed violent shaking.

"Out of here!" Curt snapped.

Henry popped the rear ramp by pulling the Emergency Evacuation lever. "I ain't goin' out the top of this mother and have it roll on me! Out the ass end, everyone!" he announced.

Curt didn't really remember getting out of Phillip, but he suddenly found himself on solid ground that wasn't any more. It was tossing him up and down like a Ping Pong ball.

His impressions were fleeting, blurred, distorted by the rush of adrenaline surging through him. Trees were swaying, and huge limbs were breaking off. The power line poles alongside the road were leaning and snapping, throwing live electrical power lines to the ground.

He couldn't stay on his feet, so he simply sat down. He discovered that the other members of his staff were having the same problem. Bit by bit, all of them worked their way to a spot where the OCV couldn't topple on them or a tree wouldn't come down on them.

The noise was overwhelming.

Curt had been in battles before and had heard the unholy uproar of combat.

But this was a maelstrom of tumultuous chaos.

The crashing collapse of buildings created a thunder that Curt had never heard before.

Through the din of a world suddenly gone berserk, he heard the screams and yells of people running everywhere, anywhere in sheer panic or crying out for help as they were trapped in collapsing buildings.

The primitive wood and masonry houses and buildings of Kurskoye were falling in rubble on the heaving roadway.

Panic-stricken people were rushing out of them into the open, falling and stumbling as the shaking ground threw them off their feet.

Over the open fields to the west hung a pall of airborne aerosol mud particles. As Curt watched in fascination, the heaving ground sent up fountains of mud and tossed large rocks high in the air.

Eleven kilometers away to the south, the 115-meter-tall multiple smokestacks of the coal-fired power plant in Novoaleksandrovsk, something that had become a landmark for the Greys, slowly swayed as Curt stared. The masonry stacks seemed to be made of rubber because they waved like willowy stalks of wheat in a strong wind. Then one of them simply collapsed in a billowing cloud of masonry dust that obscured the others.

Alongside the road, several fissures opened in the ground and propagated in random before they closed again, often with opposite directions sides at different heights. Several large pipelines paralleling the road were bared to the skies with their severed pipes spewing water and, from its smell, natural gas. They were too far out in the boonies to be sewer lines, for which Curt gave small thanks.

Some of the breaks in the natural gas line caught fire from the sparks of the fallen power lines. Several gas explosions were visible along the road.

Curt had seen many battles that tore up a lot of real estate and left hellish devastation in their path. But he suddenly realized that a major earthquake like this could do far more damage than mankind's puny wars.

The ground shook and underwent spasms for several minutes before it started to quiet down.

Hardly any of them said much of anything to one another until it finally seemed that it might be over. They were much too awed by what they'd just been through.

Finally, when the ground had steadied to the point where Curt could stand, he got to his feet, took the tacomm brick from his waist, keyed it, and called verbally, "Greys all, this is Grey Head! Anyone standing up yet?"

"Good God Almighty! Well, Henry, at last we've all been through something you haven't!" Edie quipped.

"Matter of fact," Henry replied dryly, getting to his feet, "I recall the quake of ought-seven in - Damn! That shook the hell out of me! I'm getting too old for this kinda crap..."

"Grey Head, this is Warhawk Head!" came Cal's response from the sky. "What the hell is going on down there? Looks like the whole island is shaking!"

"It is and it was," Curt told him. "I think the game has been called by a higher command. My strike order is cancelled until we find out what's happened. Stay aloft until we find out where we need you. Check with Hawley's Haulers and report their condition! We're probably going to need 'dynes to get anywhere we need to go on this island for a few days! Break, break! Anyone on the ground read me?"

"Warrior Head here! I read you!"

"Joan, what's the story! Report!"

"Things are still shaking!" his TACBATT commander reported from Sinegorsk. "Couple of our ACVs slid off the road. We've got wires down on top of a lot of our gear, and we've got broken water and gas pipes all over the place! I'll get a sit-rep in a minute if I can pull things together!"

"Any shooting?"

"Are you kidding? When the quake hit, it sort of brought our argument to a screeching halt," Joan told him. "Right now, this is a disaster area! Most of the Soviet troops are caught in buildings that collapsed on them! We're trying like hell to get to them and rescue as many as we can! You'd be surprised what great bulldozers the ACVs make!"

"What the hell. are the Russkies doing?"

"Working right alongside us! Glinka and I are talking. We know the Japs started this by screwing around with the Silver Pilgrim command freaks! But that's sort of behind us right now!" Joan's voice was hurried but not harried. She was transmitting via verbal tacomm, and the excitement of combat was gone from her voice. She was now involved in something just as serious and just as deadly, but it was rescue, not combat. "Kurotkin and Ivanovski are trapped under a building here! Can we get some help?"

"Joan, I think everyone's in the same situation you are! If you need airlift, I can get it to you!" Curt told her.

"I was thinking about getting Doctor Ruth's group here ASAP! We've got injured and wounded, both Greys and Russkies! Maybe even some dead. I don't know! I'm trying to help Glinka and Yurasov find Kurotkin! They don't seem hot about finding Ivanovski, but I don't blame them..."

Curt looked around. The three M660E Biotech Support Vehicles were still parked on the road to the north of him. He could now see people milling around them as the dust began to settle. "Wait one! Biotech, this is Grey Head! Anyone in Biotech! Report!"

"Biotech Head here! I read Joan's message loud and clear," Major Ruth Gydesen's voice came back. "Everyone okay here. We've got some smashed equipment, and I don't know the extent of the damage yet. Is there any way we can get to Sinegorsk?"

"Use airlift until we get some recce on road conditions," Curt told her. "Talk direct to Joan! Call in your own airlift! Cal is standing by! Channel Delta-niner-Mike is now an open party line. Greys all, stand down from combat mode unless shot at! Go to civil rescue mode! If there's nothing you can do in your immediate area, go to disaster public control mode! We're bound to have looting and other disturbances shortly!"

"What's the situation at Sink-Spud?" Joanne Wilkinson asked him directly as she clambered up the stirrups and started to reenter Phillip.

"Just better hope they weren't all caught in a collapse of the Sink-Spud building!" Henry said.

"Sink-Spud Head, this is Grey Head! Do you read?" Curt snapped into his tacomm.

"Colonel, I didn't exactly have time to throw a patch to put your hand-held on the Sink-Spud freak before we shagged ass out of Phillip," Edie said.

"Get back inside, check out our C-cubed-I gear, and then get on the hooter to them, Edie," Curt ordered.

"I was about to do just that," she replied and mounted the OCV behind Wilkinson.

Curt looked around and said to his regimental sergeant major,

"Henry, you and I have been through a fair amount of death and destruction together, but I think this one's sort of going to stand out in my mind for a while."

"Well, Colonel, when compared to combat, I'm not so sure I liked it. Maybe I'll get used to it the next time," the old soldier replied.

"Grey Head, this is Mustang Leader!" Lieutenant Dyani Motega and her SCOUT platoon were still up in the hills overlooking the Chinese casern at Krasnetskoye.

"Grey Head here! Deer Arrow, are you all right?" Curt asked in concern.

"Yes and no! We managed to hang on to trees that didn't slide down the mountainside," she reported. "Now that the dust is starting to settle, I can see that the Chinese column is trapped on the canyon road. Some of the vehicles were smashed by rock and mud slides. Others are buried under slides. Those that aren't have their way blocked in both directions. Mud slides everywhere! Half the mountain range must have slid over them! I'm not even sure they can climb over most of that debris!"

"How about the casern?" Curt knew that Maggie MacPherson was probably still there...unless, God forbid, she'd managed to talk her way into going along with the column.

"Whoever built that put it together to stay together in quakes," Dyani reported. "Rock slides went around one side of it. The other side got partly buried in a mud slide. But the rest of the building didn't collapse. I don't know if anyone's hurt down there, but at least one company of Chinese soldiers is still there. Maybe they're Colonel Qian's housekeeping unit. We can try to go down and find out."

"Negatory! Negatory!" Curt fired back quickly. "Let me get our efforts coordinated down here in the valley, then we'll come in by airlift to help if we can and shoot if we're not welcomed with open arms. Mustang Leader, I don't want you pulling another one of your personal initiative stunts like you did on Kerguelen or at Yuzhno-South! Hold your present position! Do not approach the

Chinese casern! That's a direct order! Do you understand that Mustang Leader?"

"Yes, sir! Understood, sir!" she snapped back. Then she added, "Now that I can begin to see things a little better, I was a little hasty in my appraisal of the situation. I don't know if we can get to the casern from here anyway! The landscape is still shaking and moving around a lot. We're having to hang on..."

Curt was concerned about that. He didn't like the idea of Dyani and her SCOUT platoon there in those mountains while real estate was moving around. There was a chance they could be buried in a rock or mud slide. "Dear Arrow, haul ass out of there! Can you retrace your steps and join the Greys in Sinegorsk?"

"I'll check it out, sir! The terrain has been changed around quite a bit since we came up the hill. I'll report often. We're all right, Grey Head. We can stay the course. We brought our sweet rolls and bed rolls if we can't make it back by sunset. Don't worry about us, Grey Head!"

He knew he probably shouldn't, but he did anyway. While he knew that Lieutenant Dyani Motega of all people was capable of taking care of herself very well in the wilderness, he was still worried because Dyani was Dyani.

However, his first concern now was the well-being of the Washington Greys and any casualties they might have suffered during the brief encounter and the earthquake. He had to concentrate on that first. Then he could allow to come to the forefront his concern over the Sultana Alzena, who was perhaps trapped in the CINCSPD building in Yuzhno-Sakhalinsk, then Maggie MacPherson, who might be trapped in an inaccessible casern high in the mountains.

In the meantime, this destructive earthquake had thrown the whole Sakhalin mission into a totally new light. The Washington Greys might be the only regiment left with enough strength to fight the Soviets, who might have lost a lot of their men and equipment in Sinegorsk, and the Japanese, who might have lost nothing but who had tried to clobber the Greys by taking control of the Silver

Pilgrims.

He found himself again in a typical emergency situation with an unknown but large number of problems to solve and an unknown amount of time to solve them. And he might be the only CINCSPD commander left with a reasonably intact unit. If CINCSPD had been damaged or destroyed, he might have to take over as the military commander of this dangerous island. The quake would undoubtedly mean thousands of people on Sakhalin in deep trouble with water, power, food, and other shortages, which could lead to looting and violence. Then he expected that thousands of people from all countries would be pouring in here to render aid and succor...and straining the limited resources left working. The tasks before him seemed to be so many and so insoluble that he didn't know what he'd do or how he'd handle them.

He'd have to take it one job at a time and hope to God that the shock of this natural disaster would defuse a potential nuclear disaster that could brew up because of Sakhalin Island, a place few people had ever heard of but a place where the future of the free world might hang in the balance.

"Okay, Henry, let's get busy. First things first..."

"Well, at least you remembered something else I tried to teach you, Colonel..."

Chapter Thirty

"General Mahathis has been injured and is out of action. His condition is considered serious but stable," was the report from Colonel Julio Castillo. "The sultana sustained minor injuries and has been released by our biotechs. We have instituted martial law in Yuzhno-Sakhalinsk, Colonel."

Curt breathed a sigh of relief. No one had been killed there. He wished it had been the same in Sinegorsk. The Greys had survived the earthquake, but they'd taken casualties in the firefight.

Lieutenant Martha C. Milton, the plain young lady from Rutland, Vermont, who had joined the ROTC at MIT because she admired the legendary Deborah Gannett who was one of her ancestors, was in critical condition undergoing surgery in BIOTECH. She had broken both hips, both legs, and sustained internal injuries when she'd been blown off the top of the LAMVA by the 53-millimeter round of the Soviet Silver Pilgrim warbot. She'd hit the armored side of another LAMVA which had torn off her protective battle helmet, and she'd sustained serious head injuries leading to possible brain damage when she hit the road; this had been compounded by head wounds from pieces of metal and composite armor plate flying around in the short battle. "She's breathing," was the only news that Doctor Larry McHenry had time to pass along to Pappy Gratton.

One of Milton's sergeants, Pamela Parkin, had been killed immediately by the second Silver Pilgrim round which hit her LAMVA right next to where she was also bore sighting the Saucy Cans.

Jerry Allen's first sergeant, Forrey Barnes, was seriously wounded, as was Milton's platoon sergeant, Andrea Carrington.

Curt couldn't help feeling responsible. He recalled only too well Jerry's chewing out Milton during maneuvers for failing to get out from behind armor and do what needed to be done with her artillery instead of staying safely back in her ACV and directing fire from there. He should have spoken to Jerry later.

"Colonel," Jerry told him, "it wasn't your fault. I've got to accept part of the blame. I'm her company commander."

Curt could only shake his head in dismay. "Three of our ladies! *Three of them!* And your top kick who could have stayed in a service job and never gone into the front line to be shot at!"

"Colonel, we all accepted the unlimited liability portion of our contract when we elected to become combat soldiers," Jerry had to remind him.

"Jerry, that doesn't make it any easier when comrades and colleagues and especially ladies are lost," Curt insisted.

"Colonel, we've lost more than a few together, haven't we? I know what needs to be done. So, let me take care of it as the company commander," the young man told him. Jerry, of course, had a role model in the form of his former company commander who was now standing before him as his regimental commander. Jerry also knew that the man had far greater responsibilities and much more serious duties, but that Curt's concern for his personnel was uppermost in the man's mind right then. In spite of the shock of battle and the earthquake, Jerry had the presence of mind to realize that the concern shouldn't fall on Curt's shoulders right then. So, he added, "You've got a hell of a lot more people and a humping big job to worry about at the moment. Joan and I have things under control here at Sinegorsk. We're not shooting at the Russkies, and vice versa; we've got bigger problems to solve, and we're solving them together. Go knit this sheep screw back together, sir."

Curt clapped him on the shoulder and told him, "Carry on, Major!"

"Grey Head, this is Gurkha Head!" came the call on the verbal circuit of Curt's helmet tacomm.

"This is Grey Head! Go ahead, Gurkha Head! What's the situation?"

"I'm with Colonel Mishida at the moment. The Ninth Internal

Peacekeeping Regiment got out of its casern when the quake started. Seems they react automatically with their regular earthquake drill. They have no casualties. We're rather deeply involved with them rescuing trapped people and treating the injured."

"What's the status of your Gurkhas?" Curt wanted to know.

"My dear Colonel, we certainly wouldn't think of letting a mere earthquake throw us into a panic!" Payne-Ashwell was obviously all right, as were his Gurkhas. "I have assigned the mission of street patrol and policing to my Gurkhas. They will do a smashing job of that, I assure you!"

Curt knew the Gurkhas' legendary fighting abilities were enough to maintain law and order in Yuzhno-Sakhalinsk and Novoaleksandrovsk. The first idiot who began looting would suffer dire consequences. Curt really didn't care what happened to looters in the current circumstances. He knew the Gurkhas wouldn't shoot; they'd pull their *kukris* first.

"Duncan, it doesn't look like there's anything much left to smash."

"I say, you're right about that! By the by, the sultana wants to know about Maggie MacPherson. We need worldwide coverage as quickly as we can get it. Miss MacPherson is just the person to get it!"

"That's the next job on my list, Duncan. Tell the sultana we're going into Krasnetskoye by air in the next thirty minutes. At last report, Maggie MacPherson was detained there by Colonel Qian. I'd like to have the Brunei Snake Eagles standing by for additional airlift if possible. But first I've got to get in there, assess the damage, and find out what can be done to help the Chinese while we still have some daylight." The days were getting short here on Sakhalin in the early fall. Curt had to remind himself that they were farther north than Quebec.

"And before it starts to rain again, old chap!" Payne-Ashwell pointed out as the staffer for air ops when he wasn't head-honchoing the Gurkhas. "The latest met data isn't thrilling . We can expect more rain within hours. Perhaps even snow down to a thousand meters."

"Dammit, Duncan, when Mahathis assigned you as air officer, we all expected you'd order better weather than that." Curt replied with a touch of whimsy.

"Well, one does one's best, you know. Sorry about that. More rain might make rescue and assistance triply difficult. Mud could become a real nightmare, what? But, as the air officer, I expect I'll fly over it..."

Curt had one more call to make from his OCV. "General, it's like Hell with the lights out over here," he told Belinda Hettrick and gave her a quick run-down on the fight and the earthquake. "General Mahathis is on the injured list. I've *got* to have some help."

"Damn. Curt, you make it sound like a job for Superman! Sorry, I can't give you any more troops! As quickly as I can get this news to Len Spencer at the White House, humanitarian aid can start on its way via military airlift," she told him, relying on the historic fact that when it came to international disaster aid the armed forces of the United States were the world's most effective organization. It wasn't just because they had the equipment and the manpower. Only one group of people had the education, training, and expertise to run very large operations involving a million or more people: the generals and admirals. Whenever big jobs had to be done in the past - digging the Panama Canal, controlling the Mississippi River, building great dams, going to the Moon - the generals and admirals slipped into civvies and got the job done. And some generals hadn't done too badly when they'd been called upon to run the United States government from the Oval Office. In fact, the first president was a general.

"I need more than that, General! This godforsaken island is a mess! And the whole bucket of slime has landed in my lap by default!" Curt told her, then admitted, "Belinda, just between thee and me, I'm a goddamned beginner at this sort of thing, and this isn't the place to learn! I need you or General Carlisle or someone experienced in big international operations to run things while I maintain law and order!"

There was silence on the audio-only net for a moment, and Curt almost feared he'd somehow said something wrong. But Major General Belinda Hettrick came back, "Curt, let me let you in on a secret. In terms of international relations, I was a raw field beanette wearing silver chickens when we went to Namibia in Operation Diamond Skeleton, and I didn't know diddly squat. I was no more prepared for it than you are right now. What I'm trying to say is that you'll probably have to do the job somehow for days, maybe weeks, or maybe longer if or until the President can find or assign someone. Right at the moment, nobody cares squat that you're not experienced; *you're there!* You've got good people to help you! You'll be getting lots of help! In fact, you'll have hundreds of people telling you what they think you ought to be doing! Figure it out according to your best judgment, then *do it!* Sometimes experience isn't as important as the willingness to tackle the seemingly impossible. Now get your ass in gear and find Maggie MacPherson! She can get you more help than you know."

"If she's still alive..." Curt added.

"So, find out if she is! Here's your chance to rescue a delectable damsel in distress...maybe."

Curt couldn't help but grin. "I'm glad you qualified that, but I'm not exactly sure what you qualified, General! Delectable, yes. Damsel, maybe. Female definitely yes! In distress - I guess I've got to find out!"

"So? What the hell are you waiting for? Or has being a regimental commander turned the iron in your blood into lead in your ass? She's probably up there in the hills, threatened by the Yellow Peril and God knows what else. Go be a big hero and get her out! Believe me, it will pay off. As you've found out, it's nice to have friends in high places...and that doesn't always mean Fort Fumble on the Potomac."

"General, I just wanted to clue you in so you wouldn't be greeted by the Big Surprise later," Curt admitted to her.

"Surprised? At anything you'd do? I've known you too long and too well, Colonel Curt Carson!"

Curt had selected his team carefully. He wanted a Mary Ann for heavy fire support and a Jeep for close-in intense fire. He wanted and got Lieutenant Nancy Roberts piloting a Chippie; Nancy knew how to fly in mountainous terrain and had proved it in Sonora's Sierra Madres. He called for volunteers and drew some flak as a result of his selection: Regimental Master Sergeant Henry Kester, Battalion Sergeant Major Nick Gerard, First Sergeant Tracy Dillon, Platoon Sergeant Charlie Koslowski, Biotech Sergeant Al Williams, and Lieutenant Hassan Mahmud.

Alexis Morgan didn't try to be tactful. "Colonel, this is an equal opportunity regiment, and I deserve the right to put my pink bod at risk, too!"

"Yes, Colonel," Captain Adonica Sweet chimed in, "some of us are better at close-in fighting!"

Major Joan Ward simply said, "I should declare some of those men essential to the jobs we've got to do down here in Happy Valley tonight."

Curt didn't reply at once but told his contingent, "Load up, men!" Then he turned to the women and said, "Ladies, I greatly appreciate your candid comments. I've taken them into careful consideration. However, we've lost one lovely lady today. So, I've decided in my infinite wisdom that if anyone else gets killed today, it will be one of our gallant men so that true gender equality may be preserved within this outfit. Major Ward, you're in command until I return! Carry on!" So saying, he slung his Novia over one shoulder and his Black Maria over the other and marched into the waiting Chippewa.

It was only thirteen kilometers from Sinegorsk to Krasnetskoye, but the flight was up a narrow canyon. Clouds now topped the ridges at two thousand meters. Curt hadn't been reluctant to choose Nancy as the pilot; she wouldn't be involved in any hand-to-hand if the Chinese were still nasty. Her instructions were to unload, get out of there, and go back to Sinegorsk to stand by.

On the way up, dodging through the canyon and flying what Nancy termed IFR – "I Follow Railroads" or roads; but in this case she had what was left of both, so she used what she could - Curt kept a watch on Dyani Motega's beacon location. Motega's Mustangs appeared to be slowly following the ridge east of Krasnetskoye.

He told his pilot, "Nancy, on the way back to Sinegorsk, try to pick up Lieutenant Motega and the Mustangs if you can find a place to do it."

Her reply was "Colonel, I'll try, but I couldn't even land a butterfly around here!"

They flew over parts of the Chinese convoy that were trapped between rock and mud slides on the road. The Chippie wasn't fired upon. The Chinese were milling around semi-leaderless in the descriptive "Chinese fire drill" or working hard to rescue comrades from slides.

The Chinese casern at Krasnetskoye suddenly came into view at the head of a U-shaped blind canyon nestled up against impossible ridges on three sides. Evidence of rock and mud slides abounded. Part of the huge, blocklike casern was buried. The rest of the big building appeared to be okay. It had once been a combination coal mine tipple and miners' barracks; there wasn't much room in the canyon to build two separate buildings.

"Nancy, put us down on that circular patch of level ground in front," Curt told his pilot. Over the roar of the aerodyne, he yelled to his recon patrol, "Looks like only one entrance in the center of the building. We'll go in there! Our objective is to find out if we can help anyone and get them down the hill to safety. Maggie MacPherson may be in the building, and they may be holding her prisoner. So, we're not going to play games with them! The doctrine is this, *I trust you, Chang, but cut the cards!* If we can't be buddies, we'll get nasty with those who want to be nasty! If we draw fire as we go to ground, I want Dillon to go in a right window and Koslowski in one on the left. I'll be primary command of Bucephalus, the Jeep; Henry is Number Two. Nick, you're to command Geraldine because she's your Mary Ann anyway, and Hassan will back you up if necessary. Everyone use the Black Maria. We may have to fire only a couple of rounds because those are kind of awesome in close quarters and may convince any nasty Chinese to stop fighting and cooperate. If we can't convince them, remember Captain Marty Kelly's doctrine: *Kill 'em all and let God sort 'em out!* Load and lock! Nancy, once we're on the ground, scat out of here and await the recall!"

They were disciplined, professional soldiers. They didn't need to be told twice. And they already knew why they were here and what their mission was. Curt had just done what any prudent commander would do: refreshed their memories.

Nancy Roberts put the Chippie down precisely, and Curt was the first one to get out. He walked slowly toward the building with his two personal weapons slung. He was followed by his five men and Al Williams, who was wearing the red cross tabard of a medic.

Curt and the others were wearing body armor under their cammies and also the bright blue tams with yellow poms that were the headgear of Sierra Charlies. Their combat helmets were thrown back and resting atop their shoulder packs. Curt wanted to give the appearance that they weren't here on a combat mission.

It also created a high pucker factor. He could take a 5.56-millimeter Chinese A-99 round in the head and never know what hit him.

It didn't happen. Maybe the remaining Chinese housekeeping troops were so startled to have the huge Chippie land at their front door that they hadn't reacted yet.

As he entered the huge double-doored entrance and walked into the two-story foyer, Curt called out in Mandarin, *"Ni hao! Wo shi Meigo ien! Wo de mingzi shi Colonel Curt Carson. W o zai zhao Colonel Qian!"*

A uniformed man wearing the rank pips of an NCO stepped slowly out into the open on Curt's right. He was carrying a Chinese A-99 5.56-millimeter submachine gun in his arms, but it wasn't pointed at Curt. Apparently, Curt's greeting in Chinese had surprised the man. But he replied to Curt, *"Wu an! Wo shi Quo Ling Wen! Ni yau shem-*

ma?"

The ensuing conversation, transliterated in English, went as follows:

"I am here to offer help. Your regiment has been trapped on the road to Sinegorsk by the earthquake. The earthquake will occur again, and your casern may be completely destroyed. We can take you down to Yuzhno-Sakhalinsk where we have food and a place for you. How many men remain here?"

The Chinese was wary, but as Curt got a closer look at him, the man seemed to be an old non-com. Something about the man's mannerisms and movements suggested that he might be the Chinese equivalent of Henry Kester. "We need no help."

"You will," Curt promised him. "We will take you out of here by aerodyne, and you can help us rescue your comrades who are still alive on the road."

"I will ask my comrades here," the man replied.

"Is the American reporter Maggie MacPherson still with you here?"

The whole building suddenly shook, and plaster dust began to fall from the ceiling. An aftershock caused the canyon to rumble. It must have scared the shit out of a nervous Chinese observer because Curt heard a yell of panic behind him. The aftershock tossed him to the floor.

A three-round burst from an A-99 sent three bullets snapping over his head.

Curt saw the Chinese who had fired on him and pulled the trigger on his Black Maria only once. The blast was like that of a 25-millimeter cannon going off. A door and the man standing in it simply disappeared in an eruption of plaster dust and wood splinters.

From behind, Curt heard another Black Maria blast as Henry Kester fired at yet another target.

Curt was consumed with the need to get the hell out of the middle of the room and find cover. It really wasn't necessary because Henry had brought Bucephalus through the door with him, and the warbot searched for targets...and found them.

A warbot didn't miss. And it didn't need a three-round burst. It fired once if it had a single target, its radar tracked the outgoing round, and if the round converged with the target, it sought another target; if it somehow missed, it corrected its aim...and the second shot normally didn't miss. This took place in milliseconds, so a two-round burst sounded like a single shot.

Then Kester and Hassan were in the foyer and up the stairs. Curt started for where Quo Ling Wen had been standing. Gerard took the ground floor on the other side of the foyer while Bucephalus followed Curt.

The sound of gunfire echoed through the long halls. It was an intense mad minute. Curt saw a form duck out of one door into another one, so he sent Bucephalus ahead to draw fire if there was any.

Bucephalus trundled down the hallway and came to a stop in front of a door. Its 7.62-milhmeter heavy-duty machine gun swiveled quickly around and pointed into the doorway which was open.

"Don't shoot!" came the panicky cry of Maggie MacPherson.

Curt broke into a run and got to the door just as he saw Quo Ling Wen escort her out into the hallway. Curt couldn't tell if the Chinese was trying to use Maggie as a shield, so as he pointed his Black Maria, he snapped, *"Bie dong le!* Don't move!"

"Many pardons, sir! I was only bringing Miss MacPherson to you. I am Sergeant Major Quo Ling Wen of the Forty-fourth Special Regiment, People's Liberation Army. I left my weapon elsewhere, the NCO said in Mandarin. The man obviously had no fear of Bucephalus because he had never seen a warbot Jeep before.

"Maggie, are you all right?" Curt asked, not moving the muzzle of the Black Maria a millimeter from its aiming point on the chest of the Chinese.

"I am now! These bastards took me prisoner!"

"Well, the tables have turned!" Curt snarled and snapped in

Mandarin to the Chinese NCO, "Turn around! Hands up on the wall! You are now my prisoner!" And he made a quick body search of the man. He found no weapon.

Then picking the tacomm brick off his waist, he called out, "Henry, this is Carson! I've found Maggie! What's the sit?"

"We've got the rest of the Chinese, Colonel!" Henry Kester's voice came back. "Shot eight of them before they could get us. Captured six, mostly cooks. They're unarmed and scared shitless. Housekeeping troops like we suspected. We've also found Maggie's crew, and they're okay."

"Oh, thank God!" Maggie breathed.

"Grey Companions, this is Grey Head! Back down to the front door!" Curt ordered. "We got what we came for, and these bastards can damned well shift for themselves until we get around to rescuing them! Let's go back to Happy Valley! Fancy Nancy, return for recovery!"

"Grey Head, this is Fancy Nancy!" came the reply from Lieutenant Nancy Roberts in the Chippewa. "I'm five klicks southeast in the canyon, and this is as close as I can get without moving some rocks! You'd better take a look outside! Things have gone zero-zero! Heavy rain squall has moved in, and the ceiling's dropped to zilch. Forecast says more of the same. Better get comfy! I can't get back in right now, and I may not be able to get back to you until this weather lifts! And you're not going to get out on what's left of the road!"

Chapter Thirty-One

Curt gathered everyone together in the huge two-story foyer. Nick Gerard, Charlie Koslowski, and Tracy Dillon had taken the eight dead Chinese outside; there wasn't much they could do to bury them because darkness had fallen, and it was raining and sleeting outside. In short, it was cold and miserable.

Carson's Companions - the combat team members had insisted that the rump platoon be called Carson's Companions because everyone except Hassan had served under Curt in the old Companions - stood around and relaxed. Bucephalus was on guard on one side of the foyer where he could look down one hallway, while the Mary Ann stood passively on the other side and watched in the other direction. The seven Chinese were awed by the warbots. Curt doubted that they'd try anything after the display of lethal firepower that had been exhibited during the initial panicky shoot-out.

"I see you found the generator and got us some juice, Henry," Curt remarked to his regimental sergeant major, probably the best jackleg gadgeteer in the regiment with the possible exception of Edie Sampson, who had a way with electronics, computers, and robotics that Henry didn't.

"No sweat," Henry replied easily. "Standard-issue Matsushita design with Chinese placards on it. Couple of thousand liters of fuel for it. Guess it shut down because of short circuits during the quake. So, I got it started again. Had to bypass a couple of blown breakers because of shorted wiring. We got power now for lights and pumping water."

"This place was built on top of some hot springs," Sergeant Charlie Koslowski added. "Plenty of hot water to take a shower...if you can stand the sulfur smell."

"I've checked the storage areas that weren't destroyed by the quake," Hassan put in. "Lots of blankets. Lot of Chinese rations."

Sergeant Tracy Dillon was the clown in the outfit today. "Well, I guess we'll have to have Chinese tonight; we can't send out for a pizza!"

Maggie MacPherson was there with her two-person mobile video crew, cameraman Joshua Bilmet, and the very plain, uncomely, and almost masculine female coproducer, Judy Delmonico. Curt couldn't figure out what Judy did except make Maggie look absolutely and unbelievably beautiful by comparison. Bilmet seemed disinterested in everything except the condition of his equipment. The coproducer acted scared. What surprised Curt was the way Maggie treated them. Other than her initial delight that they were unharmed, she treated them like they were just hired help. Maybe that was normal in Television Land, but Curt would never treat his subordinates with such indifference.

Maggie was very scared and shaky. Curt thought she'd probably undergone quite an ordeal that day. He hoped that a hot meal and some rest would help her get over whatever was really bothering her.

"Okay, troops," Curt addressed them in English, shifting into Mandarin when he needed to translate something for the seven Chinese soldiers, "here's the situation: We're staying here tonight."

"My God, can't we get out of here?" Maggie sounded panic-stricken.

"Afraid not, Maggie," Curt told her. "Here's the total situation: The road is out; in fact, the members of the Chinese regiment who weren't killed or buried by rock and mud slides are trapped on the road. I'm not about to try walking out of here through these hills at night in this cold rain and sleet. And we can't get an aerodyne in here because of the weather; I won't ask any of our pilots to risk their lives trying to get in here without approach and landing aids. This place right now is surrounded by *cumulo granite* as well as clouds that are right down on the deck and knocking at the front door. You can't even see three meters outside!"

"What are we going to do?" Maggie's question was almost a plaintive cry. For some unknown reason, she was very frightened, something Curt thought extremely unusual for a journalist who'd been in all sorts of dangerous spots.

"As I said, we're staying here tonight," he repeated. "It's the best place to be right now. Down in Happy Valley, the buildings are destroyed, the power is out, there's no running water, and the Greys are having to sleep in their vehicles...which is much better than anything most of the citizens of Sakhalin have tonight. We've got a warm, dry building with electricity, running water, plenty of hot water, a kitchen, and a lot of food. We've even got cooks who know where everything is! Hell, we've even got bunks and beds to sleep in! Our cup runneth over!"

"Yeah, a real rough situation," Henry muttered. "Count your blessings."

"I been in worse places. Much worse places," Nick Gerard put in.

Curt turned to Sergeant Major Quo Ling Wen and spoke to him in Mandarin. "The fighting is over, Sergeant Major. It stopped when the earthquake hit. We were never ordered to fight each other anyway. So, you're not our prisoners. When we get out of the mountains tomorrow, we all have a lot of work to do to help the people of Sakhalin recover from this terrible earthquake. Do you agree that we should not fight each other?"

"Colonel Carson, one of the guards was young and frightened when the earthquake aftershock came. I am sorry you had to kill him. My apologies for his behavior," the Chinese top kick replied formally in Mandarin.

Curt gave Wen a thumbs-up, a sign of approval recognized in both of their cultures. "And I apologize for the fact that my men had to kill your men. We will make certain that they receive a proper military funeral with all honors."

"I am indebted to you, sir!"

"Will you please give orders to these soldiers that we will not harm them if they don't harm us?"

Sergeant Wen laughed. He'd been very worried about what sort of relationship he should have with these Americans. "They will not fight! They are cooks! And we have much to eat here!" There was a slight smile on Sergeant Wen's face. "Because of the earthquake and the destruction, we will not have to account for everything we consume tonight. As a military person, I am sure you understand what I mean..."

Curt nodded. "I do indeed, Sergeant! Yes, tonight I hope we will eat well because it is not often that we get the chance."

"Everyone will relax and enjoy what we can provide tonight," Wen promised.

Curt saw that Wen was indeed a typical non-com in spite of his Chinese cultural background. The Orientals had no tradition of the literate non-commissioned officer equivalent to the European sergeant or boatswain's mate. They'd had to borrow it from the Europeans because it was the only way a modern military force could be run.

Sergeant Wen continued, "It will be good to relax with an American who speaks Chinese. I understand you well, although you speak my language like an American."

Curt had to laugh. He translated into English, "Sergeant Wen and I agree: We're not fighting each other. But he told me in most polite terms that I have a terrible American accent!"

Wen began talking to his cooks. Curt heard him give direct orders concerning complete cooperation with these Americans.

But Maggie was still upset. Ordinarily, she would have had cameras rolling, recording this interaction between the military personnel from two cultures for use on *Maggie's Hour*. Something was keeping her from doing it. Curt found out when she said to him, "Curt, we're not safe here!"

"About as safe here as anywhere tonight, Maggie," he tried to reassure her.

"No, no, no! You don't understand!" There was panic and terror in her voice. "We've had some aftershocks! They're minor, as usual! But within a day or so we'll get a terrible secondary shock! It could be worse than the initial one! That's the way major earthquakes are! I know! I've been through two in southern California! When the secondary hits, the whole mountain could come down on us! This whole casern could be covered by a slide! This canyon is a death trap!"

Curt now understood her terror. As one who had grown up in Los Angeles, Maggie knew something about earthquakes. And feared them. He tried to calm her. "Maggie, if we can get through the night, chances are they'll get an aerodyne in to us tomorrow morning. We'll probably be out of here and back on flat ground when the secondary hits. So, we might as well enjoy what we've got while we can. We can't really do anything else ... and *I'm* the one who's *really* got a *lot* of work to do once we get out of here! General Mahathis has been injured, and I've got the monkey on my back for this whole island when we get back!"

Curt looked at his watch and asked Sergeant Wen, "Is it possible that dinner might be made ready in three hours?"

It was. And it was worth it. Although Curt had been able to get a hot shower, he had to don his grubby field cammies. But he didn't put on his uncomfortable body armor. The shower made him feel better, even though the water from the tapped hot spring came out smelling slightly like rotten eggs. He was even able to shave the stubble from his chin with the GI issue razor in his RON kit.

As Henry Kester remarked, "It ain't often that a field soldier gets a hot meal and a warm, dry place to sleep! Enjoy it while you can!"

The meal was very good, even though it was somewhat plain by American standards. But it was filling and it was hot and there was a lot to eat.

Maggie didn't eat very much.

And Curt tried to stay away from the Maotai that Sergeant Wen brought out from some sequestered personal spot. However, Henry Kester and Nick Gerard went drink for drink with Wen and seemed to be holding their own. Curt was concerned but not worried. Henry and Nick were old hands at this sort of thing. But Curt demurred because he had a lot of things on his mind,

After the dinner was over, Curt excused himself. But he wasn't going to leave the frightened Maggie with her crew who was getting bombed on Maotai and some bourbon Delmonico had. Their solution to overcoming fear seemed to be to drown it in ethanol. They were from southern California, and now Curt knew why they were scared. But Maggie wasn't drinking even the Maotai except to take a few sips in response to toasts from Wen.

So, he took Maggie by the hand and led her down the hallway to the room he'd taken on the ground floor where Bucephalus looked down the hallway and patrolled with its sensors. Maggie said nothing. She came along not with eagerness hut with surprising docility. She was scared, and she didn't really know how to handle this situation. She was walking and talking as if she was in a stupor. None of her radiance was evident. She was scared and lonely. So was Curt. He wanted very much to go to bed and make love to her. The way she came with him indicated she harbored similar yearnings, but the old sharp, sassy edge of Maggie MacPherson wasn't there that night. So, he decided the best he might be able to do to help her that night was to console her and try to assuage her fears. But he had things to do first.

"You didn't seem to enjoy the meal very much," she observed.

He sat Maggie down in one of the chairs. "Neither did you, but I got a hot meal in me. Helps me carry out my responsibilities," he explained, taking up his tacomm brick. "First the personnel, then the warbots, then the guns, and then I can relax!"

He called up Joanne Wilkinson and Joan Ward.

Curt knew he couldn't run the operation down in the valley by remote control like this, and he trusted his people to do a good job. But he wanted to let them know that even though he was stuck in the mountains that night, he was still staying on top of the work his staff was doing.

"How goes it?" he asked his chief of staff.

"We did all we could in Sinegorsk, Colonel, so we're back in Sokol," Wilkinson reported. "The casern wasn't too badly damaged. No more leaks than usual."

His second in command, Major Joan Ward, added, "Lost a Jeep and two Saucy Cans in the fracas."

Curt then asked the question he really didn't want to ask. "How are the casualties? Give me a report, please."

From the moment of silence on the tacomm net, Curt knew the worst had happened. "Colonel, I regret to report that two members of the Washington Greys have honorably paid the ultimate price, and two others require evack to the States as quickly as it can be arranged." Her voice was strained and nearly broke. She was obviously strung out and nearing the end of her resources. Curt feared that this might be the final item of stress for her, and it seemed to be that way. Joanne Wilkinson had seen seventeen Greys pay the ultimate price since the regiment had become Sierra Charlie. She'd seen dozens of others wounded, some to return to the regiment, some to elect resignation or medical retirement. She had been one of those who'd remarked to Curt that she'd seen just about all the fighting she cared to experience in a lifetime.

Major Joan Ward picked it up because it was apparent that Joanne couldn't go on. "Doctor Ruth did everything she and her unit could possibly do, Colonel. Lieutenant Milton just had too much broken up inside."

Curt didn't feel too good about it himself. He never did. He thought savagely that maybe it had been a mistake to abandon NE controlled warbots and to put human beings back on the battlefield. Maybe it had been a mistake to allow women to become combat soldiers.

"I'll take care of the task of notifying next of kin tomorrow," he told them. "We can't do much tonight. As soon as the weather permits it, get a Chippie up here to evack us. We're all okay. We're warm and dry and fed, so we'll survive."

"Wish I felt the same," Joan Ward told him. "The place is wet and leaky and cold. The troops are bitching to beat hell."

"They're okay," Curt advised her. "Never worry about the troops complaining. The time to worry is when they stop. Get everyone as warm and dry as possible...and fed."

When he signed off, Maggie noticed his emotional state and said quietly, "I'm sorry, Curt. I didn't know her, but I'm sorry."

Curt turned and looked at her. "Martha Milton did what she did by choice. She knew she could get killed. It was an accident, but she took a risk willingly."

"I just hope we don't get added to the casualty list tonight."

"Maggie, if a secondary quake hits tonight, we don't have any control over it. We're here. We have no choice. And when you haven't got either control or choice, you make the best of what you've got. When the fox gnaws, smile."

Maggie sighed. "I ought to know better. I've had plenty of good examples to follow. So, I'm ashamed of the way I've acted. I've often heard military acquaintances say that 'to stand and be still to the Birkenhead Drill is a damned tough bullet to chew.' I've never had to face that before," she admitted, straightening up a little in the chair. "It makes me take stock of my life and think about the meaning of what I'm doing or want to do..."

Curt knew he was drawing the fright out of her by getting her to talk. But he didn't look at her. Long ago, he discovered that you should never look a frightened person in the eye. Let them talk it out or they'll lose self-respect. So, he turned the tables on her. Usually, she was the one conducting the interview. He took over that role. "And what is it that you're doing and want to do, Maggie?"

"I've always operated on the basis that I had to claw my way up the greasy pole of success and that anything worth doing was worth doing for money," she admitted. "I've known a lot of people. But of all the people I've known, I've always been fascinated by military and naval people. It wasn't just an adolescent fantasy about the glory and the machismo and the pretty uniforms. I couldn't understand why the warriors did what they did for such little money or recognition. If I didn't understand the men, I really didn't understand the women who were following a military career."

"Do you have any better idea now?"

"Yes." Her voice was growing a bit louder, a bit more confident. "There are some things worth doing just because they're worth doing. No other reason."

"Are you sure? Why are they worth doing for their own sakes?"

"Because other people have done those kinds of things...and none of us would be here if they hadn't."

"Or maybe things would have been a lot different anyway," Curt tried to add.

"Maybe. Maybe not. But as long as we think so, that's what counts." She paused, then went on with growing confidence as her fears subsided, "Maybe I've forgotten something very important. When I was stashed away in a girls' school by parents who really didn't want me, I remember reading something on the chapel wall. I haven't thought about it in years. Sort of forgot it. But right now I remember one part of it very well: 'Enjoy your achievements as well as your plans. Keep interested in your own career; it is a real possession in the changing fortunes of time. Exercise caution, for the world is full of trickery. But let this not blind you to what virtue there is; many persons strive for high ideals; and everywhere life is full of heroism...'"

"There's another part that says, 'Do not distress yourself with imaginings. Many fears are born of fatigue and loneliness...'" Curt appended the quotation. "We all have to live with fear. Sometimes a lot of fear. We learn. You'll learn. You're learning now."

After a long pause during which Curt remained looking at his boot tops, Maggie suddenly blurted, "My God! What an experience this has been! Curt, my dear, thank you! Thank you! *Dammit, Curt look at me!*"

From the tone of her voice, Curt knew he'd succeeded. And when he looked at her, it was as if Maggie MacPherson was back in front of the video camera lens. Except this time the effect was even stronger and more pronounced.

"Good! You're Maggie again, the Maggie known by millions!" he told her with a grin.

"That? The TV image? Curt, I did that because I had to! It was something I learned! What you're seeing is Maggie doing what Maggie really wants to do! For you! *Because I want to!*"

"You don't know your own strength," he told her, the desire for her now welling up through his own fears and weariness.

"Oh, yes, I do! And I'm going to use it to get rid of our fears and loneliness!" She got up out of the chair, came over to him, pulled him to his feet, and led him over to the bed. He didn't resist, nor did he hold back when she pushed him onto it and began to frantically remove her own clothes as well as his. "You, sir, are about to be subjected to the most intense and thoroughly demanding legendary MacPherson horizontal interview that's ever been perpetrated on anyone! And not because I want something from you, dear Curt, but because...just because! With no strings attached! And, my military genius, with no quarter given! You once remarked that you didn't know who was going to get who! Well, we're going to get each other! And it's not raining inside tonight! And you're going to discover that I am more than a news harpy with only a sexy, wholesome image."

She was right.

It was no image now.

It was real.

And so was she.

She was more than the sensual but now distant Alexis Morgan. She was more than the kittenish Kitsy Clinton. She was more than the educated and delightful Alzena. She was all that she seemed to be and more. Except real affection. And something else Curt sensed was missing, although he didn't know what. Nor did he really care too much at that point. She was indeed the legendary terror in the sack. It had been a very long day full of fears and terror and death and destruction. They had both been scared. Together, they forgot their fears.

And her own fears were not rekindled even when they both dimly felt a sudden jolt followed by cyclic horizontal and vertical motions of the bed, the room, and the building.

"Orgasmic! There's your quake," he murmured softly in her ear. "I've never made love to a beautiful and desirable woman in an earthquake before…"

"No, no! It couldn't be a quake. A quake never felt this good!" she gasped, breathless. "And don't you dare apologize for being orgasmic! Be orgasmic again! Unless you want Big Trouble from the news media: *me!*"

"Anything for peace," he murmured.

Chapter Thirty-Two

"I'm discovering damned fast that running a regiment is child's play in comparison to running a whole island with more than a million people living on it," Curt bitched via commlink to Major General Belinda Hettrick, who was in General Jacob Carlisle's office in the Pentagon. "What makes it even more nasty is the fact that about a quarter-million people here have no shelter, no food, no running water, and no public health facilities. General Hettrick, I don't know how the hell I'm going to cope with this!"

Hettrick nodded her head. "From what you've told us and what Maggie MacPherson reported, it was a real bastardly bitch! A tectonic earthquake, the largest in several centuries. Better than an eight Richter. It was felt as far away as the southern tip of Kyushu in Japan. Hokkaido got it, too. Clobbered Sapporo and Ashikawa. The Japanese are prepared for this sort of thing, but their relief effort has all their capabilities tied up. Nothing much is moving on Hokkaido."

"And we couldn't move anything without the Warhawks and the Brunei Snake Eagles," Curt reminded her. "The quake damaged the roads and railways so badly that land transportation is difficult if not impossible. At least in the area hardest hit, which is Happy Valley."

"Curt, the State Department thinks you took the easy way out with the Chinese," Carlisle pointed out. "Did you really have to cream them so badly?"

Curt sighed. "General, we were sent here to keep law and order by force of arms if necessary. When we tried to rescue the Chinese regiment trapped on the road to Krasnetskoye earlier today, some of them shot at our Chippies, and others welcomed the rescue. I couldn't convince the nasties to stop shooting even when I talked at them through one of the aerodyne PA systems. They were making it nearly impossible for us to rescue their non-nasty comrades. So, I authorized Major Cal Worsham to make the nuisance go away. I've got enough troubles without a bunch of Mongols who want to shoot up a place that's already a disaster area!"

"It's tough to convince Old Foggy Bottom that force of arms is often necessary when diplomacy fails," Carlisle remarked. "I take it the sultan's daughter has things in hand on the diplomatic front?"

"I don't know, General. She bugged out of here with her brother about noon," Curt revealed.

"*What?*" It was a simultaneous exclamation of surprise from both general officers.

"General Mahathis was hurt pretty badly in the quake," Curt explained. "The sultan wanted to get his only son back to Brunei ASAP so they could get their biotechnologists working on him. The sultana went along. She said she had to. She told me I should understand because I was a family member, too."

"Well, I guess the sibling bonds between twins are stronger than extra-familial responsibilities," Hettrick mused.

"That wasn't the whole story. The sultana is pretty pissed off at me right now," Curt explained. He hoped she'd get over it. The stress of having her twin hurt was something she hadn't coped with before. If he handled the situation very gently, he could probably rectify things again. But the whole Sakhalin affair was a very complex issue in his relationship with her. "Although the sultana is an outstanding diplomat, she was one of my real problems. She didn't want me to fight, but she also wanted me to run the military operation. That was all right by me. But then she talked General Mahathis into issuing orders and an ROE that would keep us from doing our job. That would have exposed our asses to injury while she tried to glue things together on the diplomatic side. Things came unglued when the Japanese shot down the Soviet air lifter with a Chinese clone of the Soviet SA-seventy-seven SAM. The Japanese hoped to get the Soviets to go after the Chinese. The Japanese want this island back real had. They still refuse to call it anything but Karafuto..."

"I can understand that. Lot of oil there. Saves them having to ship it in from Indonesia and Iraq," Carlisle said.

"If I'd followed the orders Mahathis *thought* he gave me, the Washington Greys would have been dead meat," Curt went on, then paused before admitting, "Fortunately, I wrote my own orders because Mahathis doesn't write orders; he gives them verbally and expects them to be carried out. For some strange reason, there were a few loopholes in my orders from Sink-Spud, and that little oversight allowed us to save our butts when things went to slime."

"Ahem! That's highly irregular, Colonel!" Carlisle remarked.

"Yes, sir. I used Operation High Dragon as a model, sir." That brought the discussion of orders to a halt. Carlisle had put his career on the line in a similar fashion at Kerguelen Island, and Curt had followed suit on Sakhalin Island.

"So, what's the situation, Curt? Who's watching the store?" Hettrick wanted to know.

"I am, ma'am. With the help of Colonel Payne-Ashwell and Colonel Julio Castillo. Good men to have at your back in an alley fight like this. Glad I've got them because they've got good ideas, they're good managers, and they're really hard workers if you understand them, which I do," Curt went on with his report. "We've got law and order restored. The looting has stopped. What's left of the Chinese regiment is on its way home today. The Japanese and Soviet troops are happy because I nipped the problem in the bud, so to speak."

"Oh?" Hettrick was interested in this development. "Yes, ma'am. We may not have power or water, but the Russian red-light district will be open in Yuzhno-Sakhalinsk tonight. It's off limits to the Japanese troops, but they'll have their own cultural circus shortly. I'm sure you remember Lieutenant Hassan Ben Mahmud, my best bargainer and the former holder of an unlimited credit card to the best houses in Zahedan when he was there. This morning I sent him to Tokyo to talk to the marketing department and strategic planners of the big Japanese 'social entertainment' conglomerate, The Tea-house of Great Heavenly Pleasure, Incorporated. I'm fairly sure they'll respond to the enormous, untapped market and consumer demand here. Even if they do it on an experimental basis for quick-look data, they'll help alleviate the source of our troubles..."

"Colonel, I'm surprised that an American Army officer would even think of such things!" Hettrick said reproachfully, but he could tell from her eyes that she was laughing at Curt's unique solution.

"Yes, ma'am, but what can you expect from your dumbest plebe?" Curt fired back. "If America wants this to be a temporary solution, please get them to send me some help! And it had better not be wearing striped trousers and a morning coat! We've got a bitch of a multi-cultural job to handle here, and I'm not equipped to do it right!"

"Get suitable quarters prepared for General Hettrick," Carlisle told him. "It's time she took on one of these. She's done pretty well in the past."

"General!" Hettrick said with a groan. "I've got a division to run!"

"It's only temporary, Belinda. Consider it a maximum ninety-day TDY."

"We're ready for you, Battleaxe," Curt told Belinda Hettrick and left it to her to explain her affectionate call code to General Carlisle.

He felt somewhat better about it once he'd toggled off. Help was on the way. In the meantime, he had to deal with the problems of the day.

And they weren't all related to the Sakhalin relief efforts.

Major Joanne Wilkinson waited until late in the day when most of the brush fires were out temporarily. Then she came in and put it on the line to Curt.

"Colonel, I'm going to lay it on you straight," she told him frankly, a weary look in her eyes that told Curt she'd seen too much over the past few days. He thought he knew what was coming. He was right. "I've got five months and a butt before twenty-and-out. I've thought about it, and I'm going to go for it. I've just had all the fighting and combat and chasing around I can take. I've had enough to last me the rest of my life. I don't know what I'll do, but I'll find something in the real world. I wanted to let you know as quickly as I came to a decision so you wouldn't be left high and dry with no COS."

"Joanne, was it Martha Milton?" Curt asked unnecessarily.

She nodded. "I've got twenty years behind me and haven't been winged yet; it could happen next time. Martha had it all ahead of her, and she got it on the first buck out of the chute."

Right behind Joanne came Alexis Morgan, but she had a different gimme. "Colonel, I request a thirty-day leave."

Curt looked at her. He saw the same look in her eyes. "Why?" he asked simply. She'd level with him. Or so he thought.

She nodded. "I've had it, and yet again I haven't. I need to go somewhere for a few weeks and do some thinking about everything."

"Care to confide in me as your regimental commander?"

"No, sir."

Curt got up, walked around his terminal desk, and sat on its edge to confront her as someone other than her regimental commander. "Then care to confide in me as an old friend?"

"Hell, why not?" Alexis sighed. "I thought I'd keep up the fun and games with Ahmad Mahathis while I could. But I got so pissed off at him here on Sakhalin that I damned near broke it off and became his platonic step-sister. Then he got hurt, and I don't know what happened to me. I damned near went AWOL to be with him. And I don't understand why."

"But you didn't go AWOL," Curt reminded her.

"No. I couldn't let you down. But I did get a pass from Pappy this morning when Ahmad's biotechs called up and said he wanted to see me before they flew back to Brunei. Curt, he proposed to me!"

Curt was silent for a moment. Alexis was still very close and dear to him. Finally, he asked, "Going to take him up on the offer, Allie?"

"I ought to. A girl doesn't often get an offer like that from the son of the wealthiest man on the planet." She sighed. "But I don't know. I just don't know! I'm all confused. If I don't accept, I might get it on the next trip out of the Chippie. If I do accept, I'll let down you and my friends and my regiment...and this has been a big part of my life. I was a girl when I came; I literally grew up here. But it's been too high-stress lately! So, I need time to think about it all. That's why I'm asking for leave. Adonica is ready to take the Marauders on a temporary basis. Carol Head won't let her make any mistakes..."

Curt knew this was the sort of personal problem that was often brought to commanders. In this case, it was doubly difficult for him to deal with it. He didn't have his own thoughts straight. He desperately wanted time on this one because he was full of pent-up emotions. "Alexis, I'm up to my asshole in alligators right now. Will you let me ponder this for a few days until Belinda Hettrick gets here?"

"The Battleaxe is coming? Oh, how wonderful!" Alexis chirped.

"I expect the Greys to react that way," Curt said. "I need the help of a general officer for the relief mission, and she got the job."

"You just need a motherly type to hold your hand," Alexis advised him.

"Joan Ward does a good job of that."

Alexis shook her head. "Joan's too young for the job."

"Maybe, but it goes back to beast barracks."

Alexis relented. "Okay, you're short-handed right now. You need a stable situation while you drain the swamp. I owe you and the regiment more than lip service loyalty. So, I'll stick until Battleaxe arrives. Then I'll have a talk with her! A long one! Thank you, Curt! I can live with that for right now!"

The next one to show up was Captain Adonica Sweet. She was agitated, and her request was different. "Colonel, I request transfer to the Wolfhounds!"

Curt sighed. Adonica knew that under both the circumstances and current Army policy, such a request was next to impossible to fulfill. "What's your problem, Captain Sweet?"

"I'd rather not discuss it, sir!"

"Unless you have a compelling reason for a transfer and tell me, how can I justify it when I forward it to General Hettrick, much less DSCPERS?"

Adonica thought about this and finally said, "Very well, sir, I'd rather tell you than have you get the garbled word from Rumor Control. Jerry Allen and I have split up."

Curt reached out and toggled the comm unit. "Major Allen, report to my office on the double and on the bounce!" Then he turned back to the beautiful, wholesome little blond officer. He asked her, "Oh? Really? Why?"

"He's become insanely jealous over the attention being paid me by Hassan!"

Goddammit, why did he have to adjudicate petty lovers' quarrels, too? And a small voice inside him replied, *Because you're the regimental commander!*

"Well, Hassan is indeed quite a lady killer, Adonica. How do you feel about it?" he asked, trying to draw her out.

"I request a transfer, sir!"

Major Jerry Allen popped in, saluted, saw Adonica, and stiffened. "Major Allen reporting as ordered, Colonel."

Curt looked levelly at both of them and told them in the sternest voice he could muster without getting angry, "This is a direct order! I want both of you to go off together *right now* and find some place *real private* where you can yell at each other and then enjoy making up. And if I catch wind of the two of you having this sort of stupid, adolescent, beanie-beanette, third-class spat in public again, *I* will personally find some place real private where I can figuratively spank both of you young idiots who apparently don't know that you've got it so good! Consider that you've raised the wrath of your commanding officer and have thereby had your asses chewed for conduct unbecoming officers as well as two people who love one another very much! Now get the hell out of here and carry out your orders! Dismissed!"

Jerry looked at him, shocked that his regimental commander had responded in such a testy manner. "Yessir! Colonel, what is *your* problem, sir?"

"None of your business, Mister! I can wrestle my own alligators!" Curt told him sharply.

"I sincerely hope you win, sir!"

After the two of them left, Curt realized that things were indeed getting to him...and he couldn't afford to let that happen. It was nearly sunset, so he cleared his terminal screen. He'd had it at that point. He stormed out of his office, told Lieutenant Harold Clock, the OOD, that he was going off duty, and that he'd call in telling where he could be reached in an emergency.

He let his pent-up emotions guide him through the casern. To rationalize what he was doing, he told himself he wanted to check with Lieutenant Dyani Motega. She hadn't reported to him that morning on returning from the scouting mission to Krasnetskoye. He told himself he just wanted to see that she was all right. First the people, then the warbots, then the guns, then he could go kick a tree somewhere...

Dyani's small room was in a section of the casern where electric power hadn't been restored yet. But she'd overcome the lack of electric illumination with a make-do that even Henry Kester would be proud of. Three bowls of animal fat from the nearby packing plant sat with burning rope wicks in them, providing a warm glow throughout the room. It was very primitive, but so was Dyani in many ways that Curt enjoyed.

She was sitting barefooted and cross-legged on the bed, brushing out her long, black hair. Unlike many ladies of the Greys who went on field deployments with only drab and unexciting government-issue personal gear, Dyani somehow always managed to have her own things. Tonight, she wore a fringed suede robe wrapped loosely around her and held at her narrow waist by a simple clasped belt.

Curt closed the door behind him. "Hi!"

She looked up at him and smiled. "Hi!"

"You got back okay, I see."

"Of course!" Dyani never was a chatterbox.

"How was it?"

She smiled and her dark eyes twinkled. "It was rough. My air mattress leaked!" Her sense of humor no longer caught him completely off guard.

But that did it. He quit kidding himself about why he was here. He sat down on the edge of the bed. It was the only place to sit. Junior officers didn't rate a large room with lots of furniture like a colonel.

"Let me," Curt said, taking the hairbrush out of her hand and beginning to brush her long, sensuous hair.

"That feels very, very good."

"You just washed it." It was like shining black liquid running through his fingers.

"I had to. You wouldn't want to come near me after thirty hours in the field. I was dirty."

"I wouldn't care. Underneath the dirt would be you. But now you smell delicious."

She asked him for his report to her. "How was it at the Chinese casern last night?"

He decided he'd retaliate for her humor quip about the air mattress. "It was rough. Only lots of Chinese food and Maotai."

"Did you find Maggie MacPherson all right?"

Curt nodded.

But there were several meanings to her question, so she asked, "Did you enjoy each other as much as I thought you would?"

"Can you really read my mind, Deer Arrow?"

She quietly stated facts. "I don't have to, Kida! The time and the opportunity came for both of you. But the two of us are together tonight."

He stopped brushing, pulled very gently backward on her sensual mane of hair, and looked tenderly down into her upturned face. "You're the most lovable woman I've ever known!"

"I like those words. But I know only three words to tell you what I feel for you: I love you!" That was the first time she'd said them to him. Others had done so in the heat of passion. But when she of few words said them with such sincere intensity, it totally overwhelmed him.

Maggie MacPherson was a rank amateur in comparison to what Dyani could do without any words. When Dyani added words, there was no comparison.

He discovered *he* couldn't say anything but those three words in reply to Dyani.

Without words because words weren't necessary now, she slowly turned on the bed, snuggled softly and intimately against him, and put her arms tightly around him.

After weeks of discipline, worry, concern, anxiety, distrust, stress, confrontation, tension, fighting, killing, pain, death, destruction, natural disasters, cold rain, hot tempers, frustrations, and suppressed emotions, he too put his arms around Dyani and did more than merely hold her tightly to him.

In the flickering dim light of the lamps, they caressed and shared one another with loving, passionate tenderness and an intensity only two warriors could ever know.

They'd had to withhold their emotions on the awful fields of death. Now in one another's arms, those emotions were forced out. That was force of arms they could live with.

Appendix One

THE 3RD ROBOT INFANTRY REGIMENT (SPECIAL COMBAT) "THE WASHINGTON GREYS" ROLE OF HONOR

FALLEN IN THE LINE OF DUTY ON SAKHALIN:

Second Lieutenant Martha C. Milton
Sergeant Pamela S. Parkin

WOUNDED IN THE LINE OF DUTY ON SAKHALIN:

First Sergeant Forest L. Barnes
Platoon Sergeant Andrea Carrington

Appendix Two

ORDER OF BATTLE
SAKHALIN POLICE DETACHMENT

Commander in Chief: General Sultan Ahmad Mahathis bin Muhamad, Negara Darussalam Brunei (The Nation of Brunei, the Abode of Peace).

3RD RI "Washington Greys"

Special Combat Regiment:
Lieutenant Colonel Curt C. Carson, commanding officer

Regimental Staff ("Carson's Companions")
Major Joanne J. Wilkinson, chief of staff
Major Patrick Gillis Gratton, regimental adjutant (S-1)
Major Hensley Atkinson (S-3)
Captain Nelson A. Crille, regimental chaplain
Master Sergeant Major Henry G. Kester, regimental Sergeant Major
Sergeant Major Edwina A. Sampson, regimental technical sergeant

Technical Battalion (TACBATT) ("Ward's Warriors):
Major Joan G. Ward
Battalion Sergeant Major Nicholas P. Gerard

Reconnaissance Company (RECONCO) ("Aart's Avengers")
Major Elanor S. Aarts (S-2)
First Sergeant Tracy C. Dillon
Biotech Sergeant Allen J. Williams, P.N.

Scouting Platoon (SCOUT) ("Motega's Mustangs")

2ND Lieutenant Dyani Motega
Platoon Sergeant Harlan P. Saunders
Sergeant Thomas C. Cole
Sergeant Donald J. Esteban

Birdbot Platoon (BIRD) ("Brown's Black Hawks")
2ND Lieutenant Dale B. Brown
Platoon Sergeant Emma Crawford
Sergeant William J. Hull
Sergeant Jacob F. Kent
Sergeant Christine Burgess
Sergeant Jennifer M. Volker

Assault Company A (ASSAULTCO Alpha) ("Morgan's Marauders")
Major Alexis P. Morgan
Master Sergeant First Class Carol J. Head
Biotech Sergeant Virginia Bowles, P.N.
First Platoon ("Sweet's Scorpions")
Captain Adonica Sweet
Platoon Sergeant Charles P. Koslowski
Sergeant James P. Elliot
Sergeant Paul T. Tullis
Second Platoon ("Pagan's Pumas")
2ND Lieutenant Lewis C. Pagan
Platoon Sergeant Betty Jo Trumble
Sergeant Joe Jim Watson
Sergeant Edwin W. Gatewood

Assault Company B (ASSAULTCO Bravo) ("Frazier's Ferrets")
Captain Russell B. Frazier
Master Sergeant Charles L. Orndorff
Biotech Sergeant Juanita Gomez, P.N.
First Platoon ("Clock's Cavaliers")
1ST Lieutenant Harold M. Clock
Platoon Sergeant Robert Lee Garrison
Sergeant Walter J. O'Reilly
Sergeant Maxwell M. Moody

Second Platoon ("Hassan's Assassins")
1ST Lieutenant Hassan Ben Mahmud
Platoon Sergeant Isadore Beau Greenwald
Sergeant Victor Jouillan
Sergeant Sidney Albert Johnson

Gunnery Company (GUNCO) ("Allen's Alleycats")
Major Jerry P. Allen
First Sergeant Forest L. Barnes
Biotech Sergeant Shelly C. Hale, P.N.
First Platoon ("Milton's Magnums")
2ND Lieutenant Martha C. Milton
Platoon Sergeant Andrea Carrington
Sergeant Jamie Jay Younger
Sergeant Pamela S. Parkin
Second Platoon ("Ritscher's Rascals")
2ND Lieutenant William P. Ritscher
Platoon Sergeant Willa P. Miller
Sergeant Richard L. Knight
Sergeant Louise J. Hanrahan

Air Battalion (AIRBATT) ("Worsham's Warhawks")
Major Calvin J. Worsham
Battalion Sergeant Major John Adam
Tactical Air Support Company (TACAIRCO) ("Jolly's Rogers")
Captain Robert Jolley
1ST Sergeant Clancy Thomas
1ST Lieutenant Gabe Neatherly
1ST Lieutenant Paul Hands
1ST Lieutenant Bruce Mark
1ST Lieutenant Stacy Honey
1ST Lieutenant Jay Kennedy
Flight Sergeant Zeke Braswell
Flight Sergeant Larry Myers
Flight Sergeant Adam Adams
Flight Sergeant Grant Brown
Flight Sergeant Sharon Spence

Airlift Company (AIRLIFTCO) ("Hawley's Haulers")
Captain Roger Hawley
First Sergeant Carl Bagwell
1ST Lieutenant Ned Phillips
1ST Lieutenant Mike Hart
1ST Lieutenant Tim Timm
1ST Lieutenant Dorothy Peterson
1ST Lieutenant Nancy Roberts
1ST Lieutenant Harry Racey
Flight Sergeant Kevin Hubbard
Flight Sergeant Jeffrey O'Connell
Flight Sergeant Barry Morris
Flight Sergeant Ann Shepherd
Flight Sergeant Richard Cooke
Flight Sergeant Harley Earll
Flight Sergeant Sergio Tomasio
Flight Sergeant John Espee

Service Battalion (SERVBATT)
Major Wade W. Hampton
Battalion Sergeant Major Joan J. Stark

Vehicle Technical Company (VETECO)
Major Frederick W. Benteen
Technical Sergeant First Class Raymond G. Wolf
Technical Sergeant Kenneth M. Hawkins

Warbot Technical Company (BOTECO)
Captain Elwood S. Otis
Technical Sergeant Baily Ann Miles
Technical Sergeant Gerald W. Mora
Technical Sergeant Loretta A. Carruthers
Technical Sergeant Robert H. Vickers

Maintenance Company (AIRMAINCO)
Captain Ron Knight
First Sergeant Rebecca Campbell
Technical Sergeant Joel Pruitt

Technical Sergeant Richard N. Germain
Technical Sergeant Douglas Bell
Technical Sergeant Pam Gordon
Technical Sergeant Clete McCoy
Technical Sergeant Carol Jensen

Logistics Company (LOGCO)
Captain Harriet F. Dearborn (S-4)
Chief Supply Sergeant Manuel P. Sanchez
Supply Sergeant Marriette W. Ireland
Supply Sergeant Lawrence W. Jordan
Supply Sergeant Jamie G. Casner

Biotech Company (BIOTECO)
Major Ruth Gydesen, M.D.
Captain Denise G. Logan, M.D.
Captain Thomas E. Alvin, M.D.
Captain Larry C. McHenry, M.D.
Captain Helen Devlin, R.N.
1ST Lieutenant Clifford B. Braxton, R.N.
1ST Lieutenant Laurie S. Cornell, R.N.
1ST Lieutenant Julia B. Clark, R.N.
1ST Lieutenant William O. Molde, R.N.
Biotech Sergeant Marcela V. Jolton, P.N.
Biotech Sergeant Nellie A. Miles, P.N.
Biotech Sergeant George O. Howard, P.N.
Biotech Sergeant Wallace W. Izard, P.N.

The 6TH Sultan's Own Gurkha Rifles, Brunei:
Colonel Landers Duncan Abercromby Payne-Aswell, regimental
    commander
Sergeant Major Tengah Tuanku, regimental sergeant major
Leftenant Kumar Rawat
Sergeant Gurung
Lance Corporal Bijay Rai

3RD Airborne Regiment, Army of Chile:
Colonel Julio Castillo Pinedo, regimental commander

Sergeant Major Enrico Escobar Gil

110th Special Airborne Guards Unit, The Ground Forces, Union of Soviet Socialist Republics:
Colonel Viktor Pashkavitch Kurotkin, regimental commander
Captain Andrei Gulavitch Glinka, company commander and
        translator
Major Aleksander Semonovitch Ivanovki, political affairs officer,
        (KGB/GPU)
Captain Vladimir Nikolayevich Yurasov, commander, special
assault
        battalion
Junior Lieutenant Pavel Fedorivich Koslov, commanding officer,
        first assault gun company
Sergeant Sergey Petrovich Zaytsev, robotic assault gun operator,
        first assault gun company
Sergeant Altrem Butomavich Ishkov, non-commissioned officer

9TH Internal Peacekeeping Regiment, Japan Self-Defense Forces:
Colonel Yushiro Mishida, commanding officer
Captain Hoshiro Takagi
Sergeant First Class Sabau Ito

44TH Special Regiment, People's Liberation Army, People's Republic of China:
Colonel Dao Min Qian, commanding officer
Sergeant Major Quo Ling Wen

OTHERS

The Sultana Alzena Mahathis bin Muhamad, Brunei, deputy for
        Civil Affairs, Sakhalin Police Detachment
General Jacob O. Carlisle, JCS, COS U.S. Army, Washington, D.C.,
        Unites States of America
Major General Belinda J. Hettrick, commanding officer, 17th "Iron
        Fist" Division, AUS, Fort Huachuca, Arizona
Colonel Frederick H. Salley, commanding officer, 27TH Robot
        Infantry (Special Combat) Regiment, "The Wolfhounds,"

17TH Iron Fist Division, United States Army
Major Martin C. Kelly, Operations Officer, 27TH Robot Infantry
    (Special Combat) Regiment, "The Wolfhounds" 17TH Iron
    Fist Division, United States Army
General Ivan Fillipovich Vlasov, commanding general, Far East
    Military District, Armed Forces of the Soviet Union
General Lieutenant Yuriy Palovitch Druzhinin, chief political
    officer, Far East Military District, USSR
Saltan Ahmad Iskander bin Muhamad Shah Rajang Brunei,
    ruler of Negara Darussalam Brunei
Margaret "Maggie" MacPherson, foreign correspondent, Los
    Angeles *Times*
The President of the United States of America
The Hon. Louise M. Dallas, Vice President of the United States of
    America
The Hon. John M. Clayton, U.S. secretary of state
The Hon. James B. Floyd, U.S. secretary of defense
The Hon. Harriett F. Thomas, U.S. secretary of the treasury
The Hon. Charles F. Nagel, U.S. secretary of commerce
The Hon. Joan S. Crittendon, U.S. attorney general
General Albert W. Murray, USAF (Ret), direction, National
    Intelligence Agency
Admiral Warren G. Spencer, USN, Chairman, Joint Chiefs of Staff
The Hon. Betty C. Redfield, director, U.S. Arms Control Agency
Major General William J. Barnitz, USAF, national security advisor
Colonel Dr. Osami Sakamoto, electronics warfare expert, University
    Of Ashikawa, Hokkaido, Japan, and Japanese Self-Defense
    Force
Sergeant Gunji Kirata, electronics warfare technician and graduate
    student, University of Ashikawa and Japan Self-Defense
    Force
Olga Survarova, citizen and business girl, Yuzhno-Sakhalinsk,
    Sakhalin

Appendix Three

**Attributed to Regimental Sergeant Major
Henry G. Kester
3RD Robot Infantry Regiment (SC)
"The Washington Greys"**

1. Murphy was a Sierra Charlie
2. You ain't supermen (Aerodyne drivers please take note)
3. Professional soldiers are predictable, but the world is full of amateurs
4. The side with the simplest uniform wins
5. No combat ready unit has ever passed inspection (Inspections are to readiness as field rations are to food)
6. Never forget that your was made by the lowest bidder
7. You can get shot doing anything, including doing nothing
8. If it's stupid and works, it ain't stupid
9. The important things are always simple
10. The simple things are always hard
11. The easy ways are always deadly
12. Don't look conspicuous; it draws fire
13. Marching fire usually works to keep the enemy's head down, but remember that a moving target is easier for the people with Brand X weapons to see
14. Try to look unimportant; the bad guys may be low on ammo
15. Your vehicles are bullet magnets; a moving foxhole attracts attention
16. If you're short of everything except enemy, you're in combat
17. No tactical plan survives first contact
18. The enemy diversion you're ignoring is the main attack
19. If the enemy's in range, so are you
20. If you're in a forward position, your artillery support will

fall short
21. If you make it tough for the enemy to get at you, then you can't get out of there
22. If your attack is going well, you're probably being ambushed
23. Friendly fire ain't
24. Suppressive fire doesn't
25. Incoming fire has the right of way
26. The only thing more accurate than incoming enemy fire is incoming friendly fire
27. Comm gear will fail as soon as you desperately need fire support
28. Ammo is cheap; your life ain't
29. It's easier to expend material in combat than to fill out the forms for Graves Registration
30. When in doubt, empty the clip
31. Just because your target falls silent or starts to smoke, don't assume you got the bastard; that's your signal to blast him all to hell
32. Tracers work both ways
33. When you've secured an area, don't forget to tell the enemy
34. When both sides are convinced they're about to lose, they're both right
35. You can win without fighting, but it's a helluva lot tougher to do. And the bad guys may not cooperate

Appendix Four

GLOSSARY OF ROBOT INFANTRY TERMS AND SLANG

ACV: Airportable Command Vehicle M660

Aerodyne: A saucer-shaped flying machine that obtains its lift from the exhaust of one or more turbine fanjet engines blowing outward over the curved upper surface of the craft from an annular segmented slot near the center of the upper surface. The aerodyne was invented by Dr. Henry M Coanda after World War II but was not perfected until decades later because of the predominance of the rotary-winged helicopter.

Artificial Intelligence or AI: Very fast computer modules with large memories which can simulate some functions of human thought and decision-making processes by bringing together many apparently disconnected pieces of data, making simple evaluations of the priority of each, and making simple decisions concerning what to do, how to do it, when to do it, and what to report to the human being in control.

Beanie: A West Point term for a plebe or first-year man.

Beanette: A female beanie.

Birdbot: The M20 Aeroreconnaissance Neuroelectronic Bird Warbot used for aerial recce. Comes in shapes and sizes to resemble indigenous birds.

Biotech: A biological technologist once known in the twentieth-century Army as a "medic."

Black Maria: The M44A Assault Shotgun, the Sierra Charlie's 18.52-millimeter friend in close-quarter combat.

Bohemian Brigade: War correspondents or a news media television crew.

Bot: Generalized generic slang term for "robot" which takes many forms, as warbot, reconbot, etc. See "Robot" below.

Bot flush: Since robots have no natural excrement, this term is a reference to what comes out of a highly mechanical warbot when its lubricants are changed during routine maintenance. Used by soldiers as a slang term referring to anything of a detestable nature.

Cee-pee or CP: Slang for "Command Post."

Check minus-x: Look behind you. In terms of coordinates, plus-x is ahead, minus-x is behind, plus-y is to the right, minus-y is left, plus-z is up, and minus-z is down.

Chippie: The UCA-21C Chippewa tactical airlift aerodyne.

Class 6 supplies: Alcoholic beverages of high ethanol content procured locally; officially, only five classes of supplies exist.

Column of ducks: A convoy proceeding through terrain where they are likely to draw fire.

Creamed: Greased, beaten, conquered, overwhelmed.

CYA: Cover Your Ass. In polite company, "Cover Your Anatomy."

Down link: A remote command or data channel from a warbot to a soldier.

FIDO: Acronym for "Fuck it; drive on!" Overcome your obstacle or problem and get on with the operation.

FIG: Foreign Internal Guardian mission, the sort of assignment Army units draw to protect American interests in selected locations around the world. Great for RI units but not within the intended mission profiles of Sierra Charlie regiments.

Fort Fumble: Any headquarters but especially the Pentagon when not otherwise specified.

Fur ball: A complex, confused fight, battle, or operation.

General Ducrot: Any incompetent, lazy, fucked-up officer who doesn't know or won't admit those short-comings. May have other commissioned officer rank to more closely describe the individual.

Go physical: To lapse into idiot mode, to operate in a combat or recon environment without neuroelectronic warbots; what the Special Combat units do all the time. See "Idiot mode" below.

Golden BB: A small caliber bullet that hits and thus creates large problems.

Greased: Beaten, conquered, overwhelmed, creamed.

Harpy: The AD-40C tactical air assault aerodyne which the Aerospace Force originally developed in the A version; the Navy flies the B version. The Office In Charge Of Stupid Names tried to get everyone to call it the "Thunder Devil," but the Harpy name stuck with the drivers and troops. The compound term "news harpy" is also used to refer to a hyperthyroid, ego-blasted, over-achieving female news personality or reporter.

Headquarters happy: Any denizen of headquarters, regimental or higher.

Humper: Any device whose proper name a soldier can't recall at the moment.

Ice cream cone with wings: What an airborne soldier's insignia looks like to Sierra Charlies. Airborne regiments tend to be special units active only in armies other than that of the U.S.

Idiot mode: Operating in the combat environment without neuroelectronic warbots, especially operating without the benefit of computers and artificial intelligence to relieve battle load. What the war bot brainies think the Sierra Charlies do all the time. See "Go physical" above.

Intelligence: Generally considered to exist in four categories: animal, human, machine, and military.

Intelligence amplifier or IA: A very fast computer with a very large memory which, when linked to a human nervous system by non-intrusive neuroelectronic pick-ups and electrodes, serves as a very fast extension of the human brain allowing the brain to function faster, recall more data, store more data, and thus "amplify" a human being's "intelligence." (Does not imply that the Army knows what "human intelligence" really is.)

Jeep: Word coined from the initials "GP" standing for "General Purpose." Once applied to an Army quarter-ton vehicle but subsequently used to refer to the Mark 33A2 General Purpose Warbot.

KIA: "Killed in action." A warbot brainy term used to describe the situation where a warbot soldier's neuro-electronic data and sensory inputs from one or more warbots is suddenly cut off, leaving the human being in a state of mental limbo. A very debilitating and mentally disturbing situation. (Different from being physically killed in action, a situation with which only Sierra Charlies find themselves threatened.)

LAMVA: The M473 Light Artillery Maneuvering Vehicle, Airportable, a robotic armed vehicle mounting a 75-millimeter Saucy Cans gun used for light artillery support of a Sierra Charlie regiment.

Linkage: The remote connection or link between a human being and one or more neuroelectronically controlled warbots. This link channel may be by means of wires, radio, laser, or optics. The actual technology of linkage is highly classified. The robot/computer sends its data directly to the human soldier's nervous system through small nonintrusive electrodes positioned on the soldier's skin. This data is coded in such a way that the soldier perceives the signals as sight, sound, feeling, or position of the robot's parts. The robot/computer also picks up commands from the soldier's nervous system that are merely "thought" by the soldier, translates them into commands a robot can understand, and monitors the robot's accomplishment of the commanded action.

Log bird: A logistics or supply aircraft.

Mary Ann: The M60A Airborne Mobile Assault Warbot which mounts a single M300 25-millimeter automatic cannon with variable fire rate. Accompanies Sierra Charlie troops in the field and provides fire support.

Mad minute: The first intense, chaotic, wild, frenzied period of a fire fight when it seems every gun in the world is being shot at you.

Mike-mike: Soldier's shorthand for "millimeter."

Novia: The 7.62-millimeter M33A3 "Ranger" Assault Rifle designed in Mexico as the M3 Novia. The Sierra Charlies still call it the Novia or "sweetheart."

Neuroelectronics or NE: The synthesis of electronics and computer technologies that permit a computer to detect and recognize signals from the human nervous system by means of non-intrusive skin-mounted sensors as well as to stimulate the human nervous system with computer-generated electronic signals through similar skin-mounted electrodes for the purpose of creating sensory signals in the human mind. See "Linkage" above.

OCV: Operational Command Vehicle, the command version of the M660 ACV.

Orgasmic!: A slang term that grew out of the observation, "Outstanding!" It means the same thing. Usually but not always.

POSSOH: "Person of Opposite Sex Sharing Off-duty Hours."

PTV: Personal Transport Vehicle or "Trike," a three-wheeled unarmored vehicle similar to an old sidecar motorcycle capable of carrying two Sierra Char lies or one Sierra Charlie and a Jeep.

Pucker factor: The detrimental effect on the human body that results from being in an extremely hazardous situation such as being shot at.

Robot: From the Czech word *robota* meaning work, especially drudgery. A device with humanlike actions directed either by a computer or by a human being through a computer and a two-way command-sensor circuit. See "Linkage" and "Neuroelectronics" above.

Robot Infantry or RI: A combat branch of the United States Army which grew from the regular infantry with the introduction of robots and linkage to warfare. Replaced the regular infantry in the early twenty-first century.

RTV: Robot Transport Vehicle, now the M662 Airportable Robot

Transport Vehicle (ARTV) but still called an RTV by Sierra Charlies.

Rule Ten: Slang reference to Army Regulation 601-10 which prohibits physical contact between male and female personnel when on duty except for that required in the conduct of official business.

Rules of Engagement or ROE: Official restrictions on the freedom of action of a commander or soldier in his confrontation with an opponent that act to increase the probability that said commander or soldier will lose the combat, all other things being equal.

Saucy Cans: An American Army corruption of the French designation for the 75-millimeter "soixantequinze" weapon mounted on the LAMVA.

SCROOM!: Abbreviation for "Screw 'em!"

Sheep screw: A disorganized, embarrassing, graceless, chaotic fuck-up.

Sierra Charlie: Phonetic alphabet derivative of the initials "SC" meaning "Special Combat." Soldiers trained to engage in personal field combat supported and accompanied by artificially intelligent warbots that are voice-commanded rather than run by linkage. The ultimate weapon of World War IV.

Sierra Hotel: What warbot brainies say when they can't say, "Shit hot!"

Simulator or sim: A device that can simulate the sensations perceived by a human being and the results of the human's responses. A simple toy computer or video game simulating the flight of an aircraft or the driving of a race car is an example of a primitive simulator.

Sit-guess: Slang for "estimate of the situation," an educated guess about your predicament.

Sit-rep: Short for "situation report" to notify your superior officer about the sheep screw you're in at the moment.

Smart Fart: The Ml00A (FG/IM-190) Anti-tank/Anti-aircraft tube-launched rocket capable of being launched off the shoulder of a

Sierra Charlie. So-called because of its self-guided "smart" warhead and the sound it makes when fired.

Snake pit: Slang for the highly computerized briefing center located in most caserns and other Army posts.

Snivel: To complain about the injustice being done you.

Spasm mode: Slang for killed in action (KIA).

Spook: Slang term for either a spy or a military intelligence specialist. Also used as a verb relating to reconnaissance.

Staff stooge: Derogatory term referring to a staff officer. Also "staff weenie."

TACAMO!: "Take Charge And Move Out"

Tacomm: A portable frequency-hopping communications transceiver once used by rear-echelon warbot brainy troops and now generally used in very advanced and ruggedized versions by the Sierra Charlies.

Tango Sierra: Tough shit.

Tech-weenie: The derogatory term applied by combat soldiers to the scientists, engineers, and technicians who complicate life by insisting that the soldier have gadgetry that is the newest, fastest, most powerful, most accurate, and usually the most unreliable products of their fertile techie imaginations.

Third Herd, the: The 3rd Robot Infantry Regiment (Sierra Charlie), the Washington Greys (but you'd better be a Grey to use that term).

Tiger error: What happens when an eager soldier tries too hard.

Umpteen hundred: Some time in the distant, undetermined future.

Up link: The remote command link or channel from the warbot brainy to the warbot.

Warbot: Abbreviation for "war robot," a mechanical device that is operated by or commanded by a soldier to fight in the field.

Warbot brainy: The human soldier who operates warbots through linkage, implying that the soldier is basically the brains of the warbot. Sierra Char lies remind everyone that they are definitely not warbot brainies whom they consider to be grown-up children operating destructive video games.

Other books by Timothy Imholt

1) *The Forest of Assassins*
2) *Toddler Art*
3) *The Layman's United States Constitution*
4) *China Bones Book 1 – China Side*
5) *China Bones Book 2 – The Bamboo Caress*
6) *China Bones Book 3 – The Red Pagoda*
7) *China Bones – The Complete Series*
8) *The Layman's Articles of Confederation*
9) *A Collection of Mother Goose Tongue Twisters*
10) *A Study in Scarlet with Annotations*
11) *The Sign of the Four with Annotations*
12) *Laughing at a Military Enlistment*
13) *The Hound of the Baskervilles (Annotated)*
14) *The Last World War Volume 1: Trial by Fission*
15) *The Valley of Fear (Annotated)*
16) *Degrees Book 1: Saving the Earth*
17) *The Adventures of Sherlock Holmes (Annotated)*
18) *The Memoirs of Sherlock Holmes (Annotated)*
19) *Boston, Sort of Legal Part 1 – Win Some, Lose Some*
20) *The Return of Sherlock Holmes (Annotated)*
21) *Concusstitution: Welcome to Football*
22) *A Princess of Mars (Annotated)*
23) *Fighting Spirit*